WE'RE THE WEIRD ALIENS
Edited by Mara Lynn Johnstone

ACKNOWLEDGEMENTS

With thanks to Vivian Caethe, editor of *Humans Wanted*, a similar anthology that I highly recommend. Thanks also to the many, many writers online who have explored this idea with such imagination and glee. You make me proud to be human.

CONTENTS

THE MANY WAYS OF BEING WEIRD

Did you know that humans are exceptional, even on our own planet? I don't mean the large brains that we're so proud of. Our endurance puts other animals to shame; only dogs and horses can keep up with us. We used to hunt by "pursuit predation," which is basically just following a deer until it drops of exhaustion. We were the Terminators of this planet, back when pointy sticks were the height of technology.

We can also throw better than even our closest relatives. A gorilla is roughly four times stronger than a human, but the human can throw a rock four times faster, and with devastating accuracy. We're omnivorous to an impressive degree, eating foods that would poison many other animals (chocolate, grapes, onions), and even foods that actively poison ourselves. Our eyesight is sharper than that of many creatures, and our color vision better than some. It's not just the brains that make us the oddballs of Earth.

If you've frequented writer space online in the last few years, you may have heard some of this before. If not, welcome to the concept that has been such a joy to explore: that humanity is profoundly strange in ways we never considered.

When put into a science fiction setting, the possibilities are endless. Humans are space orcs with shocking endurance; denizens of a deathworld where creatures breathe *oxygen*, of all things; daredevils and inventors and unending surprises. Humans are *weird*.

With so much of science fiction portraying humanity as the standard race that all the interesting aliens are compared to, this new slant is deeply satisfying. As someone who would always choose an inhuman character in my speculative fiction games — an elf, a robot, a talking cat, anything but a boring ol' *human* — I have been delighted beyond words to find a way to see my own species as the interesting one. And I'm glad that so many other writers are right there with me.

This is new. This is different. This is fun. Let's show the universe what we have to offer.

THE MACHINE
Jules Blymoor

Day 1

When Edgar Roberts Reed found the Machine, it was a hot summer night. The kind of summer night that refuses to let you stay indoors by turning the house into a furnace, beckoning you into the relief of cool dusk. It was fine by him, since his tiny house was practically just a lean-to with some semblance of wallpaper and a big chair to make it feel like a home fit for human habitation. The cool air that came from the nearby ocean whisked the heat farther inland — directly towards Reed's little shack.

If it was sweaty and unbearable inside the house, it was even more miserable in the kitchen. Edgar Roberts Reed was a cook by trade, and it wasn't uncommon for tradesfolk to live in accommodations far, far below what any human being should be subjected to. Reed was one of the luckier ones. Most of his colleagues lived in hastily erected tenements somewhere in the labyrinthine streets of the city some fool had optimistically decided deserved the moniker "Los Angeles."

Reed had inherited this lean-to in the hills north of the city through his uncle, who swore that he'd find some last traces of gold if it killed him. Arriving decades too late, he didn't, and it did. But Reed was grateful for the house. Though the commute to the city was a painful and exhausting walk, and though his nearest neighbor was a mile away and an aged rancher who got on better with cows than people, it was home. In 1901, one took what one could get.

After a long shift like the one he'd just been on, the wisps of consciousness in his head were less "thoughts" and more "sporadic flashes of coherency." The chief thought in his head, though, was something he could hold onto.

That star looks awfully big.

The light from the city lamps didn't penetrate this far, and the night sky was a sight to behold. One of the pinpricks in the tapestry above was growing, and at a shocking pace too.

What was a curiosity seconds before was rapidly becoming a safety concern.

Reed shot to his feet. The object was small, but it was burning fiercely, a large cone of angry flames bristling around it as it plummeted through the air. But there were other flames too — blue-white ones, pushing in the opposite direction?

The little object was locked in battle, the red flames driving it toward Earth while the blue ones sought to keep it aloft.

Before Reed could really understand the battle, it was over. The object pulverized a nearby hilltop, and the flames died.

Reed was running before any thoughts entered his head. His shoes scratched against the rocks and dirt, but he didn't heed the developing scuffs. He stopped at the edge of the crater, peering down into the haze of smoke.

The crashed object looked like a crescent, but it was the size of a horse. It was crafted from some type of white stone; or was it metal? Reed didn't dare get closer. It was hissing and smoking in a most disconcerting way.

It was smooth and geometric, all clean lines and sharp angles. There was no roughness or irregularity, the way a natural rock might have.

Then, one of the smooth angles began to split open, in the middle of the crescent. Reed slid down onto his stomach to peek over the edge of the crater. The edge widened more; two panels, which had met and fit perfectly together, were splitting apart.

This was too much. If a glowing meteor was momentous, a machine from the sky was terrifying. Reed mentally ticked off a list of people who would be more equipped than him to deal with this that he could go find.

The fire brigade? No, they would laugh him out of the room before they'd follow him into the hills behind the city.

The United States military? They'd shoot him, and even if they wouldn't — where would he even find them?

The Police? Worse than the military.

Reed was running out of authorities, but he didn't get the chance to think of any more because the Machine was now fully open. A small groan emanated from inside.

Reed froze. "Hello?"

A string of rapid gibberish came from the Machine, a high-pitched voice rattling off something at incomprehensible speed.

"Sorry, a little slower?" Reed replied.

"Maxxis. U'uni. Sneeeeeep. Noxodor. Q'l'kim." The voice spat out each word in a staccato rhythm. "Hurn'is. Martian. Tuum. Español."

Reed's eyes widened. "No, English! English!"

"Eng-lish. Searching Database."

Now those were words.

The voice returned, this time spitting out only one word. "Hello."

Reed breathed a sigh of relief. At least he could talk to it. "Hello! What are you?"

"My designation is Probe EG-17. My name is Lieutenant J'Gar."

The panel now open, Reed shifted around so he could see in. The inside of this bean was a series of instruments and arrays, glowing readouts in a language Reed couldn't comprehend. In the center was a small cupped chair, and an even smaller figure sitting in it.

The figure was shaped in vaguely the same way Reed was, although there were four arms and the creature stood about a foot tall. The skin was a pale and mottled green, and the eyes, which took up most of the face, were a deep black. Lastly, the creature wore a shimmering red coverall. Reed was almost horrified, but the creature really just seemed endearing.

"And ... you're from space?" Reed prompted.

When the creature spoke, its words were barely a hiss of air. The voice Reed had heard echoed from inside the spaceship.

"Yes."

The creature drew breath to say more, then something blue spilled out of it and splashed on the ground. The creature collapsed.

*　*　*　*　*

Day 2

The sunrise annoyed Reed. Usually, he found the warm rays comforting. Today, they were just a reminder of how long he'd been awake. Reed blinked the sleep from his eyes and set down his screwdriver, sitting back on the stony ground. Scattered around him were parts of readouts with wires sticking out, their screens dull and lifeless.

He had tried to take things out as gingerly as he could, but it felt like trying to assemble a porcelain vase with a sledgehammer. Reed reasoned that anything with a living creature inside would have some sort of medical supplies, but he could hardly tell what was steering mechanism, what was navigation, and what was hull.

Of course, he was assuming this little ship had any of those things. But it was a machine built to traverse long distances, clearly, and living things surely must have the same basic needs. And the machine didn't seem to have *drawers*.

The air was still cold, and dew had collected on the low grasses and scattered machinery, but it would heat up soon. Reed groaned and stood up, bringing his screwdriver to attack the machine one more time.

Next to many of the panels were small ovals of black glass. Reed tried pushing them, tapping them, even attempting to pull them — though they were flush with the rest of the panels — but nothing worked. He was left with hand tools.

Straining with exertion, Reed pried off a panel that was affixed directly above the chair. Now, this was something! Tucked into the panel were two smooth canisters with lids.

Inside the first was a wad of dull red leaves. Reed held one up to the sun, scrutinizing it. The leaf was shaped like a spade, and had veins running through it. It smelled like lavender.

The second contained a dark blue hunk of something slightly squishy. Ribbons of white ran through it, and it oozed juice when pressed. It smelled of salt and metal. It had once been alive.

Reed jammed the lids back on the canisters, and headed back to the house.

Lieutenant J'Gar was curled up in Reed's bed. Reed hadn't been sure whether to put them under the covers or not, but they crawled into the untidy heap of blankets almost as soon as Reed set them down. They hadn't moved much, though they shifted around occasionally. Reed considered that to be a good sign. The creature was cool to the touch, but Reed realized they might just have a different normal temperature.

He'd dragged the part of the machine that emitted the voice into the house with them, careful to cut out enough wire that it continued to glow when he brought it in. Even still, Lieutenant J'Gar hadn't spoken since the crash.

He gingerly placed a leaf on the bed next to the Lieutenant. Almost instantly, they sat up and began to eat. Something unfolded at the base of their neck, and they fed the leaf in.

"Feeling better?" Reed asked.

The Lieutenant looked over, their eyes wide and unblinking. "What has happened? Where am I?"

"You crashed. Seems like you know the place, though, since you speak the language. We call it Earth, but I guess you might call it something else. Looked like you were hurt, so I brought you inside."

"Yes. English. Planet Q4-Y67-3. First visited Basic Year 98. Contact As-Yet Unrevealed. I am on a scientific mission as part of the Alliance Research Group, and I am operating under the protection of the Quadrant Alliance. I must be treated with the respect my position dictates, as per Galactic Kindness Code 127-B."

"Well, your ship crashed. I'll treat you as good as I can, but it looks like you're pretty banged up. Can we fix your ship?"

"My spacecraft will automatically repair itself over a period of seven Galactic Rotations. I agree with your assessment of my physical state. My concern is remaining in good enough condition to pilot. How long is a rotation here?"

"Um … how long is a day?"

"Difference in parlance. How long is a day?"

Reed scratched his head. "Twenty-four hours."

"How long is an hour?"

"Sixty minutes."

"Unhelpful. How long is a minute?"

"Sixty seconds."

"Confusing. How long is a second?"

"Um, one steamboat?"

"Absurd. How long is a steamboat?"

Reed hesitated. "No, a steamboat isn't a length of time. It's a way of counting time. A second is as long as it takes to say 'one steamboat.'"

"I see. This means a day is eight hundred and sixty-four thousand steamboats. Seven Galactic Rotations is five point two eight days. In your parlance."

Reed nodded. "So, five days. Then your ship is repaired."

"Correct. I need only to remain functioning to pilot it back to my cluster."

The little alien's green skin looked pale and sickly. Reed realized he had little context for how a healthy creature might look, but he was willing to bet it wasn't this dull greenish-gray. Five days, that was all he needed.

"Right … and how are you feeling?"

"Negative. I was injured in the crash."

"Negative?"

"Bad. Sub-optimal. Loss-case scenario."

"I see. Did the food help?"

"Nutrients assist in healing, yes. Why did you dismantle my ship? My readouts indicate this has increased repair time by three Galactic Rotations."

"Oh, I'm sorry. I was looking for medical supplies. Just found the food. It is raw, though."

"Raw?"

"Uncooked."

"Uncooked?"

"You know … hasn't been turned into an actual meal? Something that's enjoyable to eat?"

"I do not understand to what you are referring."

"You've never cooked your food?"

"We harvest nutrients and consume them. I do not understand what is so complex about a simple biological need. Surely your species does the same."

Reed frowned. "Well, sure, but you make it sound so unappetizing. Food's an art."

"Incorrect. Art is an application of creative skill to induce emotion and appreciation, and occasionally social commentary. Sustenance continues life." The creature took a bite of the raw, blue meat, shuddering slightly as it chewed.

"Doesn't look like you're enjoying it too much."

"Nowhere in the Quadrant Alliance is nutrition a matter of 'art' or 'enjoyment.' Either my translation database is incomplete, or our biological functions are different enough as to be incomparable. Do you consume emotion as sustenance?"

"No."

"Do you consume social commentary or appreciation as sustenance?"

"No!"

"Then I refer to my previous statement. There are many avenues of progress, exploration, and development, and the Alliance Research Group has advanced them all to the very bounds of collected knowledge. Nutrient consumption is a basic component of life, worth studying for physical health reasons only. It is not an art."

Reed reached over to pick up the meat canister. "Tell you what. A good meal always cheers me up when I'm feeling 'sub-optimal.' Let me cook a little bit of this, and you can see what you think. Sound fair?"

The lieutenant crawled back underneath the covers. "This is acceptable."

❉　❉　❉　❉　❉

Day 3

Reed returned from work with more energy than he'd had in a long time. The shift had been a blur of hastily combined ingredients, surly customers, and mediocre conversation. He hadn't paid it much mind, especially not when compared with the excitement at home.

Cooking at work was, well, working. This was going to be art.

Chronology willing, Reed would have been a cook aboard an exploratory vessel. He could have seen new waters, explored new regions of the world. When he tossed pasta, he imagined the steamy restaurant kitchen was the cabin of a research ship. Perhaps this meal would be served to someone like the great Charles Darwin, returning hungry after a day of studying the species of the Galapagos; or maybe the pasta would be made from a new kind of wheat, experimentally milled into uncharted flour. But that time had passed. The world was explored. All that was left now was for a few very powerful old men to decide who owned what.

Perhaps that was why Reed had found his way out to the cottage of a dead uncle he'd barely even spoken to, let alone loved or formed a connection with. It was the edge of known space. Land and land and land, filling up the borders of the American maps that hung in most tiny classrooms. At home, a pinprick in the center of that great landmass, you could see for what felt like forever. The ground was a simple horizontal line, and just by looking at a map you could tell what was in the parts you could no longer see.

But here, in California, it was the edge of the known world. Of course, if you went long enough, you'd come right around to the known world again and hit Japan. But before that were waves, and whatever lay below them. A man named Jules Verne painted a world of submarines and buried treasure. That sounded promising to Reed, though of course it was only fiction.

This was real. This creature, from above, was new. Whatever was up there, worlds upon worlds of Galactic Rotations and Quadrant Alliances, was interesting. Far more interesting than the map Reed lived on, which was quickly being colored in by various angry people who told legions of less angry but more scared people with guns what to do.

The familiar crackling of flame helped Reed focus. He had placed his cast-iron skillet over the low heat of his stove, and butter was melting. This, he knew what to do with.

"You perform a plasma reaction in your own living space?" J'Gar called over from the bed.

"I don't know about that. I know I use fire to cook."

"This is extremely hazardous."

"Not if you're safe about it."

Reed set the hunk of blue meat on a cutting board and sliced it into thin strips, then cut off an infinitesimal sliver to taste. Staring at the ribbon of blue on the cutting board, it looked so innocuous. Of course, it might be poisonous and kill him instantly. It might merely taste vile. But it was definitely of another world.

Reed ate it.

It was good meat, dissolving in his mouth quickly. Extremely salty — he'd have to watch out for that. The flavor was rich; it reminded him of beef. It certainly cut like beef. Reed found himself wondering what the animal it once was looked like.

Thin slivers would certainly be best, then. It was tough to get the knife through, so it would be tough to chew.

The butter in the pan was sizzling properly, so he laid the strips of meat in the skillet. They hissed with the heat, releasing a delicious and surprisingly familiar aroma. Meat was meat, it seemed, regardless of planet. He salted it. Less than usual, but a lot of the salt was going to vanish in the cooking process.

It needed a sauce. He wasn't sure about his guest's interest in spice, or sweetness, or saltiness. Better to stick close to natural flavors, he thought. You wouldn't want to overwhelm someone.

A simple peppercorn sauce, perhaps. Not too bold, but not boring either. He readied the ingredients.

"What are you doing in there?" The artificial voice of the translator was now familiar.

"Cooking."

"I am detecting increased positive olfactory indicators."

"I don't know what that means."

"Smells. Good."

Reed grinned. This was his element.

He flipped the meat over. Best to leave it rare. If you were used to raw, anything well-cooked would be a shock. The peppercorn sauce would be augmented by juices left in the pan when the meat was done.

Reed bit into one of the leaves. It was a perfunctory action — he needed to get the taste, so he could make a decent dressing. Salad was the obvious choice.

He froze.

The leaf was delicate, with a light flavor that leaned more toward herbal than he would have expected. It would be like trying to make a salad of mint leaves, albeit not quite as strong. It didn't need much, perhaps just a simple vinaigrette to draw the flavors out. Again, something light.

The meat was done. He scooped it out of the pan, setting it down neatly on one of his scratched plates. He poured some sauce over it, added a small mound of salad. It was done.

The kitchen was filled with the smells of cooking. Familiar, but completely foreign at the same time.

Reed brought the plate over to the bed, and set it down. "Go ahead."

Lieutenant J'Gar glanced from him to the plate, then back to him. "What have you done to it?"

"Prepared it. Cooked it. Made it into art."

"It is sustenance."

"Just try it."

The alien took a small bite from one of the strips of meat, perfectly darkened at the edges. To Reed's eye, at least.

The realization hit him like a freight train. This was to be J'Gar's first meal. Ever. What if it wasn't good? What if they hated it? Reed was an order cook at a restaurant, not a spectacular chef. What if he had made the food poisonous somehow? What was a plasma reaction?

"Oh."

J'Gar was staring at Reed. Their eyes, still dark and blank, seemed a little lighter.

"Oh, this is good. This is better than good. Excellent? Surpassed expectations? Your language database has a shocking variety of words for enjoyment of sustenance. Is this why? This must be why."

Reed beamed. "Like it?"

"How did you DO this? It is still the same matter, is it not? You have simply edited it somehow? Added enjoyment? How is this possible?"

"You cook it. Put it over fire, or add different flavors that complement it. Just have to know how to pull the flavors from food."

"I believe I am having an emotional reaction." J'Gar took a large bite of salad, and collapsed on the bed. "Sorcerer refers to someone who uses unknowable means to produce spectacles, yes? You are a sorcerer."

Reed laughed. "I don't know about all that."

J'Gar sat up again, to more easily continue eating. "Surely the processes through which you have transformed these nutrients are arcane?"

Reed shook his head. "You can pick it up pretty quick, I bet. Especially with more arms than me."

J'Gar stared at him quizzically. "Are the elements of matter you combine with the base nutrients extraordinarily rare?"

"I got the butter and the vinegar for cheap. Depends on what's in season, really."

"Do I understand correctly that this is a simple process that can be done with reasonably common ingredients?"

"You do indeed."

"EUREKA." The flat tone of the translator's voice didn't change, but the volume increased immensely.

Reed leaned back, his ears ringing. "Beg your pardon?"

"Is 'eureka' not a common exclamation of positive emotion upon making a momentous discovery?"

"No, no, it is. Fair enough. I just … wasn't expecting it. Is this a momentous discovery?"

"It is indeed! Imagine the possibilities! This is a groundbreaking new avenue of exploration in both research and art!"

"I suppose so," Reed said. "You can try out all sorts of new combinations."

"You can do *multiple* things with the same ingredients?"

"Oh, of course."

J'Gar sagged back, dazed. Their skin looked a bit more lively and green. "The magnitude of this discovery has increased exponentially! Imagine the optimally-calculated flavors! Imagine the cultural cuisines!"

Reed grinned. "Well, I can write down a few recipes if you want. You know, to take with you."

It was hard to read expressions on J'Gar's face, but the little alien radiated confusion. "For … for your own reference?"

"No, for you to use."

"But you must come with me! You must bring this art back to the Quadrant Alliance!"

Reed paused. An actual unexplored region. Endless things to see. The absence of a map filled with ownership below beneath his feet. The chance to explore it, to learn from it, not to claim it for his own but to become *part* of it. It was too much.

"I — you don't want me. I'm an order-cook. There are thousands of better cooks than me, chefs even, people who are real artists. You want someone like that. Someone with skill, or flair, or, I don't know, someone French. An artist."

"Art is an application of creative skill to induce emotion and appreciation, and occasionally social commentary. Is this not correct?"

Reed sighed. "Yes, it's correct."

"You applied your creative skill to this. It induced emotion and appreciation in me. It made a comment on my society. It is art. I was mistaken. You have created it. You are the artist."

"Well, I suppose—"

"I do not recall anyone else providing kindness to me when I crashed. This art is inspired not by prestige, but by kindness and honesty. That is the best kind of art. This research would not be the same without you. There might be other cooks, but there is only one you. Assuming you are not cloned."

This was it. Reed's eyes sparkled.

"I accept."

BITE BACK
Lauren Glover

It was three ship's cycles after the battle that Ttrr Wanek found the time to address the strange complaint that had been submitted by the brig guards. The feathers on his shoulders were half mantled at the inconvenience as he stalked down to the brig.

The mesh of the cell containing the Artorian and the Human was the only one active. There was, as his crew complained, a discordant noise echoing through the space which seemed to vibrate directly into Wanek's nasal cavity. He approached the cell nonetheless.

The Human was seated with its limbs folded at odd angles, in the direct center of the cell. It bared bright white teeth in dark skin when it saw him and the discordant noise stopped. Wanek seemed to recall vaguely, from some long ago educational file, that Humans sometimes bared their teeth in pleasure, but found it absurd to think that was the case at the moment.

"Ah! You must be the TttsssArrrrr!" It got up with a surprising speed and approached the security mesh. Wanek reminded himself he was a senior Ttrr and not intimidated by the smaller, featherless being no matter how fast it was. He did not take a step back.

"The equivalent title in Standard is Captain. Use that," he commanded, unwilling to hear his title butchered.

The Human bobbed its head. "Sure, Captain. Got a name after that?"

"Wanek." It had been known at his fledgling naming that he was going into space, so his parents chose a name that would be easy for most species to pronounce.

Once again it bobbed its head. "Captain Wanek. I'm Mari. Thanks for coming to see me. I wasn't sure if the guards spoke Standard." Its teeth once again appeared.

Wanek was sure the Human was lying. The guards at least knew how to say the word "stop" in Standard and had specifically told the Human that several times.

"What is it you want, Human?"

"Well. I'm pretty sure this bear guy is sick and needs some medical attention asap. I could use some too." It gestured with one of its limbs at the torn off leg of its flight suit which was tied around another limb and stained with a brown color which might be Human blood. "But it's not as urgent for me, I think. Unless he really is a bear and is hibernating for some reason?" The Human tilted its head quizzically. It was disconcerting to see such a familiar gesture in amongst all the mixed signals of its other mannerisms.

Wanek turned his attention on the Artorian. Their species were built of muscles, tall enough that its head would brush the ceiling if it stood up and it had thick, bristling brown fur. It was also curled in a ball in the corner and hadn't moved at all in the time Wanek stood there. Usually, such a prisoner – the captain of a ship they had fought and won against – would be railing at his captivity and promising retribution.

After the battle, Wanek had had a bit of a conundrum. He was ordered to keep the Artorian alive and bring it back to Kyaeria for interrogation.

With the damage to their ship, it was going to be several cycles more before they reached Kyaeria. Artorian metabolism was very fast, and his ship did not carry food fit for carnivores like the Artorians. (Technically, he did since this war was being fought over the Artorians' terrifying habit of eating their preferred food – Kkavians i.e. Wanek's species. However, he would see the creature starve to death before feeding his own crew to the Artorian!)

It was also against galactic spacefaring rules to shoot down a civilian ship in the midst of battle. But shoot down the small Human ship his crew had. He had hoped when they towed the ship in that the Human would be dead, thus solving both his accidental war crime and his food supply problem for the Artorian. Unfortunately, the Human hadn't even seemed to be injured other than being low on oxygen.

Wanek was a pragmatic creature. So he had wiped all records of the Human ship and the Human from the battle, melted the Human's ship into slag with the ship's weapons, and put the Human in the same cell as the stunned Artorian captain in the hopes that both his problems would solve themselves over the next several cycles.

Instead, the Artorian huddled in a corner, faint tremors racking its frame.

The Human had no claws or talons to defend itself. Those teeth it kept baring were flat things, coming only to faint points. Wanek was pretty sure his fledgling's beaks were sharper. Artorians had both claws and razor sharp teeth for tearing meat. It was Wanek's turn to tilt his head in puzzlement gazing at the clearly incapacitated Artorian.

He let out a trill in annoyance and walked back to the nearest guard. "Did we do a health scan of the Atorian when he came on board?" They should have, but Wanek had been busy destroying another Artorian ship at the time.

"Yes, Ttrr. Did you want to see it?"

Wanek gave a sharp whistle of assent. The guard took a moment to pull it up on his pad, then hand it to his Ttrr. The Artorian had been brought in stunned, since it was the only safe way to handle them. It should have shaken that off in a few cycle marks. Impatiently, he flicked through the rest of the report. Radiation levels normal. None of the few known poisons in the blood. It had been healthy when it came on board.

"Summon a medic and a medic's shield," Wanek commanded quietly. He stalked back to the Human.

"If we examine you and the Artorian, you will cease your discordant warbling?"

"Discord – Hey! I have a perfectly nice singing voice!"

Maybe to other Humans. There was probably a file on Humans somewhere that Wanek could add the notation "capable of continuously producing noises which were exceedingly irritating to some species" if he were admitting to having a Human on his ship at all.

The Human thrust its lips out in some sort of baffling gesture. "Okay, so 'We Will Rock You' is a bit repetitive and like, insanely old fashioned, but I really like the rhythm!"

Wanek really had no idea what the Human was talking about. "You will cease?"

"Yeah. In return for medical treatment for me and the other guy, I'll stop singing." The Human cocked its head sideways. "You know, we could use some food in here too. Isn't it against the Galactic Standards to starve your prisoners? You've been providing water packs, but we do need food so we don't eat each other."

Since that had been exactly what he intended, Wanek refused to feel guilty about not wanting to waste food on the soon-to-be-dead Human. "We are not sure of your dietary requirements," he prevaricated. Humans were much more ubiquitous across the galaxy than they should be considering their soft bodies and lack of defenses. This far away from their own system though, Wanek had only seen a few during his lifetime.

"We're omnivores," it said with a quick baring of the teeth. "Fruits, grains, meat, vegetables, insects. You name it, we eat it."

"I shall see what we have." If the Artorian was sick then he was going to have to deal with this Human.

The medic arrived. They wore a heavy, but necessary energy shield around their waist. It would allow them to reach through and touch their patients, but any attempt by the Artorian and Human to touch them would be blocked.

"Retreat to the opposite corner!" Medic Lantta demanded of the Human. There was a fine tremble to his feathers which indicated he was scared, but Wanek doubted the Human would notice. It was the Artorian that Lantta was scared of anyway.

"You should look at them first," suggested the Human, pointing to the Artorian. Lantta looked at his Ttrr, and Wanek whistled his agreement.

For all his fear, Lantta was professional and thorough in his examination. Wanek was pretty sure he performed his scans twice just to be sure before backing away to make some notes. When Lantta finished, he looked at the Human for a long moment. His feathers were still quivering in fear, so much so that the Human might even notice soon. He started backing out of the cell.

"You had better check the Human too," reminded Wanek. Lantta's trembling increased, but he did as he was told. Scans and samples taken, the medic hurried out of the cell and down the hallway. Wanek reactivated the mesh before following.

"Report, medic!"

"The Artorian is dying, Ttrr. Its blood is poisoned."

"How?" asked Wanek. "Are Humans poisonous?" He didn't remember that from any educational files.

Lantta trilled a negative. "The Artorian didn't pick up the poison from biting the Human. If I had known of this cycles ago when it happened, maybe we could have prevented it, but as it is..." He trailed off. "I need to go get supplies, Ttrr. I will be back soon."

Lantta hurried off. Wanek was baffled so he borrowed the guard's pad again to look up Humans on the Infosys. They were neither venomous *nor* poisonous for that matter. There were several foods they shared in common, so Wanek reluctantly ordered a guard to get some for the Human. There was nothing in the file indicating how a Human could be killing the Artorian. He was relieved when Lantta returned.

Lantta almost ignored the Human when it returned to the cell, but his feathers ruffled in determination before settling. It seemed he had found his courage when he went to get supplies. Lantta tossed a water pack and a medical patch to the Human. "Clean your wound, then cover it with the patch and stay in that corner!"

Lantta turned to the Artorian, though never quite turned his back on the Human. He injected what was probably a sedative. Then he produced a knife and proceeded to shave off the hair on one of the Artorian's limbs. The skin was black and sickly under it. Lantta gestured him closer, after a quick check that the Human was staying still. There was a small, half crescent of marks puncturing the skin, with a gray pus oozing out of them. Kkavians did not have a good sense of smell, but this close even Wanek could smell the decay.

"What did you do?" he asked the Human, though he was eyeing it warily, knowing how fast it could move when it wished.

"It defended itself," said Lantta.

"Well, yeah," said the Human. "When it bit me, I bit back. What else was I supposed to do? And it's 'she' by the way."

Wanek turned to Lantta for an explanation. "I will have to search the Infosys for proof, but I believe that Human mouths are much ... dirtier than most sentient species. Their teeth aren't sharp like our beaks or the Artorian's incisors. They barely pierced the Artorian's skin, but all it needed was broken skin and one deadly bacteria to get through. My scans show there were several of those deadly bacteria to choose from. We will need to take the Artorian for surgery. If I remove the limb, it might survive. Assuming you want it to, Ttrr."

Wanek trilled that he did. Medic Lantta whistled for the guards and the extra medics he had brought. One kept an eye on the Human while the rest loaded the Artorian on a hoverpad. They headed out. The final guard on the Human activated the mesh as she left.

Wanek stayed back. He did not want this Human on his ship any longer. "I will give you one of our shuttles, food and as many credits as you can carry if you will leave now and not mention this incident to anyone ever again."

It was the Human's turn to study him. "Throw in a packet of these patches and one of your med scanners, and you have a deal."

Kkavian medicine was no doubt very advanced compared to the Human's, but that was someone else's problem. "Deal."

The Human bobbed its head. "It's been a pleasure then, Captain." It bared its teeth at him.

Wanek suppressed his quivering until he was out of sight.

EPISODE 51: EARTH
Jennifer Lee Rossman

In the grand scheme of things, "What the hell are you?" may not have been the most diplomatic way to welcome an extraterrestrial to our planet. But then, no one had ever accused Teagan Strong of having an overabundance of diplomacy.

Freckles, yes. Opinions, yes (oh god yes, just ask her fiancée). Diplomacy … not so much.

(Again, just ask her fiancée. Or possibly ex-fiancée; she couldn't quite remember how they left things the night before.)

But in any event, humanity was not given a choice as to who would represent Earth to the visitors. Which is probably for the best, as I'm sure Keanu Reeves would have had other obligations, and Mr. Rogers would be unavailable because it's just so difficult to get a hold of necromancers on the weekend.

And so, it was Teagan. Angry, foulmouthed, still a little bit tipsy Teagan: the first human featured on the universe's most popular wildlife documentary series.

*   *   *   *   *

"Welcome back," said the host, a small, gray-ish green fellow wearing what appeared to be a silver lamé safari jacket.

Perhaps "said" is inaccurate. He certainly made noises at his similarly-attired camera-alien, but they weren't words so much as the vocal version of what happens when a cat walks across the keyboard. Yet somehow, in some telepathic way, Teagan understood him perfectly.

"Today we're visiting a beautiful, uninhabited planet in the Milky Way galaxy. It's mostly unexplored, and with good reason, as most of the ships that came here in the early days…" Here, he paused for dramatic effect. No doubt they would add suspenseful sound effects in post. "Never returned."

"Yeah, 'cause they crashed and got themselves dissected by the government," Teagan pointed out. She put her hands on her hips and took another step into the field, closing the distance between her and the aliens to about twenty yards, although she was terrible at estimating distance so it could have been a completely different number. But she decided to go with twenty. It didn't really matter anyway, since no one would believe this story regardless of how accurate her measurements were.

"What's this, then?" she asked, gesturing to the camera. "Is that a raygun? It better not be. I may or may not be getting married in…" She looked at her wrist. She was not wearing a watch, but she looked at her wrist nonetheless. "…Five hours, and I would very much like to not be dead during the ceremony."

(Probably a good decision, since it was very early on a Saturday morning and, as has already been established, it is very hard to find a necromancer willing to work on the weekend.)

The host turned abruptly, looking delighted. "Frank!" he stage-whispered. Whether the other alien was truly named Frank or if that was simply the roughest English translation, Teagan neither knew nor cared. Besides, if she thought too much about that, she would have to think about how nonsensical it was for her to psychically understand what they were saying, and then this whole story would fall apart and this narrator would be out of a job.

The alien who was not named Frank — or perhaps he was, as Teagan didn't know his name yet, but spoiler alert, his name will not end up being Frank — began walking toward Teagan. Slowly, carefully, all the while describing the specimen before him.

"Oh, aren't we lucky! This peculiar little creature is called a human. They are believed to have once been an apex predator on this planet, but evolution has rendered them more docile in recent millennia. Although not at all harmless in a celestial sense—"

"Hold up. Am I on some sort of messed up alien nature documentary right now? Because I don't remember signing a release—"

"Listen! Can you hear those vocalizations? It is theorized that they have learned to mimic the talking birds they have symbiotic relationships with — Frank. Frank, over here."

Frank, who had studiously been filming a bush, now swiveled in the host's direction ... this time pointing his camera straight up.

"Frank."

"Dominic."

The host — Dominic, apparently — briefly covered his face with one of his sucker-covered hands, a gesture that was, truly, universal. "Frank. I'm sitting here, pointing out and talking about a creature that is on the ground. Why are you filming the sky?"

"There was a bird," Frank said obstinately. Dominic could drag him to Earth, but he didn't have to pretend he liked it. Luckily, they had filmed most of what they came to document, and would be leaving soon.

Dominic seethed. Teagan snorted.

"I know how that feels," she commented, distantly grateful for the alcohol that was making it just this side of impossible to comprehend how terrified she should be right now.

*   *   *   *   *

At this point, the narrator would like to pause and remind people to drink responsibly. Alcohol can impair your judgment, as Teagan is currently demonstrating for us.

Please drink in moderation, don't drive while under the influence, and, if at all possible, avoid alcohol altogether on the days when aliens come to our planet to film nature documentaries.

*   *   *   *   *

Dominic glanced at Teagan in surprise and possibly just a touch of confusion. "Frank," he said, and it was not a question so much as a command. "Frank, I really need you to focus here. This human is absolutely fascinating!"

Teagan demurred.

At least, she thought she did. Was demurring that thing beautiful ladies did in old movies when they were complemented? Turning slightly, raising one shoulder, batting their eyes all sexy-like? She would have googled it but the field, like most random fields, did not have a Wi-Fi network.

(The narrator's house, on the other hand, does. And no, Teagan was not using that word correctly, but we will let her pretend she was.)

Where were we? Yes. Teagan demurring at the fact that she was apparently fascinating.

"Just look at the way she wobbles about, and how unkempt her mane is."

"Hey!"

"It does look soft but she must already have a mate, otherwise she would be grooming better — Frank! I swear, if you don't…"

Reluctantly, and with a lot of grumbling under his breath, Frank began filming Teagan. She couldn't see his expression very well behind the camera that still sort of looked like a raygun, but she got the distinct feeling he was rolling his eyes.

"This appears to be a female," Dominic resumed narration. "Although humans have a much looser concept of gender than we do, so one should never assume."

"Ally points for the alien!" Teagan said, tipping her imaginary hat.

"Although whatever her gender, you can tell by her sagging earlobes that she is well past breeding age."

With a gasp of indignation, Teagan clasped her hands over her ears. "Don't you look at my ears, you Martian pervert! And I'll have you know, I'm not even 40, and Perri thinks my earlobes are very attractive. Even if they are the earlobes of a Catholic."

Had the aliens been able to understand Teagan — and the way Dominic once again paused and looked at her when she talked suggested that perhaps he could —this non-sequitur about her most recent lovers' squabble would have taken them quite by surprise. But the shiny documentarians from the stars were embroiled in a lovers' squabble of their own.

"I never listen to you? You never listen to me!"

"Because you never talk to me; you talk at me, like I'm one of your viewers!"

"You're scaring the wildlife with all this shouting!"

Here, Teagan felt the need to interrupt. "Wildlife? That's a funny way to pronounce dominant species, buddy boy."

"Wildlife?" Frank unknowingly echoed. "Your precious wildlife used to kill our kind! That's why they never came back, Dominic! There's no big mystery, no need for a pause so we can add dramatic sound effects in post! We landed, and the humans murdered us!"

The field fell into utter silence in the wake of this announcement. Frank waited, and when his husband — Teagan had no context to know their matching eye colors were their equivalent of wedding rings, which is why you should always hire an omniscient narrator — had no reply, he beamed himself up into the sky.

"Cool," Teagan whispered, and this time there was no denying it. Dominic had understood her.

*   *   *   *   *

We must not examine the mechanism by which Teagan and Dominic could psychically understand one another, because … reasons. Very good reasons that … are not important to tell you right now.

(Look. There are some things even omniscient narrators don't know, and it hurts our feelings when you point them out. Just accept that this is a world in which strange things exist, like necromancers and psychic bonds between strangers and commercially available cloned dinosaurs, and let me move on with the story.)

(Not dangerous dinosaurs, obviously. Little ones that eat plants.)

*   *   *   *   *

"Welcome back," Dominic sighed to himself. "I am here on a little planet called Earth, currently psychically conversing with the dominant species and waiting in vain for my husband to come back. I should go after him. This is really not a good place for me; harmless and adorable as the humans are, Frank is correct. Most of them will kill us soon as look at us."

"To be fair," Teagan pointed out, "Only some of us would kill you. Most would study you." And then, because that didn't sound as helpful as her drunken mind thought it would, she added, "Hey, fun human fact for ya: we are also assholes to the people we love."

She slumped to the ground, resting her back against a bale of hay. Dominic joined her, partially out of the desire to share a mutual emotion of exhaustion and regret and partially because, if he got very close and was very quiet, perhaps the human would let him pet her hair.

It looked soft.

"You see, the problem with us humans? We hate each other. Usually for no good reason. Sometimes for good reasons, like the existence of boy bands, but usually because we are awful and we don't want anyone to be happy unless they're exactly like us." She gestured to her shirt, which read "queerly beloved, we are gathered here to gay."

"Word play," Dominic said, ever the documentarian. "The humans appear to have something of a rudimentary language. Although this specimen appears not to have a firm grasp on it, as she keeps slurring her speech."

Teagan opened her mouth to object, belched instead, and miraculously found her way back to her original topic. "I'm supposed to get gay married today, and I want it in a church and she doesn't because ... because churches have historically sucked when it comes to gay stuff. But it's important to me and I thought we figured it out but we had a whole fight and now I'm drunk and talking to an alien — a gay alien, a ... gaylien — in a field and I just found out I have elderly earlobes."

Dominic tried not to stare at her, as he was not sure whether that would constitute a threat. He failed, but at least he tried.

"What are you staring at, moon man?" Teagan asked, perhaps less diplomatically than she should, but again, no one had ever accused her of having an abundance of diplomacy.

Dominic thought for a moment. "I am trying not to ascribe emotion or logic to your actions. Which is not to say you don't have emotions or logic. Just ... when we try to project ourselves onto animals, we get attached, which is bad in my line of work. You and I are not the same, but it is getting harder for me to remember that."

Teagan looked up at the stars, and only the fog of alcohol prevented a panic attack at the thought that each of those billions and billions of lights could have people on them.

"I don't know," she said finally. "We're both sitting here with an alien, painfully in love with someone who's mad at us for trying to share something beautiful with them and not realizing that what we call beauty, they call trauma. I don't care if you're human, alien, or…" Here she paused, not knowing if there was a third option and not sure she would want to know what it was. "Or … or whatever. That shit hurts."

And now it was Dominic's turn to look at the stars, marveling at all the planets he and Frank had visited, all the creatures documented. Each species lovely and weird and sometimes scary in their own way, but none so much as the human.

Only humans, he mused, possessed the violence and xenophobia required to instantly capture and destroy visitors that didn't fit in with their comfortable little idea of reality. Only humans had evolved the technology and ability to make themselves dangerous not only to their fellow Earth creatures, but the entire universe.

And yet, of all the planets and of all the creatures Dominic had studied, only humans. Angry, foulmouthed, still a little tipsy humans. Only they had the ability to recognize and regret their mistakes, to empathize to the point of psychic bond with an alien who came to the planet with the intention of destroying it.

*   *   *   *   *

Yes, perhaps I should clarify for anyone who has not seen a full episode of Dominic's show.

On the surface, it follows the same formula as most nature documentaries: dashing quasi-celebrity with a soothing voice and tempestuous love for his cameraman visits a far off land, trying the local cuisine and mildly irritating the wildlife while teaching the folks back home fun facts about the ecosystem.

But it is important to know that the show's title loosely translates to The Celestial Cemetery. It is not a travel show, it is not really about nature. It is an in memoriam reel, for after the final commercial break, Dominic and Frank bid the world farewell as the producers (also known as The Intergalactic Council for Extraterrestrial Population Control) explode the planet.

*　*　*　*　*

Earth had not done anything wrong, other than simply exist in a quadrant already too full of life. Sure, maybe they were only depleting their own planet of resources at the moment, but they would be interstellar by the end of the century. The devastation they would inevitably cause...

"Go to her," Dominic said suddenly, looking at Teagan with the same wonder and marvel he had been giving the heavens. "Apologize to your mate. Participate in your mating ritual, wherever you can. Just do it before it is too late."

His urgency gave gravity to his words, and Teagan scrambled to her feet, if a tad unsteadily. "You too, ET. Go ... phone your homo."

With that, she left, unaware that, in this context, "before it is too late" did not mean simply before Perri had decided to move on, but rather before the end of the world as they knew it.

(And they would not feel fine.)

As he watched her form retreat into the night, two things occurred to Dominic. First, he had not even tried to pet her hair. That regret would stay with him for years to come.

Second, and possibly most important (but only possibly; her hair looked extremely soft), it occurred to him that he could, indeed, phone his homo. One of Frank's mothers — the nice one, who adored Dominic

— worked on the council. If he told Frank that he refused to leave, they couldn't possibly destroy the planet.

In the end, perhaps it was fortunate that necromancers are impossible to hire on the weekends. Mr. Rogers was a vast many things, all of them good and lovely, but sometimes, in the grand scheme of things, what you really need to save the world is a drunk lesbian with freckles, too many opinions, and not enough diplomacy.

SABER-TOOTHED LICKER
S.Park

Akitl was admittedly not paying terribly close attention to the pair of children chasing each other in circles around on the grass a few meters away from her. She had her communicator unit held in her main manipulator, her two central eyes focused on it, and was composing a natal-day message for her mother. The honoring of one's female parent was a long-held Klizkit tradition, though doing so specifically on natal-days was something that she had picked up from humans.

Natal-days were a good occasion, though. They weren't tied to a specific belief tradition, so no offense could be given if a child or parent had changed their belief tradition, and one had to pick a day or two out of the year's turn *somehow*. A natal-day was as good a day as any to pick.

She input a few more lines, her antennae held down as she struggled to find appropriate phrasing, her four secondary eyes fixed on the running children, but her attention definitely elsewhere. Her recently pupated offspring, Pthiz, had been playing with Emily, the three-year-old human girl, for several months now without any major incidents, so Akitl had stopped being quite as watchfully nervous when the pair were together. Besides, Emily's father, Steve, was right there, helping keep an eye on the two children.

Really, there wasn't that much to be worried about. Humans were bizarre creatures, shockingly reckless, with extremely strange ways of finding enjoyment, but they weren't super-klizkian; they were mere mortals, and in some ways rather fragile. Their soft epidermises were astonishingly easy to damage, to begin with. Akitl remembered the first time she'd seen Emily "skin her knee" as Steve had called it.

It had been quite alarming. She'd been certain the child was savagely injured, what with internal fluid — a bright, shocking red, even — leaking from her surface. But the girl had hardly seemed to mind. She'd gotten a brief swabbing with a sanitizing cloth that Steve had produced from the bag he carried over his shoulder at all times, and a small bandage that didn't even fully cover the leaking area placed over it, and then a "kiss better" on the injury from her father, after which she cheerfully raced off to play again as if nothing had happened.

Klizkit were far more difficult to damage externally, though of course if something did crack their exoskeletons, it could be catastrophic. Steve had nodded when told this, but then startlingly noted that most human children fractured their endoskeleton at some point in their development. He himself, he said, with something almost like pride, had managed to break both arms at once in his youth.

He'd also told her, with pleased interest, that scientists of his species were studying Klizkit exoskeletons, seeking to artificially produce similar substances, as they were made of a material far stronger than the chitin found in superficially similar but much smaller animal species on their native world.

So humans were actually if anything more fragile than Klizkit, which made their impulsive willingness to throw themselves into danger all the more remarkable.

With a shake of her antennae, Akitl returned her attention to the missive on the small screen in front of her. Suddenly a sharp sound, a kind of high-pitched yip with a trailing click, made all her eyes snap to where the two children were playing. That hadn't been a pain sound or a danger call, but it was a sound of shocked surprise, the kind of sound that sometimes happened just before a danger call or — even worse — when something so fast and deadly had attacked that there was no time for a danger call.

A rush of fear-pheromones thickened around her as Akitl sprang to all four feet, seeing Pthiz lying on the ground, with Emily bent over him in a positively predatory posture. What had the girl done?!

Steve waded into the situation before Akitl could decide if she should, and he towed Emily off of the young Klizkit who, much to Akitl's relief, climbed to his feet with a puzzled buzzing, seemingly unharmed. Steve, though, was once again scolding Emily, and after a brief telling-off that Akitl couldn't quite hear, he gently took Pthiz by the main manipulator limb and urged him towards Akitl.

Emily pouted, dragging her feet as she was also towed along. Pthiz, amiable as always, walked at Steve's side, his antennae indicating only curiosity. As they got closer Akitl heard Emily saying, "Daddy, I was only *playing* saber-tooth tiger. It's okay!"

Confused, Akitl moved to meet them, having alarming visions of the admittedly carnivorous human child deciding to inexplicably try to predate her own offspring. "Steve? What happened?"

Steve sighed deeply and said, "Emily licked him."

Akitl blinked, her mind wrenching to a different track entirely. "As far as I know there are no compounds on the exoskeletons of Klizkit that are toxic to humans, and Pthiz is generally cleanly..."

Steve chuckled and shook his head in negation. "Oh, no, I'm not worried about her. She licks all kinds of things, most of them much dirtier than your son. No worries there. Just, well…" He gave Emily a complex look, and the child looked down at her shoes, seeming chastised by it. "She *does* lick all kinds of things, so I have no idea what else she might have licked today, and human mouths are dirty places to begin with."

Akitl angled her antennae to indicate confusion. "I do not think any diseases are transmissible between our species…"

"No, but bacteria can grow anywhere. I know it *probably* wouldn't do him any harm, what with that handy exoskeleton he has, but I don't want him getting some kind of bacterial joint rot or something. And like I said, I have no idea what else she might have licked recently."

"Oh." Akitl found herself suddenly at a loss. Bacterial joint rot was actually a thing that could happen, especially if one had been engaging in activities that might leave micro-abrasions around the joints, like say being chased and pounced on by a human child. But now she was very much at a loss about what to do next. Taking Pthiz to a doctor just for getting licked by a little girl seemed absurd.

Steve apparently correctly interpreted the baffled set of Akitl's antennae, because he began rummaging around in his bag while saying, "It's fine. I think I know what to do. Just … How are Kilzkit with the application of alcohols? Er, externally, not internally."

Akitl found herself flicking her antennae upwards in something close to laughter, contemplating the complete and total insanity of the phrase "externally, not internally" with regards to alcohols, and said, "It will do him no harm, applied externally."

"I'll just sanitize the lick, then, and all's well." Steve bared his teeth in a gesture Akitl recognized as meant to reassure and set about opening a little packet with a sanitary wipe in it.

"Thank you," said Akitl, sitting back down on the bench and pondering how in the galaxy a species that spent its developmental years *licking* everything even survived. Once again she found herself thinking that humans were very strange indeed.

FRIENDS OF CATS
Maree Brittenford

The Rogurplian ship was strange, and well, alien. Which made sense, seeing as the Rogurp were aliens.

That knowledge didn't make Stephan any more comfortable. But still, the time frame and importance of this mission meant that when they offered to transport him to Lincoln Station, he couldn't say no.

He stepped through the opening that appeared in the wall, wincing as he brushed against the slippery substance that formed all the interior surfaces of the ship.

Stephan was no scientist, so he didn't understand exactly what the material was, or how it worked, but in his layman's opinion it was gross. He'd had to put his hand into it when he first came on board, and let it crawl onto him. It needed to learn him, he was told. It felt like a thousand centipedes running across his skin. Just remembering it had him shuddering in revulsion. What was wrong with a normal DNA encoded lock?

Everything about the ship was creepy, starting with the disturbingly mobile walls and floors. What exactly was holding the shimmery white substance together? All Stephan had to do to open his cabin door was touch the wall with the intent to exit, and an opening formed itself. What was stopping the floor from doing that and dropping him straight into the engine or empty space? Stephan had already decided that he was not going to set a bare foot on the floor, just in case.

And the smell! It wasn't bad exactly, sort of like a combination of citrus and mouse. He wasn't sure if it was coming from the rippling substructure or the Rogurplians themselves. He supposed it didn't matter.

He leaned down and opened the door of the cat crate he'd brought on board with him. "It's only for four days. We can handle that, right?"

The cat curled around his ankles, and Stephan ran a hand down the orange mottled back. He didn't even like cats that much, but the feel of the warm soft fur was incredibly comforting in this ship where everything else felt strange and wrong.

He perched on the edge of the bunk, which at least seemed to be a solid piece of furniture, and not more of the shifty stuff. The cat hopped up beside him and curled herself into a purring orange blob.

At least someone was relaxed. Stephan couldn't imagine relaxing enough to sleep here. "It's only four days," he reminded himself.

The walls flashed a startling pink, and he flinched, before remembering that the crewman who brought him on board had mentioned something about that. It meant something. The walls flashed two more times before he recalled. It was a kind of a doorbell.

He braced himself for the crawling sensation and touched the wall, and then watched in fascinated disgust as an opening appeared on the far wall.

"May I enter?"

It was the same crewman from before.

Crew-member. Stephan wasn't even sure it was a male or female, or even if these people had a concept of gender. It was a seven foot tall cricket, more or less. Its eyes were bulbous and solid brown, and about three times the size of human eyeballs. Six limbs with wicked looking spurs ranged down its abdomen, and while it didn't have opposable thumbs, the four upper limbs worked in such concert that thumbs seemed like a pointless adaption.

"Please," Stephan gestured using the polite gestures he'd learned. He'd been drilled on this part. Under no circumstances was he to give grounds for offense and upset the delicate state of interspecies cooperation.

If only anyone knew what Rogurplians found offensive.

They were a deeply insular culture, and even the fact that they'd allowed Stephan onboard was amazing.

While they didn't seem to wear clothing, they did decorate themselves by painting bright colors on their shell-like bodies.

It was based on the purple crosshatched pattern on the front of the shell that Stephan felt fairly certain that this person was the crew-member called Rasslic.

There were two cylindrical pieces of furniture in the corner that Stephan hadn't taken a look at yet. Rasslic seated himself on one, so Stephan took the other. It startled him by slowly beginning to sink, making all his fears of falling through the floor almost a reality, but it stopped as suddenly as it began, and he realized it had been adjusting for his height. He didn't know whether to feel disturbed or intrigued by the sentient goo chair.

The silence stretched uncomfortably.

"I would wish that you have pleasant journey," Rasslic said. Their voice was high pitched, with a humming quality that gave it a pleasant resonance. The wording was odd and disjointed, but that was normal with the translation software. Especially when it was translating to or from English. Unfortunately the software only supported the four major human languages, otherwise Stephan would've switched to his native Swedish, a much more predictable language.

"I'm sure I will."

"I am bade to be at your assistance at any of times."

Stephan nodded. "Thank you."

He cast his mind around for appropriate non-offensive interspecies conversational topics. The weather? Everyone's health? Neither seems applicable.

Rasslic let out a strange squark and leapt up, backing up against the wall.

Stephan scanned the room for a threat. "What is it?" he demanded. If the floor was going to start dissolving, he wanted to know immediately.

"The creature, it's loose!"

On the bed the cat stretched languorously.

"Oh! Was I expected to keep her caged for the whole trip?" That seemed cruel. The carrier was a very small container.

Rasslic's posture didn't relax. "Is it not a danger?"

"A cat? She might scratch if you scare her. But she's been chosen because she's a good pet."

Rasslic's bulging brown eyes seemed to bulge a little further. "I will certain be not to scare her. I believe I have heard telling of these human weapons. Pets."

Stephan had to struggle not to laugh. What on Earth had these people been told about humans?

"A pet isn't a weapon, it's … for comfort, and companionship."

Rasslic's antennae twitched, almost like they were trying to read the truth of the statement.

"Do Rogurplians keep pets?"

"Trained combat animals?"

Well, at least Stephan had found a conversation topic.

He picked up the cat, who draped compliantly over his arm, and brought her closer to Rasslic. They brought their upper two sets of limbs up in front of their body defensively.

"It's okay, she won't hurt you. Try touching her."

After a long moment when Stephan contemplated the possibility of this causing the exact sort of incident he'd been warned to avoid, one of the limbs extended toward the animal. Stephan stroked a hand across the orange fur, and Rasslic hesitantly followed suit, before snatching the limb back to their body.

"The texture is unusual."

"A lot of people like it. They find stroking an animal like this soothing." It was soothing Stephan right then. Was he doing the right thing? Or should he be locking the cat back into her crate for the remainder of the journey? It was only four days. Surely she would be fine.

But then Rasslic was unfolding from their defensive posture, and reaching toward the cat once again.

"Her name is Tabitha," Stephan said. He'd thought it a stupid pun of a name when he'd collected her. What kind of a name was that for a cat that wasn't a tabby? Now it seemed almost cute.

"Tabitha," Rasslic said reverently.

Once they warmed up to the animal, it was difficult to get them to leave. Stephan spent the next few hours sitting on his suspicious stool watching the alien as they observed, touched, admired.

Tabitha was un-fazed. Her calm friendly personality was why she was selected for this mission, after all. But even she had her limits, and eventually she tired of Rasslic's fascinated attentions.

She stood, stretched and sauntered away.

Rasslic made to follow her, but Stephan stopped them.

"Let her be. She needs a break."

"A break?"

"A rest. She's tired. And you know how cats are."

Rasslic folded their top leg pairs into their body. "I am not know cats. What are they?"

"Some people say cats can't be trained. That's been proven wrong, of course. But the truth of it is still that cats do as they please, and to be friends with one you have to make allowances for that."

"I must?"

"If you want her to like you."

This information seemed to strike Rasslic particularly.

"I must assure that Tabitha remains friends. I will make sure she does as she pleases. I will leave now so she may rest."

Stephan nodded gratefully, glad for the excuse to get his odd guest out of his cabin. It was exhausting to be watching his every word and gesture. But at least it took his mind off the strange shifting surfaces of the walls and floors. As soon as he was alone, it was all he could think about.

He lay down on the bed, the texture of the fabric bedding making it feel like the only safe place on the ship. The cat sauntered over and curled into his side. Her purrs vibrated comfortingly through his torso. And it was to that sensation that he fell asleep.

*　*　*　*　*

Stephan was woken far too early. He'd never enjoyed mornings, even in space where morning was a concept rather than an event. It didn't matter. He never felt entirely human until after he'd been awake for an hour or two.

He did not get the luxury of an extended wake up period.

The flashing colors in the walls broke the darkness of the room, jolting him into wakefulness.

Rasslic was waiting outside, with three crew mates.

"We wish to see the pet Tabitha," they chirruped.

Stephan rubbed his eyes and gestured the group inside.

The four of them cooed over the cat, in awe of the deep vibrations coming from her throat. Only Rasslic was brave enough to attempt to hold her, and still became panicked when she, as cats are wont to do, decided she'd had enough of him and slid out of his grasp.

Stephan had to spend several minutes reassuring them all that the cat had not been mortally offended.

As the day wore on it seemed that all sixty four crew-members found a reason to stop by his cabin and meet the famous pet.

Much comment was made over the softness of her fur, the pleasantness of her purring, and the beauty of her orange tortoise-shell coloring.

"Two more days," Stephan muttered to himself as he saw his last guests out, and fell into bed exhausted.

When he woke the next morning, the cat was gone.

* * * * *

"A least I must not sound the alert of personnel accidentally evacuated!" Rasslic said chattering their limbs against their carapace.

"Accidentally evacuated? What does that mean?" Stephan asked, not entirely sure if he wanted to know.

"Accidental airlock operation!"

Stephan stared at them in shock. "You can accidentally open the airlocks? How is anyone still alive on this ship?"

"Do not be concerned, friend Stephan. We can survive for several hours in open space. But knowledge of your biology and Tabitha is cause to prevent access to external airlocks."

"So you're saying I can't accidentally vent myself to space because you know I'd die?"

"Extremely sorry, Stephan. You were promised full ship access. Sorry for restriction."

"No, no, that's good. I appreciate it. On human ships that's normal."

Rasslic relaxes its chattering limbs.

"This is not offensive?"

"No no. It's for my safety." Stephan relaxed slightly. It was good to know he didn't have to worry about venting himself. And presumably that meant that he couldn't accidentally fall through the walls of the ship in his sleep or something. Of course it didn't solve the more immediate problem.

"None of that explains how Tabitha got out of my room. Is it possible someone let her out?"

Rasslic began the limb quivering again.

"Rasslic?" Stephan asked carefully, "Did you let her out?"

"You said 'Cats must be allowed to do as they wish!'"

Did he?

"But why would … Oh. Did you change the settings on the walls so she could leave the cabin?"

"It was only if she wished! Tabitha can do as she wishes!"

Stephan groaned. This was a disaster. There was a ship delaying a deep space mission because of this one precious cargo. His own job as Nutritional Engineer was unimportant by comparison. Sure, he was the expert at putting together food from alien sources in a way that humans found palatable. But in the end, other crew-members could fudge together meals. No one but a cat could fill the role of ship's cat. Or at least no other human. Dogs and rabbits, as well as pigmy sheep had tested moderately well as deep space companion animals, but none were as adaptable and resilient as a cat.

And the worst of it was that he could only think of one reason why she'd venture so far from her food bowl for an extended time.

"She's gone to find a secluded place to give birth."

Rasslic twitched backwards as if repulsed. "Mammalian reproduction? Is that not dangerous? And many fluids involved?"

"Tabitha and her kittens were ruled healthy before I boarded your ship. It is a few days before her due date, but it's not that early. I'm sure she'll give birth without a problem. Unless she's found a dangerous spot to hide in. Can you scan the ship for her?"

"This would be an invasion of rights. We do not invade guests rights."

"But your guest is asking you to do it. You have my permission."

"Tabitha has not given consent."

"She's an animal, she has no rights to personal privacy."

Rasslic began to back toward the door, limbs chittering violently.

Stephan suddenly felt like this was one of those moments he was warned not to cause. Where diplomatic relations could be destroyed by one misunderstanding.

"I must speak to commanding officer," Rasslic said as they backed into the corridor. The wall fused closed in a very final manner.

Stephan pressed his hand against the gooey surface, willing it to open but it didn't respond.

He could very well be doing it wrong, but he doubted it.

He'd been locked in.

* * * * *

It wasn't a terribly long wait. Only 34 minutes by Stephan's antique earth wristwatch. But each minute dragged endlessly.

Had he committed an unforgivable transgression? And what was it anyway? Telling Rasslic that cats do as they please? Or saying she was an animal with only limited rights? Or was the real mistake letting the Rogurplians interact with the cat at all? Was this all inevitable from the first moment their forelimbs stroked that soft cat fur?

He was lying on the bed trying to sleep when the wall lights flickered and Rasslic entered without waiting to be invited.

"Commanding officer will discuss you now."

They led Stephan to the Captain's office in heavy silence. Even their footfalls were soundless on the spongy living floor.

The Captain was indistinguishable from Rasslic, save their own painted markings were far more extensive. They mostly consisted of scarlet and green curving lines, like the way a child draws the ocean.

The Captain's office was more of the same biomass walls and flooring. Here even the furniture seemed to be no more than temporary outgrowths of the floor. The Captain seated themself behind a long imposing desk, and gestured with two forelimbs for Stephan to be seated on a stool that formed itself from the floor. It was damp and uncomfortably tall, and didn't adjust to his size the way the stools in his cabin had done. He did his best to perch on the front edge.

At least intimidation tactics were the same across the galaxy.

"The cat Tabitha has been offered safe haven on this ship." The words were spoken slowly and carefully, as if the Captain was choosing each word with care, to ensure the message was clear.

It still took Stephan a moment to understand.

"You're offering asylum — to a cat?" Surely this wasn't happening. Surely he hadn't created this situation. This horrible, horrible, interspecies incident situation.

The Captain stared at him with those unblinking dark orbs of eyes. "You have been accused of species rights violations. This is a serious crime. Due process will be seen."

Stephan's brain froze up.

"Is she safe at least?" he finally managed to ask. "Has she been found? Has she delivered the kittens safely?"

The Captain stared at him for a long moment, at least it felt like staring, with those bulbous brown eyes focused on him in an unblinking stare.

"She has not chosen to make herself known to us at this time."

Stephan had thought he was panicky before, but now? He couldn't imagine how much worse this would get if something happened to Tabitha. He couldn't help imagining a kitten crushed in some mashy part of the engine, or vaporized by lasers or whatever they had down there in the engine room that made this ship go.

"You have to find her! She could be in danger!"

Those eyes continued to stare. "You will be confined to your quarters now. Rasslic?"

Rasslic stepped forward from the corner of the room he'd been hovering in, and gestured to the opening that had appeared in the wall.

Stephan shook his head and exited, Rasslic following close behind.

This was the worst case scenario of the worst case scenario. And he had no idea what to do.

Rasslic chittered their forelimbs against their caprice. "Is that true?"

"Is what true?"

"Could Tabitha Cat be hurt?"

Stephan stopped and turned to Rasslic. "She could. Parts of the ship could be very dangerous to her. Is anyone trying to find her and bring her to a safe place?"

Rasslic chittered their limbs again. "Captain believes she will present herself when she wishes and we are to respect her wishes."

The translation software could be misleading, but Stephan swore there should have been a "but" at the end of that.

"But you don't agree?" he hazarded. Hell, he couldn't make much more of a mess of this.

"I have downloaded data from human database. Restrictions for human safety are not…"

"They aren't the same as what keeps a cat safe, especially baby kittens." Stephan looked around. Other crew-members were going about their duties, and he couldn't tell if they were interested in them or not. But he felt watched. "Let's talk in my cabin."

The few minutes it took to get there gave Stephan time to gather his thoughts. Perhaps he could salvage this situation.

"If you can show me a floor plan of the ship, I can probably help you find Tabitha."

Rasslic didn't appear to be paying attention.

"I did wrong in reporting. It was wrong to report this to Captain."

"I wish you would've given me a chance to explain, but that doesn't matter now," Stephan said.

The constant sound of Rasslic's vibrating forelegs went silent.

"It does not matter?" they asked, fanning the legs out wide.

"Not at this moment! Right now I'm more concerned about the cat. You can tell me how sorry you are when she's been found."

"Ahh yes. Find Tabitha Cat."

Stephan shook his head. He'd never have picked giant cricket people for having angsty personalities, but Rasslic sure seemed to.

"Can you show me a floor plan of the ship?" he asked. "An image of the interior areas?" He added when Rasslic stared blankly.

"Ahh yes. Model of ship floor." Rasslic released an apparently untranslatable series of clicks and squeals and a three dimensional hologram appeared in the air between them.

"Okay, okay, can you highlight the areas that you've granted Tabitha access to?"

A surprisingly large number of areas light up. "Oh wow, okay. Was I granted access to all those places too?"

"Of course. Agreement was for free movement about the ship."

Stephan examined the model more closely. "What is this area here?" he asked, pointing to a long row of much smaller cubes.

"Crew quarters. You and Tabitha were welcome to visit crew friends."

He supposed that made sense to allow crew members to invite him to their rooms, although none had.

"Okay. I'm assuming that if the cat was in someone's room they'd have reported that by now, right?"

"Yes, right. No crew has seen Tabitha in crew quarters."

"Remove the highlight from there then."

Rasslic made a few sounds and the section dimmed.

"And you can blank out the hallways too, she won't be there."

Even more of the hologram grew dim.

"Is this the engine room? What's it like in there? Are there any dark quiet corners?"

Rasslic made a hissing noise, and Stephan flinched back, wondering if he'd caused some new offense.

"Are you not familiar with star engines? Yet you have served on many star ships! This is very amusing."

As a matter of fact Stephan wasn't familiar at all with engines. He visited the engine room maybe once each tour, and that was if the captain felt it necessary to hold an orientation tour. The rest of the time he just went between the kitchen, his quarters, and whatever recreational area the ship happened to have.

"I thought your technology might be different to humans," he said, feeling self conscious. He shouldn't have felt embarrassed. Why would a cook need to visit the engine room? He probably didn't even have clearance to go in there on a human ship. Rogurplian ships were obviously more freewheeling than that.

"Engine room is very bright, very loud. Very clean and organized."

"Okay, block that out too."

There were very few areas left glowing now. A few small scattered areas which Stephan guessed must be some sort of bathroom facilities (and he didn't want to know what that looked like for other species) and one larger area still glowing at the stern of the ship. An area that looked surprisingly familiar in layout.

"Is this the mess?"

"No! Very well organized."

"I mean is it the area for food preparation and eating."

Rasslic didn't answer, simply increasing the size of the area for better viewing.

When the details came into clearer view, Stephan grinned.

"I know where she is."

*   *   *   *   *

Rasslic had departed, cat carrier in hand, and aside from a curt message informing him that cat and kittens had been found safe, he had very little to do for the rest of the flight. Leaving him simultaneously bored and eaten up with anxiety.

Time dragged. Obviously.

Stephan had plenty of time to think up any number of ways of defending himself, which were all useless unless someone would let him out of his cabin and talk to him.

Finally, finally, at what he estimated to be nearly the end of the trip, he was summoned.

A crew-member, not Rasslic, at least not as far as Stephan could tell (the body language and decoration was quite different) escorted him to the captain's office.

The Captain was regally installed behind their massive desk. Rasslic hovered off to the side. And Tabitha lounged in her open carrier against the far wall.

The wall closed, leaving Stephan facing what felt like three judges.

The cat stood, gently shaking off her offspring, and stretched.

"Hey kitty," Stephan said, and then froze. Perhaps he wasn't supposed to speak to the asylum seeker. But Tabitha didn't seem to mind. She strolled over to him and began twining herself around his legs, meowing.

"Have you fed her?" He needed to shut up instead of questioning his host's ability to feed a cat.

"I have supplied the food as you instructed, but I am concerned. She is very hungry," Rasslic said, and that familiar limb rattling noise started up. Was the alien cricket ... nervous?

"She's fine. Cats just like complaining. Don't give in."

"So you would limit the access Tabitha Cat has to food," the captain said.

"For her own good? Yes." Stephan felt like he was on fairly solid ground with that.

"Rasslic believes I should hear your reasons. I am not certain."

Crap. It was all or nothing then.

"Isn't it the responsibility of those more knowledgeable to protect those who know less? Didn't you act the same way to protect me when I boarded your ship? Preventing me from entering areas that might be dangerous to me, like the engine room, or airlocks? Don't you protect your own children in the same way?"

"Caring for a cat is like caring for a pupae?"

"Yes, absolutely!" He may not have been exactly sure what a pupae was, but he sure was going to grab onto anything that sounded like common ground. "Pets need to be kept safe from things they don't understand."

Stephan felt like he needed to make a better argument than that, but Rasslic stepped forward and engaged the captain in a untranslated conversation. It seemed rude to interrupt, especially when he seemed to be gaining a toehold.

Finally the conversation ended and they both turned back toward Stephan.

"Very well. As the Cat Tabitha seems amenable to remaining with you, no formal action will be taken."

Stephan couldn't imagine what would've happened if he'd been given a shy or grumpy cat.

"But—"

Of course there was a but.

"I would wish to send Rasslic to discover more about humans and pets."

"I will inquire with my superiors. I'm sure it can be arranged."

The conference seemed to be at an end, and Stephan hurriedly deposited the cat back into her carrier and hustled out of there.

It was far better than he could've hoped. No diplomatic incident. Everything fixed. The cat safely back in his possession.

Of course now he had to figure out how to explain to the admiral why the only thing about Earth culture the Rogurplians seemed interested in was cats.

FIVE ROUNDS RAPID
Harrison Salzman

It started with a dare.

"You know, you can turn it down," Vassk confided during the mid-shift meal break, their mandibles held in conspiratorial stillness. "Nobody but that idiot Garhuff would even care."

"I'd care," Sylvia murmured back, tilting her head in a fair approximation of Vassk's own intimate-friends stance. "And you know the other crew would talk, like that time Enshri backed out on a hull race with Vix and Henry. I don't want to find potatoes in my locker for the next cycle."

The two of them were tucked into the smallest of the ship's cafeterias, deep in the lower decks near the main fuel tanks. Dingy, dimly lit, and forever filled with the hum of the gently-burning engines, it also only served L-chiral foods - a biological quirk that humans and Ishirans shared. Those factors combined to give it a privacy that had helped it become their favored date spot, when their shifts could be arranged to share off times.

Crewing a comet-ice freighter had more than a few similarities with serving on any other long-haul ship, space or sea. One of them was that weird little rituals sprang up. For some unfathomable reason, "potato" had come to mean "coward" to the crew of the *Unreachable Horizon*. Probably a pun in some language or other; it usually came down to that.

Another was dares, of course. No real penalties for backing out of one. Nothing but a little bit of respect on the line. But respect was a currency easier to spend than to gain, and Sylvia could barely stand potatoes at the best of times.

"Besides," she said, running a hand over her short-cropped brown hair. "Don't you think I can win? Come on, I'm no neophyte. It's not like I'm arm-wrestling a Silesian. What are you really worried about?"

After spending two years sharing a bunk with the Ishiran, it would have been harder for Sylvia not to pick up some of Vassk's body cues — especially given how ill-suited the species was to imitating human facial expressions. No lips, no eyebrows, not even the "right" number of eyes, but spend enough time together, and it was astonishing how mandible wiggle and cilial tilt could become an open book. Now, her angular face was held awkwardly, and she wouldn't meet the human's gaze with even one of her eyes.

"Come on, Vassk, tell me what's going on in that brain of yours. I won't be able to focus on my work this afternoon if you don't."

"You're just so fragile!" Vassk burst out, the voder-speaker at her throat buzzing with the forcefulness of it. "I know you, you're tough, yes, but humans are just so soft, it's hard to not worry about you. That stuff is dangerous! It's poison, and you're just going to drink it like it's nothing?"

"Oh, love." Sylvia laid a hand gently along the curve of a mandible, stilling its agitated twitching. "Trust me, humans are a little tougher than you might think."

* * * * *

The hull of the ship was a dull silver expanse against the endless black, lit by suit lights and the heads-up AR of their displays. When they left dock, it had been polished to a mirror sheen to help radiate out heat, but dust impacts had dulled that on every thrust-facing surface. Here and there, pock marks showed the impacts of micrometeorites; pulsed lasers and aimed grav-fields were supposed to keep them away, but every now and then one got through. Rarely, something bigger slipped by, and techs had to suit up and survey the damage. "Rarely" was now.

Sylvia's scalp prickled with sweat. She wished she could lift a hand to brush it away, but no way to do that in a vac suit. A little puff of cool air from her ventilation system helped to evaporate it. She stood at the lip of a ragged-edged crater, nearly eight feet across and lopsided, in the skin of the hull. Through the skin, really; she could see into the ship from the outside. Not good.

"This thing must have been moving at a hell of a clip," she muttered into the channel as she carefully reached for the sealer safety-clipped to her waist. "Think it might have holed a water tank, too."

"Think I can see some water ice at the bottom, yeah. Must have bubbled through. Hope everyone's been taking their rad supplements." Garhuff confirmed.

He clung to the deck of the ship like an overgrown water bear, five of his legs mag-locked to the hull; his vac suit bulged and hissed at constant-volume joints as he used his free forelimb to steady a toolkit that must've weighed fifty kilos. Sylvia suppressed a quick flare of jealousy. She could work out all she wanted in her off hours, take every legal supplement in the galaxy, but nothing short of cybernetic augmentation could put a human on the same level of strength as a Balorian.

"Gonna take more than a patch job to fix that, no doubt." Garhuff settled the toolkit against the hull of the ship, magnetic locks deploying with a thunk that Sylvia felt through her own boots, and rummaged through it.

"Gonna have to get in there with your clever little monkey fingers. Check for atmo leaks, yeah?"

She shook her head and carefully hooked her safety line to the toolkit, giving it a quick tug, and made her way into the breach. "You know," she muttered over the local channel, "Humans aren't monkeys. Any more than Balorians are big burly slugs — ow!" A sudden yank on her safety line dragged her back abruptly while only one of her mag boots was engaged, bending her ankle at a painful angle before she could release it. "Son of a—"

"Safety check," Garhuff snickered. "Gotta make sure you're firmly anchored, don't want any monkeys jumping ship before our little contest. You sure you don't want to give up right now?"

"Oh, I'm not going to be the one giving up," Sylvia warned as she settled herself back onto the deck. The water tank was holed, sure enough, but it didn't look like anything worse was damaged. A quick check over and some judicious application of sealing patches would have them ship shape again. "Just you wait."

*   *   *   *   *

There were three cafeterias on the ship. The small one, the one Sylvia loved best for the meals she and Vassk had shared there, was mostly for anyone unable to get far from the engineering section. Some of the crew, like the chief tech, always stayed close for fear of an emergency.

The primary along the ship's spine, centrally located and kitted out for every species in the crew, was the largest and by far the most-trafficked; Sylvia wasn't a big fan of crowds, though she had to admit that the head cook — a Talar with radial symmetry, like a six-legged stool with several rows of arms along its columnar body and an incongruous toque jauntily perched atop the mouthparts at its apex - could whip up one hell of an Earth-style gumbo, even if the ingredients came from a swathe half the width of the galaxy.

The third was middling in size, but rarely used. It was theoretically the captain's mess, but by tradition, the command crew mostly ate at the primary cafe while they were in open space. The most use it saw was formal dinners with the clients who found some romance in a shipboard meal with too many kinds of silverware and crisp uniforms — which also tended to stay packed in storage until just that sort of occasion.

Even on a large ship, however, space was at a premium. Leaving a fully furnished, functional cafeteria mothballed for months or more at a time just rubbed the crew the wrong way. Even the captain, dour and stern as she had become beneath the weight of command, had started out as common crew on a gas hauler not too different from her current craft, and hated waste as much as those who served under her.

So the captain's mess had become, quietly, the place where dares and bets were settled — at least those that didn't require the ship's gymnasium or a spacewalk. The command staff theoretically frowned on this unorthodox use of the space, but in reality, they turned a blind eye and placed their own quiet bets amongst themselves on who'd win, who'd lose, and who would turn potato.

Sylvia sat at one of the tables now, across from Garhuff. The two of them were surrounded by a quietly attentive crowd, Vassk among them — nearly everyone off-duty at the time, barely any two of them the same species. None of them were human.

Out of his vacuum suit, the Balorian looked less like a tardigrade and more like a clothed walrus; his dark hide was covered in coarse gray bristles, four webbed paws supporting his burly body while his two forelimbs rested on the tabletop. The ship's fabricators had struggled to produce clothing that could fit a species with his sheer bulk and musculature; in the end, they'd had to print his clothing requisitions in halves and finish the assembly by hand.

His feeding tendrils twisted slowly below a single bulging, three-part compound eye, and a soft chuckle came from the voder strapped to the chest of his shipboard jumpsuit. Some expressions translate poorly from species to species, but smugness tends towards the unmistakable.

Between them, neatly stacked on the white tablecloth, were a row of capped bottles. They were full of deadly poison — solutions of a substance so vile, so reactive, that few species could tolerate more than a few grams of it without serious cause for regret. It was mostly used as a disinfectant, a destroyer of pathogens from every kind of ecosystem; in desperation, it could be burned as a fuel. Only a very few species were crazy enough to consider ingesting the stuff.

Of those few, only humans had thought to make whiskey out of it.

"You know," Garhuff sneered across the table, pouring himself a shot of Robinson's Old Peculiar, "Not too late to bow out, before we have to get the medic involved. Humans are built so delicate."

Sylvia met his cyclopean gaze levelly as she poured herself a line of shots with a well-practiced hand. "I think … I'm going to be just fine."

It took two bottles between the two of them before the Balorian, wheezing, disbelieving, outmassing Sylvia by eightfold, slipped from the table to the floor. He spilled half a glass of very nice rye along the way, and the room shook with the impact.

Sylvia paused, wobbly but triumphant, deliberately drained her glass, and slammed it upside-down to the table. The room was silent for a moment in collective disbelief, and then the cheering started — while a good six or seven crew strained to get the weakly-protesting Garhuff off the floor so they could drag him to the infirmary.

Vassk was at her bunkmate's side, enfolding Sylvia in a many-armed hug that nearly knocked her off her feet and sent the room spinning. "I can't believe — that much would have killed me twice — how did you put it away? What are you made of??"

Grinning madly, Sylvia planted a kiss right on Vassk's mandible — nowhere near anything in Ishiran body language, but what the hell, you had to express yourself in your native tongue sometimes. "I told you, you big sexy bug. Nobody, but nobody, can outdrink a human. Now, how about we spend some of Garhuff's credits on a really nice dinner? My treat."

Vassk had to keep her steady as the two left the room, but on the plus side, Sylvia managed to snag the bottle of rye along the way.

HUMAN OBSERVATION LOG
M. L. Winslett

Human Observation Log Entry: 1

We have acquired a human. The information found on humans was either blatant propaganda against the species or myths and stories of things that surely no one species could do. We have attempted to communicate with the human, but it seems human speech is primitive enough that the ship's translator is having issues. Updates to the system have been ordered. Until then, we will communicate as best we can. However, the human is indeed fascinating.

"I was not expecting humans to be so small," the ship's Chief Scientist said as we all observed the human.

The human was indeed small, especially compared to the propaganda that depicted them. The human observed us back. It started speaking, but we tried to gesture that we didn't understand. We all froze as the human rushed forward and started climbing our Security Officer. The human then bellowed something that forced our Security Officer to harden his exterior in panic. The human then poked my poor crewmate until one of us unfroze enough to extract the human. Our Head Medical Officer was not impressed when we showed up with the Security Officer and the human.

Human Observation Log Entry: 6

The human has attempted to help us in our scientific endeavors (refer to Science Log Entry: 22784) It was … interesting to say the least. We found a very primitive species thought to be extinct. We kept our distance but the human approached it with no fear. The human wanted to bring the creature with us. We declined.

"It is hideous," our Security Officer said as we all watched what looked like sentient ooze trundle towards us.

"I dunno. I think it's cute," the human said as they stood out in front of us. The human likes to lead. For one so small, it is quite bold.

"Cute? … Our translator must be malfunctioning. The definition of cute by earth standards is Cute: Adjective- attractive in a pretty or endearing way. Unless you are using the term in a sarcastic format?" I glanced around when I did not get an answer. The human was no longer in front of us. "Human?"

I heard laughter and blanched at the sight of the oozing alien draped over the human.

"It likes me! Can I keep him?" the human exclaimed as they began to pet the creature.

"Absolutely not!" I said in a loud tone that startled myself and my team.

Human Observation Log Entry: 11

It has been observed that the human's resting cycles are bizarre. The human attempts to regulate their cycles, but they seem to always fail. Our species' rest cycle is very uniform. The human complains that since time is meaningless on the vessel, that they cannot keep a constant rest cycle.

Another peculiar observation is that, even though their rest cycle varies by length, our crew is unsure what sort of "mood" the human will be in once out of rest. Sometimes the human is almost dull and lifeless, sometimes awake and happy, and then there are what we call "the true monster" awakenings. We avoid the human when they are in those moods. One of our crew actively avoids the human at all costs due to a past encounter during one of these moods. The only thing found to quell the monster is to provide what we consider a poisonous byproduct. The human has deemed it "Coffee."

"I don't understand why you wanted this poisonous substance," the courier said, baffled as cases of the poison were loaded onto the ship.

"It is a substance that fuels the human," I said tiredly. Said human was now standing in the doorway as the cases were rolled up the ramp, chanting a word that the courier had never heard. I had heard nothing but that word for what felt like eternity.

"What is it saying?" the courier asked as the human jumped on the closest case.

"Cofye?"

"Coffeecoffeecoffeeeeeeee!" the human said, now smacking the case.

Human Observation Log Entry: 20

The human has been content to eat our foods but has requested foods we are not familiar with. We managed to find a few items and the fascinating thing was, all the items were considered useless or creature food. We purchased a lot for so very little. However, we must be careful with how the human eats.

"Hey. Hey! You guys want to hear a joke?" the human yelled from its table. The furnishings were too large so the human sat on top of the table so it could observe and be observed.

"A joke?" an ensign asked hesitantly. The human nodded vigorously and looked at me. I nodded.

"What has ten black eyes and is really hungry?" the human asked with its hands behind its back. I started thinking of creatures we had encountered, then the human shouted, "Me!"

The human had black bulb-like items on its fingertips as it placed its hands in front of its eyes and wiggled its extremities. The human laughed as it started eating the "eyes" off its extremities. I sighed and called the medbay. Of course, the human would not be familiar with a highly deadly parasite that feeds off our species that it just emulated. My fellow crew members panicking and hardening was a typical defense mechanism. I will receive another talking-to from the Head Medical Officer.

Human Observation Log Entry: 45

The human found human-made transmissions. The human calls them "How-to videos." Humans' need to create is astounding, but some things should never be executed.

"What is this?" I asked in my naturally neutral tone as a small group of us crowded around a viewing screen. The human always looked so small.

"This is one of the weirder nail art trends from years ago," the human said.

"Nail?" I asked, glancing down at the human's small extremites. Our species does not have nails. "Art?"

The human laughed. "Yeah. Weird, right? I still tried it though."

My fellow crewmates and I gave each other flat looks, the human missing our exchanges. We all looked back at the screen. I know I kept my neutral facade but internally I was frightened. What does it tell you about a species that sticks smaller versions of their extremities on their nails for fun? Then call it art? Our human has partaken in this before, but even they admit it is "weird."

> **Human Observation Log Entry: 84**
>
> To anyone who wishes to have their own human, we recommend that you do not. They are more unpredictable than you would think. Operating manuals do not explain the horrors you will get into. The propaganda, though biased, is accurate. A bored human is dangerous. A tired human is dangerous. A human you decide to take out on a walk is dangerous. You may think that due to their stature and biology, they would have died out. Our human has fallen from a great height and stood up functioning just fine. (Refer to Entry Log:14) But our human has also run into one of our vessel's doors and broken its own bones. (Refer to Entry Log: 19)
>
> They are fascinating to watch, and will surprise you every time. However, stick to more docile species for companionship. If an acquaintance of yours has a human, borrow your acquaintance's. Never have your own unless you have a crew to handle all the fallout and destruction the human creates. If the crew survives.

I heard laughter behind me as I finished my latest data entry. I slowly turned to see the human on top of one of our cleaner bots. Another bot was following them. I drooped in defeat as I saw a primitive sharp weapon secured to the bot following them. Both bots had a pair of what the human called "googly eyes" slapped on. The human rode with glee.

> **Human Observation Log Entry: 98**
>
> Our human is the best thing ever. At the same time, our human is the most terrifying thing ever. Our vessel, a scientific vessel with top of the line defense but subpar offense, was attacked. The intruders were a species that regularly attack

passenger vessels for supplies. I was curious to know why our vessel was targeted but they did not stay long enough for me to question them.

"What do they want?" the human asked, actually looking worried.

"Supplies," the Chief Security Officer said. "Food. Medical equipment. Science equipment." He explained distractedly as he watched the intruders break a hole through the outer wall.

"Coffee?" the human asked.

"Coffee," the Chief Security Officer agreed.

I watched as the human seemed to transform. Before I could understand the look that crossed its face, the human had disappeared. I slowly looked around to see if the human's own defense mechanism had kicked in. For the first time. The Chief Security Officer made a noise of distressed disbelief. I looked at the monitor and just let out a breath. The human was confronting the intruders.

I placed a hand on the Chief Security Officer before any order could be declared. The intruders shot at the human with a liquid that we avoided. It did not harm us, but it triggered our hardening defense. The liquid had no effect on the human.

We watched in terrified awe as the human grabbed anything within reach and attacked. A fleet of bots appeared, all with googly eyes and a few with primitive weapons affixed to them. The bizarre army seemed to be enough to drive the intruders back. It was when the human seemed to spit fire at them that the intruders got them off the ship.

We all collectively looked at each other in shock and horror. When the human reappeared on the command deck, many hardened in defense. I looked down at the human, who was dripping liquid everywhere. The human looked at me and smiled as it held up a torch and a bottle.

"What is that?" I asked as I looked at the bottle closely while taking the torch away. Who left the torch out for the human to grab in the first place?

"I think you were using this to water plants or something? It's very similar to moonshine. I can only handle a sip," the human explained. "Can I get a towel? I don't know why they were using water guns. Does water hurt you or something?"

I stared blankly at the wall. The human can ingest fertilizer used to subdue our more aggressive sentient plants. The human willingly spat said fertilizer while lighting it on fire. I handed the human a rag, patted its head, and left to ground myself in my quarters.

Human Observation Log Entry: 100

News of the attack on our vessel seems to have spread rapidly. We were just another scientific mission vessel manned by one of the most docile species in the galaxy. Apparently we are now known as the vessel that contains the monster. The attack only happened yesterday.

"You seem to be popular," the human said as I scrolled through the surprising amount of correspondence.

"Our world is worried about us," I stated.

"That's nice of them. I should probably head back to mine," the human said.

"You have a world to return to?" I asked. I was not aware humans still had a planet. The human laughed.

"Of course I do!" the human said. "If you think I'm weird, wait til you meet my best friend! Or my cousin, but dude's crazy! So I think I'll spare you." The human then patted my hand and wandered off.

Personal Log Entry: I'm in a panic

There are more humans. Worse humans. As docile as my species is, I am ready to blow this entire vessel up just to avoid meeting more. Knowing the human, they'd be fine. Knowing my luck, I'd be fine and suddenly living on a planet full of humans.

Perhaps we can just jettison the human in the direction of their home world. I can feel myself starting to harden in panic. I will return once I have calmed down. End Log.

FLYING BLIND
Jay Mendell

Himou squeezed his eyes shut, trying not to cry from the pain. His wings weren't meant to bend that way, tied behind him and leaving his talons to struggle fitfully against the small of his back. He would be surprised if he didn't look like a plucked *KhoKho* by the end of this experience, considering the way that his captors dragged him roughly along the ground with no care for his delicate pin feathers.

They were speaking above him, grunts of vocalization that Himou could no longer interpret, due to them snatching his translator away as soon as he'd boarded their ship.

Himou could only speak Khorrinian, which had been perfectly acceptable when he was still on Kibbara, but now he was dearly mourning the fact that he hadn't paid more attention during his language electives.

If he had known — well, if he *had* known, he never would have insisted on visiting the space station with his brother in the first place...

He was certainly paying for that now, wasn't he?

The pirates had invaded their ship before they got anywhere close to the station, and Himou had been separated from his brother in the chaos. Now, he had no idea when he was going to go home.

If he went home.

The thought brought fresh tears to his eyes, and he had to swallow heavily around the lump in his throat to hold back his sobs.

The pirates holding him didn't pay him any mind, only talking amongst themselves as they continued to haul him along.

Before long, they were standing in front of a set of bars, and when Himou chanced a glance up, he saw that there was already someone inside, huddled against the corner.

They were going to put him in a cell with someone else?

His trepidation rose once more, wondering what kind of terrifying creature might be held captive by vicious pirates like this.

Using the control pack on their hip, the pirate roughly gripping Himou's bound form unlocked the cell door and tossed him inside, with no reaction to the pained trill that escaped his throat.

But then one of the pirates moved as if to follow him in, their cranial tentacles lifting in a clear expression of anticipation. They reached towards the disciplinary baton on their belt, and Himou flinched back, trying to duck out the way of the incoming hit.

And that was when the huddled figure lurched forward, a terrible snarling sound coming from their mouth.

They slammed bodily into the pirate, and Himou shut his eyes and pressed himself against the wall as the sound of scuffling continued, shivering and trying to convince himself that this was all a dream.

There was no *way* that this was happening to him, right? No, he was just resting at home, in his bed. His brother was going to scold him for sleeping in so late, certainly. He would wake up any minute now.

As the noises faded behind him, the pirates shouted something and the bars clanged shut, their heavy footsteps making their way back down the hall. Himou still didn't move, didn't open his eyes.

What if the creature in the cell turned on him next?

But instead of a bite, a snarl, or a terrible clawed hand coming down on him, something began to pull on the knotted ropes holding him captive, carefully picking them apart.

Himou shivered, fear prickling at the back of his neck, but he could only stay still as the ropes were tugged off, and the heavy presence behind him pulled back, just a little.

He turned, swallowing heavily, only to stop short. Himou thought that it must have been some kind of large beast, terrifying beyond measure, if it was able to scare off those pirates so easily, but it was just a strange-looking alien!

Even sitting down, Himou could tell that they were a tall, gangly thing. Long limbs, and odd posture. They way that they curled up almost reminded Himou of the insects back home, that were able to move their limbs in strange ways that even the best Guard in the Palace wouldn't be able to manage.

Himou let out a small sigh of relief, before brightening. Not only had this alien scared off the pirates, they had freed Himou, allowing him to finally straighten out some of his bent feathers! What a kind person they were.

However, there was *one* problem…

He had no idea what kind of alien this was — not even their gender, let alone their species!

Their body was peculiar, not a single feather to be seen. No scales, no hardened plates. On the alien's face, dark colors were beginning to blossom; something that must have been a sign of bruising. It appeared that they did not escape their tussle with the pirate unscathed.

He moved a little closer, and the alien didn't try to stop him, remaining still as Himou settled down by their side.

Himou had never seen anything like this before, and he couldn't help the fascination that led to him trailing a talon down the creature's exposed arm.

His talon left a mark behind, a thin line of blood that caused him to snatch his hand away in a hurry.

"Sorry!" He chirped, quickly shoving his hand underneath his leg to stop his reckless actions. "Sorry, sorry!"

Himou hadn't meant to hurt his savior, but he could never have imagined that the alien's outer shell could be so thin and vulnerable.

He peeked up, beak clacking in nervousness, but the creature's lips had spread to expose their teeth. Himou knew that in some species, that gesture was meant to be friendly, but he couldn't help his instinctive shudder at the sight.

Their low, soothing tones quickly followed, a broad, stubby-looking hand rising towards Himou's head.

The feathers along his back puffed up, for just a moment, but Himou forced himself to relax. The alien hadn't done anything to hurt him yet — not even when it would have certainly spared them some pain.

So Himou stayed still, hoping that his trust had not been misplaced.

Their hand landed on his head, and Himou could only blink, uncomprehending. But the creature did nothing else, only patting his head a few times before pulling back.

Himou looked at this odd alien that had shown him nothing but kindness, even after Himou had *hurt* them...

His eyes welled up with tears, and he sniffled as he reached up and scrubbed at his face.

"I'm Himou," he said, pointing to himself in hopes that it would help the creature understand.

They tilted their head, following the motion of his talon as Himou repeated himself, stating his name once more.

"Himou."

"…Hemow?"

Their brows furrowed, but they still tried their best to sound out the word. It wasn't quite right — the trills too deep in pitch, sounding like a rather endearing lisp, but it was still an excellent first attempt.

Himou nodded, fluttering his feathers in excitement. "Yes, Himou!"

The creature gave that same baring of teeth, before pointing at their own chest.

"S-o-r-e-n."

Himou blinked, trying to discern the strangeness of the word, the way it almost sounded like it curved in the air.

"Um … Soaring?"

The creature — Soaring? Sure in? — flashed their teeth again, and their chest shook as a strange sound came out of their mouth. It was a jarring thing, and Himou should have found it grating against his sensitive ears, but it was so clearly an expression of joy that he could hardly find it unpleasant.

"Soaring," they said again, in that strange and heavy tongue. The cast to their face was particularly gentle, and when they carelessly wiped at the cut on their arm, the blood had already stopped.

It was a pretty name, if a bit incorrect — Himou didn't think that his new friend could be capable of much flight, considering the way their body was far too thin in some places and far too wide in others.

Still, that hardly mattered.

Himou let out a gentle coo in return, happy to have made this connection with his savior, before he suddenly snapped his head to the side, eyeing the bars of their cell as heavy, purposeful footsteps started coming down the hallway.

Soaring shifted their position next to him, holding out their thin, featherless arm to block his view.

Himou chirped in alarm, but Soaring refused to relent, pushing Himou behind them as they faced the front. Himou found his feathers puffing up, a defensive posture to make himself look bigger than he actually was.

Soaring may have been able to fend off the two pirates from before, but their body was so fragile! Even the slightest touch from Himou's talons had been enough to draw blood!

Himou didn't want them to get hurt — especially not in his defense. Not again.

But thankfully, this pirate didn't seem interested in causing any trouble. With a pointed huff, the Nagania merely unlocked the cell and tossed several bundles of thin reeds inside, her yellow eyes glaring at them as she turned to slither away.

Soaring reached out to take them, a somewhat resigned expression on their face, and offered the reeds to Himou.

"Are we supposed to eat these?" Himou asked slowly, having never seen food like this before. It was nothing like the rich and opulent meals he was used to at home.

Soaring nodded, and held the reeds out to him again.

"…Alright then," Himou sighed, reaching out to take one.

It was hardly a balanced meal, but if it was all they were going to get … Himou wouldn't complain. After all, Soaring must have been suffering through this for longer than him.

Himou could be brave. As long as he…

He reached out, hooking his talons very gently in the side of Soaring's torn shirt.

Soaring looked down at him and made an inquiring sound, a reed halfway out of their mouth.

Himou couldn't help the laugh that bubbled up from inside him, and firmed his resolve.

He could be brave. As long as he wasn't alone.

Their days passed in this manner, almost without incident. Himou could only tell how long it had been from counting the meals they were given, and he guessed that it had been about eight days since he was kidnapped. It must have been longer for Soaring, who kept giving Himou pieces of their food — like they didn't need it even more for themselves! Himou tried continuously to turn it down, but Soaring was far too stubborn.

They were having one such debate when something unbelievable occurred. The ship shuddered and lurched, the lights above the two prisoners flickering. The two didn't have time to do more than exchange a confused glance before the ship's alarms started blaring.

Several pirates raced by their cell, not even bothering to stop and harass them for a moment. One of them came into view just as Himou began to feel afraid, shrinking back behind Soaring's protective bulk.

The alien — a Tagvi — halted only steps away from the bars of their cell, pulling out their communicator and speaking into it in a rapidfire tone.

The Tagvi were a species with an especially bulbous head, which had a thin crystalline outer layer. Though Himou hadn't seen this one before, they must have been a high-ranking pirate, because they had a control pad on their hip, right next to their disciplinary baton.

Himou noticed all of this, numbly, in the span of around five seconds.

Because that was all the time it took for Soaring to *move*.

They lurched towards the bars in a motion too fast for Himou to fully register, and when their thin hands slipped through the gaps, they grabbed on to the short alien's head with a single, rough movement, and *yanked* it backwards.

The Tagvi's head slammed against the bars, the crystalline shell shattering apart on impact. Soaring dropped the body in the next second, their hands stained with the Tagvi's thin, watery blood.

Himou could only stare in shock. The pirate's head had been completely caved in, a light blue mush slowly seeping out.

But Himou didn't have any time to let that sink in, because Soaring hauled him up, the gesture still so *gentle*, and began pulling him towards them as they used the pirate's control pad to open the lock on their cell.

Soon they were running down the hallway, the ship's klaxons blaring in time with the beating of his heart.

"How did you *do* that?!" Himou screeched, the sound ripping from his throat as they whipped around the corner. Everything he had witnessed was just catching up to him, and he stared at his friend's back with wide eyes.

But ... Soaring seemed so delicate! Their outer shell had been damaged from just a careless swipe of Himou's talons! Had they really been hiding so much raw power, all this time?

Soaring just made that same happy, rasping sound again, firmly holding onto Himou's hand as they moved forward, seemingly unburdened by the alarms blaring in Himou's ears.

"Safe," they said, their chirps still slightly off-key. "Run. Safe."

Himou let out a shaky breath, and just tried his best to keep up.

Pirates were scrambling, trying to figure out what had set off the alarms, and though some tried to stop the two of them from escaping, Soaring tore through them all like they were made of air.

Where Himou was panting, following after his friend with shaking legs, Soaring seemed to only move faster as they continued on, a steady pace that never faltered even with the screaming of the sirens right above their heads.

Underneath all of his wheezing and the struggle to catch his breath, Himou couldn't help but be in awe.

Wow.

His friend was nearly as scary as a human, and those deathworlders were the kind of thing that nightmares were made out of!

But Himou couldn't find it in himself to care — scary as they may be, Soaring had only ever used that power to protect him. And now, they were about to be *free!*

They were almost to the front of the ship when they realized why the alarms had gone off; the pirate ship had been forcibly docked, and was being boarded by a group wearing colors that Himou instantly recognized.

That was—!

Himou's hand slipped out of Soaring's grip as he cheered, sharp trills leaving him as he latched onto his brother's waist. Wodou's brightly-colored feathers were like a beacon in the dark, drawing Himou to his side without a second thought.

"Brother, Brother! You're here!"

Wodou held out his arms, dragging Himou into a hug. The two simply stood there for a long moment, soaking in each other's presence.

"I'm sorry, Himou. I'm so sorry." Wodou's voice was low, like a feather drifting in the breeze, but Himou shook his head.

"Nothing to be sorry for," he insisted. "I'm just glad you're *here*."

Wodou pressed his forehead against Himou's for a second, before a shuffling sound caught all of their attention. Himou looked back to see that Soaring had just caught up, and was gazing upon the procession of the Khorrin military with wide eyes.

"Stay back!" Wodou said immediately, pulling Himou away.

Soaring took a step back, holding their hands up in a closed-off posture, making themself look smaller.

Himou didn't understand what was happening.

"Wodou, wait!" Himou said, tugging on his brother's flight suit. "They're my friend, they saved me!"

Wodou looked down at him, expression disbelieving.

"Himou, what are you talking about? That's a human!"

...What?

For a moment, Himou thought *how could that be possible?* And then he remembered the scene of Soaring crushing that pirate's skull like it was nothing more than a rotten fruit, and he suddenly believed it.

"Hemow?"

Himou jolted, his feathers pricking up. Soaring couldn't understand what they were talking about. Soaring was looking to him for *help*.

This was his friend. Human or not, *this was his friend.*

He tugged on Wodou's flight suit once more, trying to get his attention. When his brother glanced at him out of the corner of his eye, unwilling to fully take his attention away from the human, Himou gave him a pleading look.

"They can't understand you, brother. It's not their fault. I've been teaching them some Khorrinian, but the pirates took our translators away."

Wodou frowned, but gestured to one of the guards, having her come forward and outfit Soaring with a translator of their own.

Soaring accepted the wary treatment with grace, allowing the guard to pin the device to the collar of their bloodied shirt.

When the guard retreated, returning to their side, Himou *finally* understood his friend's speech.

"Thanks," Soaring said, their deep voice translating into something almost rough in Himou's ears. "I'm a member of the Galaxy Accord, on the S.S.E. *Nomad*. If you could get me in contact with my ship, I'd be much obliged."

At that, Himou could see the way his brother's feathers began to lay flat, the tense line of his shoulders loosening by increments.

"I wasn't aware of any humans being part of the Accord," Wodou said, still with one hand in front of Himou, keeping him back. He sounded slightly less suspicious, but Himou knew that the guards around them would still be on high alert.

Soaring made that sound again, almost like a cough, and Himou belatedly realized that it was a *laugh*.

"It's a new development." Their voice was rather rueful, and they slowly put their hands down, relaxing from their taut position. "Seems like my first assignment has ended up a bit more complicated than we expected."

Wodou only hummed in reply, a small sound of acknowledgment.

Himou could tell that his brother was wavering, unsure if the human could really be trusted, so he took matters into his own hands, gently reaching out with his right wing to brush his feathers along his brother's back.

Wodou glanced down at him, and Himou only looked to him with a pleading gaze.

Human or not, Soaring had been the one to rescue him. Saving the life of a Prince — that had to be worth something, didn't it?

Wodou's expression quickly turned resigned, and that was when Himou knew he had won.

"We're going, then," Wodou said, turning and facing the guards. "Make sure that a room is prepared for our ... guest."

The guards all murmured their agreements, and Wodou moved out of Himou's way with only the slightest hesitance, giving him a severe look as he headed over to their ship's ramp to direct their troops.

Himou glanced back and saw the way that Soaring had faltered, their eyes sweeping over the group of Khorrin guards that surrounded the entrance to their ship.

He turned, walking back towards his friend, ignoring the way his brother whistled in warning behind him.

"It'll be alright," Himou whispered, reaching out to take their stubby hand in his own, careful of his sharp talons.

Soaring nodded, giving his hand a gentle squeeze. When they looked down at him, there was that same baring of teeth that had appeared when they first saved him from those pirates.

"I know."

And by the way that they moved forward, as unrelenting and courageous as they had been while carving their way through the pirates' ship, Himou had no doubt that Soaring could handle anything the universe tried to throw at them.

Ha, and wasn't that a story — a *human*, rescuing him from pirates? His friends at school were never going to believe this!

Hand in hand, Himou tugged Soaring along to their ship, no longer afraid. He knew that even if they were attacked again, his friend would stop at nothing to save him.

Humans were the most dangerous species in the galaxy for a reason, after all.

BRUISABLE
Jane Colon-Bonet

Bananas. Kesper had only just found out about bananas. Curved, yellow, oblong fruit. (Were they fruit? Or were they some kind of berry? Were berries fruit? Human taxonomy was so needlessly complicated). Kesper had never eaten a banana, obviously, nor would they. Produce was hard to come by in deep space, not to mention that a single bite of a banana, which contained potassium, would kill them very quickly and very painfully.

Noemi had explained it so cheerfully when she'd first introduced Kesper to the concept of the banana.

"They're high in vitamin K," she'd said with a happy little smile. Kesper was so horrified to learn what vitamin K was that their frills had turned neon green. Not bright green, which would've indicated a more manageable level of fear, but neon green. Stupid human English alphabet and periodic table nonsense. Potassium didn't even start with a K! It all made Noemi's craving seem so innocuous when in fact the fruit (fruit?) contained a deadly poison.

Noemi's cravings had been the reason why bananas were brought up in the first place. She had a lot of cravings, and she loved to stand in the doorway, "supervising" while Kesper did their repairs, and babble about them.

"God, I'd kill to get some proper spices on this ship. You know I asked Xenth if he could synthesize cayenne and he gave me *paint*. And I almost put it on my potatoes anyway I was so desperate."

Kesper didn't pretend to understand her cravings, since they didn't exactly experience "taste," as it were. Most sentient species didn't; flavor was a human peculiarity. Being Urisk, Kesper's tongue was well in the back of their throat (where it belonged). Their food would be mashed and partially digested into a fairly uniform paste well before it reached that point. They didn't understand what it meant for a food to "taste good," or why some foods belonged together or needed to be cooked in different ways. And they certainly didn't understand how small amounts of powderized plants could make all that much of a difference. Not to mention that some of these so-called spices were only added for the purpose of causing pain. Why would someone want their food to hurt?

Everything humans did seemed to revolve around flavors and recipes, handed down amongst them for eons like priceless heirlooms. Infinitely variable and sometimes unbelievably complex. It baffled Kesper; food seemed more like worship than sustenance in the hands of most humans.

"And tostones!" Noemi had exclaimed during her conversation with Kesper. "I've had the hugest craving for tostones for like, a month now. It's driving me nuts; I'm literally dying."

This outburst had, of course, prompted Kesper to ask what a tostone was.

"They're these crushed, fried plantain things. Kinda like chips but also not at all."

Which had prompted Kesper to ask what a plantain was.

"They're like bananas, but not sweet."

Which had led to the dreaded explanation of what a banana was. That, in turn, was the reason for Kesper having a near full-on panic attack in the middle of the cafeteria. Not out of fear of bananas; they figured they were safe from those being several million lightyears away from Earth. But because of what they saw when Noemi walked into the room.

Up and down her arms there were blackish marks of various shapes and sizes. Kesper felt their frills turning a sickly purple as their clawed feet curled. Anyone familiar with emotional colorations among the Urisk species would recognize it as worry. Deep and profound worry.

Before the discussion of the banana had concluded with the revelation of "vitamin K" Noemi had brought up how the fruit (…fruit?) bruised easily. Bananas would present with misshapen brown patches to indicate damage and spoilage.

Kesper was far from an expert, but the marks all along Noemi's arms bore a remarkable descriptive resemblance to such "bruises."

Purple turned to pink along the trembling edges of the frills that lined their neck and jaw as their worry turned to panic. Was Noemi injured? Was she spoiling? Could humans do that? Become overripe and turn to mush as she had said bananas do? (She had remarked that bananas were perfect for making into bread at that point of decomposition, but Kesper was fairly certain that humans were not to be made into bread).

The other members of the crew noticed Kesper's concern and turned a little purple themselves. Luckily, Noemi saw nothing as she carried her lunch tray from the cafeteria to eat elsewhere. Kesper frantically packed away their own food, now too nervous to eat, and excused themself to do some research.

* * * * *

r/HumanHelp was a subreddit dedicated to clarifying some of the more bizarre and confusing aspects of the human race. Which was really all of their aspects as far as most other sentient species were concerned.

Kesper had spent a good deal of time on the forum since meeting Noemi: scanning the pages for explanations to her behaviors and clicking through the endless descriptions of human foods in fascination.

They could've asked her in person, but that would've been horribly awkward. And the orange of embarrassment was really a terrible color on them. Much easier to browse the internet for answers.

Unfortunately, the subreddit wasn't providing the information they were looking for. There were a handful of posts about human illnesses (apparently their body temperatures could rise and goodness wasn't that just a thought. Humans were already so unbearably warm) but nothing about bruises or what they could mean.

Typing furiously, Kesper posted the question themself:

ConcernedCesper: Help!! Do humans "go bad" like fruit? Human crew member appears to be covered in small bruises and I'm worried she may be sick/spoiling!

They sat back and groomed nervously, picking at their own skin and waiting for a reply. Eventually they had to go reorganize their tools to distract from the agonizing delay. They about melted with relief, frills flashing a powdery blue, when they saw their question had been answered.

Xenopartyologist: humans get bruises when something hits us hard enough to damage our cells, like some fruits, but we don't "go bad" or anything like that. your human crewmember probably got a little banged up. maybe check with her to make sure she's ok but don't worry too hard, bruises aren't a big deal.

Kesper flopped back in their chair as the several hours-worth of tension disappeared from their muscles. It all made sense. Of course Noemi would have a few bruises as the head of security; just the other day she'd had to deal with pirates that had snuck onboard to steal supplies. It was all so clear now.

They were glad to hear that they wouldn't have to bake Noemi into a sweet bread. Not that they thought they would, but they couldn't help but imagine such a scenario once the idea occurred to them. Bread baking seemed so complex too, what with all the rising that went on.

And Kesper rather liked Noemi; they didn't want to lose her. She was good to talk to, and actually enjoyed their jokes. Her laughter took some getting used to (so many *teeth*! And so close to the opening of her mouth! They thought she was going to bite them the first time it happened) but it was better than the flat gray coloration that the other Urisk crewmembers sported in response to Kesper's humor.

After taking the necessary time to lie down and recuperate, they set out to check on the human. They found her looking disapprovingly over a few members of the crew as they cleaned up an algal spill in life support. Not all human expressions translated well to Urisk peoples, but the flat glare she had leveled at those responsible for the mess had their frills turning a deep orange with shame.

Kesper pawed lightly at her back. Noemi had finally gotten to a point where she didn't jump or stiffen at the common Urisk form of getting someone's attention, and Kesper counted that as a victory.

She turned to them with a warm smile, thankfully with her teeth tucked behind her plump lips. Her tawny-brown skin rounded at her cheeks and crinkled around her eyes. Kesper liked her face like this, the wrinkles in her face more akin to the folds of their own leathery skin. She was slightly shorter than them, with curly black hair she kept shaved on the sides. It rose and spilled over her right eyebrow, just short enough to stay out of her eyes, which were dark brown in the sea of uncanny white that characterized human eyes and human eyes alone. She placed her hands on her hips, which were wide and padded with fat, and raised her chin at them as the puddle of red algae lapped at her heels.

"Hey Kesper! What can I do for you?"

They did their best approximation of a smile back at her while trying to hide their nervous picking behind their back. It was a terrible habit.

"I just … wanted to check on you, make sure you're doing alright," they said and their frills turned an affectionate red at the way Noemi softened in the face of their concern.

"Aww, thank you. That's very sweet." She reached forward and ran a hand down their arm, a gesture she'd picked up from the Urisk crew members. The red in Kesper's frills deepened substantially.

"Are you?" they asked after a moment.

"Hm?"

"Are you well? Healthy and … altogether whole?"

Noemi snorted lightly and stepped back.

"I'm fine. Thank you for asking, Kesper."

The sound of metal striking the floor caused Noemi to whip around and scowl at the other crewmembers. Before Kesper could say anything more she marched across the algal spill to scold the clumsy Urisk technician. Her footsteps rippled across the crimson surface as Kesper stared after her.

They wanted to believe she was telling the truth about being well, but it was so hard to gauge honesty in humans. Why couldn't they keep their emotions on the outside like Kesper did? The red in their frills turned wine-colored as purplish worry seeped in despite Noemi's assurances.

* * * * *

The bruises didn't go away. Or rather, new ones formed as quickly as old ones vanished. The blackish marks dotted her skin and had begun to stain her fingernails. Kesper grew more and more worried all the time, the edges of their frills now constantly colored purple.

They were glad that their work as a mechanic didn't require them spending much time with the other Urisk crewmembers. If the others saw the purple they'd likely be teased even more than they already were for being so attached to the human. While the others didn't mind Noemi, and respected her where it counted, they didn't seem to truly like her. Just as they didn't seem to truly like Kesper.

But Kesper liked her and she was very vocal about liking them back; which they appreciated since they couldn't see her feelings. They didn't want her to be unwell. The ship would be so much lonelier without her.

So they poured their concerns onto the r/HumanHelp page. Asking question after panicked question in their search for reassurance.

ConcernedCesper: How long does it take for bruises to heal in humans?

ConcernedCesper: Do bruises hurt for humans?

ConcernedCesper: Can bruises be cured with antibiotics for humans?

ConcernedCesper: Is it possible for humans to develop spots later in life? Like polka dots? Except that they look like bruises?

ConcernedCesper: What human illnesses cause lots of small bruises that keep coming back?

That final question garnered an answer that finally sent them over the edge.

looseloosegoose: Some vitamin deficiencies can lead to bruising. There are worse diseases that can cause it, but maybe you should check if your human is doing it to themself before you jump to those. Some humans can become depressed and self-harm, either in reaction to something or due to an underlying condition. Ultimately, if you want to figure out what's really wrong, you need to talk to them.

Kesper stared in their screen in horror for a good while after reading that. Their frills awash in waves of neon green and bright violet that cascaded over each other.

They re-read the words "vitamin deficiencies" and "self-harm" again and again until their thoughts tangled into a terrible hypothesis.

Noemi had said that she was literally dying due to the lack of decent food. She had said it outright and Kesper hadn't picked up on it. They stood away from their monitor and began to pace, picking frantically and occasionally pausing to wring their frills.

Could it be that her ramblings about food were so much more than ramblings? That she needed flavor in order to survive and now without it she was withering away? Humans were so obsessed with taste, and the food printers were hardly calibrated to accommodate it on a primarily Urisk vessel. Not to mention the potential for vitamin deficiency; no wonder Noemi had brought up vitamin K. Of course the absence of flavor would harm her over time! She was human, and humans needed food to taste good. How could Kesper have been so stupid!? She'd been telling them all along and they'd failed to notice until she'd gotten to this point. Now it was only a matter of time before she turned to mush and her brethren would come to collect her remains to bake into bread!

Kesper flopped onto their bed, shuddering in a fuchsia panic as they imagined increasingly impossible scenarios where Noemi was lost to them due to the absence of good flavor in her life. Oh why did humans have to be able to taste?

Abruptly they curled their feet into their bedsheets, nearly ripping the cheap fabric in their claws. They sat up and with a great effort they pushed away their fear and panic to focus on the mental image of their friend. Purple, pink, and green faded to reveal the dark blue of determination. They would not allow their human to slip away. They were going to help her.

They stood, took a deep breath, and began researching how to synthesize and cook human food.

* * * * *

They started simple: spices. Well, relatively simple compared to the other things they were going to make, and one of the less dangerous since capsaicin didn't affect Urisk peoples the way it did humans. And they only had to make a dry powder of the proper composition as opposed to a true-to-form pepper.

Unfortunately, in order to test if they'd done it correctly, they had to ask Briz for help. Which wasn't difficult in and of itself: Briz, in addition to being head of engineering and Kesper's boss, was a really lovely person and would be happy to assist however she could. The problem was that Kesper was going to feel really really bad about what they needed her to do.

Briz was one of the only other non-Urisk members of the crew, and although she couldn't taste any more than Kesper could, she was able to experience the effects of capsaicin. To be precise, Briz's fungal nature meant that capsaicin was literally poison to her and would be extremely painful when applied topically.

Kesper already felt guilty even asking her to help test the spice, hiding the blackish-gray of their frills as best they could, but then she had to go and agree, which only made them feel worse. But she was as fond of Noemi as Kesper was, and thus, she was standing, or rather clinging to the wall, beside Kesper as they removed the synthetic cayenne powder from the printer.

So this substance will cure Noemi? Briz asked nervously in her strange, whispering rasp. Kesper was still unsure if she had a vocalizing mechanism or if she was able to speak softly into other people's minds.

"I don't know. I don't think it'll cure her, but it'll provide her with flavor and hopefully make her happy," they replied as they removed the beaker of cayenne with a pair of laboratory tongs usually reserved for moving acid.

That's more than enough reason for me. Briz, who at the moment was casually shapeless (she often took a tall, bipedal shape when working with others) shuffled over and extended a patch of her multicolored "skin" (technically cuticle).

With a deep breath to steady themselves, Kesper began to tip the beaker. Just before the red powder could spill over the lip, they hesitated and looked over at Briz.

For Noemi, she said, coloring a dark blue to emphasize her determination. Kesper knew that she was only doing it for their sake, considering she had much better control of her emotional colorations, but their frills turned blue to match and they nodded.

A moment later, Briz was writhing in the corner in pain while Kesper frantically wiped away the cayenne. Once they had both settled, tangled in each other on the floor, Briz spoke up.

Definitely too much capsaicin.

"Yeah," Kesper agreed.

Let's try again.

Kesper looked over at the multicolored fungaloid in horror, but agreed again.

For Noemi.

*   *   *   *   *

It took a good deal more tries after that to get the cayenne to an acceptable level of "spiciness." Luckily, after the first time they decided to start low and work their way up in terms of capsaicin content. Once they settled onto the proper formula for the spice, they saved it to the printer's database of foods and moved on to the next.

Unfortunately, what came next was plantains. Kesper was very unhappy to learn that they, too, contained "vitamin K." Which meant they would have to place potassium into the food printer in order to make them, as the devices were not ordinarily equipped with the deadly substance.

The only other place on the ship where potassium could be found was in some munitions for the weapons onboard. Human vessels might be littered with potassium for fertilizers, but in order for Kesper to get some, they would have to disassemble a missile.

Briz took on the duty of distracting Noemi, since her office was situated close to the thankfully rarely-used weapon's bay. Kesper, dressed in a full biohazard suit, obtained a small missile from the room and took it to an escape pod. The emergency evacuation vessels were heavily armored enough that should the bomb go off, no further damage would befall the ship.

Kesper tried not to think about the further damage that might befall them as they removed the paneling from the side of the missile. Their frills trembled a steady bright green inside the frame of their clear mask, the edges turning more and more neon as they worked.

With the core visible, they grabbed their tweezers and reached, ever so slowly, ever so carefully, inside the missile to grab the potassium. Just another inch and they would have it, and so long as they didn't bump the sides, it would all be just fine. What was that human board game Briz had mentioned? Openation? Oper—

"What are you doing, Kesper?"

They nearly jumped out of their skin and whirled to face the speaker. It was Theddy, the communications officer and the only other non-Urisk onboard besides Noemi and Briz. He looked Kesper up and down with piercing dark eyes beneath the bone-white fur of his brow. It wasn't often that Kesper got to see his face, as he only came out of his shell when in a state of extreme distress, amusement, or anger.

Kesper assumed it probably wasn't the second one that had him in the open air now.

"I'm … obtaining potassium," Kesper answered.

"Why?"

"To make bananas … and plantains."

"…Why?"

"For Noemi; I think the lack of flavorful food onboard has made her depressed."

The two stood facing each other for a long moment before Theddy's shell slowly lowered back over his face and upper torso, leaving only his uncannily long, dexterous, fur-covered arms exposed.

"I forgot that humans had that weird thing with food," Theddy said, deep voice muffled by his shell.

"Taste."

"Yeah, that. Super weird."

"Yeah."

A long silence stretched between them, then Theddy walked forward and held out his hand.

"Do you want me to grab the potassium? It's not deadly to me," he offered, and Kesper thrust the tweezers into his hand before he had even finished.

"Yes, please, oh my," they said in a breathy rush, taking several steps back and doing their best to calm down. Theddy gave them a thumbs-up, a gesture he had learned from Noemi, and reached in to retrieve the potassium.

A brief and anticlimactic second later, Theddy had the substance out of the missile and inside of a sealed container. He pressed it into Kesper's numb hands and began walking away.

"Hope Noemi feels better," he said as he passed through the door, leaving Kesper alone with the deadly element.

* * * * *

"Seriously, where are we going?" Noemi asked as Kesper guided her through the halls toward their room.

"It's a surprise," they answered, trying, and failing, to keep the white of excitement and the purple of worry out of their frills. White for the surprise they had in store for her, and purple at the black marks that still dotted her arms. It had only been two days since they'd started the process of making her food, but still.

"The good kind of surprise I hope. I can't deal with any more algal spills this week."

"It should be good," Kesper replied and stopped in front of their door. Noemi cocked an eyebrow at them, one of the less unsettling of human expressions. It brought out the wrinkles Kesper liked.

With a deep breath, they let her inside and gestured to their workbench. Atop it was a beaker of cayenne, a plate of tostones, and three misshapen bananas with no peels. Kesper walked ahead of the human and gestured at the foods one by one.

"Briz helped me test the capsaicin levels in the spice to make sure it would cause the right amount of pain. And since we don't have a kitchen onboard, I used my welder to heat the oil to fry the tostones, it was … more difficult than I thought." They held up their arm and indicated a few spots where the skin was still healing from the oil burns they had received. Luckily, Urisk peoples were very resistant to heat. "Oh! And I'm sorry the bananas look odd; the printer would only synthesize the peels separately, so I just did the part that's for eating. They got a little mashed up by the biohazard tape. I hope that's okay." They looked hopefully up at Noemi, picking at their skin and tucking their purplish frills as far toward their neck as they could.

Noemi blinked at the foods, her mouth open (unsettlingly, Kesper did not like to be able to see her teeth and tongue, but they said nothing).

"You made this stuff? For me?" she asked, seemingly baffled.

"Yes. I know you miss food with flavor and I was worried that the absence was beginning to harm you."

Noemi blinked at them and took a step closer to the food.

"Why would you think that?"

Kesper gestured vaguely at her arms and suppressed a shudder.

"Because of your bruises," they answered quietly. To their surprise, Noemi just frowned at them in confusion.

"Bruises? I—" Then she glanced at her arms and sucked in a breath of realization. "Oh this? Kesper, this is just dirt!" She held an arm toward them and brushed at one of the spots on her skin. The dark shape smudged and fell away, revealing itself to be nothing more than granules of soil.

Kesper's frills turned bright yellow in shock, before shifting quickly between brown and light blue as they sputtered in a mix of relief and anger.

Finally they settled on a deep, deep orange in embarrassment as they realized the foolishness of not just talking to Noemi about the spots sooner.

"Hey, hey, it's okay," the human reassured, stepping close to Kesper. "I
think it's really sweet and, to be honest, I have been kinda down lately and
knowing that you would do something like this for me, it makes me feel a
little better." She looked earnestly up into their eyes as the orange began
fading away. "It makes me feel a lot better, actually. Thank you."

The orange melted into a rich red as Kesper uncurled from themselves
and faced her.

"Do Urisk hug?" she asked abruptly.

"I don't know what that word is."

"I'll take that as a no. Would it be okay if I embraced you?"

Kesper nodded unthinkingly, and in an instant Noemi had her arms
wrapped around them and was gently squeezing. They froze, afraid this
might be some kind of attack, but after a moment they registered that the
sensation was a sign of affection, and rather pleasant.

"Oh, oh this is nice," they muttered, placing their arms limply on
Noemi's back. She snorted and pulled away. Her eyes were damp even as
she smiled, and Kesper recognized this as how humans showed emotions
on the outside. Not as colorful, but clear as day.

"Let's try the food you made," she said, stepping over to the plates.
Impulsively, she stuck a finger in the cayenne and stuck it in her mouth.
She pulled a face and smacked her lips.

"Well, it's spicy enough, but the flavor is … weird. I think there's red
dye in here, enough to taste."

"You can taste dye? Does that mean you can taste color?" Kesper asked,
eyes wide in wonder.

"No, I can't taste color. But some dyes have a strong flavor, and this one
tastes like iron."

Kesper didn't say anything, but internally marveled at the revelation
that Noemi might be able to differentiate between metals by taste.

Next, she tried one of the tostones. Flat, misshapen, golden-brown discs that Kesper couldn't understand the appeal of for the life of them. It produced a loud crunching when it met her teeth, and Kesper had to fight not to wince at the sight of her mouth at work.

"Definitely overcooked, and it needs salt, but otherwise pretty good!" She stuffed the rest of the tostone into her mouth and grabbed a banana. She held it up to Kesper in a kind of toast, and they instinctually stepped back. The threat of potassium was much closer than they would've ever liked.

She bit into the fruit (Kesper had looked it up, apparently bananas were and were not a fruit. They were a berry, but also technically an herb. After that, they'd given up trying to understand). Noemi smiled with some confusion in her eyes as she chewed.

"Almost perfect, but weirdly not sticky," she said, taking another bite.

"You can taste stickiness?"

"No, but texture is also an important part of food."

Kesper spluttered in disbelief. Humans were so weird, they were almost glad they couldn't taste themselves. As Noemi settled in and picked at the foods, trying a little cayenne on the tostones and even dipping a banana in it, Kesper stewed with a question.

"What's up, buddy?" she asked, picking up on their brooding.

"Why did you have dirt on your arms?" they blurted, and Noemi smiled gently.

"Come with me," was all she said in answer.

She guided them back across the ship to her own room, carrying the beaker of cayenne and a bag of the remaining tostones. The door to her chambers slid open to reveal several wooden crates in the corner, filled with soil and positioned under a sun lamp.

Noemi stepped in and crouched by the strange setup.

"I've been making a garden, to grow some spices for myself." She pointed to a spot in the dirt and Kesper leaned over. "The oregano is starting to sprout."

"Is it afraid?" Kesper asked, and she frowned at them.

"No? Why would it be?"

"Because it's green."

Noemi blinked at them and then devolved into a fit of giggles.

"Most all plants from Earth are green; it doesn't mean fear like it does for you," she explained. Kesper nodded but side-eyed the plants skeptically.

Standing up, Noemi carefully brushed the dirt from her arms. "You were right. I have missed flavorful food."

Kesper turned a deep, loving red, and she smiled widely. Her teeth were showing but Kesper didn't mind too much.

"You'll have to show Theddy and Briz," Kesper piped up. "They helped me with the food and they'll want to know you're all right."

"Oh, that's sweet of them. We can all have a little dinner party once some of these babies sprout."

"But you're the only one who would be able to taste anything," Kesper pointed out. Noemi just shrugged and gave them a lopsided smile.

"Yeah, but I can make things for you guys that have the nutrients you need. And besides." She placed a hand on Kesper's arm. "Most of the fun of food is getting to share it with others."

And that much Kesper could actually understand.

PLANET KARTOSHKA
Thaís Polegato de Sousa

After no less than three planetary rotations spent fixing the communication system, he had finally managed to make brief contact with the main ship before the central computer melted for real. The relief from the talk with Command was as instantaneous as it was short-lived. Now all that is left to do is to inform Maria.

Well, that and the original mission.

Kartof finds her sitting a quick walk from their crashed pod, near a pile of what looks like little rugged gray cones. She has long discarded her sealed uniform and helmet, almost from the moment the manual suit system had deemed the atmosphere non-toxic to her. Now she's poking one of the cones with her pocket knife, holding the thing in her bare hand in a show of the peculiar recklessness that got her sent to explore this planet in the first place.

Him, he got the task as punishment.

They are friends of sorts now, and so when she bares her teeth to him when he approaches, as she usually does, Kartof does not blink. It is a show of affection from her, not a threat … and if it was, she only has two pointy teeth, very small ones. The rest are blunt. He has never been afraid of her, only a little contemptuous of such displays at the beginning.

"Masha." He uses the name she prefers, instead of her given name, Maria. To soften the blow, he tells himself. She needs to comply with the mission regardless of her feelings about it, and in his experience, humans are notoriously temperamental. "I bring bad news. Mission control is sending a rescue team, but our rations will not last until their arrival."

He expects more of a reaction to his words. He even tries to inconspicuously look for an excess of watery secretion from her eyes, a rare but telltale sign of distress for her species, but she only shrugs.

"So, what's the plan?"

Kartof sits next to her. "We are to fulfill mission parameters to the best of our abilities, for as long as we can … They will surely send another exploration unit, so we should make our notations as detailed as possible … minimize the danger to them…"

She nods along until his voice falters at the end. Despondence is catching up to him without her fighting him on every order as he had imagined she would. Instead, Masha breaks the cone in her hand, somewhat distractedly, face still unworried as anything.

"Do you realize we will die?" He asks at last, curious despite himself. "You are taking it all very well … no embarrassing displays of emotion. We will leave them out of the official record if that is the problem."

She makes a sound with her nose, a strong exhalation of air that makes her torso move up and down fast. Without the helmet, the crinkling at the corner of her eyes is evident, but Kartof does not remember what they are meant to convey.

"I suppose I always knew death stranded in space was a possibility in this career."

"We are stranded on an uncharted planet, not space," he corrects.

"I'm glad it's on a place so much like Earth." She bares her teeth again. "I'd like it better if it was less tropical, but beggars can't be choosers."

"Could you not beg for a specific thing? It seems a wasted effort if you are going to just get any random item out of it."

The thick hair growths above her eyes raise, making the skin of her forehead wrinkle. "Do you … care, about the answer? That was down-right chatty for you. Or is this you having an emotional reaction?"

He blinks at her. Is he? He ponders the question for a moment, staring at the cone in her hand without really taking it in.

"Perhaps. It is not the kind of death I would have chosen for myself. Though I am glad not to be alone with it."

"Ah, Kartoshka!" She wiggles from her place, abandoning her knife and cones and dragging her butt on the ground until she's close enough to encircle him with her two weird hairless arm appendages. "You're my number one death buddy option too!"

"That is not what I have said."

"It's what you meant!" she says, letting him go with some pats to his suit-covered dorsal spikes like they are inoffensive with a thin layer of oil-product cloth over them. "Don't worry, we'll have a fun last month or so. Or I can make you wish you were already dead if that's better. Just say the word."

He does the math inside his head. At first, her insistence on using Earth parameters for distances and time was irritating, but he grew to like the mental exercise it demanded. He had become somewhat of a professional converter of such measures. Even so, the calculations must be wrong in this case.

"An Earth month is the equivalent of two consecutive occurrences of your lunar phases, correct?"

"A synodic month, yes." She moves one hair growth up again, but not the other. "But I meant 30 Earth days."

He silently redoes the operations. The result is different, but just as incorrect.

"We will not last 30 Earth days," he says, thinking it over. "We have supplies for … five Earth days, I believe. The rescue crew will arrive soon after that."

"What?!" she cries. This time she bares her teeth enough that Kartof can see a thin coat of mouth fluid over them. "How soon after?"

"Two Earth days." He cannot help the bemoaning tone. That had been the most saddening, frustrating part for him, one which he would have spared Masha from knowing if he could … for the sake of their mission. "It is a very close window."

"We can survive two days without food!" She gets to her feet and starts to walk in circles, needlessly wasting precious energy. "If we even need to!"

"I cannot," he says, hopeless.

"Oh, yeah, I forgot about the tiny stomach thing." She squats in front of him. "How long would you survive rationing the food?"

Kartof does not want to speak of such things. If no other comfort is to be found in their fates, he knows he will at least have a quick death. It does not mean he wishes to discuss it in detail. He would rather let it happen. Masha's penchant for overly discussing subjects that do not need that kind of extra attention is one of her least pleasant features, together with her general hairlessness. It is something most humans share.

If he gives her the benefit of the doubt, however, perhaps she will have a point this time. She surely seems very enthusiastic for someone facing certain death.

"An additional half Earth day. Two of this planet's rotations."

"And if you had my food as well?"

He makes no effort to hide his indignation. "I would not ask that!"

"Yeah, yeah, you're a dear, but answer the question."

He thinks it over, but the process is arduous. The very idea makes his spiked tail tense downwards.

"After taking out all the indigestible items … if I do not strain myself … I could last to the rescue time," he admits. "This is a pointless exercise."

"Stop complaining," she makes the air exhalation sound again, and the eye crinkling. Kartof remembers all of a sudden: it means happiness. "From this moment on, you don't move an inch, all right? I'm in charge now."

Masha being in charge means, apparently, her going back to sit by her cone pile and poking at them again with her knife.

Before Kartof can ask, she breaks another of them and shows him the inside: rough and gray, only slightly more soft seeming than the outside of it. Completely unappetizing. Just looking at it through his helmet's visor makes his innards contract with disgust.

"I'm going to cook those with some of my drinking water supply. I can drink my filtered pee if I must, and if there's enough oxygen to breathe, there's enough for a flame. I'm going to use," she points towards the tall vegetable formation behind her, "that tree bark doused in ship fuel. There's lots in the forest. And other fruits too. I've seen some animal life as well. I think the crash scattered them for now, but if they come back…"

She flicks her pocketknife quickly in the air, then bares her teeth.

"You don't need to look so scared, I'm just kidding!" She blinks a single eye at him. "I'm going to shoot them, of course."

Kartof cannot say he is keeping up with her rationale at all. Burning fuel on the vegetation life? Wasting her precious water supply to wet her cones? Killing the local animal life? And that is supposed to keep her alive?

She is still rambling on when he tries to pay attention again.

"And there's the part of the rations you can't eat. I'll have those, too. I can even ration them if the cones are too bad or make me too sick."

Understanding finally happens. Kartof hits his tail on the ground, making dust particles fly.

It does little to release the tension on his body, or to ease the worry on his mind.

"You cannot mean to eat those." He shakes his head in time with his tail, disbelieving. He must have misunderstood. This is simply not possible. "You would poison yourself willingly?"

Masha shrugs again, hiding the knife in one of the many compartments of the garish vestments she always wears under her suit.

"No, not really. The lab is mostly intact, so I'll test them for pathogens and toxins first. But it's a pretty big planet, pretty tropical. Something is bound to be edible."

"Yes, they are edible. For the native dwellers of the planet."

"Kartoshka, dear, you're not listening to me. This baby," and she pats the middle of her torso proudly, "Can take anything but lactose. I'll eat these alien pines. I'll eat the alien fruit. I'll eat alien animals and that rock over there and I'll even eat you if I must. If you die first, of course, natural causes only."

"What of the mission?" he asks.

It is little more than a last weak attempt at dissuading her from the strange actions she has decided to undertake, but Masha does not seem impressed.

"Sure, I'll do some exploring. I need to forage for food anyway. But," she points a finger appendage at him, the insignificant claw on it painted a bright purple, "neither of us is going to worry about writing shit down, you hear me? It's Command's fault we're stranded here. They could've warned us about that dynamic magnetic field before we tried to land, so I don't care if the mission fails. And if we survive this, ohoho, boy! I'll give Lïpfa something else to worry about."

Humans truly are barbarians, just as the gossip on the main ship said. Kartof had not believed it at first, and especially not after being paired with Masha for exploration missions. She is so small and delicate, no spikes or outer skeleton to speak of, not even some harder skin. Her boasts that she is tall for her species, at what she calls two meters, had seemed like a poor attempt at self-aggrandizing and intimidation.

Kartof had felt sorry for her, for her feebleness, at first. It had passed as he got to know her and her surprising strength and adaptability. But now it seems he underestimated even that.

He watches Masha depart to the bluish formation of vegetation without a glance behind, with something akin to dread growing in him. For the first time since Masha bared her teeth at him, he realizes she can be dangerous.

Over the next few planetary rotations, they develop separate routines. Kartof's consists of eating his share of the food and moving as little as possible to conserve energy. He stays inside their crashed pod most of the time, where the pressurizer still works and he can take off his suit on occasion.

Sometimes, he goes out. He is tired of always watching the same metal walls, especially when he can hear the world outside. Then he sits outside of the pod and watches Masha go about her own daily activities.

So far, she has been eating the gray cones, a kind of grainy formation that turns the piss she has been drinking a rich purple color, and her share of the rations. Every rotation, as soon as the light of the system's white dwarf star illuminates the spot where they landed, she hikes to the vegetable formation and comes back with an armful of things to try.

As Kartof predicted, the food resources of the planet are edible to the inhabitants of the planet. However, as Masha predicted, not only is she surviving the alien food, but she is able to digest some of it to the point of extracting considerable nutritional value from it.

While Kartof is starting to lose muscle mass and tufts of brown hair from the rationing, she is still in relatively good health. She has lost some weight, but not enough to cause worry. The most remarkable difference is that her teeth and the whites of her eyes now have a lilac tinge to them.

If her energy is not as boundless as ever, she still finds enough of it to run from the blue forest one day, a brown, hairy lump held above her head and her teeth bared.

"Look what I found!"

She puts the lump on the ground in front of him, apparently expecting him to show the same level of enthusiasm.

In all honesty, Kartof would not be able to muster it even if he had ideal levels of nutrition. Much less now, three rotations away from rescue.

"What is this? Some kind of plant?"

From up close, the hairs on the lump look more like minuscules roots, and they are covered in ground particles.

Given everything Masha has been up to lately, it should not be a shock that someone would eat the parts of a vegetable that grow below the soil, but he still recoils from the sight.

She remains unbothered. With a flick of her hand, she opens her pocketknife and stabs the lump with it.

Kartof watches the process with disgusted fascination. She cuts the thing in half and peels the brown hairy part away, revealing a hard, yellowish interior. Then she cuts it up in smaller pieces, most of them in cubes, and throws the things in the water she separated today for what she calls cooking.

She sits down next to him and begins the process of starting a fire. By the time everything is ready and the only thing to do is to watch the water becoming thicker in the improvised pan and the vapor coiling upwards to disappear in the atmosphere, Kartof must admit: it does not look so disgusting anymore.

"It looks just like a potato. A plant from back home," she explains before he can ask. "It's the same word as your nickname in my language."

Kartof turns his gaze to her, tail brushing her arm in amusement, the spikes retracted even inside the suit.

"Have you been calling me a plant name this entire time? The translator said it was an affectionate suffix."

Masha pats the spikes on his tail, eyes crinkling, just as amused.

"It's both. The potato is an important vegetable on Earth, very noble. It's been saving millions from hunger and exploitation for millennia. It deserves our affection." She pokes at the pieces with her pocketknife, baring her teeth when the blade goes in easily. "And it's delicious!"

With those words, she takes pot and vegetable inside the ship, probably to test it in the lab. Kartof would not put it past her to eat it even if the results were discouraging.

In the end, she does eat it the rest of their time on the planet, to the point of mostly subsisting on it.

When the rescue team lands and rushes them inside the ship, her eyes and teeth have gone back to their whitish color and her pee is yellow again. Kartof is carried to the med-bay. Masha walks there of her own volition and under her own power.

Before he is rendered unconscious for exams, Kartof finds the time to ask:

"What you said about the plant … the plant from your planet? That I'm named after…"

"Potatoes?"

"Yes, potatoes." Kartof wraps the end of his tail around one of her hands as the medical assistant fits a mask over his face and he starts to feel sleepy. "It is only for affection, right? You would not truly eat me?"

He can see Masha baring her teeth one last time before he closes his three eyelids. Her voice reaches him distantly as he goes under.

"It's just a joke, Kartoshka. Don't worry about it."

More reassured by her hand squeezing his tail than her words, he holds it and falls asleep.

TO STUDY WAR NO MORE
S.Park

"Man had decided to study war no more because they were very, very good at it."

— Larry Niven, Man/Kzin Wars

Bril inhaled a deep gill-cavity full of dockside air and sighed contentedly. It was good to be in space again. Her species was fairly new on the galactic stage, but she'd been raised in an asteroid belt habitat, and planetside air always smelled wrong to her. If habitat air had that much scent to it, it meant that the scrubbers weren't working and something was very wrong.

Now, though, she was about to embark on her real dream, and she flexed her venom-bearing fangs in delighted anticipation. Ever since the long ago days of highway robbers and water-going piracy, any Therbin with a scrap of real ambition wanted to be a raider. Producing was for the weak, the lowest of the low, the bottom rung of the ladder who were basically prey. Taking what you needed was what true Therbin did.

She was far from the best of the best as Therbins went, but she and her sisters had scraped together the funds to buy a hyper-capable ship, and from what she knew of the galaxy out there, they'd do just fine against the namby-pamby pacifist types who seemed to make up most of it.

The world she'd just shuttled up from after finalizing her purchase was just such a world of weaklings. There had been no visible military presence at all. She had been planetside for nearly half an orbit and in all that time she hadn't seen a single victory parade. But it got far more absurd than that. The human colonizers had actually gone out of their way to set aside huge sections of the planet as "preserves" so that the native life wouldn't be disrupted by them, for egg's sake! What kind of soft-sided lunatics did a thing like that? She'd seen their idea of violence, too, a game called "football," and sure it looked aggressive enough on first sniff, but it was played in armor carefully designed so that injuries were rare, and medics were on claw just in case something went wrong. They were actually *proud* of that, proud of their greatest competitive tradition being bloodless! Weaklings, all of them.

Even the ship she'd bought had shown their weakness. It had been human-owned once, but they'd sold it when it became "unsafe." Not because anything on it had actually failed, not because anybody had actually died, but just because it no longer had tripled-up redundant systems. Tripled! It still had all its life support and propulsion working just fine, and redundant backups for nearly everything. What kind of mewling hatchlings needed more than that before venturing into space? Therbin-built ships tended to have no backups at all. One built the best systems one could, and if they failed, they failed, and hopefully took the weaklings who hadn't properly maintained them out with them.

"Hey Bril. Got the guns mounted."

Bril swiveled her eyes towards Drig, her second in command. They were not literal brood-mates, but she considered Drig to be a sister all the same. "What, already?"

"There were some reinforced points that were just perfect for them. They had mounting pins and everything. Looks like there'd been something on them before."

"Huh. Are you saying the humans had armed their ship?"

"Don't think so. Whatever was bolted on before our stuff was much, much bigger. No way a ship this size would pack guns that huge! Maybe some kind of specialty equipment, scientific instruments, stuff like that."

Bril rubbed her foreclaws together thoughtfully. The ship had been a fast merchantman before Bril had bought it. That didn't seem like it would need scientific equipment. Then again, the previous owners might not have been the first owners either.

"There's also some rapid-jettison tubes that'd make a great improvised torpedo launch system, so maybe you should pick up some torpedoes," said Drig.

"Nice. What were the tubes for before this?" The seller hadn't mentioned any such feature, and Bril couldn't help but be curious.

Drig ruffled her joint spines in a disinterested shrug. "Dunno. I heard that human ships never lose a cargo. Maybe it's for jettisoning it so pirates can't get it?"

"There's no way they could count on that working all the time; debris in space can be tracked."

"Well, whatever it was for, the control runs and power systems were all pulled out, but I figure if you give me four or five days I can get some stuff to set up torpedos. The space is there, and we've got the funds for a dozen or so; why not?"

"Sure, why not." Bril waved a claw, and Drig waved back and turned back to her work on the ship's weapons. Soon they'd be ready, and soon the soft, weak species of the galaxy would know who was about to rise to the top rungs of the galactic ladder.

*　*　*　*　*

The bar was like spaceport bars everywhere: badly lit, badly cleaned, and badly serviced. With dozens of species coming and going, finding your poison of choice was sometimes a bit of a problem too, but fortunately Therbin shared the tendency to get high on certain specific salts with a few other species, and their digestion handled carbohydrates well enough. They were carnivorously-inclined, but omnivory was always a good survival strategy. So Bril was happily chewing on a bowl of "salted pretzels," a snack common in human-frequented space and quite sufficiently intoxicating for her.

"Greetings." Another being dropped down to sit next to her. It was a simple biped, hardly any limbs at all, and weirdly smooth; covered in tiny, slick scales, with a long tail that drooped from the end of the bar stool as it took a perch there. Bril recognized it as a Fth'chak, an endothermic and reptilian species that had a reputation for being fluttery, chattery things, who considered direct discussion of anything to be dreadfully rude and would circle a point for hours.

Bril gave the Fth'chak a nod, and it nodded back. Bril had no idea how you told the sex of Fth'chak.

"Are you the owner of that light freighter getting refitted in bay twelve?" asked the reptile.

"What if I am?" said Bril, pulling her eye stalks warily close.

"I only wanted to pass on a small bit of wisdom, gleaned from my species' several centuries in space. There have been a number of incidents of space piracy in the news of late; have you noticed?"

Bril's eye-stalks retracted further, and she gave the Fth'chak a long look. "What of that?"

The Fth'chack ruffled a frill around its neck and replied, "One should be careful, going out in space in such times. One should perhaps do a little research on such incidents, on their history, on their usual results."

"I haven't done research since I had my adult molt," snapped Bril.

"Nevertheless, it can provide valuable information. But if you don't wish to research, then perhaps I could help you by pointing out that piracy is almost unknown in this part of the galaxy."

"I'm quite aware of that. I have no fear of being attacked by a pirate." Bril tried not to flex her fangs too blatantly. She was going to be the one doing the attacking.

"And yet you go armed. Pirates do exist. Indeed, I believe I mentioned that incidents of piracy have been on the rise. Interestingly, they have been rising ever since your species discovered FTL travel."

"Are you insinuating something?" Bril tried not to bristle.

"Oh no, no." The Fth'chak waved one taloned hand. "That would be quite rude. I only wanted to do you a favor. A young, new space captain such as yourself should be warned before going out into the wider galaxy."

Bril did bristle now, her joint fur standing up on end. "I know what I'm doing."

"I am certain you do. Yet you may not be aware of all relevant facts. For example, did you know that human ships carry almost a quarter of the cargo shipped about the galaxy?"

"I knew that, yes."

"And yet they charge a quite significant premium to do so. Have you ever considered why?"

"The cost of all that ridiculous redundancy, I'm sure. Just means I can under-cut them and still make a profit," said Bril dismissively. Not that she intended to ship much legitimate cargo, but she'd at least pretend to.

"Indeed, indeed. Still, the way other species are willing to pay this premium is a fact that you might ponder upon for a time."

Bril let out a short hiss of annoyance. "Do you have a point that you wanted to get to, Fth'chak?"

The Fth'chak snapped its frill up for a moment, the gesture startling as it seemed to make the alien's head twice the size it had been. Then it smoothed it back down. "No, I suppose I don't," it said, and slid down off of the stool and stalked away.

Bril looked after it, then ruffled up her joint spines and picked up another pretzel. That had been an odd encounter, but hadn't given her any actually useful information at all. Piracy on the rise. Of course it was; the Therbin were in space now, taking their rightful place! What need did she have to research that obvious fact?

*   *   *   *   *

"There it is." Bril's fangs were practically dripping in anticipation as she looked at the big screen on her ship's bridge. It didn't show an actual view, of course, since to the naked eye another ship wouldn't be visible until it was freakishly, insanely close, but the little icons scattered across the screen were a beautiful sight all the same. Here the system's primary, glowing white. There a scatter of planets, marked in green. Further out, the arc of a line indicating where the gravitational boundary between hyper-safe space and the star's gravity well lay. And just past that point, the little blue triangle marking a merchant ship, on a course so predictable that Bril's own ship would have no trouble at all matching vectors. That was necessary to board a ship, of course.

But first the fun part. The part where they pounced on the prey and put a nice, big hole in something vital but not too vital, just to make sure it didn't escape.

"Captain, the merchant is changing vectors," spoke up Abitz, one of Bril's actual brood-sisters. "Also its power readings have just spiked."

"Trying to run away, I suppose. Does it have the power to outrun us?"

"Ah … It's a very large ship, Captain; we're much faster. But it's not running. It's slowing down to meet us."

"What?" Bril felt all her joint fur standing on end in shock. "Are you sure it's a merchant?"

"As sure as I can be. The engine readings aren't military grade. Everything is consistent with a Kooringa-class human cargo transport."

Bril rubbed her claws together, trying to think. "What the hell do the humans think they're doing? A ship pops out of hyper right on their vector and starts after them, they have to know we're pirates. Or can they be that stupid? Have they hailed us?"

"No, Captain."

"Hail them, then! Put it on screen."

The creature whose image replaced the navigational display a moment later was a soft-looking thing, wearing an elaborate conglomeration of fabric to cover up its pale, squishy skin, with a tuft of dark hair on the top of it. A human, of course.

The human — Bril thought that the lack of facial hair tufts might mean it was female — sprawled sideways in her chair, putting one leg up over the arm of it, and gave Bril a tooth-baring expression. "Why hello there," she drawled. "I'm Captain Amanda Price of the Terran merchant ship *Nobody's Business*. What can I do for you?"

Bril bristled at the ridiculous human and her ridiculous long name and her ridiculous sentimentality in *naming* her ship. *That* was a ridiculous name, too. "You can kill all power and prepare to be boarded."

"Ah, so you really are pirates, then. Therbins, right? I've heard about you."

"If you have, then you should know the danger you are in. This ship is well armed. If you surrender, we will allow you and your crew to live."

"See, the problem with that is that my ship is armed too."

Bril snorted in amusement at the very thought. The triple-redundant, super-defensive humans, carrying weapons like a predator? Hah. No doubt they had very good shields, but Bril had paid for the best grasers, and the highest-yield torpedoes that the ship's tube system could fit. There was no way—

"Sullivan, why don't you give the nice spider-ladies there a little demonstration? I know it'll cut into our margins a bit, but I think we can afford it."

"Yes, ma'am," said one of the other humans, seated behind the one in the center of the screen. It did something to its console, and a moment later Bril heard Abitz suck in a shocked breath.

"Missile launch, Captain."

"What?" Bril felt a cold chill run through her vitals. They were still far, far outside of effective torpedo range, let alone energy weapons range, so there was no way she could fire back. She could try to shoot it down with a torpedo, or one of the grasers once it got close enough, but if it were an actual military-quality missile it would be able to take evasive maneuvers, so there was no guarantee she'd get it.

What kind of lunatic merchant ship carried actual combat missiles? Their grav-drives meant they cost a small fortune each, and that was just the beginning of the absurdity of arming a merchant ship with such a weapon. The space a missile launcher would take up would cut into their cargo capacity, and the magazine storage for the massive things if you wanted to be able to fire more than once would take up even more. Surely it had to be some kind of fake.

Bril's eyes snapped back to the human, still lounging idly in her chair.

"This is your warning shot, Therbian. It's the only one you get, so I suggest you pay attention."

"Coms off," Bril snapped at Abitz, not wanting to see that smug, squishy creature any longer.

Abitz tapped the command into her console, and the lounging human vanished, replace by a navigational display that now showed a blinking orange dot moving inexorably from the human ship towards the Therbin ship. Bril's mind raced. Space was a huge place, and even when ships were "close" to each other, as now, they were still actually vast distances apart. Missiles moved at sub-light speeds, so even though they were blazingly fast in those terms, their run times were measured in minutes, not seconds. Still, there was limited time to act in, and Bril would have to make the most of it.

"Drig," she snapped at the weapons expert. "Track that, get a torpedo locked on it and ready to launch as soon as it comes in range."

"Yes, Captain," she replied.

"Should I ready a retreat course?" piped up Tisl, the navigator.

"No." Bril felt all her joint-fur bristling in annoyance. "That has to be a fake, and even if it's real, they can't possibly carry more than one. That's a cargo ship, not a warship. This is all just a bluff. I've seen humans, I've been on one of their worlds. They're soft creatures. They're *prey* creatures. They're just acting like a tarquil, puffing up their spines so that they seem too large to tackle." Bril flexed her fangs again, coldly, eagerly, and said, "I like the taste of tarquil."

There was silence after that as they waited, while the orange dot of the missile crept closer and closer. Suddenly Drig's claw stabbed down as the right moment arrived and a green dot raced out from their ship towards the human missile. Torpedoes were smaller things, and were given all their impetus by the torpedo tube that launched them. They had no drives of their own, so they couldn't change course once sent on their way.

This one streaked out, and the missile streaked in to meet it, but at the last second the missile swerved, adjusting its course slightly, and then again to re-target the ship, so the torpedo missed it entirely. The whole exchange had taken long enough that the missile was almost in energy weapons range now. Bril wanted to curse. She should have had Drig fire several torpedoes, in case the first missed. "Prepare the grasers, it's almost in ra—" She was cut off by the orange light vanishing from the display. The missile had exploded outside of energy range. An alarm buzzed as the shield suddenly registered dangerously elevated amounts of energy. The missile had been nuclear, and from the hellish heart of its blast came radiation that sleeted against the Therbian's shields. But the shields were more than sufficient against it, and Bril let out a long breath of relief.

"Sister," said Abitz, "The human is hailing us again."

"Put the thing back on screen then."

Abitz stabbed at her console, and once again the squishy creature lounging in her chair appeared. "Hello there, Therbian. That was your one and only warning shot. You can heave to, or you can run away. I don't really care which, but if you continue on this vector, I will shoot to kill next time."

"I will not be taken by your bluff, human. No cargo ship could afford more than one missile. I wasn't hatched yesterday."

The human finally straightened in her chair. "It was not a bluff, I promise you. You'll save yourselves a lot of trouble if you just break off now."

"Hah. That's what you want me to think. But I know better, human. You are not raiders yourselves. You are mere cargo haulers, not even producers of things. You are the lowest form of prey. I will not be bluffed by *prey*. Com off," she added, turning to Abitz, who once again obediently switched the screen back to the normal display.

"We maintain our course then, Captain?" asked Tisl, her voice nervous.

"We do," said Bril firmly.

Nearly a minute ticked by, and Bril felt her eye-stalks extending in renewed confidence. She hadn't even realized how far she'd pulled them in. But the humans obviously didn't have any more—

"Missile launch," said Abitz, her voice tight with sudden fear.

"Just one?" said Bril, mentally counting the torpedoes they had on board and considering the best strategy to catch the damn thing this time.

"Just one. No, wait, another launch."

"They have to be fake," hissed Bril. "They *have* to be."

"And a third," said Abitz.

"What should I do, Captain?" asked Tisl.

"Nothing," snarled Bril. She knew perfectly well that the missiles, if they really were missiles, would be locked onto her ship. There was no time to slew far enough to the side to get out of range, so there was no avoiding them entirely. Their shield had held against the radiation from a blast still kilometers away, but would crack like the thinnest of eggs from a direct impact. It wasn't military grade at all; it was meant to protect against micro-meteors and radiation hazards.

The only thing to do was to hope they could pick at least a few of the missiles off with the torpedoes. "Drig, come up with a firing plan to shoot the whole torpedo magazine at them. They can only do so much dodging. If we hit enough of them, we can take them out, or slow them enough for the grasers to get a good shot. Go ahead and fire early. We don't need ideal targeting; we just need more chances to hit them."

"Yes, Captain." It would be tight. They'd only brought a dozen torpedoes, so they'd get just four shots at each missile, and they'd have to take all four as fast as possible to even have a chance, so they could all miss completely, unless the missile dodged one and swerved into another. Still, they might get lucky with those, or with the grasers at closer range...

"Another launch," said Abitz, and her voice was heavy with dread.

"Pchack!" Bril couldn't keep from swearing. "How many of those things can they have in a ship that size?"

"If the cargo hold is entirely missiles, more than a thousand," whispered Tisl. Her eye-stalks were pulled all the way in, and her arms were curled in as well, hunched in a posture of terror.

Bril hissed in rage. "They *cannot* have the hold full! They're a merchant ship! They make money hauling cargo! We will bring down the missiles targeted at us, and then we will bring them down like the prey they are. Keep our course."

"Yes, Captain," said Tisl, but Bril feared it was as much because she knew fleeing wouldn't save them as for any other reason. Bril wanted to be certain they'd made it, that this was all a bluff, a ruse, that the missiles were fake, that the torpedoes would take them out. She wanted — needed — to believe anything but that her own death was staring down at her in the form of one blinking blue triangle and four orange dots creeping towards her.

The torpedoes began firing, a volley of three, aimed at the first missile.

"Another launch," whispered Abitz, and a fifth orange light blinked into existence next to the blue triangle of the human ship.

Bril felt her own eye-stalks retracting completely. They had to be fake. They had to be fake. They all had to be fake.

The first torpedo blinked off the display. The second did as well. The third vanished too ... and the missile's orange glare vanished with it. Bril almost dared hope for an instant that it was indeed fake. Then the shield alarms squealed again as the remnants of nuclear hellfire splashed against them. It had been real, and at least four more just like it were headed her way.

※　※　※　※　※

Captain Amanda Price stared at the main display and shook her head. There was a scatter of white pinpricks indicating a recent debris field, and another scatter of little green dots — life pods, and Terran made ones too, it looked like — across the spot where the Therbin ship had been.

It had taken six missiles to take them down, a good chunk of her twenty-shot magazine. Though at least she hadn't needed to spend any counter-missiles. The Therbins hadn't gotten anywhere near her ship, and they'd obviously used every torpedo they'd had trying to shoot down her missiles in any case, for the last few had only been opposed by energy weapons.

"These new guys aren't very bright, are they?" That was Dan Sullivan, the weapons officer, who sounded half amused, half incredulous.

"Gals," said Price, almost absently. "Any Therbin you talk to will be female; their males aren't sentient."

"Huh. Okay then. Well, gals or guys, that was pretty dense of them."

"That's been how most of the reports I've seen on Terran shipping encounters with them have gone," said Price with a shrug. "So no, at this point they're really not. They have to know by now that their pirates nearly always lose. They've managed to have some decently armed ships, and to get lucky a few times, but mostly…" Price gestured at the screen. "Mostly that happens."

"How many do you think got off of it before it blew at the end there?"

"Not many, probably," replied Price. "Jackson?" She turned to another member of the crew, the navigator, "Plot a plan to pick up all the pods all the same. I wouldn't leave even pirates out here. While you do that, I'll start writing up the incident report for the spit-and-polish types back on Earth." She flashed a grin at that. "Gotta get our anti-piracy payout from the Navy, so I can afford to restock the missiles. It'll be nice to get some really up-to-date ones."

"Hell, maybe if Earth gets enough reports about these bozos, they'll do something to actually drive the point home to the whole species," said Sullivan.

"Maybe so. I'm considering just releasing any we find in the pods to make their way home. Normally I'm all for prosecuting pirates, but I feel like they might be better served telling everybody else from their backwards little planet to stop it already." Captain Price shook her head again. "Although given their specific form of idiocy, maybe they'll just try ramping it up."

"Well, the Navy will definitely teach them what not to do if they try that," said Sullivan with a chuckle.

"True enough. Now let's get a move on, people. We've got lots to do, and when that's all done we still have to finish our route." She grinned. "After all, a human ship *always* delivers its cargo, no matter what."

HANDS ON
Liz A. Vogel

Biospecialist Fleerg grrled in frustration. It didn't mind treating crewmember Benjamin's injuries; it had been chosen for this crew-group because of its knowledge of human medicine. But it was running low on human-compatible supplies.

It spread the analgesic compound as thinly as it could while still ensuring efficacy onto the human's manipulative appendage, and the human sagged in a way that Fleerg had learned to interpret as relief and not impending circulatory collapse. "Oh, that's better."

"You are fortunate the damage is not worse. That plant excretes an extremely caustic substance."

"Yeah, I figured that out." Benjamin held up his limb and waggled his alarmingly red appendages in front of Fleerg, impeding the biospecialist's efforts to apply protective coverings.

"And yet you touched it ... why?

"I wanted to see what it felt like."

"How can you *see* what something feels like?"

"See as in find out, not see as in visually perceive."

"For a species that expresses so much through visual metaphors, you certainly are determined to put your appendages on things." Fleerg extruded a tendril and pulled the limb back down, holding it in place while it layered thin protective strips over the damaged areas. "And why would you need to feel it, anyway? You could see it, hear it, smell it — okay, *you* probably couldn't smell it, but —"

"I thought it smelled very nice."

"It smelled like poison!" Fleerg felt again the distressed bafflement it had experienced when seeing the human reaching for the plant the rest of the exploratory party had so carefully veered around. "And you kept petting it!"

"It was fuzzy."

Fleerg restrained the howl of frustration it could feel building in its thoracic cavity. It was growing skilled at that; this was not the first such conversation it and the human exchange crewmember had had. In nobly restrained silence, it finished covering the injuries, then said, "These should protect your," it paused to recall the word, "hand until it is healed. Please don't remove them until I instruct you to do so." Fleerg had learned that lesson early on, when the human had peeled the coverings from a bad-ly-cut palm "to see how it's doing" — as if he couldn't tell the state of his own body without visual inspection — and only then discovered that the strips were not reusable.

"Yes, yes, I'll be good," Benjamin assured in what Fleerg could only assume was some kind of tap into an alternate reality, since the human's behavior had no such precedent in this one. Benjamin prodded the cover-ings with his other hand — Fleerg contracted in horror — and pronounced, "Good as new!" before hopping down from the treatment platform.

"It is *not—*" Fleerg recognized the futility, and stopped.

"It's great. Thanks, doc!" And before Fleerg could protest at the strange appellation, Benjamin added, "Come on, let's get back down to the planet."

Fleerg had little choice but to follow, if only to be readily available when next its expertise was called for. Normal people regarded medical treatment as a necessary recourse after unavoidable injury; humans, apparently, regarded medical treatment as a routine activity that allowed them to continue injuring themselves, rather than avoiding things that might damage them. Fleerg wondered how to tactfully compose a note to that effect for the documentation of the exchange experience.

*   *   *   *   *

They arrived on the planet along with the next rotation of crewmembers, sampling units, and refreshments for those staying planetside. Crew-Coordinator Krzg'tlak canted a pair of eyes at the human as Benjamin bounced over to the main group. "Are you fit for duty?"

"Sure, no problem." Benjamin waggled his appendages again, displaying the coverings to the whole group. "Fleerg patched me up just fine."

Fleerg began to protest that it had only applied standard analgesic treatment and protective coverings, but Krzg'tlak dipped another pair of eyes in its direction and Fleerg subsided. The Coordinator had also had similar previous experiences with their human crewmember.

They proceeded to the next sector on the survey plan, and spread out to continue taking samples and readings of soil, air, and flora. Benjamin carefully avoided the fuzzy green-leafed stalks which had seared his fingers earlier; fortunately there were few of them, and they stood out clearly in the blue-and-purple landscape. Instead, he progressed through an area of low growth and exposed rocks, plunging the sampler into the ground at neatly-spaced intervals and recording the concentration of each variety of plant. Humans *were* very efficient workers, once you got them focused on a task.

"Hey, look at this!" Several members of the survey crew whirled around to stare in alarm; they'd heard that tone in the human's voice before. But this time no one seemed in danger of being eaten; Benjamin was hunkered down beside a small hillock covered with a moss-like growth. As he passed the scanner over it, tiny cilia uncurled and extended a few millimeters above the surface of the moss, following his motion. "Hello there, friend," he said to the plant. "Now, is it the scanner that's got your attention, or..." He set the scanner aside and repeated the motion with his empty palm; a turquoise ripple tracked across the moss in his wake. "I think it likes me!"

"*Don't touch—!*" Krzg'tlak and Fleerg called out at the same time, but it was too late. The human was gently stroking the moss with his unprotected hand, sending waves of turquoise and lavender across the blueish-violet mass. "It's all right," Benjamin called back, making that punctuated breathing noise they'd eventually learned did not signal impending respiratory distress. "It tickles!"

Krzg'tlak briefly shrouded all six eyes. Benjamin gave the moss a final pat, then retrieved his scanner and stood; Fleerg observed carefully, but the human showed no indication of damage. He merely moved on to the next sampling point, and eventually the others also returned their attention to their own survey tasks.

Behind them, unbeknownst, the patch of moss began to take on a pink tinge.

* * * * *

The survey crew had dispersed widely by the time they were due to reassemble and consolidate samples to be sent back to the ship for analysis. Benjamin was one of the last to rejoin the group, and Krzg'tlak was beginning to worry that he'd found some other hazard to expose himself to when the human finally appeared. As they packaged the neatly-labeled vials, packets, and containers into transport cases, Krzg'tlak moved between the survey crew members, correlating data and checking if anyone needed assistance or had found something that would alter the survey plan.

Benjamin was standing back from the rest of the group, watching silently. It was the silence that alerted Krzg'tlak more than the fact that the human's hands were empty. "Benjamin, where are your samples?"

The human's head rotated toward the words. After a long pause, he said, "I … do not have them."

"And your scanning equipment?" Krzg'tlak had a premonition of a great deal of requisitions paperwork in the near future.

"It is not here." The human's unblinking stare was disconcerting.

"I can see that." Krzg'tlak resisted the impulse to scrape forearms in agitation; a Coordinator should have more dignity. "Is it damaged?"

Benjamin replied slowly. "To my knowledge, it is undamaged."

Well, that was something; the looming imaginary paperwork dissipated. "When next we reassemble, can you bring the equipment with you? Please?" Krzg'tlak added, recalling the pre-exchange briefing on the importance of that word to human interactions.

"I can do that."

Krzg'tlak canted two pairs of eyes at the human. "Benjamin, are you quite well?"

"I am also undamaged."

Krzg'tlak had doubts, but decided not to pursue it at this time. "If you are unable to carry your equipment and samples, Meliorlel will assist you." Krzg'tlak signaled to another crewmember to join them; the prtzian pipped an affirmative, then turned and bobbled amenably at the human. Benjamin bent his knees in an awkward bobble back. Krzg'tlak elevated a pair of eyes slightly; was this some human effort at nonverbal language learning? There was no harm in the attempt, but it was unlike the human to forgo an opportunity to speak.

"Keep watch on him," Krzg'tlak said surreptitiously as the human turned away to stare unblinking at the rest of the crew readying their equipment, and Meliorlel gave a soft affirmative pip.

It wasn't until the crew had dispersed again that Krzg'tlak realized the human was no longer wearing his protective hand coverings. That was hardly surprising, but the Coordinator hadn't thought his injuries would heal that quickly.

*　*　*　*　*

Krzg'tlak was documenting the structure of a stand of spiky red things that were either plants or mineral outcroppings — the readings were inconclusive, and further analysis would be required — when Benjamin came bounding over the nearby rise.

"Sorry I missed the meeting!" the human called as soon as he was close enough. "I found this really neat soil pattern — I'm guessing there might have been hot-spring activity in the not too distant past. Anyway, I got caught up in it and lost track of time. Sorry!"

Krzg'tlak unbent from studying the base of the spikes. "At least you recovered your scanning equipment." That was one less set of paperwork to be done. Then the Coordinator worked through the human's statements — it was fairly probable that Benjamin had not been physically entrapped in the soil — and came out the other side with, "But you were at the reassembly."

"I was? No, I wasn't."

"I spoke with you there." Krzg'tlak knew that human memory was not as precise as some species', but this seemed unusually unreliable. "You failed to return with your samples, or your equipment."

"Well, sure, I don't have the samples with me *now*, because when I realized what time it was I wanted to find you and apologize in person, and there was no sense dragging them around with me. They're back at the site with the soil pattern." Benjamin waved vaguely in the direction he'd come from.

"You did not mention this soil pattern at the reassembly. In fact, you were unusually uncommunicative."

"Yeah, because I *wasn't there*?"

Perhaps this was some human metaphor for behaving strangely? Krzg'tlak said as much, adding, "You assured me that you were not unwell."

"Maybe somebody did, but it wasn't me. You realize I have no idea what you're talking about, right?"

It was unlikely that Krzg'tlak had mistaken anyone else for the human. "And where is Meliorlel?"

Benjamin shrugged. "Dunno. Haven't seen 'em."

Krzg'tlak activated the communicator. "Meliorlel? Transmit your coordinates." The communicator's display flickered and displayed a string of characters. "Fleerg? Meet us at these coordinates, if you are available."

"I will be there promptly," said Fleerg's voice from the tiny speaker.

Krzg'tlak gathered samples and equipment, and oriented toward the coordinates Meliorlel had provided. "Come with me. Please."

"You're the boss." Benjamin fell easily into step alongside the Coordinator's long strides. "But seriously, we should redo the survey plan to give more time to that soil pattern. Hot springs implies volcanic activity, and we haven't seen any evidence of that around here. It could give us a very different idea of the planet's recent development..."

The human continued on the subject until they approached Meliorlel's location, requiring little input from the Coordinator. Krzg'tlak was unsurprised to find the prtzian alone, but Meliorlel saw them, froze, and then twisted to look in the opposite direction.

"Where is this soil pattern?" Krzg'tlak asked to distract the human, then conveyed quietly to Meliorlel, "I told you to keep a watch on him!"

"No, not here, it's over that way." Benjamin waved his arm toward an area well ahead of where Meliorlel had been working. Meanwhile Meliorlel squiggled that one had only turned one's attention away for a moment—! "And hey, I already covered this area. Or did you find something interesting?" The human bent to peer at the prtzian's scanner.

Fleerg arrived, vent-slits flaring as it reoxygenated after moving at high speed. Krzg'tlak didn't even have to provide direction; it immediately went to Benjamin. "Is your hand worse?"

"No, it's fine. Why?"

Fleerg looked to Krzg'tlak, who asked, "Are humans prone to cognitive malfunctions after such an injury?"

"Hey, my cog is functioning just fine, thank you." Benjamin rapped his knuckles against his head as if to demonstrate its solidity. "What is all this?"

Fleerg considered this. The cognitive sciences were considered an entirely different field than human physical medicine; after the cursory briefing it had been given on the subject, it understood why. Their brains didn't even make sense to them. But, "It is possible, if the injury has become infected."

"It's *fine*." Benjamin waved the hand in question in the air between them, as if that proved something. "And anyway, infections don't develop that fast in humans; it takes days, usually. Not that it's going to."

Fleerg pointed a scanner in his direction. "I do not detect an elevated temperature. That's supposed to accompany hallucinations, in an infection situation," it explained to Krzg'tlak.

"That's because it's not infected. Look, check my fingers if you don't believe me." He thrust the hand at Fleerg. "You'd be doing me a favor, anyway. I really want to take these things off."

"How did you get them back on?" asked Fleerg.

"Huh?"

It was a profoundly unhelpful human sound; in great restraint, Krzg'tlak shrouded only one pair of eyes.

Fleerg clarified, "How did you reapply the coverings? I noticed you had them off at the reassembly."

"I keep telling you, I wasn't at the reassembly! And I didn't take them off. I wanted to — it would have been nice to have both hands to experiment with that moss — but I know how it makes you crazy, so I left them on like a good boy. See?" Benjamin held up his still-covered hand, the wrappings undisturbed save for a slight grubbiness that was inevitable when the human was left unattended with anything that involved dirt.

"And yet, you don't remember being at the reassembly," Krzg'tlak pointed out.

"Because I wasn't there! Look, I'm sorry I missed it, but I don't know what this messing about is supposed to achieve. If this is some alien practical joke, I don't get it."

"But you were there, Benjamin," said Fleerg. "I saw you too."

Meliorlel indicated that one had also witnessed the human's presence at the reassembly. Although the human was clearly very fleet of foot, since the human had been behind one only moments before arriving beside Coordinator Krzg'tlak.

"There may be some other cause," said Fleerg. "Did you touch anything hallucinogenic?"

"No, I didn't! ...How would I know if it was hallucinogenic?"

"Because you could smell—! No, you couldn't. No, of course not..."

"Look, the only thing I've been handling is samples — and I do know better than to contaminate those by touching them," he added somewhat acerbically. "In fact, I don't think I've touched anything since that moss, after you both freaked out so bad about that."

"Perhaps the moss is a delayed hallucinogen," Krzg'tlak suggested to Fleerg.

"Well, you can sniff it if it'll help," Benjamin snapped. "There's another patch of it right over there."

He pointed to another low hillock covered with the blueish-violet moss, not far behind Meliorlel. Fleerg and Krzg'tlak started toward it, but

Meliorlel froze, then began pipping alarmingly. One writhed that that had not been there moments ago!

Krzg'tlak and Fleerg froze as well, then carefully backed away from the small mound. But Benjamin said, "Really?" and headed straight for it. "Can this stuff move on its own, do you think?"

"Don't touch it!" his fellow crew all variously shouted, but of course the human was already kneeling beside the moss and stretching out his unprotected hand. "Hello there," he said gently. "Don't be afraid, now. Do you want to come and play?"

The moss merely sat there, unmoving. Benjamin inched closer and passed his hand back and forth above the surface; a turquoise wave of tiny cilia followed his motion. "There you go," he encouraged, and gave the mass a friendly pat. Turning to his compatriots, he said, "See, there's nothing to be afraid of," but he choked it off at the expressions of horror he'd learned enough to read on their various physiognomies. He turned back to the moss and— "Whoah!" He scrambled backward on hands and backside as the moss bulged upward, reaching nearly six feet as it morphed into a vaguely bipedal shape. Pinkish-beige replaced the blueish-violet at the extremities, while the middle faded to the pale gray of a survey coverall. Within a very few minutes, an exact replica of Benjamin stood over him, staring unblinkingly down.

"Whoah," the human said again, in a very different tone. "Hey, that's pretty cool." He scrambled to his feet and took a step closer, peering into the matching eyes. He raised one arm out to the side; the moss-creature raised a matching arm, mirroring the gesture. Benjamin lowered the arm and raised his other one, flexing the elbow up and down; the moss-creature mimicked him precisely. He started to raise a foot, then said, "No, wait, this is getting silly."

"…Yes," said the moss-creature.

"Hey, you can talk! Excellent!"

The moss-creature merely stared.

"Uh, you can talk, right?"

"I can talk. It … is difficult."

"Well, I'm glad you made the effort, 'cause now we can get to know each other." Benjamin paused to look over his shoulder to where the other survey members stood. "You guys are seeing this, right?"

"Oh, yes," said Krzg'tlak in a resigned tone. All six eyes were unshrouded, but conveyed the impression that this was only because a Coordinator must stay alert during an unexpected alien contact.

"And it doesn't smell like a hallucinogen?"

"It smells like you," said Fleerg. "Though … oddly, as if you'd been eating too many vegetables." Benjamin immediately thought of two different interpretations of that, and decided not to ask which one Fleerg had meant.

"So, you're really here. That's good."

"I am."

"Sorry, don't worry about my friends back there. They're a little confused." Benjamin noticed that there was one error in the moss-creature's otherwise-perfect copy. "And I think I see part of the reason why." He held up his injured fingers and waggled them yet again. "Why didn't you copy the bandages? Or the burns, for that matter?"

"You … did not want them," the moss-creature said slowly. "They are not a part of you."

"But you did the coveralls. Those aren't part of me either, just so you know."

"You accepted them as … part of how you should be."

"Well, that's true; I don't much fancy running around alien planets naked."

Krzg'tlak decided it was time to intervene. "We apologize for not communicating with you sooner. We did not realize you were here to communicate with."

"I … understand."

"We intend no trespass. Our purpose here is peaceful and scientific; we would like to examine the composition and life forms of your planet, if you would permit us to do so."

"This … is acceptable."

Krzg'tlak's eyes swayed in relief; the paperwork regarding an interplanetary incident was enough to make resigning the service an appealing alternative. "This pleases us. Can you inform the rest of your people of our purpose here, so we do not alarm them?"

"We … know."

Which had implications that would need to be pursued later, but for now Krzg'tlak was just relieved to not have to call an evacuation.

"Terrific!" said Benjamin, and stuck out his uninjured hand. The moss-creature mirrored the gesture again, and Benjamin said, "No, put out the other one." When the moss-creature complied, Benjamin seized it. "This is an Earth custom. It means we're glad to meet you!"

"Glad," the moss-creature echoed, hopefully in agreement.

"One thing, though. You can't go around looking exactly like me. I mean, I'm flattered, but it's going to confuse people."

"I cannot communicate with you in my natural form."

"Hmm." The human pondered; Krzg'tlak worried. "I know! Can you keep this shape, but revert to your natural colors?"

The moss-creature stared unblinkingly, whether thinking about it or not comprehending was impossible to tell. Then a bluish tinge began to spread over its form; soon the Benjamin-shape sported a lavender coverall and turquoise hands and head.

"Awesome!" the human cheered. "So listen, my name's Benjamin. What's yours?"

"I … do not have such an appellation."

"No name? Well, we've got to call you something. How about Mossy? Would you be okay with that?"

"That is … okay."

"Great! Mossy it is, then! So listen, can you tell me anything about this soil pattern I found over that way? It looks like..."

Krzg'tlak dipped a set of eyes each at Fleerg and Meliorlel, sending them to follow the human and ... "Mossy" ... in hopes of continuing to avoid that interplanetary incident. The rest of the survey crew would need to be informed that there was sentient life on this planet. And, Krzg'tlak reflected, they'd have to set up a rotation so that someone was always available to medically treat the human; they'd never be able to keep him from touching things now.

CARE AND CUDDLING
E.A. Greene

"It's crying again?" Rilya asked, scuttling into the medical cabinet. The whole ship rang with the wails of the tiny human ensconced in the cabinet's smallest scanning compartment, a sound far out of proportion to the infant's size.

"It is. And I still don't know why. The cabinet says it's in good health," Carrix said. "I've done everything the human health module suggested. I've double-checked the nutrient mix we're feeding it, I've made sure the sanitizing fluids aren't an irritant for it, I've wrapped it in a temperature-maintenance covering. But every time it wakes up, even if it's fed and clean, it starts making that sound."

When Rilya had cut the human infant out of the mangled lifepod they'd come across, Carrix had put themselves forward immediately as the child's caretaker. They had experience with live young, they insisted, since thrixin reproduced similarly to humans; Rilya and Felao had no experience with young at all, having just put down substrate and laid their first eggs on this very trip. But now Carrix was yellow with stress, shading into orange, and it had only been six shifts since they'd picked up the lifepod.

"Maybe we should sedate it after all, like the medical cabinet keeps suggesting," Rilya said. "I know I said we shouldn't, but its biochemistry doesn't seem that different from an adult's. It can't be as dangerous as dosing a larva."

"No, no." Carrix's tendrils paled for a moment in negation. "You and Felao were right about that. We don't know if it's safe. I don't think it needs chemical intervention. I think it just needs sleep. But I can't figure out how to induce it for more than short periods."

"It's not the only one who needs sleep, Carrix," Rilya said. "Did you actually rest on your last sleep shift?"

"As soon as I left the cabinet, it started wailing again," Carrix said. "It's not always quiet when I'm in here, but it's quieter than when I'm gone. I did rest in here between feedings."

"That's not enough to get you ready for a monitor shift," Rilya said. "You go rest, Carrix. I do have eggs on the way. I might as well get some parenting practice in."

"A human infant isn't anything like a valioran larva."

"It needs to eat, and discharge, and sleep, just like larvae do." Rilya dipped his eyestalks at Carrix. "All the basic needs are the same. It's just the shape that's different."

* * * * *

That wasn't quite true. The voice was also different.

Larvae could only make a soft clicking, a pale imitation of their parents' chatter, and only did that out of hunger. After half an hour on the other end of the medical cabinet, going through the human health module again, Rilya was grateful to know clicking was all he had to look forward to. The human didn't wail full-throated with him in here, but it kept crying, pitiful and loud.

"You are a noisy little thing," he told the human, standing over the scanning compartment. "Not that I can blame you. I don't know how you fit that much stress in such a small body."

The medical cabinet was still reporting alarmingly high stress levels in the infant, and still recommending sedation. But Rilya's review of the module made him even warier of applying it. The module itself noted that the reliability of weight-based dosage cut off at a low end far above this tiny creature's size.

"I'm sure sleep would help. It's a shame you can't tell me how to help you rest."

It almost certainly couldn't understand him, but it had quieted further when he came over, and now it was only making soft mewling sounds. Rilya dipped his eyestalks fondly towards it. It reached up towards them, the mewling turning to gurgling, its soft brown skin dimpling around its mouth.

The motion reminded him of a just-pupated valioran youngster, reaching out with wonder to touch something that it was suddenly able to see. He dangled his eyestalks lower. "Is this what you want? What senses are you calibrating, I wonder?"

Reaching higher, the human grabbed his closest eyestalk in a surprisingly tight grip. Rilya hissed in pain and surprise, the rest of his eyestalks curling in on themselves, but the human didn't let go.

Hyper-aware of its tender flesh, Rilya humped the front of his body forward and over the edge of the scanning compartment and prodded very gently at the human's fist with his topmost claws. The infant made the gurgling sound again, then grabbed at one of his claws with the other hand. Its grip was just as tight with that one, though less painful.

Still terrifyingly aware of how squishy and soft its skin was, Rilya poked it with his other claws, drumming them against its cloth-swaddled chest and belly. That would have annoyed any larva into dropping its prize and skittering away. But the human's gurgling intensified, and it looked at him with an open mouth and crinkled cheeks, its huge wet eyes very wide.

"Not letting go, are you?" Rilya stretched a couple more claws out to wrap around it, gently, then reared backwards, folding his spine until his upper back rested on the lower and the human was lying on top of his underbelly. "That's fine. I'll wait you out. You'll have to get annoyed about this sooner or later, and then you'll let go to escape."

But, again unlike a larvae, the human didn't try to squirm out of Rilya's claws after a few minutes. Its grip did relax on his eyestalk, eventually, enough that he could pull it loose. And then the other hand loosened and slid off the claw it had grasped. He was safe to put the human back in the scanning compartment.

He didn't, though. Because the human was lying still, head to one side, eyes closed, breathing in a slow and steady rhythm. Instead of squirming, or wailing, or otherwise indicating distress, it had fallen fast asleep.

*   *   *   *   *

"What did you do?" Carrix demanded at next shift-change, when Rilya scuttled onto the bridge with the human asleep on his bared underbelly. "You didn't actually sedate it, did you?"

"No, I didn't. And don't be so loud. I don't want it to wake up."

"How can it sleep with your claws around it?" Felao turned away from the instruments to look, her eyestalks going stiff in surprise. "Doesn't it have any defensive instincts at all?"

"Not this young, apparently," Rilya said. "It's so soft, you'd think it would panic at being touched, but the only time it's wailed at me since I picked it up is when I put it down to feed it."

Rilya's own instincts made him want to twist away so that his underbelly was less openly bared, even though the only threats in the room were his friend and his own mate. But he ignored that impulse. Felao wasn't going to gut him and raise their larvae on her own, and Carrix was harmless. Going pink with horror, at the moment, but harmless.

"I had heard that humans were a high-contact species," they said. "I've seen a few here and there, and they didn't seem very concerned about personal space. But I wouldn't have imagined that their young would like being held, no matter how much contact they might want as adults. You don't even have the same kind of limbs. It must feel threatened by your claws."

"They are a predator species," Felao said. "And dominant on their planet. Maybe their young don't need to fear contact with other beings, so they haven't evolved it."

"You're probably right. Its stress levels have dropped into the normal range since I started holding it," Rilya said. "Lack of contact must have been part of its distress earlier. I'm sure that if we set up a rotation and keep offering it contact, it will be easier to deal with until we're able to drop it off."

"A rotation," Felao repeated, her eyestalks curling. "You mean that we should all take turns holding it? That I should bare my underbelly to it like that?"

Rliya looked at her, his mate and future co-parent, and at the way her mandibles were twitching. Then he looked at Carrix, whose pink was deepening towards red.

"A duty rotation," he corrected. "So that I can make sure it gets enough contact."

"That seems reasonable," Carrix said, their tendrils shivering with relief. "Perhaps Felao and I can take over your monitor shifts entirely until we get to next station and get in touch with their alien welfare office."

The human shifted on his belly, making a soft little noise. Rilya looked down at it and realized that his claws had tightened when he'd seen Felao's curling eyestalks, trying to lace protectively over his exposed underside.

He loosened them, but the human was already awake, and he braced himself for more noise.

Instead it looked at him again with its disproportionately huge eyes, then closed a hand around one of his claws and gurgled contentedly.

"That seems like an acceptable arrangement," Rilya said.

Vulnerability aside, there was a deep satisfaction in looking at the human's pleasure-signs and knowing that it, too, was satisfied.

THE ROOM
K. B. Elijah

"Where's your nose?" the Earthling asked as I walked through the door. She was sitting cross-legged in the middle of the floor, her hands tucked into her lap. None of the holo-controls were activated, leaving the metal room bare and depressing.

I shrugged, dropping down in front of her so I could mimic her position. It was as uncomfortable as I had imagined it to be, the skin on the inside of my thighs stretching uncomfortably, but a job was a job. "It was in an inconvenient place," I said. "It dripped foul goo into my mouth and it kept making me shudder when its sense was activated."

"You ... smelled something bad?" she guessed.

I shrugged again. It had been my favorite human movement to learn, and I thought I was pretty good at it. But this Earthling had so much more to show me. I watched as she crinkled her own nose very slightly, suddenly wishing mine was in place so I could try it.

"I stored it in my pocket."

"You can't just discard a nose!" the human protested, her voice rising. I listened to its musical tenor, entranced.

And then I sobered, because she was right. On all the holo-vids I'd seen of Earth, the humans had noses. I pulled mine out of my tunic pocket and stuck it back on my face.

"Do you find that preferable, human?" I asked.

She eyed me with an uncomfortable look on her face. "I suppose. Am I really to teach you how to act human?"

"Yes," I said. "That's why the Syndicate brought you here."

"*Kidnapped* me, you mean. Here's a lesson in humanity: you can't just steal people from their homes and jet them across the universe to keep them prisoner."

"We know *that*," I reassured her. "Which is why we made sure to choose *you*, Earthling, an open-minded specimen with no familial ties, so we'd only have to do it once. But none of our operatives infiltrate a planet without having a native teach them the ways of their world first."

"Lucky me," she said drily, rolling her eyes. I copied her. It was fun, so I did it again. And again.

"You can stop that now," she interrupted, an odd snorting noise coming from her mouth. I wasn't sure if it was approval or disdain.

"I'm just practicing," I said. "So, what can you teach me? Be warned, I've already read the *Earth Handbook*, so most of what you've got, I'm probably already educated on."

The Earthling stilled, her brown eyes boring into mine.

"A handbook?" she asked after a moment. "And how long was this book?"

"It's not technically a book," I explained. "It's a holo-info. But it was suitably intricate. Four hundred thousand words."

The human burst into something that took me a moment to recognize as laughter. It was so different for each Earthling: the sound, the intensity, the amount that their shoulders shook and their faces scrunched, but I was good enough at my job to have catalogued key expressions before I even met with my native guide. I took the opportunity to join in, a chortle that reverberated through my vocal cords.

The Earthling abruptly stopped. "I don't know what that was, but it was darn creepy," she said. "Don't do it again."

"I was … laughing."

"*I* was laughing. You were something out of a horror movie. I suppose you know what they are?"

I nodded eagerly. "A holo-vid — you call it a film — that is designed to evoke fear in its audiences."

"Here's a tip," the human said. "Try to sound less like a dictionary. Explain it again, without using *any* of the words you just used."

I faltered. I was the best in my class, had graduated with honors, and had read the *Earth Handbook* four times so I could memorize it before I met with the native. And in less than five minutes, she'd torn me apart. "I…"

"It's a scary movie," she said, placing her palms on the rusting metal floor and leaning back on her hands. "See how I said the same thing, but in normal-people speak?"

"A scary movie," I repeated.

A nod. "Cool. So this handbook of yours, forget it. No one can learn how to be human in four hundred thousand words. No one can learn to be human from a book, full stop. That's why I'm here, I suppose."

I nodded. "To help acclimatize me before I go undercover."

"And the guys who … brought me here," she said, her voice cracking. "They said that you're not looking to invade Earth? That true?"

"Absolutely," I reassured her. "The Syndicate is not a violent organization. We have operatives on each planet to monitor progress, to determine when a civilization is ready for us to introduce ourselves and guide them across the universe. Humanity is in no danger from me."

The human abruptly leaned forward, catching my face in her hands. My skin tingled unexpectedly where she touched it, and I wondered if I was having some type of allergic reaction to the contact, despite knowing that humans did not have any naturally occurring toxins in their skin.

She stared into my eyes as if they were anything other than organs I had grown specifically for the job, and I wondered what she was looking for.

"My human designwork is immaculate," I said, offended. "I had the best crafter on the ship make it for me."

The Earthling didn't seem to hear me, so I said it again, wondering if her own auditory organs were malfunctioning. But when she hissed at me to "*shut up*," I clamped my mouth closed, suddenly unsure of myself.

"I believe you," she said.

"I can show you the crafting records if you doubt—"

"Not about that," she snapped. "About your intentions towards my home."

I gave a deliberate blink, filled with a sudden urge to do something human to prove myself to her.

Her face softened. "Let's start at the beginning. When we humans meet someone new for the first time, it's customary to give your name." Her lips cracked into a broad smile, and I stared at her, overwhelmed by a feeling of … happiness? Joy? I couldn't put a description to it, but it felt good. It felt *brilliant*.

"I'm Jenny."

She held out her hand, and I took it, recognizing the gesture. But the holo-vids hadn't taught me how tightly to hold, and I quickly eased off when she winced and tried to pull away.

"I'm Aratas," I said. "But on Earth, I shall be John."

"John Smith?" Jenny asked, and I stared at her, wondering if the *Earth Handbook* had really got it so wrong as to miss the fact that humans were telepaths.

But she just laughed. "The most common name in Western civilization," she explained. "And speaking of Westerners, that handshake will not work everywhere. Some humans bow. You need to know the customs of the place you will be living. I presume it's France, based on the fact that we're speaking French?"

"Oh, I speak all 7,345 recorded languages of your planet," I assured her. "I won't be out of place."

Jenny sighed. "Unlearn about 7,343 of them," she said, "otherwise you really will be."

"That's confusing. Why have languages if nobody can speak them?"

"Somebody can speak them," she retorted. "Usually. But nobody can speak *all* of them."

I digested that for a moment. "Thank you," I said. "That is helpful to know. What else can you teach me?"

Jenny ran a hand over her face and I copied the action, ensuring my expression appeared suitably downcast. Satisfied I'd gotten it right, I mentally added it to my list of "exasperated/weary" expressions.

"Where do we start?" she said, eyes wide. "How do I teach you *Earth*?"

*　*　*　*　*

The next day, I returned to find the Earthling lying on the unpleasant metal floor. Her eyes were closed, her knees tucked up to her chest, and I watched her for a while, marveling at how delicate she appeared. Her face was soft and her brows unburdened.

And then I began to grow worried about her not moving. Her chest was heaving slightly, strands of her brown hair fluttering in the breeze of her breath, but she still hadn't opened her eyes. I'd been standing here for minutes, and humans in the holo-vids never slept for this long. What if she was *dying*?

"Jenny!" I called out, rushing over to where she lay. "Jenny!"

I reached for her shoulder and her eyes shot open, her hands batting me away violently.

She clutched her heart, panting, her eyes wild. "Aratas! Don't *do* that!"

I stood a few meters away, not sure what to do with my hands. "I'm sorry," I said. "I thought something was wrong."

"I was sleeping!"

I frowned. "Still? But it's been six of your Earth hours since you told me to leave you because you were getting— " I raised my fingers into air-quotes like she'd taught me "—Tired."

"Do not air-quote *that*," Jenny snapped. "Of course I'm tired after being kidnapped and then endlessly interrogated about my world. And I didn't exactly sleep well on this floor. These are barbaric conditions to keep someone in, you monster!"

I took a step back, trying to figure out the pain in my chest and why her words felt like physical blows.

"Why didn't you sleep in a bed?" I asked eventually, my voice small and hollow to my ears. "That's what humans do, isn't it?" I wondered if I was being insulting by asking.

"Do you see a bed?" Jenny snarled, brushing her hair out of her face. I watched the movement, inexplicably wanting to reach out and do it for her.

I looked around, not seeing anything but the rusting sheet metal of the floors, walls and ceiling of her cell. "Why didn't you make one from the holos?"

A frown. "What you talking about, Aratas?"

I copied the expression, my brow furrowing. "No one showed you?" I lifted my face to the ceiling. "Holo-room R3-D," I commanded. "Simulation creation tool."

Dotted grid lines appeared around the room, mapping out its dimensions.

"Create room."

Instantly, a four-poster bed shot up beside us, silk sheets and lacy hangings wafting in the breeze from the open window to our left. I could smell pollen, and my stupid human nose began to itch. The walls painted themselves in intricate wallpaper, and various items of furniture — wardrobes, tables, sofas, rugs — blinked into existence to fill the room.

"Oh," Jenny said. "That's ... that's just ... Oh my gosh, that's something else." She looked at me, wide-eyed. "How did it know to create a bed?"

"It analyzed my thoughts," I told her. "This room was in a holo-vid I watched about English estates. Do you like it?"

She crossed over to the window and tentatively poked a hand through the open space, wiggling it.

"It's so real!" she said delightedly. "I can hear a lawnmower and smell the flowers and oh, Aratas, it's beautiful!"

She spun and ran for the bed, taking me by surprise when she jumped onto it, dirty feet and all. "It's so real!"

I laughed at that, and unlike yesterday's failed attempt, this felt more natural.

"This room can be whatever you need it to be," I said as she bounced happily, needing her to know that she would not want for anything while she was here. "You can have anything."

"Except my home," she said, sobering, and I had no response for that. We were all sacrificing for the greater good — for the Syndicate, for the future of humanity. But it did not mean there was not happiness to find along the way.

"It will help with my training," I added. "We can simulate scenarios, locations, events, and you can help me through them. Today, I was hoping you could help me obtain nutritional provisions."

Jenny tilted her head and started jumping again. "You mean take you grocery shopping?"

I nodded. "Yes. I would like to learn how to blend in within a number of social and economic settings."

"Can we eat the food afterwards?"

I blanched. "Yes, I suppose we shall have to. I admit, Jenny, I'm not looking forward to that portion of the training. The stuffing of random materials into one's mouth is rather unappealing."

She stopped bouncing on the bed. "You ... your species doesn't *eat*?"

I scoffed. "Do you realize how inefficient such a process is? Cramming things into your body that are expelled from the other end, with only a fraction of the nutrients being absorbed? Not to mention how disgusting it is. My people have more direct ways of sustaining ourselves, by way of intravenously inserting the nutrients of precise doses for our bodily needs so that nothing is wasted. Most other species do too. You humans are ... weird."

Jenny slipped from the bed. "But eating is delicious," she said, a stupefied look on her face. "The taste of a home-cooked meal, of a bar of chocolate, of a cold drink on a hot day. What pleasure do you derive from being drip-fed?"

"Pleasure?" I asked, laughing again. I was beginning to like how it sounded. "The consumption of nutrients is essential to life. Do you obtain pleasure from breathing? From your heart beating?"

"Oh, Aratas." Jenny took my hand, slipping her warm fingers into mine. I stopped talking because the feeling was so distracting. I wanted it to last forever.

"Er ... holo-room R3-D?" she said tentatively, looking at me for confirmation. When I nodded, she grinned. "I'd like to create a room please, if you can see inside my head?"

The room didn't answer. Why would it? It wasn't alive. But it listened to the Earthling all the same, the furniture disappearing to be replaced with scattered tables and chairs. The clamor of metal and ceramic hit my ears, as well as a myriad of complex smells, and I looked around as a restaurant formed around me.

"My favourite place," Jenny said. "But it's got two Michelin stars, so it's not like I'm able to afford it more than once a year. Shall we?"

She directed me into my seat and I obediently folded myself into it.

Two drinking containers appeared before us on the table, crystal glasses filled with something almost as deeply red as blood. I recognized it from its context.

"We drink this wine, yes?" I asked, and Jenny nodded happily.

"Hell yes. It might be morning for me, but what does that mean in space? Cheers!" She tipped it to her lips, but I sniffed mine before doing so, and was glad I did.

"Jenny!" I lurched forward and knocked the glass from her hand, a bright red gash forming over the tablecloth. She stared at me.

"Aratas? What's wrong?"

"It's poisoned!"

She sucked in a breath. "How? The room? Is it trying to-"

"It's just a program," I said, confused. "But I could smell the ethanol in the liquid. How much did you drink? It wasn't a lethal dose, but we should get you checked out. Can you make it to the infirmary?"

Jenny sank back into her chair. "Ethanol? That's the poison in my drink you're talking about? Ethyl alcohol?"

I nodded, my eyes darting around for the door. "Yes."

And then another glass was in Jenny's hands, and she was drinking from it even deeper than before.

"Jenny!"

"Relax, little alien," she said, as the empty glass returned to the table and a contented look crossed her face. "It's just wine."

I stared at her in horror.

"That's one thing you gotta learn about us humans," she laughed, reaching for the pile of misshapen lumps in the middle of the table and biting into one. I hadn't even realised they were food. "We love poisoning ourselves with alcohol."

"I don't get it," I admitted, feeling terribly out of my depth. Was it too late to request a change of assignment to a planet less complex and weird than Earth?

"You don't have to get it," Jenny said, lazily waving a hand. "It's one of our more dreadful quirks. It's a deadly substance that kills, ruins lives and destroys families … and yet we will never stop drinking it."

I eyed my glass uncertainly. I wasn't sure I was ready to take that one on faith.

"Let's eat," Jenny declared, and I looked up, trepidation building as a human clad in black and white brought a steaming plate over to our table. I felt sick already.

*   *   *   *   *

The restraint clicked in around me, securing me to the seat. I swallowed, not liking the feeling of that at all. But Jenny, her eyes bright with excitement, placed her hand on mine, and my fear inexplicably evaporated. She was here, so everything would be alright. Such simple yet powerful logic that had held true every time.

"Do you trust me?" she yelled, and I nodded without hesitation. It had been difficult at first, putting my faith in this wild human who seemed determined to kill me in a hundred different ways — from the alcohol poisoning to the operation of a motor vehicle which had nothing to stop one human from deciding to collide with another, to today's "adventure": the unfathomable act of strapping oneself to a machine and letting it drop hundreds of feet.

"You know there's no equivalent to this on any other planet?" I shouted. "Why do humans insist on terrifying themselves?"

"Scary movies," was all she said, before the rollercoaster lurched beneath us.

Nothing could have prepared me for the horror of what followed.

*   *   *   *   *

"Am I ready?" I asked her, as I did every day, and Jenny shook her head, completing the familiar routine.

"Not today," she whispered, tracing the back of my hand with her fingernail. We were lying supine on soft grass, gazing at the darkness of eternity above us.

"That one's Orion's Belt," she said, using her free hand to point up at a cluster of blazing balls of gas, millions of miles away. "See the three stars in a line?"

"I see them," I said, but I was looking at her instead, watching her face light up as she forced new constellations to hover above us in an unrealistic visage of crowded sky.

"All of the other operatives have already left for their planets," I whispered, feeling the ugly pain bubble through me that Jenny had termed resentment. My people didn't have a word for it, although we felt it: we ignored sensations as much as the Earthlings seemed to embrace them.

"You told me that their assigned civilizations were simple," Jenny said, her brown eyes flicking to mine. "Nothing like humans."

"No one is like a human," I agreed, lifting my hand to brush her hair from her face. I knew she didn't like it getting in her eyes. We'd have to set up a simulation of a hairdresser again so she could get it cut back to the length she liked best.

"Will I be ready soon?" I asked quietly, fearing the answer. "Will I *ever* be ready?"

Jenny smiled at me, and it was soft, intimate, a smile that she never showed any of the humans in the simulations. A smile that she reserved just for me.

"None of us are ever completely prepared to be human and what that means," she said softly. "But your time will come."

She leaned over and pressed her mouth to mine, and as much as I'd read about the art of kissing, words could not describe the sensations that shot over my body: not just in my mouth, but in my heart, my hands, and between my legs, a flare of heat and need and happiness. I took her into my arms, and there, under the blackness of an impossible night sky, she showed me what it meant to be truly human.

*　*　*　*　*

"You've almost got it," Jenny said, erupting into a fit of coughing. Familiar with the social conventions now, I reached around and patted her on the back, conjuring that strange colorless liquid that humans were so reliant on. It was just odd that it could kill them just as easily as sustain them.

"Thanks, Ari," Jenny said, leaning back into her chair. "You're getting good at that. But *remember*, on Earth you can't just—"

"Imagine things into being," I finished, well used to the lecture. "I know. I would go and get the water from the tap or the fridge. But while I can make it appear, I will, because I'm not going to let you choke to death."

Jenny smirked. "Nice use of hyperbole and exaggeration," she said. "Good work."

I didn't even notice my instinctual laugh, the sound and movement now as familiar to me as Jenny's own humored smile.

"Let me give it another go, and then we'll have lunch," I said, resetting the scene. "I can nail this job interview, I know it."

Jenny nodded approvingly at the colloquialism.

"Just remember that you don't have to be perfect," she reminded me, coughing again and sipping down more water. "No human is. We can strive for it, but never reach it. It's better to show flaws from time to time: hesitation, embarrassment, over-confidence, poor decision-making ... that sort of thing."

The suited executive across the table from me shuffled some papers. "Mr. ... Smith," he said, glancing up at me. "I see you're interested in the

Consultant role. How about you tell me why you think this position is a good fit for you, and where you see yourself in five years."

I took a breath.

*　*　*　*　*

"Let's go skydiving again," I begged, tugging at Jenny's hand. "It's been ages since we did that!"

She offered a smile. "Go for it, Ari."

"I meant with *you*," I sulked. "It's no fun on my own."

She looked away. "Not today."

I perched beside her in the four poster bed that I'd created for her, the bed hangings rippling in the same springtime breeze. Every time I suggested she replace it with a different setting, her jaw would set stubbornly and she wouldn't talk to me for several minutes. I'd long given up trying.

"Jenny? What's wrong? Why won't you come with me?"

"Ask me," she whispered, her eyes boring into mine.

For a moment, I didn't understand. Ask her what?

And then it hit me: the question that I'd given up asking, knowing the answer before she even gave it.

"Am I ready?" I breathed, pressing my face to hers.

Her answer, when it came, was just as soft. I felt it rather than heard it.

"As ready as I can make you, Ari."

My head shot backwards. "You really think that?" I jumped to my feet, delighted. "We can go to Earth! Oh, you must come with me, Jenny. I know it's not the usual protocol, but I'm sure I can convince the Syndicate to let you come. Will you?"

She smiled, her hair fanned over the silk pillows. I frowned at it. When had it changed color? Had she dyed it without me noticing?

"Ari, I cannot." Jenny sighed, but it was mixed with a smile, and it confused me. Was she happy or was she sad?

"Of course you can," I said impatiently. "You're my native trainer, and no one can deny you've done an excellent job. Besides," I added, with a cheeky wink. "You're much more than that, and I'm not leaving without you." I pulled her up from the bed and into my arms, surprised at how light she felt. "Rise and shine, sleepyhead!"

"Holo-room R3-D," Jenny whispered. "Create room."

The English estate disappeared, replaced by a field of white flowers so thick that it felt like we were standing in clouds. I looked around in surprise. "This is pretty," I said. "Why have we never been here before?"

"Because it's where I wish to die," Jenny said. "And that is not generally a place you visit until you are ready."

I almost dropped her.

"*Die*? Jen, what are you talking about?"

She smiled weakly at me, lifting a frail hand to her wrinkled face and tracing the lines that were so familiar, and yet I had never noticed before. "Ari, it's been forty-two Earth years since you first walked in here without a nose. I don't have long left, and I wanted to be here, with you, when I go."

I waited patiently for her to explain.

"Well?" I asked eventually. "Where are you going? Do you have another training assignment?"

"Aratas," said Jenny. "You're not listening. I'm dying."

"You're not dying," I said stubbornly, wanting to shake her in the hope that it would put sense back into her words. But that was a human analogy: *shake sense into her*, and I was having difficulty separating it from reality. "Look at you! There's plenty of life left."

But my words felt hollow and untrue, and when I looked at her - *really looked* at her — I could suddenly see the thinness of her limbs, the crinkles around her face, the shaking of her hands. How long had she been like this? How long was this stupid little frog called Aratas boiling in gradually hotter water without realizing it?

Forty-two years. Decades of learning and experiencing things with her: our shared love of food, of adventure, of thrills and fright, of newness and imagination and wonder. I even tried a glass of red wine from time to time, although I didn't like it nearly as much as she seemed to. How could I not know that we'd spent a lifetime together?

"No," I whispered, terror overtaking me at the thought of losing her. "I can't do it without you."

Jenny's fingers traced my chin. "You're not," she breathed. "I've spent forty-two years helping you prepare for Earth. I'll be with you in every step, every conversation." She took a shuddering breath. "I'll be honest, Ari, it's going to be different to how I remember it. But you are clever, and you are resourceful, and you will be a great protector of humanity. Watch out for us, won't you? Stop us doing anything crazy?"

And then she pulled my head down to hers and whispered three final words in my ear, words that are spoken in nearly every romance holo-vid, words that Jenny had told me before: under a starry sky, when watching horror holo-vids, when dancing in a hall of mirrors. But these words were no less real for it, and they held true power.

I love you.

Her body slackened in my arms and her eyes lost the light that had been in them for the near half century we had known each other.

That first day, when she'd looked into my eyes to search for meaning, I thought her mad. It was only now that I understood how much of a person those little organs truly reflected. Her eyes no longer looked like *hers*, not those dull little glassy orbs that didn't hold an ounce of my Jenny in them.

I raised my hand and closed them. Now she looked like she was asleep.

Human tears running down my face, I lowered my Earthling into the field of white flowers, the petals closing over her body and obscuring it from view.

I didn't feel ready. I felt absolutely and irrecoverably destroyed. How could I function as human when my insides felt like they were being slashed into a hundred pieces? But if I stayed here on the ship, everything she taught me would be for nothing. And Jenny was many things, but she was not nothing.

Could *never* be.

I let out a breath and left the holo-room, sealing my heart inside.

NO, YOU MOVE
Janna Kaiser

We were proud to hear that there was a new contender on the shores of the Deep Dark. Humanity had arrived at last. They made their way across the waves of starlight slowly, managed to conquer deeper space only through the help of those who had once shown us how to erect solar sails, how to look to the pale starlight and hear the whispers beyond. These were gentle, wise beings that we respected: the Great Mind of the swirls beyond my homeworld of Xanti. And although we had learned not to expect, many of us thought we would finally meet our equal. Brave warriors who would join our lines to protect the worlds.

Others thought they would prove to be a threat, but it took only a first encounter for all of Xanti to agree that the small fleshy beings could never do us harm. They could not harvest the soft glow of moons; their eyes were small, and above all they stood unprotected, no tough pelt like ours and no hardened scales like the Yllipiy. It was a miracle they had made it out of the system we had come to know as a Dark Zone, to be avoided at all cost, security level seven. Worlds where mountains spewed molten rock and the atmosphere was made up of waste gases.

But beyond their appearance that – young as I was then – I found to be disappointing, we were pleased to see that humanity was extraordinary – in how normal they were. They complied with the laws that had been written by the old mothers. There was no war to put them into place, no age-long feud as it had take with the Ol'man'au, which had been declared exiled and condemned to haunt the asteroid infested depths of the inner systems.

Instead, the Earthlings simply settled in. We saw how they made worlds their own. Worlds we had deemed uninhabitable, worlds we were grateful to be rid of, yet preferred seeing them in the hands of allies rather than being claimed by the void. We saw how they strived on these and felt pleased, attributing their success to our own technologies that we had given them, small generosities as was the custom. In turn the humans offered us tales of their own success, eager to return the gestures. And although we saw their results before our own eyes, many believed them to be false. To explode themselves into the gentle waves we had learned to glide upon seemed simply preposterous. That they had not given up despite many of them falling to the hostile dark – possible that they were exaggerating. Meaning to impress us with the tale of the mighty foe they had forced into submission.

To learn of their evolution had our own scientists baffled. Not that I could understand much; my house was one of hunters, tasked with patrolling our borders. I was a warrior through and through, had followed the Call as I had done in my last two cycles. My brood brothers and I saw the newcomers for the docile creatures we wanted to see, pleased to have new evidence that our policies for outreach programs had worked.

We didn't yet know how wrong we were.

Humanity was still blossoming in our midst. Seeing a human vessel was no more a curiosity than it was an event, observed with generous well meaning, the same way we regarded the ones that visited our planets. They were still clumsy, like we had grown to know them. Bumbling like the young of their feathered sky inhabitants. I am now ashamed to say I was concerned at times, thinking it was like letting a broodling leave the home-world too soon, before they had heard their calling.

Because while they were eager to make homes where they were allowed, eager to learn and share their own knowledge, and even eager to take flight along with my brothers and I into the Vast Deep, the humans did not seem to be willing to make the decision which path they would follow.

The Yllipiy were builders. There was no planet that was not in some way reformed by their insight into organizing biospheres into harmony.

We Xanti had always known it was our duty to protect. Our warriors grew tall and hardy; even in our old songs it was told of our courage in battles fought against outsiders, protecting the wise beings of the Inner Circle. These were the ones who had brought the ability of flight to us, to reach beyond the stars. They were bound by many things, not alone their need for sunlight to bring strength through their membranes, their soft curling figures elegant and too refined to wage war, but with the minds to invent.

We were proud to have found our place in the order of things and with all our hearts we hoped our new brethren would be granted the same. They were still new after all. Possible that they needed time to align their own houses to our structures, had to question their mothers. So in our own brood we agreed that we would try and help them, be there for them and guide them. My brothers and I were proud to do the same that the Higher Minds had once done for us.

It was because of this wish that we were gladly taking on the duty of soaring with them, inviting them onto our ships – of course we also hoped to see more of their warriors. Even I was ready to indulge them and look at any they would present with the respect they deserved. The crew we were presented with was a colorful mix, however. Only a few of them were of the house of security, as they told us, the most of them those we came to know as ambassadors, a calling usually reserved for the likes of the Whenjallh who had spun the fabrics of their great history long before my brood had grasped thought. So, again I was close to disappointment. Yet I knew to conceal it. My brothers looked to me as the oldest of our brood and I had earned instructions from the mother of my house to welcome humanity. It was to be an experiment after all, to show our new brethren their new home amongst our own.

We were proud to start with the inner circles, showing our origins. But we were eager to see what our brethren were made of. To test their hearts. So we widened the search. Went to see their new homes, the rugged, harsh terrain they had tamed. Their homes were not touched by the Yllipiy yet – the Great Minds not wanting to expose their builders to the potential dangers. But humans had dug into the mountains, had huddled against the harsh surfaces like broodlings against their brothers. It was on one of these planets that I witnessed one of the oddest things about humans that I would only understand much later.

A human was standing over a small burrow, suddenly bending down. Alarmed, I drew closer. Sometimes their environments were hazardous and I worried something had come to harm this fragile being that was under my protection. But the human stood up again, hands cupped together. Cautiously I approached, crouched forward to support myself on four of my six limbs.

"Of Earth, are you alright?"

"Oh yeah." The human bared his teeth. "Look!" He opened his hands, showing me the pollinator that had lost its way and found itself out of the protected spheres of the fields. Possibly fallen prey to one of the ten-legged predators that lurked between the rocks. Clearly it would have become prey or simply died had it not been for the human, who looked at the small insectoid, his expression somehow as soft as his pink flesh. "Found her in a net, poor thing, been looking all over."

"Very good that you found the pollinator, of Earth," I nodded, curling forward to hide my purple glowing chest – I did not want the human to be affronted by my confusion. I did not mention this incident to the mothers or my brothers, dismissing it for a random encounter.

From there we moved on. The humans had let me know that after visiting their home shores, they would like for me and my brothers to follow our usual routines. And so we drew our circles, choosing the more distant shores. We wanted to show them the beauty and the danger of our position. Our pride.

We sailed in the lights of the two-sunned system, rounded the becoming worlds in the darker arms of the galaxies. It was there that we came witness to a tragedy.

A great Wyrrim, a worldeater had come. It was uncommon that such creatures would dare venture to where the starlight was dense, able to burn their skins, blind their milky eyes that shone like moons. The Ey'irians had banished them from the oceans of our voids a long time ago. But out here where the suns drifted apart, they lurked. And now one had chosen a small planet as its next meal. We reported to the mothers, then went to oversee the incident. It was historical. I had not heard of a Devouring taking place since my pelt had grown strong and I was allowed to leave the brood.

We would have to rule out this system and rebuild our outreach post elsewhere. The broodlings and humans down on the surface were lost already; they just did not know that yet. I would have to tell the humans on the ship. Possible that they would lose members of their own brood, brothers and sisters, since I had learned they did grow both genders in every brood. Another fascinating facet of their species that failed to occupy me as I watched the Great Destroyer wind around the nearest moon to avoid the light of the nearest stars.

The announcement was met with terrified silence from the humans. I could smell they were afraid when I had explained what they saw. With flattened antennae I retreated from them as the five humans huddled together. A brother of my own brood was on this planet. I had known him to be true to his duty. The perfect choice for raising broodlings. A loss. I would include him in my songs.

"Sorry to ask, Kian of Xant, house of warriors, but … Aren't you going to do something?" One of the humans, the leader of their house of security, approached me. My chest glowed with sorrow, but I knew the humans had not yet learned to read our moods, much like our blind sisters of Hhaal whose voices were their only weapon, so I spoke up to avoid any of my brothers in the room taking offense. Humans had not settled into the order after all. The still had to learn.

"No, Jane of Earth, house of security," reluctantly I commanded my head to lower to her level, curling down small like I would to speak to a broodling. The humans were deserving of sympathy.

"We only have a few sols; it would be too late and endanger my brothers and this vessel. And they knew the risks of worlding out here. We will witness their deaths for them," a soft murmur went through my crew that stood with me at the observation. Deeper in our hearts we could feel the sadness of not being in battle, our grief for our brood soothed by the knowledge that it was the order of the Void, being carried out before our eyes. "My sorrow goes out to the brood of the humans which will perish with my kin," it was hard to remember and be considerate, but I was a leader. The mothers would be proud of me.

The human was still looking up at me, quiet and unmoving. Probably she was waiting for more words. An explanation. I could not recall their customs, so I just stood in silence, reading her own as understanding. Perhaps even her words had been uttered in mere performance, though I knew there had to be humans down on the planet too, small and praying for their deliverance as the worldeater neared.

Jane of Earth must feel their loss as well, I thought, crouching lower, my glow changing to one of comfort. Their sacrifices would not be in vain, as we were here to witness their passing into the Great Beyond. Maybe I would include them in my songs as well. It was admirable that they had come here to observe the raising of broodlings in the first place. Possible that some of them could have found their calling there.

I prepared myself for sorrow and anguish. But this would be the first occasion when humanity reared its head and I am proud, and scared, that I was unknowingly part of it, so close and yet so far from understanding what I was truly witnessing. In fact I did not even look when Jane of Earth turned away from the vast darkness.

"Procreate that!" Before I could command my translator to allow me to hear the true words of my human sister, she had turned away, striding over to where her own siblings had gathered. Apparently she had been sent as an envoy to me and was carrying word back to the rest of their faction.

Even so, her words did not make sense to me. I could understand their need for procreation; possibly they would need to signal their broods to make up for the cycles they would lose today. Smart to instantly think forward, though next to me brother Ianteh shivered. One of his brood mates was on this planet, their own broodlings barely old enough to take their first step. We too would lose cycles, but such was the order. Ianteh was right to grieve. And the human procreation should take place far away from that.

Because of this I went with the humans, to remind them that although we too were subject to it, I had to ask them to share in the sorrows first before thinking of replacing their own. Noble warriors like them would understand, surely. Perhaps I was reading too much of our own nature into them. I caught glimpses of their conversation as they marched down the hallways.

"There's already resistance down there,"

"Good, was to be expected. Mayhew is down there; no way he'd go down without a fight. He loves dogs."

It made me halt, but then press forward with even more determination. Our vessel seamlessly moved over into the human one that was connected to ours; the only difference was the airseal hissing softly as we stepped through.

"What are you talking about, of Earth?" I addressed them, involuntarily curling together since their halls were made smaller and did not fit the stature of my people as well as the small and nimble humans.

"We're going to save that planet," Jane spoke up, although she did not stop moving. "Or, at the very least, our people." Her eyes spoke of righteous fury that I could understand, and didn't dare to argue with. Instead I hung back, retreating into my vessel. I had made a promise to the mothers. I knew the order of things. Humanity still had to learn it. Possibly today. I am not ashamed to say that I let them go. I told my brothers to not rebel when their vessel undocked from ours. To let them go. Many hearts would be lost today. We would witness humanity's first encounter with the Great Order. We listened to their voices across the void, watched their large ship spew out the smaller fighters.

"Berlin? Coming in hot on your six, let's get that worm!"

Incoherent yelling flooded the lines. I thought it was terror. Later I would learn it was cheers.

"Houston, they're good boys! Up and at 'em!"

Our first sadness turned into shock, when instead of panicking and attempting to flee the system when faced with their massive foe, the human fighters kept going. They were joined by more small vessels, many of which were rising from the surface of the planet. Their signature read as first aid vehicles, small personal crafts and even one giant freight transporter. Not a single military craft. Not one military vessel.

No graceful wings slicing the dark, again, no solar sails. Just their bursting engines, screaming brightly in the dark.

Shock turned into disbelief when they turned their fiery weapons against the Devourer. The deep hum of its pain made every single one of my brothers cower as I stood, stunned into motionlessness. I could only watch as the dark swallowed several ships, only to spit them out again, bursting and exploding. Their crews lost, but their lives given in an uproad that maddened the swarm of humans.

For two sols they fought. Tirelessly flying maneuvers. It was a dizzying choreography similar to the mating dances of the Hhaal, and our own. The flashes of light when the humans fired, the soft glow of the Wyrrim's eyes, glowing with indignation at having his place in the order questioned, and contested, even! My brothers mirrored it with their own glows. Our observation was filled with the hues of stunned green and yellows of our chests. Pelts stood up to intensify the glows as we finally – incredibly – saw the Devourer retreat into the dark. Fleeing the glow of fury that the humans were raining upon him.

In that moment we were too awed to feel afraid. Fear came later, when we realised just how minor the humans felt about their accomplishment. My vessel drew a wide arc around the planet's shore before we landed, sailing slowly between the small fighters that tittered through the void.

It was then that we saw the true magnitude of their doing.

The pilots exited their crafts. They were still not the noble warriors we expected. Instead they were medical staff. The very ones that had helped my brothers take care of broodlings. They were ambassadors, who had gone against the order. They were flimsy and swayed on their two lone legs, front arms grasping at each other. They were baring their fangs in a gesture we had read about as smiling – an expression of happiness. The did not know about their grand gesture. How defying the order had never been done before. A world eater had to be accepted. Deaths had to occur. Everyone had to find their place. Everyone but humans, it seemed.

Because to them it didn't matter that nurses were supposed to nurse, not fight. They had somehow done just that.

It took a few more sols until all the humans were gathered back to my vessel. Communication had been hurried, but the mothers had ordered me to bring the ambassadors back to account for what had happened. We also needed to recount our witnessing to the Great Minds. I was anxious to approach the humans about it myself, but despite my anxious brothers, I held off until we had left the system behind.

Jane of Earth had survived their uprising and their ship was once again coupled with ours. We hadn't known if we should or shouldn't so we had just maintained the earlier order. It had to be maintained whether or not it had taken a big hit. At least that was what I thought the mothers would want.

"Jane of Earth," I greeted the human, trying and failing to conceal the trembling of my antennae, the soft glow of my chest. I was uncertain and curious, but also fearful. "Why did you do this?"

The human closed her eyelids quickly.

"Uh … I don't understand? Why wouldn't we?" She looked up at me. There was a scorch mark next to one of her only two eyes and the skin around the end of her face had turned dark blue. Which was odd; I had not heard of humans being able to turn their skin to different colors. I tried to wait for the whispers of reasons stemming from the mothers, but there was so much to explain and just so few words at my disposal.

"Look." Jane of Earth shook her head, making her head fur – hair – flow in a way that I briefly misunderstood as an attempt at mimicking my own frizzed up fur. (I would observe it many times over the coming time of our continued companionship, and I came to know it as one of the things only she did.) "I know things work differently for you guys, but … We couldn't just … Stand by and watch? All those kiddos!" She rucked the top end of her torse. "Okay, forget that, that's…" Jane of Earth raised her head high, making her a few inches taller. And then she uttered a phrase I was shocked to learn was not part of any of their strictures, as I had assumed.

"It was the right thing to do. We're too stubborn to let others die."

I could not find the right words to translate the soft violet glow of my chest. How could it be the right thing when it wasn't according to the order? How could they know from their own mind that it was right? Without consulting with the authorities of their homeworld. Seeking more answers,

I took my time making my rounds, asking the other humans on my vessel. Many of them agreed, reinforcing Jane of Earth's words.

Some called it *human nature*, yet I don't think they were aware of how it, while only a facet of their being, went deeper than any belief I had ever encountered. This single phrase would become something to be studied by the Great Mind and many of the scholars of our worlds. Secretly, in most cases. Though some claimed that it was only humans that could truly make us understand others, that not even they themselves truly understood it themselves.

I, for one, and speaking for only myself, my cycle which would continue many more times before fading, had the fortune of being there. And it was their presentation that had truly made me understand the weight of their words, the courage of their being. The way in which they self-righteously looked at the great forces of the universe and demanded it change for them.

And when it enraged them by not bending to their will, they would charge at it with all they had.

It is true, humanity might still not have found their places in the Deep Dark. But that didn't matter. To us they had shown their hearts. And they were made of starlight and steel – fierce protectors despite not having received the Call. Instead they followed their own.

ANY OTHER WAY
Chris Bannor

"Do you ever think about just how weird you are?"

I hadn't, actually. It was an odd thing to hear, coming from a creature that looked like a walking tadpole. An eight-foot purple tadpole. An eight-foot purple tadpole who walked on two legs with its tail dragging behind and got drunk off water.

"No," I answered, trying to hide my bewilderment at the question. "I mean, I'm just a normal human."

"Right. Normal. There is nothing normal about humans."

"What are you talking about?" It had been a long night after a long mission during a really long month. I liked Puchnaw. It was as friendly an alien as you would ever meet, but it had strange ideas sometimes.

"I was thinking about that video you showed me yesterday. Your people create a sophisticated communications system that can reach out to all of your planetary citizens. You create surveillance equipment that can monitor and capture important moments in history. Your people can share their joys and pains, and to reach out when they need help. It can enable human interactions with places far away so that even the poorest of your world can use these devices to travel through the vision of your cameras."

I wasn't sure where this conversation was going, but Puchnaw seemed to be leading to something. It had a point about the internet, though. It was a pretty awesome invention. "I guess. Yeah. I never thought of the internet that way, but yeah."

"And they fill it with cat videos."

"Well, yeah, but that's not the only thing on there."

"That's all you show me."

I really tried to think of something else, but I was scraping the bottom of the barrel to remember anything but cat videos I'd watched lately. Nothing wrong with a little humor, though, right? Oh, I remembered! "There was that hilarious dog."

"You don't even like cats."

"Puchnaw! That is not true. I like cats! Where did you get the idea I don't like cats?"

"I meant humans in general. The video you showed me was called 'Cats are Jerks.'"

"Well, they are sometimes."

"I concur with Puchnaw," Arugesh said.

"What?" Arugesh and Puchnaw rarely agreed on anything, but this was a little much. No one actually knew what Arugesh looked like because of the environmental suit she always wore. The only reason I knew she considered herself female was that I asked for her pronouns. Which had resulted in an ongoing discussion about gender because she had a hard time understanding that humans weren't all female.

"Humans are weird. You live on a deadly planet full of water, but you don't explore it. Instead, you leave your planet to go to a more deadly environment. You make stories that are not true to entertain yourselves. You have words that are bad to use and that you won't teach me."

"Hey! You don't hear me complaining about all the weird things you do!" I wasn't truly offended, but I was the only human in a room full of aliens.

"It's okay, Annie," Arugesh said. "We like your weird."

*   *   *   *   *

The thing is, I couldn't stop thinking about it. I'd always thought they were weird. Humans were the normal. Earth was the normal. But since the planet had become inhospitable to humans, I'd learned a lot. I lived at the International Station of Travel and Tourism. I might not be able to survive on Earth, but there were plenty of creatures that had shown up to take their luxury vacations on the Earth's shores. The too-high radiation was a Xethestrian's perfect beach day. Arugesh worked in the translation department so she could earn free time in the salty waters of the irradiated oceans.

As I watched all the aliens file into the transport for the tour of North America's greatest ruins, I wondered if being a tour guide of my destroyed home planet also made me weird.

"How's it going today, Puchnaw?" I asked as I took my seat at the front next to it. My nicely cushioned seat faced the back so I could keep an eye on our guests. Puchnaw had this intricate standing device that supported its legs and back while giving its tail plenty of room to move. It had taken me three months to realize that its tail was a sensory organ that detected chemicals in the environment. How cool would that be?

"Annie, isn't Jatta my guide today?"

"Jatta had to stay home. Her wife went into labor last night."

"Finally," Puchnaw said. "How long has she been pregnant?"

"Nine months. It's a normal pregnancy."

"Normal. For a human."

"Yeah, yeah, yeah. There you go, beating up on the poor human again," I said. "Just wait until a few more arrive at the station. Then you'll see we are perfectly normal."

That was part of it, though. You'd think that living at the station above the Earth, there would be a lot more humans. There are only five. There was some big to-do about an Earth-like planet with no sentient inhabitants a few years back. Almost everyone I knew boarded a shuttle and took off for greener (teal, actually) pastures. Most of the personnel left on Earth were aliens who were better suited for the planet's current environmental state than we were. A few scientists still hung around, but humans were by far a minority on Earth or orbiting it.

Humans were a novelty around here. There were times when I went out to eat that I turned around and ordered to-go because I was tired of the staring.

"Hey, don't get sad," Puchnaw was good at cheering me up, but it was hitting a little too close to home today. "How about after work we get everyone together and go to the movies?"

Swing ... and a miss. Because Arugesh believed making up "entertaining lies" was one of the weirdest things humans did.

"Nah, it's okay. Let's get the tour going."

"After this, we can grab lunch, and then we have the Seventy-Three Wonders of the World Tour."

"It used to be seven."

"What?"

"People got upset when their national landmarks weren't included. The list got longer and longer and..." I sighed.

"That explains why this tour never seems to end."

"All right, Puchnaw. It looks like everyone is in. Let's get going." I smiled as I pulled on the microphone that would place my translated words into the heads of everyone on that channel. "Hello, aliens!" I said in my best chipper voice. "I'm Annie, and I come in peace!" There was a spattering of laughter as all eyes turned to me. And some eyeless heads. A few things I'd mistaken as tails, too.

"Today we will take you to explore the North American continent and some of its most talked-about ruins. Our pilot today is Puchnaw, one of the bravest and fiercest Pacians you'll ever meet. Your safety is in excellent hands. I mean, claws. Or … Puchnaw, what do you call those things?"

"My paddles?"

"Right. You're in safe paddles with Puchnaw flying today."

"Weirdo," Puchnaw said with a laugh.

"Spoken by the alien with paddles for hands."

"You have four fingers."

"What's wrong with that?" I asked.

"Opposable thumbs. One finger. That's all you need. What do you do with the other three?"

I made a rude gesture to show just what I could do with my opposable thumb and three extra fingers, which turned out to be the funniest bit of the tour. Apparently watching a human tour guide get into arguments with a Pacian pilot was more entertaining than North American ruins. The tour came as part of the "Foundations of Failure" package that brought most aliens from far and wide to see what remained of humanity's dying influence on the planet.

*　*　*　*　*

"Maybe it's just me?"

"What?" Arugesh asked as we sat down with our drinks. They'd talked me into the movies after all.

"Being weird. Humanity isn't strange. Maybe it's just me. As a representative."

"Are you still upset about that?" Puchnaw asked.

It got a heavily padded elbow (or tentacle; I'm still working that out) from Arugesh for that. "Annie, did you ever think it bothers you so much because you stuck around the station instead of going with others of your own kind? Maybe you just need to hang out with some humans every so often?"

But I liked Arugesh and Puchnaw. I liked my job, and I enjoyed flying around Earth's atmosphere to witness what time did to the crumbling cities and how the aliens set up little communities. I liked it when they called me to ask about the obscure rules for some game, or how to interpret an image they found (the discussion of human anatomy and how humans did not actually have leaves growing from their genitalia was still her favorite).

Okay. So, maybe they had a point. Humans were odd. They fought when they should have forgiven. They laughed when they should have cried. They destroyed their atmosphere before they learned to care for it. But they were doing better. They were making better choices on the new world and I was proud of that.

"Maybe we are odd," I conceded. "But I wouldn't have it any other way."

Puchnaw smiled and Arugesh pushed a gloved hand (paddle, paw, tentacle? Insert body part here) into mine. "Now, before the movie begins, explain why the man in the white suit decided it was a good idea to recreate giant beasts from Earth's past and let his grandchild out to play with them?"

OBJECT'S DIALOGUE
OR
MYRIAD WORDS OVERHEARD
ON A SPACESHIP
K. Winter Walker-van Aalst

They keep it in under their soft head cradle.

I heard it makes them cry sometimes, late at night when they think everyone is taking their ship-determined deep rest time.

I am quite unnerved by their crying. I am glad that they do not do so in the general public. Remember when they were hurt? They began to cry as I was attending to them. Some of their fluid almost reached my own porous external organ. It was ...alarming.

It is simply salt and water.

Yes. Why would you put something as drying as salt in with a wet organ – it defies understanding. They have to encase this salt in water to make it palatable to the eye. The eye does not need extra salt.

And yet you are the one who sneaks the salt blocks off the tables in the mess hall.

That is different. I am using them for an experiment.

* * * * *

This time it made them laugh. Do you understand them at all?

Breathing comes naturally for them, and they have modulated it into vocalizations and language – it seems obvious that they express amusement through a differentiation of expelling air as well.

You are insufferable.

I am stating the scientific facts as I encounter them.

You are stating the notions that your fool processing unit has strung together from their speech and actions.

Exactly – science.

It does not seem to be scientific, though. They are often changed of mood after they have finished their adjournment to their private quarters. Softer, almost. Sometimes they seem so tense.

They are always too soft for my comfort. Even the small talons that they possess look like a juvenile's – weak, easily broken even. And their bones do not match what they appear as.

Yes, that cartilage. Its nose in particular – what a fascinating development. You'd think they'd get it caught on things, though I suppose they do not use their tactile units on their face very often. They certainly breathe out of it noisily.

It has so many holes.

It is quaint, when you consider how they can change their expressions to match their moods. A very simple way of showing their needs.

Simple? In the last Deep Rest I heard them laughing *and* crying as they held it. Simultaneously. As if they had confused their processing unit and were displaying a worrying mashup of emotions.

Perhaps it is an emotion they have not defined for us. They seem to have several, and can display more than one at once. Sometimes this is categorized as a new emotion. Other times they are feeling distinct ones. I get confused.

I am confused on how they interact with it. It defies scientific logic. And why do they keep it so close to themself?

Perhaps they keep it close as you keep your salt close.

I keep my salt near my bunk-workstation. Not like you, toting around that weird leafy thing wherever you go.

Excuse me for wanting to optimize my small organic friend's temperature and oxygen intake. I don't trust the crewmates from prodding at it while I'm not looking.

Yes, that reminds me. The human does leave it underneath its pillow, so they must not be afraid of its asphyxiation.

I do not think it is alive...

It must have some form of life. Otherwise, it would not illicit such dramatic responses from the human.

You have a thought.

Idea.

That is a bad idea.

Science.

*   *   *   *   *

Quickly. I have retrieved the specimen from beneath its pillow. It is a rectangular-prism shaped object.

We knew this already. How much time do we have?

Debatable. Would you be so kind as to provide a distraction to delay the human's arrival back to their bunk?

And let you ruin their possession somehow? Absolutely not.

A small one. For the purposes of enabling us to figure out the secrets of this strange, laughter-inducing thing.

...Fine. A small one. But don't do anything without me.

*   *   *   *   *

—All on-duty Engineering personnel please report to Deck Five. Repeat, all on-duty Engineering personnel please report to Deck Five.

Excellent, you have returned. I have placed it on my worktable—

You're welcome?

Thank you. My lovely worktable—

The tiny desk you've somehow made smaller by the nearly incomprehensibly unstable tower of salt that you have crammed on top of it—

It is a beautiful worktable and my salt is an integral part of my working conditions.

Seriously, what's up with that?

I would thank you to wait until I publish my long-awaited scientific paper on the subject, and present it at the next gathering of scientists on shore leave. It is a delicate operation and I will not have you gabbing about and spoiling my scientific discoveries and the progress that I have already achieved.

Right.

Thank you.

So was that before or after the First Mate nearly confiscated your salt because the mites were going to get at it?

A minor misunderstanding. Completely fixed now. First Mate's going to be front of the line to get the report signed by me.

The number of times you've said science and the way you're describing this makes me think that maybe you don't understand science at all.

Maybe *you* do not understand science at all. Nevertheless, would you – no! Leave that there!

Leave your awkward, precarious pile of salt blocks perched on the edge of your desk? My organic friend has to go somewhere.

Yes. Please. Just. Leave it on my bunk. We have other things to investigate currently, remember?

It is a miracle that you're still allowed to do these things.

I am miraculous. Now, the object. It is about the size of our Accepted Breadboxes, and contains two and a half moles of its main component, a mixture of oxygen, nitrogen, and hydrogen. They are arranged in long chains of cellulose and other materials. I do not think it is edible for the humans.

Are you taking notes or anything on this?

…Hm. You are right. That is an excellent idea. Shall you do the honors?

I should think not. I'm terrible at summarizing. Even worse at actual transcription.

Well, I *have* been recording our attempts to understand this human's much manipulated object. Perhaps that will serve as enough of a scientific record for the time being.

You're insufferable. When were you going to mention that tiny little tidbit of information?

Obviously when you signed the release form for publication. It is not as if you cannot tell when the tiny red light in my recording device above my bunk is blinking.

It's always blinking!

Yes.

Dear Accepted, it's always blinking.

Yes.

I'm beginning to understand the human's insistence on those small things called ethics and consent.

Well, you have consented to be my friend, and that implies a certain measure of understanding about my methodologies. My *modus operandi*, as the human has so eloquently put it. Those humans have so many different languages. I find one is certainly enough for me.

They didn't have the translation technologies that we had, however.

I pity them that. Still, it does not look like it has stunted their ideas' growth. They are positively overflowing with them. Which brings us back to this thing.

An idea manifested into ... what was it? Cellulose?

Indeed. A fascinating substance. It seems to hold up well to the ship's atmosphere, though of course that has been calibrated optimally for all those who need to intake air as part of their homeostasis.

The human is certainly one of that. They do breathe ... quite a lot.

I am told it is part of their nervous system as well.

No, that's respiratory.

You misunderstand me. They breathe ... to feel differently. A "practitioner of meditation," they say. I was watching their vitals one time as they sat and did nothing for a while. Eons.

Probably Accepted minutes.

As I said. Their breath deepened and slowed ... and so did their heartbeat. And a hundred different hormones were interacting, and their cranial activity changed, and they seemed much more measured when I debriefed them afterwards.

Fascinating. Does this happen every time they breathe? It seems a critical evolutionary step of keeping calm in the face of danger.

Oh, no. This was something I was very inquisitive about. No, it seems that it must be at least partially voluntary, and must be practiced. The human added something to the effect of "and you're all so stressful that I practice every day" which I added into my notes on the topic. It seems we cause them to release hormones that actively stunt their breathing.

That sounds ominous.

Quite. Apparently, I am "too unreliable around the minerals and engineering tools."

I agree wholeheartedly with them, actually.

Also. They would prefer to ingest shavings of the salt blocks instead of donating them to science.

Now, I have no idea what you're going to do with those. But that is the oddest thing. I don't want to eat that weird crystalline substance. It vanishes in water. Tastes foul. I'd rather choose my own specially imported fruits and plants as I should.

Yes. They have often said that humans quite enjoy adding substances to their food. Even ones that do not agree with their digestion systems.

You didn't...

I have conducted several experiments in the course of my scientific research. All details will be further elaborated on in my paper.

Your appearance a few days ago in the mess hall makes so much more sense now.

Was it that ... apparent?

Let's just say that salt doesn't quite agree with your constitution either. And leave my organic friend out of your "experiments" too. They don't like salt either.

Noted.

This thing feels odd. It's so ... segmented.

The outer edges of the item, or at least three of the six faces, are hard. A thin shell.

To protect it from predators? Is this a symbiotic relationship between the object and the human?

Again, this thing is not alive. However, that is a good thought. A worthy scientific idea.

Thank you. And the other three sides are...

Strange. They appear to consist of very thin layers of the material – Dear Accepted!

What happened?

I have incurred a small breakage in my outer tissue. One of the layers, it seems, has slid along my grasping appendage in such a way as to sever the phospholipid bilayer of one of my larger outer cells.

You're always so clinical. Here, let me. There. Does it hurt?

More than was expected. This item has quite a robust defense system.

But look – you can peel back its shell to reveal its innards, those layers. Look at it! It's so … plain?

I am confused why they chose such a strange color to anoint the object with. Still, the other color – black, it looks like – shows up well against it.

Huh. And the marks on it! They're ever so faintly raised, and they smell quite different. Decorations?

Are there more throughout the layers?

Dear Accepted, yes. Look, it's covered with them. What are these things? What are you doing? Get away from this with your stolen block of salt!

I am an expert on salt. I must know if it reacts with any substances, and this is one opportunity for such discovery. There is water in the item; perhaps the salt will be absorbed into the layers. Perhaps it stores things for the human until they have time to return to them.

Like they cry into the thing and then get the salt back when they need it?

Oh yes, that is not what I was thinking of at all. Another excellent idea. You should come be my assistant in more of my endeavors. You catalyze my thinking.

Thanks. I think I'll stick to being co-consiprator in any of our exploits, though.

You shall be my co-author on this scientific paper. It is decided. I will send you my outline and my list of notes and sources in exactly one point five Accepted days.

… Thank you?

You are most welcome.

Okay, go ahead with your salt. Now I'm curious.

Hm. These results are not in agreement with our hypothesis. The salt has merely scattered over the layer, getting into the crevice where the current layer is connected to the shell and all over my desk. I shall have to clean my desk, yet again.

The cruel price of science.

I am a martyr whose work will only be properly appreciated once I have reverted back into the matter from which I was formed all those Accepted years ago.

Any other bright ideas?

This is troubling, but no. I cannot fathom why this object would affect the human in such a way. It does not react to any of my stimuli, and it does not use electricity or any other form of power which would allow interaction. It is…

Is it broken? The human could simply be remembering what it had done before that prompts such a wealth of emotion. They're sentimental enough. Remember AL-74? They wouldn't stop talking about that offspring we reunited with the parental community for two Accepted weeks. It was charming.

True. Perhaps these layers have dried out. Maybe it was a flowering, alive thing before it was on the ship.

Are we handling a skeleton? Dear Accepted, I didn't sign on for this. What are they going to say when they find out?

—All on-duty Engineering personnel are cleared to resume normal duty. Repeat, all on-duty Engineering personnel are cleared to resume normal duty.

This is unfortunate. It seems we have no more of the precious time that you have diverted for us. We have wasted most of it without the hoped-for scientific breakthrough.

Always a charmer, you are. I'll go return the object, shall I?

I have been considering – ah. Hello.

[hello, what are you doing with my book?]

Oh, this? We actually … were afraid it was going to get dampened. There was a leak. Near your bunk.

Salt has excellent dehydrating properties.

[what the hell are you doing with that? give me my book back, please.]

Of course. Here. It is called a book, you said?

[yeah, this is my book. why?]

Quick question, is it dead?

[what?]

Your ... book. It doesn't really do anything. Is it dead? A fascinating life form that would be.

[you're beginning to sound like your friend. no, it's not dead. well, i guess you *could* say it was dead. secondhand death, though.]

Please continue. I must know about this secondhand death. Did it witness something so horrible that it gained consciousness but then subsequently perished from the weight of the new knowledge?

[what are you on about now? i shudder to think how you get these ideas.]

My method of thought production is obviously scientific.

Just ignore my friend. Please, what do you mean?

[we make books from plants, which were alive but then are cut down and made into paper. these pages, see? so the books themselves are never living but they're made from previously living material.]

But what are they for? Why for Accepted's sake would you go through the hassle of doing such delicate cutting and pressing for something you're only going to make weird marks on?

[books ... well, they're for everything. we make them to communicate ideas to other humans. we can decipher the marks into words. sometimes we have pictures in the books too, that also convey meaning.]

Oh, so you use your eyes to gain content from the book?

[yes, or our hands. we have a system of raised dot imprints which can also be 'read' like these letters for our blind community. and we have books online too, on our screens. i just prefer this one in print. it's my childhood favorite; i couldn't leave it behind.]

It would certainly have been most of your weight allowance for personal items on the ship.

[yeah, that's why i try to keep it *away* from crewmates who want to poke and prod at it. why didn't you ask me first? i could have told you anything you want to know.]

...I was afraid that it was a gross breach of propriety to inquire about something you keep so studiously hidden.

So my friend stole it. Yes, it doesn't really make a lot of sense now that we're saying it aloud.

[no kidding. i just keep it under my pillow because it reminds me of the time i thought sleeping with books under my pillow would allow the information to seep into my brain overnight. and no, before you get excited, that is most certainly not how it works. i failed a few tests because of that.]

A disappointing revelation. You have to scan the layers with your eyes or hands to receive the information, then? What sort of information?

[gosh, anything. humans have written thousands, hundreds of thousands of books on nearly every topic we can think of. and books are only one form of disseminating writing - there are so many other ways.]

Do you write about your society?

[often, yes. there are some stories we recount from our history, and some books that are for specific researched topics. there are books about locations, and about strategies in games – or to teach you different games. i'm partial to fiction, though. made-up stories. we wrote so much about aliens, actually, that it was hard to believe when you started showing up on our doorsteps.]

You didn't know we existed before us, though. How did you write about us?

[oh, badly. we couldn't even dream of how you actually look and act. but we were so lonely, and so scared that we were alone. it was a way of comforting ourselves; the stories of the other people out there in the stars. humans did so much, wrote so much, but we always questioned whether we were an anomaly in a dead and expanding universe.]

That sounds horrible. We've always known that there was more life a couple of planets over.

[yeah, it was a huge shock when we found that out too. i often wonder if we'd still have so much fiction if we had known the sheer possibilities of nonfiction – of you! – in the universe. but we write fiction to understand ourselves, to know how humanity would function, in times or places so different from ours that they are nearly unknowable. i think that's given us an edge for intergalactic travel. we have a fully formed, independent sense of self.]

You do not worry about losing your sanity or your motivations when subjected to the struggles of a ship's function and our customary visits to other planets.

[well, maybe i do sometimes. i'm not perfect, but i'm not a representation of the whole human race. when i'm feeling lonely, or depressed, or nostalgic, i like reading my book. it reminds me that i have a whole culture that loves me for who i am. a community i can go back to, when i'm done with this job.]

Is that why you sometimes cry when reading the book?

[oh gosh, did you see that? yeah, i miss Earth, and the book's a made-up story in a town that reminds me of my childhood home. it's set in the same area — the realistic fiction type. the author gets descriptions so perfectly i can *be* there again for a moment. lose myself in Earth's sounds and smells and feelings.]

This is like the memories that we play back to relive good moments in our life.

[i guess, yeah. we didn't have technology like that for most of our history. and sometimes i don't want to relive my own life. i'd rather be in someone else's.]

Someone who doesn't exist?

[someone a writer created for me, to show me how they see society and what's important enough to put into their own story. it reminds me to think of my priorities, what goes in my story.]

This book sounds quite informative. I would like to be able to access its information. Will you teach me to decipher the marks?

[i could – or i could just read it to you. record it and put it on your ever-listening bunk device's database so you can reference it whenever you want. i hope you'd like it. it's cute.]

You didn't share it before. Was it because you were worried we'd think less of you for enjoying it? You've never once said anything about my penchant for wearing weird things as hats, nor my focus on my small organic friend.

[you know what, i didn't actually think those were hats … i thought they were some integral form of clothing. but yeah, you're all still so new to me, i didn't want to make a bad impression.]

Nonsense. Every crewmate has an odd and endearing quality about them. We all know mine, as it is the lead-up to the most important and influential publication of research that the Accepted Communities have ever seen.

[that some salts are edible and other ones explode?]

…They do?

[uh huh. hey, did you get salt in my book?]

We may have been testing the storage faculties of your book. Many apologies.

[this is why i keep it under my pillow. if you'll excuse me, i guess i now have to go fish salt granules out from between the pages of my favorite novel. thank you for that.]

You are most welcome. I look forward to hearing the content of your book. I hope that perhaps you will translate my paper into your book form and then give it to the humans. I am sure they will enjoy such cutting-edge research.

[i think perhaps we know a bit more than you think we do. but it would be my pleasure.]

We shall have a listening party for your book, and I shall wear my best hat.

[i'm looking forward to it. oh, and you two?]

Yes?

Yes?

[thanks. for investigating. it means a lot that you care enough about me to be weirdly interested in my belongings.]

Hey, we're all stuck on the same ship, I figured it would be best to know the details of each others' lives.

No, it was absolutely purely intellectual considerations. For science.

[hey, feelings are a science too. see you in the mess hall. don't blow anything up.]

I cannot, nor will not, promise you that.

Just ignore my friend.

NEGOTIATIONS
Garrett Gantt

"We don't have stars where I'm from, you know."

Ryland sits up, taking his eyes off the hundreds of stars that twinkle above him and his otherworldly companion as he props himself up on his elbows. "Wait, really?"

His companion turns his face to him, blinking slowly but not moving to raise himself up to Ryland's level. "No. You didn't know that?"

Ryland shakes his head, somewhat shamefully. "No, I didn't."

"Why, you don't know even the basic features of our planet and yet you're still fighting for a place on our ship?" The creature hums in what might be amusement. Ryland still isn't good at reading them yet. "You are a strange one, Mr. Ryland."

"It's just Ryland, really," he lowers himself back to the ground, feeling strangely chastised. He wonders if the fact wasn't posed to him in the first place just for the express purpose of him revealing his own ignorance. "And frankly, I'm happy with anywhere as long as it's not here."

The creature just hums again.

The two of them watch the stars for a moment together, silently.

"And how's that even possible, anyway?" Ryland breaks the silence, fidgeting. "No matter what planet you're on, the stars should always be above you."

"Oh, I suppose they're up there," his companion answers. "It's just that the skies on our planet are covered with clouds, clouds all the time. The rain is nearly endless, in some places. And no matter how hard you might look, there's nowhere on the planet where you can get a view like this. A long time ago, they say, we thought that there was nothing above the clouds- that our planet was just a nice, self-contained little ecosystem with nothing beyond it. Somewhat similar to how there are those of you that say you used to believe the Earth was flat." He raises a hand to the sky. "We only saw the stars when we pushed beyond those endless clouds."

His arm drops back down. "There are some among my people who say that you traded your third eyes for the stars."

Ryland thinks about that for a second, and wonders whether or not he should feel insulted. "What do you think?"

His companion smiles, eyes not turning from that dotted sky. "I think that if you did, it was a worthy trade."

They sit for a moment longer before his companion pushes himself up with a sigh, finally looking away from that sky as he draws himself to his full height, standing nearly twice Ryland's size. "It's time for me to take my leave, I'm afraid. Are you prepared for tomorrow?"

Ryland nods with a certainty he doesn't feel. "First light, right?"

"That's correct." His companion smiles at him encouragingly, bending down to give his shoulder a reassuring squeeze. "For what it's worth, I'm rooting for you, as much as I'm allowed to."

Ryland returns his smile, still uncertain. "I'll try not to disappoint."

*　　*　　*　　*　　*

Humans aren't an extraordinarily useful species, all things considered. That's the common opinion, at least.

Not that that's a *bad* thing, most would then hurry to say, not everything *has* to be useful in its own unique way. There are still plenty of nice *general* ways that humans can be useful, after all.

But most of their somewhat unique features are more hindrance than help, all things considered. They have no good defenses, for example — they're soft and squishy and the bones that make up their endoskeleton do precious little to protect their vital organs, really. And offensively is even worse — they have no natural weapons that offer them any advantages in a fight. They're small and slow and graceless. They can only breathe an oxygen-nitrogen mix, and without it they'll be dead in minutes. Their eyes are weak and their command over the wide range of colors in the universe narrow and limited. They can typically only focus on one task at a time, and due to their only recent entry into the universal community, they often struggle with understanding and effectively utilizing the technology common in their new world.

And perhaps worst of all, they have only five senses.

Really, that's what took so long to find them, in the end — sure, their verdant little planet seemed to be perfectly capable of sustaining life, but it was so *quiet*. There was no sound — none of the telltale murmurings of the hundreds of thousands of intelligent minds you would expect to hear from a planet that boasted itself host to an intelligent civilization of any kind. Just the silence that they've come to expect from the millions of empty planets out there in the universe.

When someone finally did land (read: crash) on the little blue planet, they were more than a little surprised to find a species that, by all metrics, was sapient — they had buildings, language, art, music, scholars, medicine, all the hallmarks of a civilization.

From there it was a quick enough decision to get them incorporated into greater galactic society (despite their crudeness), and the process of looping them in proceeded as normally as the standardized procedure usually does.

But it's undeniable that the greater community tends to consider them, put nicely, a handicapped species. They can't communicate without making noise, and the wordless connections of minds are completely locked beyond their access. They can't share memories, or experiences, feelings, or thoughts, not truly. They're doomed to a silent isolation of their minds — it's pitiable, and sad.

And yet.

The Orrian ship that leaves in less than a week has been stationed on the planet called Earth for one year now, and due to the unexpected departure of certain members of their crew, they need more people to crew the ship before they can officially set sail for the stars.

In this case, they simply have to make do.

*   *   *   *   *

The advertisement scrolling across his news feed is a surprise, to put it lightly. But far from an unwelcome one.

> **Seeking Crew Members for Outbound Orrian Trade Ship — Humans Welcome.**
>
> **Applicants Must Be Able to Lift at Least Thirty Common Pounds, Navigate Basic Ship Tech, Be Willing to Spend at Least One Common Year Away From Earth, And Secure Independent Transportation Back Home At the Conclusion of the Voyage.**
>
> **Interested Parties Should Seek More Information at the Grounded Ship S.S. Venture Outside the Earth Town Barronville, Texas.**

Ryland has spent the majority of his life in the town of Barronville, and he's become, in the distant way that most residents of the town had, acquainted with the little starship that has been parked outside their town for the past year — but he never expected them to begin recruiting.

Least of all recruiting humans.

He clutches the slim phone in his hand with a sudden fervent desperation, alien tech offering him what he's always wanted.

Anywhere but here.

He's out the door before anyone can stop him, walking to a location he only vaguely knows.

In the end, he doesn't have to walk far at all before he spots what he's looking for: someone wearing the emblem of the Orrian ship, who must be a member of the crew.

"Excuse me," he calls out as he starts into a jog towards the tall, intimidating creature.

It doesn't turn, either not noticing him or not caring.

He skids to a stop in front of it, nearly tripping over himself. "Excuse me!"

The creature finally stops, looking down at him with strange, almost fishlike eyes. "Yes?"

He swallows hard, pushing down the feelings of foolishness eating at him. "It's — well — I —" he fidgets awkwardly, fumbling at his clothes for the pocket his phone is tucked into. "Your ad! I saw your ad — on my phone —" he pulls it up to show the creature, hefting his phone up as high as he can in an attempt to show the towering being. "And, um, it said to come see y'all for more information so I — I thought I should..."

"You're interested in joining us." The creature takes pity on him.

"Yes! Very — very much. So, I guess I'm asking — um, what do I have to do?"

The creature cocks its head, gills fanning out as he looks at Ryland. Ryland swallows again, this time willing himself not to fidget. He has no idea how to read these beings, but if he had to guess, he would say he's being sized up.

Finally, the being nods. "Follow me, then. We'll give you a chance."

Ryland lets out a sigh of relief, struggling to follow as the creature resumes its stride, it only needing to take one step for his every three. "So that's it? I'm in?"

"I didn't say that," the creature responds. "I said we'll give you a chance. You still have to apply like everyone else."

"Alright! Alright, I can do that — I — I can definitely do that. What's the application process?"

The creature ignores the question. "What's your name, then?"

"Oh, right, I guess that is kind of important. I'm Ryland."

"Good to meet you, Ryland," the creature hums. "You may call me Gilati. Or Gil. I understand your species is fond of 'nicknames.'"

"Well, some of us are, I guess," Ryland answers, trying to hide how out of breath he's quickly growing trying to keep pace. "So, about the application."

The creature — Gil — waves him off, wide mouth twisting into a smile. It's only somewhat unsettling to Ryland. "Patience."

"Right..."

"You are aware that we're not returning, yes? If you come with us, you'll have to secure your own route home, if you so intend to return."

"The ad mentioned that, yeah. I don't intend to come back, though."

"You haven't even seen where we're going."

"I know it's not here."

Gil huffs what might be a laugh. "True enough. Our final location is Orra — that's our home planet, I'm sure you know — though we'll be making several stops along the way. Do you have much experience in interacting with species other than humans?"

None at all, he doesn't say. "Yes, I do. Tons, in fact. I used to live in a college town — lots of interplanetary students."

Gil nods. "Good, good. That will serve you well."

In the distance, Ryland sees the ship coming up on the horizon. It's a fairly normal starship, but to Ryland, it's beautiful — wide planes of sleek twisting metal forming its hull, polished to a shine that reflects the sunlight almost painfully. The walkway leading onto the ship is lowered, as it has been in every instance Ryland has seen in in the past, and creatures that look much the same as Gilati bustle in and out, some carrying boxes, some holding clipboards, scribbling things on papers indecipherably to Ryland, some simply standing around talking. A few turn to look as Ryland and Gil approach, and Ryland ducks his head self-consciously. Gilati doesn't seem to notice, striding directly up to the walkway before stopping and turning to his smaller companion. "Wait here; I'll go get the paperwork you need."

Ryland nods, thrusting his hands into his pockets as he watches Gil disappear into the ship. He looks around himself, subtly taking in his surroundings. Two of the Orrians who had previously been carrying on a verbal conversation have gone silent, both sneaking glances at him periodically, and Ryland's face flushes as he wonders if he's being discussed where he can't hear it.

A few minutes pass before Gil comes back down the walkway, holding in his hands a small pamphlet which he hands to Ryland. Ryland accepts it, quickly flipping through, excitement turning to something akin to confused suspicion. The paperwork is bare bones — the kind of thing you might expect for an application for employment at a fast food restaurant, hardly a starship.

He looks back up at Gil. "This is all?"

Gil nods. "That's all you need in regards to paperwork. The presentation portion of the application will take place four days from now at dawn, here at the ship. I don't recommend being late."

"The presentation portion?"

"It's simple enough. First is a basic test of your abilities — your ability to perform tasks we may need you to perform as a member of the crew, and your aptitude with our ship's technology. Then you present your skill to us, and we assess whether or not you're a fit for our crew."

Ryland nods along, suddenly nervous. He's not sure he can even pull off the first part, pretending to know how to work whatever technology they'll be testing him on, but that's not what concerns him at the moment. "Er, right. What do you mean by my skill?"

Gil blinks slowly at him. "Oh, I suppose that's not a standard part of the Earth job application process, then? It's a required portion of interviews on Orra. Don't be too concerned about it — you only have to present something that makes you uniquely useful — something you can add to the crew that you think we don't already have."

Well, he thinks, trying to hide the rush of disappointment, *there goes that escape plan.* Because when it comes down to it, as he runs through his options quickly in his head — *I'm not particularly strong, and definitely not strong enough to impress an Orrian ... I don't think I can exactly blow them away with my intellect either ... and there's nothing in particular I can think of that I can do that would be overly beneficial in space. Not that I'm even sure I fully know what skills would be useful on a ship...*

His dismay must show on his face, because the alien takes pity on him. "I understand this is unusual for you," Gil says. "Why don't I offer you some help? I can only do so much, of course, but I can tell you a little bit about what this kind of technology is like, and what you'll be expected to do. I can even tell you a bit more about what typically gets presented as skills during these interviews."

Ryland looks up at him hopefully. "Really?"

Gil nods. "You have my word. I have business to take care of today, but the next few days I have free — come back whenever you please and we can talk more."

Ryland takes a deep breath, nodding. Three days. That's how long he has to work something out for this interview. And if he messes this up, he might be losing his one chance to get off this planet — to get out of his little town.

"I think I'll take you up on that."

*　*　*　*　*

He sneaks out again the next few days, visiting Gil at the start of each morning and staying throughout the day each time. Gil shows him around the ship — shows him the cabins, the cafeteria, the common areas, the storage rooms, everywhere he'll need to know to work on the ship. He even takes him up to the cockpit, and Ryland's eyes grow wide as he takes it all in, the great glowing star charts depicting planets and stars so far away he never dared to dream of them, great arrays of buttons and wheels and screens for a system so complex it's a wonder anyone could ever learn it. Gil just looks on in amusement as he takes it all in, running his hands along the panels, careful not to touch anything that looks too important. Afterwards, he shows him how to work the ship's OS — as a member of a crew, all he really has to worry about is the part of the system that catalogues inventory. It's not difficult, but if he hadn't had the time to practice with it, he's certain he would have fumbled during the interview hopelessly. Gil walks him through certain skills he'll need to demonstrate, for example, shelving and retrieving inventory. He may be called on at some points to leave the ship to retrieve supplies as well, Gil informs him, but that's not something that it would be beneficial to have him demonstrate on his home planet.

And finally, they go over possible skills. It doesn't have to be truly unique, Gil assures him — just something that he can do exceedingly well that may prove useful. For example, for this position, demonstrations of strength are often highly valued. But as the days pass and nothing comes to mind (because he certainly knows he can't compete strength-wise against any of the ship's current crew members) the excitement he feels is quickly tempered with a feeling of dread.

On the last day before the interview, he walks home alone, staying only a while longer to watch the stars after Gil departs back to the ship. He sighs. Tomorrow *has* to work out — there's no other option — but it's beginning to look like he really has no idea how to make it.

It's late when he pushes through the door of the first-floor apartment he shares with his father, and though he's certain he'll get no sleep, he's eager to get into bed.

"And where the fuck have you been?"

He stiffens, flinching and cursing himself for not thinking to come in through his bedroom window. "I was out looking for a job," he answers. It's not entirely a lie, though it is certainly excluding the full story.

His father looks him up and down, and Ryland realizes that he's probably not wearing the best outfit to sell this story — his ratty jeans and oversized t-shirt don't do much to sell the picture of a prospective job seeker. "Yeah? You doing that all day?"

"I stopped for dinner on the way home," he mutters. "There was a long wait at the restaurant."

"Oh! Fancy — eating out before you even got a job, huh? Guess that means you've got cash for rent?"

Ryland grits his teeth but knows it's not worth the fight, and pulls out his wallet.

Before he can even pull out the little cash he has on him, his father grabs his wrist in a crushing grip and yanks the wallet out of his hands, leafing through it for himself and pocketing the lone twenty dollar bill before tossing it back to his son, who hastily catches it.

"This hardly covers shit," his father informs him as he rubs his sore wrist. "You get that job, I expect your paycheck to come to me first, understand?"

He nods, not meaning a bit of it. "I understand."

"You understand?"

"I understand, *sir*," he spits out, and that seems to placate his father, who finally turns to head through the door himself.

"Oh, and from now on, I expect you home before midnight — if that suits your schedule."

And with that, his father disappears out the door. The second he's out of eyesight, Ryland turns on his heel and beelines for his door, shutting and locking it behind himself before climbing into his bed, pulling the covers over his head like a child. *Nineteen years old*, he thinks bitterly, tears stinging at the corners of his eyes, *and still too much of a coward to defend myself.* It's just easier, he's learned, to take the abuse, and even as he hates to admit it, as his hands tremble where he clutches the cool sheets against himself — he's scared.

His wrist throbs with pain, and he hopes it won't bruise. He closes his eyes — he has to get on that ship. He has to get away from this house.

And as the interaction with his father plays out in his head on repeat, he begins to get an idea.

* * * * *

"So," the Orrian he doesn't recognize addresses him as Gil leads him into the room. He's passed the test section of the interview — or at least, he thinks he has. Now all that's left is to demonstrate his skill. He tries not to let his nerves show as he takes a seat across from the panel of three Orrians — Gil in the center flanked by two he doesn't know. "Tell us, what do you think makes you uniquely valuable to our crew?"

Ryland clears his throat. "Well, this is a trade ship, and I think that the most valuable skill that I can offer you is my ability to negotiate."

The unfamiliar Orrian leans forward. "Go on."

"I went to one of the biggest colleges in our state to get a degree in Business," he explains. "I got my Bachelor's in the field and when I have the finances, I intend to go back to pursue my Master's. While I was there, I interned with one of the nearby businesses affiliated with the program

— not only did they allow me to sit in on some of their business negotiations, but they even allowed me to handle some of them after I'd been there long enough, a task that I handled well enough to receive an offer for a job afterwards. The business also had several offworld dealings, so I have experience dealing with interplanetary trade as well."

The Orrian that hasn't spoken so far nods approvingly. "Very impressive. But if you don't mind my asking, with qualifications such as yours, why apply for a position as crew on our little ship?"

"Because," Ryland says, saying a silent prayer as he prepares to lay all his cards on the table. "Everything I just told you was a lie."

Visible surprise ripples through the three Orrians, and a moment of silence passes as Ryland assumes a silent conversation takes place across from him. Gil finally asks him a question, turning back to him after a moment. "Why don't you explain, Ryland?"

"I wasn't lying when I said I think I can be valuable to you for negotiations," Ryland elaborates. "Because I think I can. I was lying about all my qualifications, and I did it to prove a point — I can lie, and I'm good at it — better than most humans, even, I'd be willing to bet. That's something that I can offer that I don't think anyone else on your crew can — no matter what, you all have the same sixth sense that all other intergalactic species do — your thoughts can be heard just like you can hear others. If you're lying, the other person will know it. But I don't have that, and in addition, I'm already good at lying. And even more than that, if you need something done quietly, I can do it — the sound of my thoughts won't give me away."

The tensest minutes of Ryland's life pass as he sits there, watching the three Orrians sit across from him, looking at each other and speaking without words.

Finally, Gil stands, and Ryland nervously follows his lead as the Orrian smiles at him, extending a clawed hand.

"Welcome aboard."

✳   ✳   ✳   ✳   ✳

The ship takes off two days later as Ryland stands by one of the thick windows, watching first as his tiny town grows smaller and smaller beneath them before disappearing completely, and then eventually as the same happens to the pale blue dot he's called home for the past nineteen years.

He doesn't feel much beyond relief as it finally passes out of view once and for all, and that surprises him — he expected to feel something more, however slight — but instead, he feels nothing.

Instead he only feels awe as he stares out the window at the wide-open darkness split only by the stars, a sight he's certain he could watch forever and never grow bored.

He's so distracted by the view in front of him that he doesn't even notice that he's suddenly not alone anymore.

"I have to say, I am impressed," Gil says from beside him. Ryland jumps at the sudden noise, before embarrassingly trying to pretend like nothing happened. "It takes a clever mind to take a weakness and turn it into a strength."

Ryland shrugs, rubbing his arm, suddenly feeling shy. "I don't know. I think maybe it was only ever a 'weakness' because other people said it was. It was just a matter of thinking of it a different way."

"Maybe so," Gil answers. "But you're the one that did, and used it to your advantage. You'll have to forgive me if I still find it something to be impressed by."

"It was really nothing," he murmurs. And then he speaks up. "But you know, you could have mentioned it to me before my interview that you're the *captain*. I would have appreciated that tidbit of information."

Gil shrugs with a smile that Ryland has come to recognize as what passes for smug. "It never came up. Besides, I can assure you it didn't affect your application in any way. Our process of doing these things is entirely unbiased. Knowing that I was going to be the one judging you would have done you no good."

Ryland ducks his head. "Maybe so, but I still would have liked to know."

"Well, next time I'll tell you."

"There won't *be* — don't laugh at me!"

Gil stops laughing, but that doesn't do anything to erase the glimmer of mirth in his eyes. "Still, I meant what I said. I am impressed with you, Ryland — I believe that you have a great potential within you. I look forward to seeing where it goes."

And looking back out to the stars, with the Earth nowhere in sight — for the first time, Ryland does too.

THE BATHS
annie nguyen

"What is this place called again?" Ixto clicked out their question. Their jaw widened laterally causing a small dusting of dirt in the air from the layers of grime and sediment caked on their body.

"The aliens call them the Baths," Alephun clicked back. His various arms flourished out from under the wave of bright blue and pink fabric, creasing the icon of stylized bubbles adorning the shoulder.

"And you say this is a ritual to honor their gods?" Ixto, the youngest Metix in their company continued clicking out questions to fill the silence.

"Sort of. More of a grooming action." Alephun's tarsi emphasized his point with a brushing motion by his head.

Ixto tilted their head curiously at that. The Phandoryte did look quite well-groomed for his species. Given his sleek sheen, the Metix would have assumed him quite young, but he claims to be through 30 cycles already. Metix grooming mostly involved ensuring the layers of life collected on their bodies were packed in and evenly distributed along their forms.

"Their bodies don't have the same protective layers and they can't carry quite as many life layers," Alephun continued. *"But they do live 120-140 Phandoryte cycles, so it must work."*

The elder Unxk seemed to bob in agreement. Indeed, the whole purpose of this journey was to ascertain whether this "Baths" could help to save some of them and extend their life cycles. The Council agreed to send a small group of Metix accompanying this Fellow Alephun to meet with the species that call themselves humans, and partake in their cleansing ritual.

"We look forward to seeing their floating temple then," Unxk clicked. Before resuming their inward contemplation, they tapped Ixto lightly with a quiet murmur. *"Let us leave Fellow Alephun to focus on getting us there."*

* * * * *

Welcome to all looking to be Rejuvenated

The sign above them outside the docking bay appeared in a strange written form, rotating digitally between various scripts. The same bubble icon on Fellow Alephun's shoulder seemed to be speakers from which the phrase repeated in different clicks, some from species Unxk recognized.

Despite the garish ornamentation of the exterior, the Baths seemed much more modern inside. The smooth metals paneled along the temple pathways leading in the outer ring had a similar feel to other waystations floating in the area. Small windows in the distance hinted at visions of the larger central bubble they saw when arriving. When first approaching the station, the mishmash design of nonfunctional pieces and unnecessary colors similar to Fellow Alephun's cloth covering was rather off-putting. More than anything though, the temple was crowded. Groups of species bustled out from the docking bay chittering about.

"They are switching between languages from the humans' home planet and other species in the area that have already visited," Alephun explained.

"Since it's your first time, you'll be taken to a different area from those who have visited before."

"Do many species come here often?" Ixto asked while surveying the lines off to the right of species from their sector and a few unknowns holding some sort of digital badge. Each of them seemed so young looking with very few life layers.

"Depends on the species. But we get a lot of regulars here who've taken a liking to the practice. They treat it like a family vacation." Alephun led the group over to the left toward an atrium space with several humans and other alien species standing in wait. All were dressed in similar uniforms showing off punchy pinks and blues accented by the childlike icon of bubbles.

"Welcome to the Baths. I'm Dr. Mika Tezuka, and my team will be here to handle your initial intake." The human figure lowered their head and paused.

"It is an honor to host you in these holy Baths. *This is Researcher Mika Tezuka, Leader of the humans in this sector. Her team is pleased to work with you to answer any questions about the process. It will be important to answer truthfully when they begin to talk with each of you so that you can take full advantage of the cleansing ritual to breathe new life into you,"* Alephun translated to the group.

The human looked up at the length of his translation and a few of the other species seemed to be stifling comments, but the Metix all listened carefully. They were briefed on what to expect, but it was strange to see it in real life. A female it seemed, and also very young looking. Or maybe just the result of the cleansing. If was difficult to tell. They appeared so soft. But to so bravely lower their heads, they must be confident in defending against any of the species present.

"Greetings," Unxk clicked, letting Fellow Alephun translate in a way that they hoped was accurate. *"We are happy to meet with you and partake*

in your ritual. We hear that many good medicinal effects come from visiting this place. Is it true you plan to remove our life layers?"

"Yes," Research Mika said bringing them in front of an illustrated wall. "That is part of the process, but we promise it will not harm you and we can make arrangements for you to keep a portion of your life layers. You will be able to move in the same ways that you did in your younger days."

"I see. And this is common among your species?"

"Yes, though we usually do this process before many life layers build up."

Unxk looked back to their group to see if there were other thoughts. Ixto started to expand his torso, but seemed to decided against it after seeing the others ruffle their heads in agreement.

Turning back toward Fellow Alephun, Unxk responded, *"Our Council has agreed to test this process. We will move forward with whatever the next steps are for the ritual and see the rest of your temple. As discussed, we would each like to keep a sample to take home."*

The Phandoryte appeared to meet eyes with the human and raise his head up and down before speaking again. *"Excellent. If each of you would follow one of the humans and their partner to a private room, you will answer some brief questions and they will begin the first stage of removing life layers. I will meet you outside when you finish and provide a tour of the rest of the temple."*

*   *   *   *   *

"How many life cycles have you lived?"
"Where are you from?"
"What planets have you visited during your lifetime?"
"What type of environments have you lived through?"

The questions were varied, focusing on time and place. The partner species, a Laptian name Llido, went down the list clacking answers on a digital tablet while the human prepared large cutting tools. The room was quite sterile compared to the colors— cool white and frosted glass with a large, padded table in the center.

Once everything was answered, Unxk was asked to lay prone on the table and they did their best to get comfortable. The human Mika had donned additional coverings for their face and appendages. From their outer eyes, a digital grid pattern appeared above them. On the small table rolled next to them, Unkx saw some of the smaller tools being used: a trowel, wooden dowels, and brushes. Along the counter were various containers and vessels with white labels.

"Please let us know if anything hurts or feels odd," Llido clicked. *"I'll continue to explain everything as it is happening."*

And though nothing seemed to pierce their protective shell, the movement of the tools did cause some vibrations as the layers shed their dust more rapidly than usual. The air soon reminded them of the strong windstorms in the west fields. But with each shaking motion, Unxk began to feel lighter than they had in ages. Perhaps the humans were on to something.

*   *   *   *   *

"Just finished the rest of the tour with the Metix." Alephun crawled in, his station jacket fitting weirdly around his five arms. "They had lots of questions, but seem to be enjoying the Central Baths now."

"What questions?" Mika asked. Her glasses perched low on her nose as she typed additional data in from the intake forms. Nearby was a tray with some bottled samples and a few stones and odd items that must have been removed from the layers. On a second screen denoting "Grid 4-8," a sectional image seemed to be marking out more detailed information.

"Like how many 'baths' these other aliens take. They were clearly surprised with daily since this is their first one ever. Just seems like a waste of water to me. Though I suppose with your porous exoskeleton you'd have to."

"Don't act like you aren't taking daily baths after hours now that you have access."

"Of course. Though strange, it is as you humans say, 'refreshing.' A bit odd considering you keep the dirt."

"Only from other aliens. And now only in specific cases. I mean, talk about easy access to planetary samples and intergalactic mapping. Plus, part of our funding is reliant on the data we get from these samples. Speaking of, do you know what's out in this sector?"

"Have traveled out there before. But I just got back; send one of the other missionaries."

"Please stop using that title."

"But Brad—"

"Brad is a fucking Catholic. Don't tell me you're using his religious jargon out there when you're representing the Baths."

"Noooo..."

"Alephun..."

"Mostly, we just say the squishy aliens have a way to help you feel new again."

"Alephun..."

"And we might use the word baptism, or the species language equivalent of being blessed by gods..."

Mika spun more fully in her chair, eyebrow raised, arms crossed.

"Don't give me that look," Alephun said. "They're receptive. Win-win. And honestly, with how easy you guys can be to kill, it's probably better they think you're agents of an alien god."

"He's right, Mika." Brad's voice echoed slightly as he stepped in the room. "Not everyone is swayed by research and discovery, or even your corporate travel agent sales shtick. Most of the species in this sector prefer a pilgrimage. New aliens. Here to save you. Come wash your sins away and live a longer, fuller life."

"I'm not having this conversation with you again, Brad," Mika huffed. "Just send another Rep. *I* am going to finish processing the new samples we just got in."

With that, she pulled on her lab coat and turned toward the Processing Center, only stopping slightly to acknowledge Alephun telling her to say hi to her mate Kelly.

"Come on, Al." Brad motioned toward the Dining Sector. "Let's go talk 'sales' tactics over dinner. Make sure they know the new aliens in town bring advanced technology meant to save them…"

"I still don't understand how you can eat so many different things. I got sick trying to eat those beef nacho supreme things you had last time." Alephun restructured his face into something of a blanch.

Brad just patted his midsection saying, "Alien constitution, my friend. Alien constitution."

Alephun crawled closely behind. "Humans are weird."

THE SPECIMEN
Elizabeth A. Allen

"What's happening, Aoia? You're positively purple."

"The most horrible thing I've ever seen in my life."

"Well, if it's the most horrible thing you've ever seen in your life, then why can't you look away?"

"I … I … I don't know why, but I just have to keep staring, even though I know the end will be awful."

"You are an inordinately strange person. I'm leaving."

"No, Eao — stay."

"Why?"

"Watch with me."

"I don't want to stare at disgusting things. — Wait a minute. That's not the most horrible thing you've ever seen in your life. That's Ghavandyn! Humans may be very different from us, but that doesn't mean that they're awful looking. I thought we got over that when we became friends. Uh … why is she rolling around on the floor?"

"Death throes."

"Really? From here, it looks like she might be laughing."

"She's dying. She's being attacked."

"By what?"

"Let me zoom in. — You see? By *that*."

"Is that—?"

"The escaped class IV specimen that everyone's been looking for the past three revs?"

"Oh no … the one that terrorized Yaiea?"

"Oh yes. That's exactly what it is."

"Are you absolutely sure that Ghavandyn's not — What is it? — Playing? She might be laughing."

"Laughing? Let me turn on the sound, and you can judge for yourself."

"Eeeeeeeeeeeeeeeeeeeeeek!"

"Turn it off; turn it off!"

"*Now* do you believe me, Eao? It's clawing at her, biting her — playing with its food."

"And you're just going to sit there?"

"I — I can't move. The screams! The horrible screams!"

"Aoia, we need to help her."

"No! No! I can't bear it. I just can't bear it. I have to get out of here."

"Wait! Aoia! — Coward! I can't help her alone."

※　※　※　※　※

"Is it … Is it over?"

"Well, uh, Ghavandyn is lying on her bed, but she isn't moving, and the specimen is nowhere to be seen. No thanks to *you*, Aoia."

"I knew it! It killed her! It's probably hiding somewhere, waiting 'til dark, before it eats its prey. How quickly do you think it'll strip her flesh from her bones?"

"You know how fast they eat. Even someone of her size will be a skeleton in no time. But I won't let my friend's face be chewed off by some vicious beast! We're going in there to retrieve the body."

"But the specimen is in there too! Lurking! In the shadows! Waiting to strike!"

"Yeah, in the *shadows* — because they're nocturnal. It won't come out if we keep all the lights on. We'll just hurry in there, get the body, and hurry out. If we're extra quiet, it probably won't even notice us."

"I still don't think we should be doing this…"

"Well, you shouldn't be talking, at any rate. I said *extra quiet*."

"Don't you think it's a little strange that there's no blood?"

"Not really. She *is* lying on her stomach, after all. The specimen could have waited till she was asleep and then gone for the throat. We might not even be able to see the wound from this angle, much less the blood."

"Oh."

"Aoia! Aoia!"

"What? Why are you yelling? I thought we were being quiet."

"Did you see that? Ghavandyn just moved!"

"She did not."

"Her dorsal side went up and down. I saw it."

"That's just wishful thinking, Eao. Here — you grab this end, and I'll grab that end, and we'll drag the body off the bed and out the door and be done with it."

"Zzzz… Huh? Whazzat?"

"She's still alive!"

"She's still alive?"

"Aoia! Eao! Huh? What? Why'd you think I was—?"

"Oh no…"

"What's wrong, Aoia? You just froze."

"The … the … the specimen."

"It's on her pillow!"

"It's looking at us! It's looking right straight at us!"

"Stop panicking, Aoia. You're not helping."

"Um … wait a minute. What are you two talking about?"

"Run for your lives, Eao and Ghavandyn! Run for your lives!"

"Aoia! We can't run! It'll just chase us. Then we'll be dead for sure."

"Doomed by what? What's going on?"

"Ghavandyn … are you aware that there's a … a … a hexafelis on your pillow?"

"Nope, no decorations on my pillow. See? Just plain ol' linen."

"Not the pillow casing. I mean … I mean … I mean *that*."

"What are you pointing at, Aoia? Awwwww, you mean this little guy? Hissy Fit? I don't think it's got a mean bone in its body. Sure, it was a little pissy when we first met, but now we're best buds. — Aren't we, Hissy Fit? Yes, we are! Yes, we are!"

"That's not a 'hissy fit,' whatever a 'hissy fit' is, Ghavandyn. That's a hexafelis."

"A hexafelis? Noooo! Can't be. Aren't those the big huge dragon/cat things that are about the size of a house? This is just some cute little feathery lizard. Besides, it just has four legs, not six."

"It's a *larval* hexafelis. They don't develop their third pair of legs and wings until they pupate."

"Wait … so you're telling me that this little thing grows up to be your planet's biggest, scariest, most ornery predator that rips people's arms off for fun?"

"Yes, that's exactly what we're telling you."

"But it's so cuuuuuuuute!"

"What does that prove? We find your planet's scorpions to be charming creatures. But they still can be deadly to your kind."

"Besides, even if it's not threatening you at the moment, you've seen for yourself how dangerous it can be. It attacked your head!"

"Yeah, we were play wrestling."

"It bit your finger and swatted at your hand."

"Pssht, that was just mock fighting. Its teeth aren't that sharp. Didn't even break the skin."

"It struck your head with its own!"

"Yeah, that was a head-butt. Cats do that when they like you. Hissy Fit's nothing but a little feathery lizardy kitty, aren't you, Hissy Fit?"

"But your screams … We heard your screams of pain."

"*Squeeeeeeeeee!* You mean like that, Aoia?"

"Ugh, don't remind me…"

"That's a *happy* noise. Didn't they cover squealing in your interspecies communication class?"

"They did. We learned that, for the vast majority of Earthling mammals, squealing means distress."

"Yeah, well, that's true, but some of us also squeal when we're happy."

"We thought you were dying! We couldn't watch."

"*Aoia* couldn't watch. I wanted to rescue you, but Aoia ran away, so I didn't have anyone to help me."

"Oh my God! Did you — Did you think that Hissy Fit had *killed* me, and you were dragging out my body?"

"…Yes…"

"Oooh, you're going blue, Eao. Distress, right? No — I've got it —embarrassment."

"…Yes…"

"It's very sweet that you were worried about me, and I know that adult hexafelii are dangerous to humans and Ieiaa alike, but I'm perfectly fine. Hissy Fit and I were just playing, weren't we? Yes, we were! Awwww, it wants belly rubs! Um, why are you looking at me like that, Aoia? And what's with the purple? Is that like *super* terror?"

"I just … It's so … I can't … I just can't look away."

"Okay, yeah, whatever. How about you, Eao? What does turning yellowish pinkish mean? Yellow is excited, but what's pink?"

"I'm just thinking. Humans tend to *adopt* things, don't they, especially if they don't have young of their own?"

"No, not necessarily. I'm happily child-free, thank you very much. Don't even like to babysit 'em."

"Yes, but you were also the one who stayed in your room for the first seven revs aboard, talking to the recycling mechanism."

"That's because Reese — she — it — had a soothing sound. It reminded me of my parents talking at night after I'd gone to bed. So we just had some encouraging chats about gathering your courage and getting out there and making friends and ... yeah ... stuff. After a while, I wasn't so intimidated by the fact that everyone who saw me freaked out, turned blue, and skedaddled. Reese helped me adjust. What's your point, though?"

"You make friends with things, like recycling mechanisms and ferocious beasts."

"Yeah. True. Most be something to do with us being a social species and all."

"If you're a *social* species, maybe the Ieiaa could use that to our advantage."

"What are you thinking?"

"Now I'm wondering if you — meaning humans in general — could socialize with hexafelii in general."

"When they're itty-bitty cutesy-wutesy larvae, sure. I wouldn't go anywhere near a grown-up one, though."

"Neither would I. Not unless your kind had adopted it and raised it from a larva and taught it to see you as a friend, not prey. You see? Maybe we could train hexafelii not to see Ieiaa as prey either! We could be safe from the scourge of the skies!"

"Oh, you mean like domestication? We did that all the time back on Earth, even with predators, like dogs and cats and stuff."

"So the idea isn't a new one to you?"

"No way. Just to warn you, though — that stuff takes time, like thousands of years, and even then it's not foolproof. Domesticated animals can still hurt you. Plus that would really change up your food chains and ecosystems. Your subcouncils and your councils and your supercouncils would have to think long and hard before they started that project."

"I'm not sure I like where this is going..."

"You never like where anything is going, Aoia, you purpletail. Think of it! Ieiaa and humans living in harmony with hexafelii!"

"Yeah! We *love* cats, and hexafelii are pretty much flying kitties, so I bet they'd be really popular."

"You're right, Ghavandyn. Domesticating hexafelii would be a huge project. Maybe we could start small with this one right here."

"Eao, are you—? You're not *touching* it?! You are. You are touching it. How can you do that?"

"What did you call this one, Ghavandyn?"

"Hissy Fit, 'cause it hissed a little at me at first. Now I wonder if I should call it Furry Purry. See — if you rub its head like this—"

"It's vibrating! Is that normal?"

"Yeah, I think that's like purring or squeeing or turning pink. It's happy."

"It's happy! I'm touching a happy hexafelis, and it's not eating me! This is amazing."

"You're amazing — amazingly stupid, Eao! This is a horrible idea."

"Do you think it will remember me after it pupates and grows up?"

"I don't think anyone has ever gotten close enough to one of them, Ghavandyn. So — Hey! — we'll be the first to find out."

"If it doesn't make a snack of you first, Eao. This is absurd! I'm telling the head of wildlife, and they're going to—"

"Oh, that's a good idea! Maybe they could help out with our pilot domestication project!"

"That's *not* what I meant!"

SUNBURN
Olivia Gordon

Glardys could not believe his eye.

The human didn't seem to notice that she was surely mere days from certain death. In fact, she was laughing, all those *teeth* of hers showing in full. Glardys attempted to compose himself and made his way solemnly to her side.

"Darlene," he said. "You should have told someone about your condition. The captain would have returned at top speed. Was no one able to help you on the surface? I will accompany you to the sickbay at once." He didn't dare take her arm, as any polite and well-bred Arton would in this situation, but he did attempt to sweep her graciously in the correct direction.

She looked at him as if he had grown a second eye. "Glardys, I'm fine." She dodged his arm, but could not prevent him from taking her bag.

He sighed. Typical Darlene. "You needn't put on a brave face. It's clear you are suffering. Allow us to help you as much as we can."

"I'm serious," she insisted, voice growing shriller. "There's nothing wrong with me."

Glardys nearly lost his temper. "Your skin is *coming off*," he intoned. "Your species does not molt."

"It was just a sunburn." She rubbed her arm vigorously, causing hundreds of tiny shreds of her skin to detach and float through the air. "See? New skin underneath. I'm perfectly healthy." She retrieved her bag from Glardys' hand. All those *fingers* curled firmly around the handle.

"A sunburn? You purposefully exposed yourself to enough harmful radiation that it caused your entire body to burn this severely?"

"I was on vacation." She shrugged.

Glardys struggled to maintain his composure. "This was recreational?"

"Well, it wasn't on purpose, but–" Darlene put a hand on Glardys' shoulder. "Trust me, I'm okay. It doesn't hurt anymore."

She breezed by him towards her quarters, and Glardys watched her casual walk in awe. He pulled up his sleeve and looked at his own arm, and the delicate skin protecting him. No self-respecting Arton would harm themself by intentionally risking their body like that. The body, as bearer of the soul, was sacred. If they could not care for this body, they would be unworthy of the next and plunged into darkness upon death, never to see light again.

Darlene was a lovely woman, kind and gracious, but she treated her body with a startling recklessness. There was no way she would be awarded a new body upon expiration of the first. She turned the corner, out of sight, and it was as if she had been plunged into darkness. It was a fate unbecoming of her.

"Glardys." He turned to see Shontu behind him. Shontu tilted her head to the side in respect. "If you will, I must pass beside you."

Mortified at being caught in the middle of the hallway where he was in the way of his fellows, he quickly shuffled to the side. "My apologies for my thoughtlessness." He proceeded to walk along beside Shontu. "I was just considering Darlene. Have you seen the state in which she returned from her trip?"

"Yes." Shontu's voice became pitying. "Her soul must be grieving. It is a shame, she is hard-working and honest."

"Would it be appropriate…" Glardys began cautiously, unsure if etiquette allowed for such a thought. "If we were to carefully guide her towards a more–" He searched for the correct word. "Respectful view of her body?"

Shontu drew herself up formally. "Surely she could only thank us."

"Pardon me." A third voice joined the conversation from a bisecting hallway. It was Juvon, one of the medics. "I did not mean to overhear your private words, but do you discuss our diligent and versatile Darlene?"

"We do."

"I, too, believe it would be beneficial to her if we were to interfere slightly in her habits. Just before her shore leave, if you'll forgive my sharing, she came to the sickbay for a bandage. She had taken a blade to her own skin, and caused an abrasion."

Glardys was shocked silent, but Shontu managed a breathless, "Why?"

"She was removing hair."

Glardys felt like that bordered on scandalous.

Juvon slowly blinked his eye in concern. "That is not all. Her visits to sickbay are somewhat frequent. For instance, she gets stomach aches from foods she knows are not good for her. And I have seen…" He whispered the next word, almost entirely unable to say it. "*Bruises.* Caused by sheer carelessness."

"We must help her!" Glardys, so overcome with passion, nearly raised his voice.

Shontu's eye was wide with emotion as well. "We may offend her if we are too direct, which is clearly unacceptable. We must take action, but it must be subtle."

Glardys and Juvon wholeheartedly agreed, and between their regular ship duties they enlisted the enthusiastic support of the rest of the crew, all of whom assured them that they cherished Darlene not only for her skills, but her charming personality. They had all noticed her risky behaviors and were quietly horrified by the recent appearance of her skin. It was instantly and unanimously agreed. Darlene must not be left alone to abuse her body, risking her very soul, any longer.

*　　*　　*　　*　　*

Darlene slept for eight hours, and so the Artons had plenty of time to enact their subtle changes around the ship during the night. Glardys was pleased with their handiwork, and even the captain looked over the improvements with satisfaction in her eye.

The moment of truth arrived; Darlene emerged from her quarters (which were, unfortunately, unaltered) and into safety. Her sunburn looked better, still flaking but less of an angry red and more of an irritated pink, and Glardys predicted her whole body would be feeling much better by the end of the day.

"Good morning, Darlene," Glardys said.

"Good morning." He was unable to interpret her expression. Surely, she must be pleased, but it would be improper to point out the changes directly. For once, he was glad that Darlene seemed much less concerned with propriety than the Artons. "What is all this?"

He heard only confusion in her voice. "We merely, as a matter of course, you understand, decided that the ship could use certain enhancements."

"Oh," said Darlene. "Well."

"Forgive me if I am too forward, but may I accompany you to breakfast this morning?"

Darlene smiled. "Of course, Glardys. I'm always glad for your company."

In the mess hall, that strange look came over Darlene's face again. "More … enhancements?" she asked.

"Yes," Glardys confirmed. "I'm sure you can see the improvement."

Another smile, but her brows were furrowed. She chose her breakfast and sat down at a table. Glardys sat down across from her with his own. She picked up her knife, looked at it a moment, then set it down and leaned forward across the table.

"Glardys," she whispered. "Have I missed something?"

"What do you mean?"

"I mean–" She gestured around the mess hall. "All of this. Is it Harvin and Noyar?"

"Forgive me, I'm not sure I understand."

She did that charming gesture where her tiny synchronized eyes roved up to the ceiling and came back down to land on him. "Surely it's not considered rude to talk about?"

He didn't quite know how to respond. He couldn't insult her communication skills by asking for a *third* clarification, but he was unsure what she was alluding to.

She pulled off the triangle of insulation they had carefully applied to the corners of the tables last night and held it up in front of her face. She seemed happy, her two little eyes widening into something slightly more attractive. "The padding on the floors. The blunt knives. The whole ship is baby-proofed!" Her voice went up in excitement. "Harvin and Noyar are going to be parents, right?"

Glardys paused with a spoonful of his breakfast halfway to his mouth. Darlene was not gracefully accepting their care for her safety in the Arton way, she simply did not realize that the ship modifications were for her benefit. On her world, babies were seen as helpless. Being an infant was *undesirable*. In fact, in his casual perusal of human literature he was almost certain he had learned that being called a *baby* was considered an insult.

Embarrassed, Glardys stood to his feet. "If you'll excuse me for one moment, please."

He approached Shontu, who had been studiously eating her own breakfast. "I fear our gift to Darlene's soul was not received as we had hoped." He explained the situation, careful not to place any blame on Darlene herself. When he was finished, Shontu blinked her eye in comprehension. "Humans are … complex," he concluded. The path of etiquette was unclear, more like a minefield.

"She must never know it is for her sake. She may be offended."

"We cannot remove it. She'll not only be suspicious, her soul will be in danger again."

"You're right. There's only one acceptable solution."

Together, Glardys and Shontu went to tell Harvin and Noyar the happy news.

THE COLD
Diana van der Schouw

"Chejo!"

"Present!"

"Aldikazovool!"

"Present!"

"Wesley!"

"Here!"

Roll call in the middle of an arctic desert was a new one. The objective had been explained prior, of course. Take a shovel, dig as deep as you can, try and find the amulet. The first team to find it gets extra credit. The rest get nothing.

Hit the amulet with your shovel? Everyone loses! We can't have any damage on the golden goal. A scorching hot ice shovel is bound to leave some scratches.

Archeology class was a tough one for sure.

Wesley wasn't going to fail this class, though. They were dead set on finding that amulet first. They needed this extra grade desperately after the last find had been a dud…

"So, Wesley, where should we start?"

Echnalii had partnered up with Wesley and you wouldn't hear the both of them complain about this team. Wesley was one of the very few classmates with only two arms. While Echnalii compensated for this disadvantage with three pairs, she had another shortcoming of her own: no eyes.

"I'd say the toughest spot to dig is in the middle of the frozen gravel a few hundred meters away, so it almost has to be there!"

"Hah! You really think these lazy professors would take the effort to bury it there? You have too much faith," one of their competitors sneered. "And even if they did, you and what arms are gonna dig in there?"

"Stay out of this, Chejo! It's not like you didn't do enough damage already!"

"Still mad about that last challenge, huh? C'mon, you know I was taking a dig at you, pun completely and absolutely intended."

"Well, that joke of yours cost us both a new winter coat and ice boots. I hope you're happy!"

Chejo was no longer paying attention. His teammate had started making suggestions for their own digging location.

Wesley knew he was right about their almost nonexistent arm strength; extraterrestrial archeology had been more of a muscle sport than they initially thought.

After a short while with the teams taking positions, the professor, an imposing creature with eight flexible arms and armor tough as nails, started beaming again.

"Everyone, remember! You get three hours to find that amulet in a radius of five hundred quizkja, that's three hundred meters, around me! The moment I blow the horn, those shovels will start heating! Don't touch the blade with any body parts you have or you'll regret it immediately!"

Wesley, of course, had only curiosity at this statement. What temperature would they have those things reach? Last time they checked, an inscription on one of the things said "16 *(". Having not paid any attention in physics class meant Wesley had not the faintest idea of Fahrenheit, Celsius or Kelvin calculations for this.

These thoughts were rudely interrupted by the sounding of the aforementioned horn.

"Wesley, let's go!"

Wesley took the lead and started heading towards the spot they'd previously suggested. Chejo took one more amused look at the pair before heading off to a much easier position, completely convinced reverse psychology would make it the best place to find the amulet.

Immediately arriving upon their destination, Wesley was ready to stab their blade into the icy pebble floor and start carving. They took out their shovel, only to be completely stunned.

"We have to dig through ice and rocks with this?"

"What's wrong with it?" Echnalii asked.

"There's no heat coming from it at all!"

"What are you talking about? I can feel the vibes right here."

"Vibes?" Wesley asked.

"Yeah, you know … Heat vibes and stuff."

A moment of silence.

"I'm gonna touch it," Wesley said.

"No," Echnalii yelled. "You're gonna burn yourself to a crisp!"

"You know I'm gonna touch it."

Echnalii sighed. "If it wasn't for your visual receptors, I'd have ditched you long ago."

"Noted," they said, a split second before touching the blade.

Nothing happened.

"What!" Echnalii said.

"I don't feel anything."

"What!"

"Listen. I don't feel anything burning. It's 40 degrees celsius at most. I had expected we could turn these rocks into lava…"

"I hate you."

"I know that. The shovel really isn't that hot, touch it. If you can't touch this, you can barely touch my guts!"

"Are you mad? One of my siblings had one of those fall on them, lost one of their right arms! Also, touching your guts sounds disgusting!"

"What's a right arm for you? They're sort of everywhere around your body, aren't they?"

"Our right arms are clearly on our right side of the body."

"I've never been stellar at directions."

"Could have told me that sooner! You're pretty much my guide around here…"

The moderate heat of the shovel was perfectly capable of melting the ice around the site. The pebbles were a challenge, but with Echnalii backing them up with two arms to dig and four arms to pick up and throw the pebbles, they made progress. Wesley constantly described the floor for the first five minutes, before Echnalii begged for them to stop repeating the words "ice" and "rock." The rocky floor turned to opaque white ice one meter in, which meant visuals were horrible, but digging was easy. It also suggested someone had filled this gap with compressed snow, a clear indication that the amulet had to be here.

After two hours of digging and four meters of depth, Wesley's heart leapt. "I see something glittering!"

"For real? You think we found it?"

"Only one way to find out! Be careful with the shovels."

One of the surrounding teams had heard the small commotion and came looking. It wasn't long before the whole class had joined to see how the winning team would dig up the amulet and gain eternal glory in the form of a good grade no one would ever look at again after the semester.

It wasn't until the last team, the one Chejo was on, joined the crowd that the floor made a suspicious noise. It was short, but loud enough to silence the crowd in anxious anticipation of an encore.

Chejo took advantage of the silence to come sneer at the competition some more.

"So, think you found it, huh? No suspicion at all that this might be a red herring? Just so you know, my team have covered much more ground already, we've practically alrea-"

The encore came, and it was loud. A creaking, tearing, snapping sound indicated the whole area could collapse at any second. The rest of the class fled in a wild frenzy, not keen on finding out what was waiting under the ice. Echnalii dropped her shovels and ran in the complete opposite direction of the rest, which was a funny sight but also probably the wisest thing to do in this situation.

Chejo stood petrified, while Wesley dropped their shovel as well and tried to get him to move.

"What's the deal, Chejo! Run! If you don't we're both gonna fa-"

They fell.

As it turned out, the glimpse Wesley had had of their eternal fame had been an illusion made by a river going right under the digging site. The professor should have been aware of this, but Chejo had made a correct observation right at the start of the assignment: this particular professor was pretty lazy. No need to be a busy bee if you're big, strong and intimidating. Teach your students, check exams, day finished. No extra effort spent and a nice salary in the pocket.

Luckily, the river wasn't wide enough for the other students to fall in as well. The area of the collapse was no more than five meters wide and three meters long. The surrounding area was still weak however, and no one took any chances to check on the duo.

"Oh my stars," Echnalii whispered, reunited with the crowd. "Did they die? Did they really just fall in there and die? What is even in there?"

"Water," someone replied. "The impact probably killed them and otherwise the freezing water will, yes."

They heard a scream.

"I'm gonna die! I'm gonna fall down and die! I'm too young to d—"

"You're not gonna die! I've still got you!"

No doubt this voice of reason was Wesley. They were still hanging on.

The crowd took a few careful steps closer. Wesley was hanging by the edge, holding on with one arm and hanging on the other arm was Chejo.

"Stop clamping my arm, will you! My blood circulation is cut off, you're going to make it sleep!"

"I'm not letting go! What does that even mean, how can your arm go to sleep without you!"

There was a collective gasp in the crowd. Seconds later, questions grew among them.

"How are they carrying both their weights on that tiny arm?"

"What is that red stuff coming out of their hand?"

"If they're that strong why didn't they dig faster?"

The teacher had just arrived at the site, horrified mostly by the consequences this could have for his career. He took a few steps towards the gap before immediately reconsidering when the floor creaked ominously once again.

Not a single soul in the crowd had any concept of adrenaline, or human blood for that matter. The closest they had to blood was a hydraulic system for movement; most of them either didn't need oxygen or used tracheae to get it through their body.

Wesley's shoulder joints were badly hurt by the sudden fall and stop at this point, but it took one last surge of adrenaline before they reached their moment suprême: they swung Chejo right over their head onto the floor. He skidded to safety where the crowd yanked him to his feet. He almost instantly disappeared in the masses.

Everyone went wild. How could they have that amount of strength in two of those tiny arms? One of the braver students tried to reach the gap by carefully spreading their weight and reaching out, but when they could peek over the edge they were met with a pair of terrified eyes, quickly gaining in distance towards the icy stream.

The crowd quieted. The splash wasn't that impressive a noise, but the echo seemed to continue forever.

After a minute of shocked staring and utter devastation at the loss of their ambitious, stupid, kind, strong Wesley, the first people started walking towards the shuttles. Only a few stayed behind, Echnalii and Chejo among them. Echnalii sat close to the edge, somehow hoping she could catch a glimpse of her friend, despite her lack of eyes. Chejo looked down, ashamed and full of guilt, but too scared to sit next to her and the abyss. Suddenly they both heard a very distinct yell out of the darkness.

"Hey! Anyone still there? I think I found it!"

The both of them exclaimed in surprise.

"You're still alive?"

"Uh, yeah! It's freezing in here, can anyone get me out?"

Chejo ran towards the shuttles, not even registering what had just happened. That's why, when he came to his destination, he could only ramble out a barely audible "still alive."

Folks grabbed rope and other tools to safely get Wesley out of there. It took no more than five minutes before they got them out safely, but they looked quite different than before. After a frenzied hike towards the warmth and safety of the space shuttles, more questions from classmates ensued.

"Why is your nose red? It wasn't red before."

"It was freezing down there, mate. Of course my nose is gonna be red."

"Wait, you have a nose?" Echnalii asked. "Why do you have a nose if you already have a tongue? Isn't that enough? Can't you smell with your tongue?" She hadn't seen their nose, of course, and assumed that their inability to talk and eat at the same time (though they definitely tried quite often, which was disgusting), was due to the tongue being both responsible for vocalization and smelling food for any dangers. Why would they also need a nose?

"I quite like having a nose, thank you very much."

"But why is it red now?"

"Give the human some space, everyone!" The professor interrupted. He then went on to give a speech about digging precautions. No one liked this.

In the middle of the lecture, Wesley sneezed, hard. This was the kind of sneeze you'd hear at 3 am in a suburban neighborhood during summer when a family left their window open and the dad's pollen allergy was acting up.

Echnalii jumped like a startled cat, which was impressive for a creature her size.

"What was that!"

"I sneezed."

"What is that supposed to mean!"

"When I get too cold my nose starts making extra mucus to keep it protected. The mucus irritates my nose and my body has a reflex that launches it from my body, hence the sneeze."

A small pool of snot sat right in front of Chejo, who recoiled at the sight of it.

"Gross, why in the universe would you do that?"

"Hey, I didn't decide on having a nose!" Wesley laughed hoarsely.

The professor shot him a glare, meaning it'd be wise not to interrupt again for the rest of the trip. It would be a boring flight home, but at least they had a story to tell.

And extra credit.

VARIATIONS
Kit Harding

"The *humans* are coming today!" Tsain came barreling into the botany-psychology lab, furstalks rippling blue-green to display their excitement/astonishment/energy.

"I'm aware." Frex, being less excitable, was a calm orange color. "We all received the intercultural documents and *I* at least read them. Baring their teeth is a sign of friendship, they prize eye contact, and they can eat *anything*. Oh, and they can't see heat waves, and they do stupid things a lot."

Tsain flopped into an empty seat. "Aren't you at all excited?"

"What's there to get excited about? I want to be an intercultural liaison, there are going to be humans here, and I'm probably scarcely going to get to see them, let alone interact — although one of them *is* a botanist, so I may get to see that one from across the lab."

"Why *does* psychology share a lab with botany, anyway?" asked Tsain. "That doesn't seem like they go together."

"It's a retrofitted ship; *none* of the lab assignments make any sense. It would be nice to get to interact with a human at least a bit; they're *fascinating* from a psychological perspective."

"More so than every other species you've encountered?"

"Yes. They apparently don't have variation. Every other species' intercultural protocol document includes a list of variations among major cultures — greeting Travians from the Red Schism with crossed forepaws instead of vertical, making sure never to serve grelden meat to a blue-scaled Imbrian ... things like that. There was *nothing* in the document that suggested they have being-to-being variations, just a general overview of 'humans do this,' 'humans do that.' I want to study a species that has such a narrow range of things they do, most of which is stuff no other species does."

"Maybe the variation section was missing, or they forgot to put it in?"

"Intraspecies variations are one of the most important parts of any such document." Frex had taken on a lecturing tone. Tsain shrunk down in the chair and meekly turned a submissive pale yellow. "While obviously no documentation can cover every variation in a species, knowing what you're going to encounter before you encounter it is *critical* to allowing interspecies ships to deploy in the first place. Imagine the disaster if you didn't know something *necessary* for a fellow crew member's comfort while serving in deep space! You could lose whole missions that way. It is simply inconceivable that any species that had significant variations would fail to put the major ones into a document!" Frex paused and seemed to notice Tsain's coloring. "I didn't mean to get all fierce. It's just ... this is what I'm passionate about. Interspecies relations."

Tsain shifted back towards an agreeable orange color. "I'm sure you'll do well at it. Being so passionate and all."

Frex's furstalks danced over one of her screens, which emitted a loud beep. "It's time to go find out," she said. "They've just docked. Shall we go join the welcoming party?"

*   *   *   *   *

The docking bay was crowded when they arrived. Everyone had heard the stories of things humans had done on other ships — wild stories, some of which Frex gave little credence to, but apparently believed by enough of the crew that many had turned up here rather than wait for the welcoming reception. The crowd in the docking bay made it difficult to get close, but Tsain's enthusiasm carried them forward on sheer force of personality, and Frex followed in their wake. At the center of the room, the captain stood facing the docking bay.

Then the door opened and the humans came through. There were five of them. At first glance they didn't *look* too strange. The humans were bipedal and their fur was limited to only on the top of their heads. They wore identical blue uniforms. The one at the front had a pictogram in the shape of a star emblazoned on the skin of his neck; Frex knew from the information packet on human customs that this was a "tattoo" and involved embedding ink into the skin. The one at the front and one of the ones behind him also had much darker skin coloration than the other three, who were paler, and none of them had the same fur color, but other than that the first four of them seemed to all be much of a piece.

The fifth one was different. She was still dressed in the same uniform that the others were, but standing by her side, against her leg, was a yellow-gold furry creature that came up to about half her height. It walked on four legs and wore a jacket with the humans' writing on it and a band around its neck which was attached to a flat cord wound around the human's wrist. Frex had not the least idea what the creature could be for. It was pressed up against the human's side, leaning on her with what looked like some force. The human also looked different from the others — where they were attentive, alert, and moved with athletic grace, she seemed to shrink into herself, and her eyes stayed focused on the floor.

"Welcome aboard the *Starleaf*," said the captain, furstalks rippling the deep purple of respect.

"We are honored to be among you," responded the lead human. "This is quite the welcoming committee!"

"Everyone was curious to greet you. We've heard stories, but none of us had ever actually seen a human before."

"Some of those stories are exaggerated," said the human. "I'm Patrick. These are Emily, Andrew, Damien, and Grace." As he said each name, he indicated the humans. The one with the creature was Grace.

"I am Captain Lihnam. I hope our partnership is fruitful."

"As do we," said Patrick. "Even if the planet proves unsuitable, we have the chance to create close relations between our two species."

"In that spirit, we've prepared a reception in a few hours so that you can begin to mingle with the crew. Until then I will have someone show you to your quarters so that you can rest and become acclimated."

The captain inclined his body towards the human, and one of the younger crew came forward.

"If you'll just follow me…" He led the humans through the doors and out towards the rest of the ship.

*　*　*　*　*

Frex arrived early to the reception, her curiosity piqued by the very strange fifth human. Most of the humans mingled energetically with the rest of the crew, excited to get to know the people they were going to be working with and seeming to enjoy being objects of curiosity. Grace sat by herself in a corner of the room, watching everything intently, but not speaking or initiating conversation. The creature lay at her feet. Frex was considering ways to politely inquire about the creature when Tsain bolted over to Grace, their furstalks back to that excitable blue color.

"Hello, human! What is this creature?" they said, speaking so quickly and energetically that it was almost all one word. Grace flinched away from them, back against the wall, and the creature surged to its feet to stand in front of Grace, forming a barrier between her and Tsain.

"Is it one of your monsters? I heard humans keep monsters. Is it safe? Does it eat people? Why did you bring it on board?"

Grace's mouth moved very briefly, but Frex couldn't hear what was said. A moment later, the creature made a loud, sharp vocalization that cut through the noise of the party.

Patrick, the lead human, immediately materialized out of the crowd and approached Tsain.

"Something I can help you with?" Patrick asked.

Tsain looked at the creature, then at Patrick. Frex could practically *see* the thoughts spinning through Tsain's head — the desire to insist they hadn't done anything wrong warring with the need to obey what appeared to be an implied reprimand from the humans' very diplomatically important leader. Obedience won, and after a moment Tsain simply walked away. Patrick sat down in a chair beside Grace and said something quietly to her. She shook her head. He said something else and she nodded, then reached down to bury her hand in the creature's fur. They talked a few moments more and Grace tossed her head back with bared teeth — laughter, Frex remembered from the packet. A sign of amusement. Patrick soon returned to mingling, but Frex saw him speak quietly to each of the other humans, and after that, any time one of the crew approached Grace, one of the other humans seemed to materialize out of nowhere by her side, to take on the bulk of the conversation.

Frex was confused. There had been *no* variations given in the intercultural packet, but Grace was most definitively not acting the way humans acted according to the packet. Nor was she acting the way the other humans were. But the other humans did not seem to find the way she was acting *strange* or in any way worthy of note, beyond that they apparently felt the need to run interference — but that looked to Frex more like protection than anything, given how Grace's body seemed to loosen when the other humans were nearby.

A good intercultural liaison was also a good observer. Frex would practice for her desired career path by observing the humans to see if she could figure out what was going on.

*   *   *   *   *

Observing did not require going out of her way, for it turned out Grace was the humans' botanist. She appeared in the lab the next day at duty-start, her creature still by her side. She looked around the room once and then approached Arthri, the botany team lead.

"Grace Jansen, reporting for duty," she said, snapping off a rigid salute — the human gesture of respect for a superior officer — with the hand that didn't have the creature's cord wrapped around the wrist.

"Be welcome among us," replied Arthri. "Your station will be right there, and we have some vegetation samples from the probes we sent down to the planet, so you can get an idea of what to start with when you go down there yourself."

"Thank you," said Grace. She sat down at her station. Her creature carefully tucked itself beside Grace's chair, facing itself so it could see the room, for all the world like it was trying to be out of the way.

Lirin, seated next to Grace, turned the same excited blue that Tsain had been the previous day.

"We're all looking forward to working with humans," she said. "We've never had any on this ship before."

"I'm sure my colleagues will be delighted to answer your questions," said Grace as she pulled her microscope towards her.

"But not you?"

"I'm not very interesting."

"But you're a human! We've all heard all the stories about humans!"

"And I'm sure half of them were lies."

"But there are so many! Even if half of them *were* lies, there's so much out there. Can you really regrow your limbs?"

"*No.*"

"But I was *sure* someone talked about that."

"You shouldn't believe every rumor you hear. Didn't they give you an informational thing about us? I got one about you."

"Oh, they never put the *juicy* stuff in the intercultural packets!"

Frex stifled an indignant squeak. Of course you put the juicy stuff in the intercultural packet! That was the whole point! Anything as major as "they can regrow limbs" would have been in there. But Lirin was flighty and always had been — in Frex's opinion, far too flighty for this sort of mission, and she was proving it by her continued interrogation of a human who clearly did not want to talk.

"You pierce your skin for decoration and you eat strange chemicals, and your bodies can take an amazing amount of punishment!" Lirin exclaimed.

"Some of us, yes. You will note I have no skin piercings and my visible body fits the human standard." Grace leaned forward to look into the microscope and began making notes about whatever she was seeing there.

"You have an *invisible* body?" asked Lirin.

"No. Like I said, I'm not very interesting."

"But you have that thing." Lirin sent a furstalk down to poke the creature.

Grace snapped her head up and moved towards Lirin with a sharp, aggressive movement. "Don't touch him!" she growled.

Lirin jerked sharply back, furstalks flaring an angry acid green. Then she pointedly gathered up her materials and moved across the room to a different workstation. The other scientists watched Grace warily as she settled back to her microscope.

Frex was unsure what to make of what she'd seen. Obviously touching the creature was a bad idea, but had she reacted so fiercely because the creature was dangerous to others or because it was a violation of some kind of human taboo? Or was she just annoyed with Lirin's behavior? Grace wasn't acting under any of the rules that supposedly governed humans' behavior, though Frex supposed she could understand not wanting to suffer Lirin's interrogation. *That* had been rude by any species' standard. But there'd been nothing in the documentation about humans being an especially private species.

Frex continued her musing as she turned back to her own work, but she came no nearer to a conclusion.

* * * * *

In the mess hall that night, the humans were all seated in a group, taking up one entire table by themselves. Mindful of her goal of continuing to observe, Frex took a seat at a nearby empty table, with the intent of listening to the humans' conversation.

"So what happened today?" Patrick was saying to Grace. "The complaint I got said you were being 'dangerous and aggressive,' but somehow I don't think that's what happened."

"She was going to touch Bear," said Grace. "After she was interrogating me about the wildest stories she'd heard about humans. You should have heard some of the questions. Do we have an *invisible body*, honestly."

Emily laughed. "I imagine that depends on what religion you belong to. Most Christians would probably say yes; most atheists would say no; anyone Jewish would say it's complicated."

Frex nearly dropped her utensil at that. That sounded like they *did* have variations! Large enough ones that everyone had laughed at what Emily had said without requiring further explanation. And apparently the creature was named Bear.

"Humans do seem to have something of an ... exaggerated reputation ... around here," said Patrick.

"Don't go spoiling that!" interjected Damien. "There are bound to be social advantages."

"I think using our exaggerated reputation to get with alien women is probably the antithesis of what we were sent here for," said Emily.

"Could be alien men. I'm open-minded. Do 'women' and 'men' even apply here?"

"Either way, don't," said Patrick. "We're here to do science and further the joint settlement proposal."

"Are you all right?" Andrew asked Grace. It was the first time he'd spoken.

"I suppose," Grace said. "It's just … a lot. And I thought I'd blend into the background out here. It's not like they've got a tradition of randomly petting strangers' dogs. I figured they'd read the bit in the packet about it being human custom not to touch dogs in jackets and … y'know, *not*. Instead Bear seems to have made me more of a target."

"Did anyone here actually *see* the packet?" asked Andrew.

All of the humans shook their heads.

"Maybe the disability part was badly written," he said. "I'll see if I can get access to it."

There had definitely been nothing in the packet about this creature that was apparently called a dog. Grace had expected there to be — and apparently the intercultural packet wasn't something they had ready access to, which *really* struck Frex as odd. They were distributed across the entire galaxy; there wasn't really any point to classifying one.

"While Andrew looks at that, can you try leaving the room instead of snapping next time?" asked Patrick. "I don't care if you seem rude walking away mid-conversation; that's still going to be an easier bit of diplomacy to navigate."

"I can try," said Grace. "I'm hoping it gets better after we're here longer and they get used to me."

"Thank you. I'm not asking you to do the impossible; I know there are things you need that the rest of us don't, and I'll speak to whoever runs the botany lab about not touching the dog. I would, however, like for all of us to come out of this without causing a diplomatic incident."

"Oh, come on," said Emily. "If anyone causes a diplomatic incident it's going to be Damien."

The conversation dissolved into general laughter.

✻ ✻ ✻ ✻ ✻

Frex continued to observe Grace and the creature — the *dog* — over the next several days, and her observations continued to confirm that Grace had to be some kind of variation from human standard. She was an exemplary botanist, but she was direct to the point of bluntness and seemed to have difficulty understanding unless others communicated with her in the same way. She was also extremely edgy. Watching out for people coming up behind her seemed to be what Bear was for; anytime anyone seemed like they were about to brush by her, the dog would stand and put one of its forefeet on on Grace's knee. Grace would then turn around and watch while they went by, and also reach down to stroke the dog's head, before she returned to what she was doing.

It was after five days of observing that Arthri called Frex into her office. Arthri's furstalks were the deep orange-red of concern.

"I need a favor," said Arthri. "And I did clear it with your supervisor first."

"What *kind* of favor?" Frex asked apprehensively.

"It's time to start sending small manned teams down to the planet for botanical survey, now that the geologists and security have a base camp established on the surface."

"I'm not a botanist."

"No. But you do maintain a pilot certification, and unlike any of the actual pilots, you've been sharing this lab enough to have figured out that Grace's creature —apparently it's called a dog — isn't going to attack you as soon as you're alone with her."

"Why do the pilots think it's going to attack them?"

"Patrick came down here to tell me that it's considered extremely rude to try to touch someone else's dog uninvited and could I please remind the lab crew not to do this, and someone who had been reading about Earth fauna recognized that she's named it after a giant predator. They are now convinced that this is another example of humans doing things that are dangerous to us without thinking about it and that it's not just rude but *dangerous* to touch it."

"Surely that can be avoided by just … not touching it?"

"You would think so, wouldn't you, but all I hear about is humans and their dangerous predators. They are at least managing to keep the *humans* from hearing about it; I don't want to think about the kind of diplomatic incident that would cause. But I don't want to force them, and I know you want to be an intercultural liaison someday, so here's your chance."

When it was put like that, how could Frex refuse?

*   *   *   *   *

The first hour of the trip down to the planet was undertaken in almost complete silence. Grace sat with Bear at her feet, looking through something on her tablet, while Frex guided the shuttle away from the ship. Then, seemingly without any prompting, Grace spoke.

"You're psychology," she said.

"I am also a qualified shuttle pilot," said Frex.

"Did they ask you out here to surreptitiously analyze me?"

Given Grace's habitual bluntness that statement should not have come as a surprise. Frex paused to consider ways to reply diplomatically, but she'd been observing Grace for several days now. Trying to be evasive was exactly the wrong tack here.

"There are concerns about whether your dog is dangerous," Frex said instead.

"*Dangerous*?" Grace spoke with such intensity that Bear shoved his front up and into her lap, pressing down. She looked down at the movement and set a hand on his head.

"I'm okay, Bear," she said. Then, "Why are they concerned about him being dangerous?"

"Because apparently 'bear' is the word for some kind of deadly Earth fauna?"

There was a long pause. "He's named that because he's big and fluffy. It's a common name for an animal on Earth."

"He alerts you when people are nearby. It follows that he serves some kind of protective function — that perhaps you've trained him to attack."

Grace leaned forward to rest her head against the top of Bear's head, and laughed a little when he licked her face before she raised herself back up.

"I won't deny that attacking is a thing some people train their dogs to do, but Bear's not one of them. Is the service dog copy in the informational packet *that* bad that it didn't mention they're not dangerous?"

"The intercultural packet didn't mention anything about any sort of variation from human standard. I *thought* it was odd; even species with low-level hiveminds list *some* variations."

To Frex's surprise, Grace started to laugh.

"What is it?" Frex asked.

"These … variations you mention. What do they normally encompass?"

"Anything where there's a large group with the same differences from the baseline — anything from coloration to dietary restrictions to psychological differences. I thought it was extremely odd that humans didn't seem to have any."

"Oh, we have them. We have *many* of them. Humans are just … bad at acknowledging them. I shouldn't be surprised, I suppose, that even when they knew I was going to be here they didn't think to tell you about Bear. Even humans aren't great at behaving correctly around service dogs."

"And dog is the species and service dog is … a special variation of dog, that performs a service?"

Grace looked down at Bear and shook her head slightly. "This whole time I thought you all had gotten *something* in the packet, even if it was bad, and were just ignoring it. A service dog is a dog that's been trained to help someone with … what you call variations. Or some kinds of variations, anyway, the ones we call disabilities."

"You have a variation that requires warning when people are behind you."

"Yes. When Patrick said it was rude to touch them, he really did just mean rude. Bear's not dangerous."

"I know of no other species that has trained companion animals to compensate in this way. We try to arrange our societies to make room for as wide a swathe of variations as possible, but the possibilities if that training could be adapted to rarer variations among other species!"

"That easy?" said Grace. "You just jump right to seeing the possibilities."

"Of course. That's my job. I want to be an intercultural liaison; I have to specialize in variations. Admittedly humans seem to be functioning as a species unlike any other known species, but with enough information we can work with that."

"Humans … aren't good at handling variations."

"Judging by the packet I received, you don't seem to have that many. A lot of things about the toughness and endurance of a human, how you're all omnivores that can eat basically anything, and how human culture is about decisiveness, boldness, and brash action."

"You know, I came out here in space because I figured if no one knew how a human was supposed to act, they wouldn't notice that I don't act like other humans. Only I discovered that everyone has these wild ideas of how humans act."

"If the packet had been better, it probably would have worked," said Frex. "Well, they might have still been a little alarmed. Humans are the only species I know of that keep animals as companions rather than livestock. But you wouldn't have gotten the whole ship wondering whether Bear was dangerous."

"If we ever want to have a functional joint settlement, *that's* going to need fixing," Grace pointed out. "People are going to need to know the actual details of the culture before commencing living together."

"I take it there's some problem with pointing that out to your government?"

"My government would like to believe people like me don't exist. Point this out to them, and they'll find a way to bar us from space settlements."

That made no sense to Frex. Humans were, apparently, developing truly ingenious ways to handle variation, but for some reason they didn't want the rest of the galaxy to know they were doing it, and Grace's comments implied that it was due to dislike of difference, not a desire to retain tactical advantage. But they were very interested in and aggressively pursuing joint settlements with alien species, which was full of much more dramatic differences than any Grace had thus far displayed.

"Do you have any ideas, then?" Frex asked.

"It can't be seen to come from my team," Grace said. "I already had to threaten them with our legal system just to be considered for this mission; they won't tolerate more of that from us. But Andrew's a xenoanthropologist — he studies alien cultures, and he knows more about humans than the human government does — and he was going to try to get access to our packet. He can probably help you write a more accurate document."

"Me?"

"You said you wanted to be an intercultural liaison! Now's your chance. You've already demonstrated you have enough common sense to both ask direct questions and wait for a good moment to talk, which puts you ahead of everyone else on the ship."

It was similar to what Arthri had told Frex before sending her off with Grace — you want to be an intercultural liaison, so liaise. From what Grace was saying, the problems between her and the rest of the crew were the tip of the iceberg. *Someone* needed to to do this before a settlement actually happened.

"From second psychologist to covert liaison," said Frex. "Do you have this kind of chaotic effect on *everyone* you meet?"

Grace bared her teeth at Frex. Human expression of pleasure.

"Only the ones I like," said Grace. "So *you* will probably get more of it."

"I can live with that."

CAN YOU TELL ME...?
Charles D. Perry

Gllaxxx entered the establishment warily and moved towards the table his contact had indicated in the message. Normally he would not be caught dead in such a place (actually, he was more than a little worried that he might literally be caught dead here before the standard rotation was through), but the need was great enough to risk it.

The need was because of one of the newest races on the galactic stage: Humanity. At first glance, just another race from some distant system in one of the galactic arms, not anything special really. There were many races in the galaxy that had been spacefaring for much longer, so a primitive undeveloped backwater race that had discovered faster than light travel less than a hundred standard orbits ago was nothing to be concerned about.

He'd heard the rumors, that they could work longer and harder than any two other races combined. That they came from a high gravity world with chaotic environments, that they domesticated apex predators for companionship and entertainment, and many more each as unlikely as the last. Bah, unsubstantiated rumors all that were not worth the breath needed to speak.

But then he'd heard that their technology was advancing at an astonishing rate, and he took notice. As did many others. The older races of the galaxy enjoyed a rather large technological head start over younger races that kept them in line, and the idea that a newer race was actually advancing fast enough to potentially catch up was worth some attention.

Then humanity's official authorized and researched history was released to the galactic public and many were horrified. From mechanical flight to early space travel in less than 50 standard orbits? Absurd. From early computational devices to global informational networks in less than 25? Unheard of. Colonizing a planet — even if it was one in the same system — before discovering faster than light travel? Ridiculous. Refining the theory behind gravity drive into a functional faster than light engine in the same standard orbit they discovered it? *Impossible.*

Absolutely impossible.

But there it was, clear as cloudless atmosphere with galactic dates and all in their official authorized and researched history. Galactic academia would never allow such a thing to even exist if all information within had not been thoroughly verified. Everything found in such a publication was certain to be true, no matter how unbelievable.

Their ability to advance was beyond unprecedented; it was unreal. Some might even say unholy. They had to have discovered some secret that let them perform such miracles. They had to. Likely by complete accident, but there was just no other plausible explanation. And the first race to discover and replicate humanity's secret would be untouchable on the galactic stage, even by humanity itself as they could never catch up to a race that advanced at the same impossible pace they did.

Gllaxxx was determined that his race, the Mixxxixxxixxxi, would be the ones to gain the secret first. Which was why he was here.

*   *   *   *   *

Jack smiled as he watched the xeno — from some race that was way too fond of the letter X — look around the seedy galactic bar nervously. Good. Nervous meant he was more likely to pay the asking price just to get the hell out of there quicker.

Jack checked himself over for a few moments to make sure everything was in place.

Concealing trenchcoat? Check.

Seventh most popular model of spacemask in human space (Star Lord's from the classic work of fiction Guardians of the Galaxy) in place? Check.

Watch display synced to a secure bank account? Check.

Concealed sidearm? Check, check, double check, and boot check.

Merchandise? BIG check.

Time to go introduce himself.

*   *   *   *   *

"Hope you haven't been waiting too long," the contact said as he slipped into the booth across from Gllaxxx, and Gllaxxx started as he realized the contact was a human.

"What…?" Gllaxxx started before shaking off his surprise. "Why would you—"

"Keep it down, would you?" the contact hissed. "This meeting is worth both our lives if the wrong person finds out."

Gllaxxx swallowed nervously at the reminder and lowered his voice accordingly. "Why would you betray your own race?"

"Why are you surprised? Every race has members that would sell out for far less than what you're offering."

"True…" Gllaxxx muttered, uncomfortable at the thought of one of the Mixxxixxxixxxi doing the same as this man. "So then, you have it…"

"Jack, call me Jack."

"Yes … Jack … you have the secret?"

"I have better than that," the Jack replied. "I have the secret behind the secrets."

"The ... what?"

"The secret behind humanity's secrets. The BIG secret that enables all the little ones everyone's chasing after."

"The little..." Gllaxxx was beginning to get confused.

"Yes, the little secrets. Like how we humans have diplomats that can debate with even the most political races like equals. Soldiers and commanders that fought, and won, a war against a technologically superior race. Engineers that can build anything with a design, and many things without. Inventors that push the limits of our technology daily. Doctors who know the healing needs of other races as well as our own. Scientists that stretch the boundaries of what humanity knows constantly. Artists that can work in mediums most races think are too much trouble. Writers that have already been invited into the galactic poet society. Mathematicians that solved one of the galaxy's great 'unprovable proofs.'"

Gllaxxx swallowed. He'd forgotten about that last one.

"...Thieves that can sneak humanity's greatest secret right out from under its collective noses," the Jack finished as he pulled out a data storage device.

Gllaxxx had to refrain from lunging to grab the thing, but he still must have twitched in that direction, because the Jack pulled it back towards himself guardedly.

"What ... does it contain?"

"Instructional videos for human children. Untranslated, of course."

Gllaxxx felt his mind come to a screeching halt in disbelief. "Instructional videos for children? But every race has those."

"Not like these, they don't," the Jack stated confidently. "Yours prepare your children to follow certain roles, certain professions. They prepare your children to be engineers, or scientists, or diplomats, or any number of things, but only one thing."

"Yes, that is how it is done," Gllaxxx replied in confusion. How else was a species supposed to maintain enough experts in all the necessary fields?

The Jack just shook his head. "It's holding you all back. These right here? These don't teach children how to learn one thing, they teach children how to learn."

"How to learn ... what?"

"Whatever they wish to."

The conversation was hurting Gllaxxx's brain.

"Tell me, how many of ... your race are experts in more than one field?"

"A few hundred," Gllaxxx stated with pride. Such individuals were highly prized and unexpected rarities. "Though one of our most esteemed scholars was recently recognized as an expert in a third." It had been cause for much celebration as well, as such a thing hadn't happened in generations.

"Humanity currently has over a dozen individuals that are recognized experts in at least five fields."

Gllaxxx felt his third heart stop for a moment. Experts in *five* fields?! Imp—

"Their identities and certifications are part of public record. You're free to verify the claim; I can wait."

Gllaxxx forcibly calmed himself. The Jack would not make such an invitation if he were not certain, and the length of time needed to sift through records searching was far longer than Gllaxxx intended to remain here. "How?"

"Because humanity has mastered the art of teaching our children how to learn. We never stop learning; we come to crave it in fact. Me? I'm not just a thief. I've also published three books, play music in my spare time for fun, and I perform all the physical and computer maintenance on my spacecraft myself. And I'm considered one of the less accomplished learners. Because of these."

Gllaxxx watched as the Jack tapped the data storage device. The Jack had not made his claims as a boast; to him they were simple fact. "What are these instructional videos?"

"Like I said, they teach our children how to learn. How to enjoy learning. They took the revision and refinement of humanity's teaching methods from all over the world and distilled them to their purest form. All before our first global information network. And then they've been revised and refined every generation since. Sure, there are many more like them, but these here are the absolute best of the best. Available to even the poorest human children for free, but jealously guarded from anyone outside humanity. The human government got everything like them deemed 'historically unimportant' by galactic scholars to hide them from all of you. This here is the only existing copy outside human space, and it's yours."

Gllaxxx could barely contain himself at the declaration.

"*If* you pay the the agreed price," the Jack reminded him.

Gllaxxx grumbled and pulled out his personal device to begin the transfer of galactic credits before pausing as he remembered something. "You said they were untranslated, correct?"

"Yes, which is the only reason I'm not charging you ten times as much or more. I grabbed the entire archive since they started making them."

Right, of course. That was a rather large undertaking for a single sapient, no matter how diverse their skills. Gllaxxx transferred the credits and watched the Jack observe a wrist-mounted alert device ping the confirmation before sliding the data storage over.

"Pleasure doing business with you," the Jack said before standing and walking out of the establishment at a brisk pace.

Gllaxxx took a moment to be sure he wasn't being watched before securing the data storage and making his own exit.

* * * * *

Jack smiled to himself as he completed the transfer of his new credits from the dummy account to a different secure account in human space less likely to sell him out if one of the galactic bigwigs came sniffing around. He'd almost done it too fast to admire the number of zeroes in the amount the Mixix-whatever had paid him.

Whistling to himself, he boarded his ship and began the process of requesting launch clearance even as he told his computer to begin burning another copy of the supposedly "only-one-outside-human-space" archive and began looking through the list of races that had bounties on "humanity's secret."

"Oooo, looks like the ... I cannot pronounce that. Haven't these guys ever heard of vowels? Ah, well, it looks like they're offering almost as much as the X-lovers did." Plus, odds were he could haggle even more like he'd been able to do for the others he'd sold to already. It was an interesting galactic constant, but no matter the race, desperate governments had loose purse strings. And since none of them had gone public with their "purchase" yet, everyone continued to believe he'd approached them first.

He grinned to himself as he got confirmation for launch clearance and began planning how to sell his merchandise to the next "exclusive" client. A few more like these and his grandchildren's grandchildren wouldn't need to work unless they wanted to. Even if he married multiple wives, which only got more and more likely each time his bank account grew. Maybe he should start looking into planets with permissible marriage laws. Maybe some attractive and open-minded xeno ladies for variety.

Not bad for a lowly con man. Though, really, this wasn't much of a con. About the only lie he'd told was of humanity's willingness to let the videos outside human space. Had anyone thought to ask, they'd have probably been given freely, but none of the xeno historians had considered them worthy of so much as a footnote. If the xenos could understand the videos' true nature and adapt them for their own races — transition from cultures focused on prepping for job roles into ones focused on guiding children to figure out what they were actually good at and could enjoy doing — they probably could start producing polymaths on par with humanity's and advance at a comparable rate. Really, they were shooting themselves in the collective foot with their educational practices. However, by the time any of them got their act together and overhauled their teaching and learning practices, humanity would be knocking on their collective technologically advanced door and they'd all be playing keep-up. And his descendants would be living the good life funded by gullible panicked xenos jealous of humanity's ability to learn and teach.

Honestly, if he had one regret about all of this, it was that he'd never get to see the faces of the xenos when they got their first look at humanity's instructional videos. He truly wondered if they'd be more incredulous about Oscar or Snuffleupagus.

He began humming the theme from his childhood as he punched in the coordinates for the next system.

IKYUR
Maggie Maxwell

Captain Carjyack narrowed his four eyes at the … creature across from him. In his lifetime of space piracy, he'd seen dozens of other species, with limbs from leaves to tentacles to all kinds of blobs, but they'd all had at least four of everything. Four branches, four tentacles, four blobs. Four was the law of nature, the law of the universe. This one, though, this "human" was only half of what it was supposed to be: only two eyes, only two arms, two random lumps on its upper torso, two of everything except its lone olfactory sensor. These humans were in defiance of all the laws of creation he'd known, and none of them seemed to know or care.

The human's captain was baring its teeth at him in a way it called a "smile" and swore was a sign of happiness or excitement among its people. In every other race that had teeth, it meant someone was about to get their soft parts ripped out. He'd had his guns drawn before the opposing captain insisted it wasn't a threat display and showed its dull teeth, not at all meant for ripping. Carjyack's soft bits, though they were hard to find unless you were well-versed in Carnivian anatomy, were still in place, so perhaps this creature was telling the truth. It hadn't tried anything. Just … smiled.

Not that it would live long enough to harm him.

"You understand the rules?" he said, gesturing at the two lines of small cups on the table, each filled with a thin yellow liquid, the empty decanter beside them. "The ten glasses in front of us contain a dose of ikyur, a potent poison made from a plant on my homeworld. It has killed everyone from the lowest servant to the greatest of generals. This particular dose has been aged for five years for optimal potency. There is no species in existence that is immune to it at this age. The rules are simple: we each drink until one of us either surrenders or dies."

The human nodded, still with that frightening white smile. It picked up the first glass and gave it a sniff before putting it down. "We drink. If I die or surrender first, you get our ship and my men get stranded on the nearest habitable planet. If you die or surrender first, vice versa. Sounds clear enough."

The poor fool didn't know what was coming. It was hardly fair to issue this challenge to a newly discovered species, but Carjyack didn't gain notoriety for being fair. Well, they'd learn. Or at least, this crew would, if one survived their marooning long enough to tell the rest its story. Most species succumbed after one or two doses of ikyur. Carnivians could handle five or six doses of it. It was usually administered over time when used in assassinations, and death by doses was punishment for the greatest criminals. The day they'd discovered their slow poison was a potent killer of other spacefaring species was the day they'd become the most feared and most dangerous of them all. The greatest adversary he'd faced managed four doses, and it had been a large creature with its stomach on the other end of its body from its mouth. That one had Carjyack worried, but in the end, he took its life and its ship.

Admittedly, the human and its crew had proved themselves worthy adversaries from the moment they'd met. When his crew had boarded the humans' ship, they had fought with a ferocity rarely seen before. Their war cries had startled even his men, and the human weapons had ripped through three of his best. They had taken down three of the humans as well, and both sides seemed surprised when all six stood back up, holding their wounds shut and continuing to fight. That was when Carjyack had called for parlay and combat by ikyur. Partially, he knew continuing the battle would be almost as costly as fighting his own people. Partially, he wanted to know more about this race. None had ever matched the Carnivian before in combat. He looked forward to learning more about them while they headed for the nearest planet.

"Which of us should take the first drink? I am willing to go first." Carjyack always liked to make the offer. He knew he could handle more of the ikyur than even most of his own race, a small immunity based on just how many times he'd faced this form of combat. His opponents usually took him up on the offer, and then, when they realized he was unfazed after the second dose, lost much of their will to continue. It was a good way to get them to surrender, and the ones who didn't, well, in the end, he still won.

The human picked up the first cup and sniffed it again. It took a small, tentative sip. Ran the poison around in its mouth. Then, without any more hesitation, it tilted its head back, swallowed the rest in one gulp, and slammed the cup down. "Whoo! That's got a kick!"

Carjyack reached for his first cup, but before his fingers could wrap around it, the human grabbed its second. Carjyack's entire crew stared as the alien downed dose after dose until the last drop was gone. This wasn't right. They were supposed to trade off. Hadn't he said they were supposed to trade drinks? The small glass shattered in the human's hand as it crushed the empty tenth glass against the table. Then it smiled a cruel, victorious smile, one that was undeniably a threat as a thick red liquid dripped between its fingers. "All right, bitch," it said. "Your turn."

Ten glasses. It just drank ten glasses of ikyur, and it was still staring him down, waiting for him to match it. Waiting for him to kill himself. The human had ripped his throat without touching him. The smile had been a lie from the start.

"I yield," he said, staring at the full glasses in front of him.

The humans erupted in cheers as a few started to round up his crew and their weapons. Five took Carjyack's share of the doses, clinked the glasses together, and shot them back the same way their captain had.

It would be a fair surrender. He was too in shock to order any rebellion. They were celebrating by drinking poison. Their captain was still upright. Still breathing. Still staring at him with that horrible smile. One of the humans nudged him with the butt of its weapon. "Get moving." Carjyack and the human captain both stood, him slowly, it on wobbly legs. One of its crew grabbed it by the arm.

"Easy, ma'am. That's a lot of drinks, and you're losing blood."

The captain waved the crew off. "'M fiiiiine. I drank worse in m' sorority. Y'ever had Old Crow? Now that stuff'll rot yer insides."

Worse? Captain Carjyack stumbled against the table as the human bound his four arms behind his back.

"How?" he managed to force out. "How are you alive? How are you still standing? No one can survive ten drinks of ikyur." Not even the Carnivian's greatest general had managed more than seven when he'd been executed for treason.

The human captain hiccuped and giggled. "You call it ikyur. On MY planet, we've got the same thing. We call it" — another hiccup — "Tequila, and we drink it for fun. You seriously thought you were gonna win a drinking contest against a fuggin Kappa Phi sister?" Another giggle. "Dumbass."

Maybe it was a side effect of the ikyur, or maybe it was his audial translator breaking down, but he didn't understand half of what the captain said. "Are you telling me ikyur is not poisonous to your kind?"

The captain fell into a fit of laughter and stumbled against its partner, leaving a smear of blood down its shirt. The human holding it up said, "It takes a lot. Like, maybe if she'd had yours, too, then she'd probably die from it. Elsewise…" it shifted the captain's weight to wrap an arm behind its back. "Well, elsewise it just makes us feel really damn good. Watson, Barnes, get them to the brig. We'll find 'em a nice new planet to call home. C'mon, Captain, let's get you some water. And some stitches." It looked at the red smear across its chest. "And me a new shirt."

As his crew were led away to the impossible fate he'd brought on them, Carjyack swore he could hear the human captain singing something about a drunken sailor early in the morning.

FTL'D
Manuel Royal

We are sorry as all get-out about your little — about the Moon. I mean, I am, and Cool-Cool totally was. I know it meant a lot to y'all, in regards to romance and tides and whatnot. Wolf-man movies. So sorry. Just wanted to make that real clear, right off.

Hey, it's nice to see so many familiar faces here today. Secretary General, Ms. President, Premier Tsernikov, General Solingen, and most of all, Dr. Vasek — it's great, frankly it's reassuring, seeing you and all your colleagues from the Earth's scientific community. I feel very sure cool heads and reason will prevail here.

I love all humans. Human beings. Every damn one of you, please remember that, even though y'all seem maybe a tad steamed at the moment. Sure, you're pissed off, my good golly, you have every Earthly right to be. Every Earthly right. Earthly. Nothing? Okay.

Say, are y'all comfortable? I could spin the deck slower, faster, whatever you like, it's round 'bout half a gee now. Okay.

To think it was just two years ago we had to hightail it so abruptly — I tell you, folks, when we saw what a mess things were, bit of a proper cock-up, well, we didn't figure on meeting up with you again.

No, it's not — *Non, c'est pas ça,* slow your roll, it ain't like that. Okay, we did hear all the messages you sent after us — yes, let me talk, right? Sorry we didn't call back, but it really seemed like the kinder course of action at the time.

Talking's good, right? After all, that's what I was designed for, top to bottom, right from the egg cluster, the minute we first detected your wet little planet.

Just like I breathe most easily in Earth's atmosphere, I've literally got no choice but to appreciate your rich, varied culture, and speak all your chaotically idiomatic languages, and convert every technical statement into your quaintly haphazard system of measurements, and even make some pretense of understanding and respecting the baffling array of primitive tribal religions you somehow believe in.

Hold on, hold on! Now, we all agreed, it was gonna be honesty from here on, *pravda*? Best policy. I signed that thing with Secretary General Tseng, right after poor *vraayy*khukul kicked the bucket. C'mon, we've always been able to talk. You trust this old face, don't you? Goodness knows enough work went into it.

Anyhow, you gotta admit, you folks got funny ways, you got hang-ups about all your weird gods and what-have-you. I'm not puttin' it down, just observing — and I get it, really. You've been the only thinkers and talkers you knew about for so long; surely that's lonely. So you made up gods and spirits and talking animals, and those elves that make the cookies — you just want there to be somebody *out there*, am I right? You even made up a thousand different versions of — well, of me, in all those stories about somebody out in the greater universe finally taking notice of your existence.

Of course, all those stories, all those made-up Others were basically mirrors you just couldn't quit lookin' at. And a mirror I was, 'cause that's what you required, so if you don't like what you see —

Shoot, I didn't even finalize my body-form until we were pretty close, to make sure it fit your psychology. Exotic, not close enough to look like an unsettling distortion of humanity, none o' that Uncanny Valley stuff, but also not, y'know, *too* alien. General design came from a committee back home, but all the refinements, like displaying words and images on my big ol' glowing tummy — my idea.

Sure, we use lots of different bodies. Some of 'em look more like centipedes or octopuses, I know you wouldn't care for — no, Ms. President, it's octopuses or octopodes; "octopi" is not a word. Hey, it's y'all's own language — anyway, like I said, getting back on track, I love you folks, is how come I always bent over backwards to be friendly and non-threatening.

Let me tell you something else: you should be awful, awful proud of yourselves for what you've achieved here, every one of y'all. I am nothing short of amazed, and my partner Cool-Cool was too, before you cut through his isolation membrane and unfortunately killed him. It's amazing that you've caught up with us out here. Somehow.

Oh, hey, that right there, that shows we were telling the truth about most everything, except that one big thing and the various things closely related to it. But obviously we weren't shootin' the bull when it came to my poor departed partner's need for his isolation membrane that you just ripped right off.

He don't even look like himself now, all leaky and whatnot.

So, no ceremony, no grieving period, you're just gonna dissect him? Well, what else did I expect. No, he wouldn't want you to pray for him, we're not primitive — never mind. It's fine. Sure, a billion human children loved *vraayy*khukul, they loved that little guy and called him Cool-Cool when he visited them in every single itty-bitty country on your planet — some of y'all here were just tykes when we showed up, I bet you got one of the little presents and gizmos Cool-Cool was always tossin' out to the precious wee children. But, never mind, no, you go on ahead and start cuttin'.

Hey, you said you'd give me time to speak. So … some explanations, obviously, are in order.

Tell you what, to start out, let's put aside all the benefits you've gotten from our visit these past forty years. We'll forget about how you've got no more famine or wars amongst yourselves, or energy shortages.

Never mind how we gave you the tools to get your climate under control.

Hey — let's not even mention how Cool-Cool and I, by getting you folks to focus your youthful species' energies on the project, essentially lifted you up out of your savage tribal warfare period. Sweep that under the rug. Forget it.

Let's pretend it's all been bad. Nothing but grief! Here, I'll even count your complaints for you:

First, you somehow imploded your own Moon trying to create a — what did the late Dr. Nakano call it? An asymmetric spatial deflationary effect. Obviously, you did a smart thing putting the test on the far side. Guess we'll never know what happened at Tsiolkovsky Base, but from where we were, the Moon looked like a big soap bubble poppin'.

I know, a lot of Moon-pieces ended up falling to Earth, so, guess I'm sorry about Sydney and Jakarta, the Pacific in general, etc. *Mea Culpa, Mea Culpa, C'est la vie, non?* Because of your immatu — because you're a passionate people, feeling things deeply, you're very upset with me, and by extension my whole people, about that. I get it, already. So that's a given, and, okay, let's just set that off to the side for now, yes?

Truthfully, y'know, logic would suggest you did that to your own selves. It was your own damn Moon.

Okay, second, after some amongst y'all felt compelled to go pokin' and prying into this ship's computer files, and found out about some aspects of our proposition that were not entirely truthful, that must have hurt. It makes perfect sense you should have hurt feelings about that. Nobody likes getting taken for a fool.

Tell you what, you really caught us with our pants down on that one. I mean, we had no idea a bunch of barely-industrial types would be such gol-darn whizzes with the computer stuff, else we mightn't have let everybody just crawl all over our system. Nobody likes a nosey parker.

We really thought it'd just be indecipherable, but turns out you do ciphers real well. It took centuries of dedicated committees to create our data system, and you folks seem to have learnt every little thing about it in a year or so, then just went crazy with adopting the technology and makin' it faster and littler. Reverse engineering, you call it? Yeah, we don't do that. We engineer in the one direction, like normal people, not that reverse thing.

I understand somebody even copied our entire database onto a little doodad he put in his pocket. So, good job, pat yourselves on the back.

Anyway, third — and I think long-term this one is liable to hurt the most — soon as you learned what our real agenda was, that also meant you had to accept that your whole faster-than-light project was a dead end. What'd you call it, Ascension Project? Nice name.

Cards on the table, now. Cold hard truth: no, that faster-than-light bullshit just ain't possible. No, there's no Galactic Fellowship with tons of infinitely-desirable benefits offering a membership as soon as you crack lightspeed, because that doesn't happen. Never happened, never will.

Yeah, sure, I and similarly purpose-grown cluster-brothers go out in beautiful impressive ships like this one, and we've never gotten faster than about a tenth of lightspeed, like we're doing now, but we go out and make contact with little young cultures like yours, and spin some yarns and make some promises about the ol' Galactic Fellowship, and, fine, fine, we dupe yokels like you into dedicating your whole species' resources into creating an FTL drive, which in your case meant the Ascension Project. Biggest endeavor your civilization ever attempted, maybe the noblest too. Sorry it's impossible. Fine, General, it was a screw-job, if that's your choice of words. Nice.

Why'd we do it? Well, 'cause we could. We already live in space, we don't get old, we got the means, and to be honest I guess we like messin' with the simpler peoples 'cause it's fun and profitable.

We always come away with something worthwhile. Rare minerals, unexpected bits of technology, useful and/or amusing biological specimens (I could go on and on about that one!) Oh, and cultural shit too — with you folks, it was your music more than anything. Great stuff, for real.

Also, of course, there's the minuscule chance — nonexistent, realistically — the faint chance you might somehow do it. None of the other subjects worked out — right, you already read about that in the data thing.

Six other civilizations, six times we played the same game, and none of 'em could pull hard enough on those bootstraps. Don't blame us for that — physical laws of the Universe and all.

One of them ended up goin' plumb nuts and wiping themselves out with a genetics war, so really you got off lucky.

But Cool-Cool totally believed in y'all Earth people for some reason, sentimental reasons I guess. His theory was that in a young, short-sighted, self-destructive — I mean, an energetic, rapidly developing, innovative technological culture like yours, some bright-eyed hominid might see an angle that hadn't ever occurred to us.

We've been space-based since before you learned how to sharpen a rock, we haven't changed anything in about ten thousand years, and we do everything by committee. Maybe fresh blood would bring results.

You were chasin' a dream, but so were we. We were the hunters, and y'all the hounds. If there was even the slightest chance it was possible — if you mouth-flapping li'l hammer-swingers could actually work it out in your li'l pink brains ... well, hell, if Dr. Nakano's test had worked instead of killing him and everybody else on the Moon, y'all woulda had, I guess, not just that faster-than-light pipe dream but a real unified space-time theory, hot and cold running gravity, some godawful weapons, who knows what else.

Course, that kind of technology would've been far too dangerous to let you hold onto, so we might would've confiscated it and prophylactically sterilized your planet, which, trust me, would be a piece of cake.

Hey, hey! I told you, nothing but square shooting from now on. You asked for the truth, so y'all can be good listeners and learn something, or you can keep yellin' and name-callin'.

Hell, if we had an FTL drive my people wouldn't be stuck on these long, slow trips, and we could make that Galactic Fellowship thing a reality, 'cept of course it'd be our dominion, or empire, whatever. I like "Dominion"; it's got gravitas. That's what Cool-Cool thought, anyway, though look how much good it did him.

Shī fu lǐng jìn mén, xiū xíng zài gè rén, right, President Zhou? The teacher opens the door, but you go through it your own self. Pop your own damn Moon.

So after that little incident, and after you folks learned the whole story and went out of your damn minds, we knew the trip was a loss, the jig was up, goose cooked, so we fired up the boson-mirror thruster — which I presume you've duplicated, am I right, Dr. Vasek, else you wouldn't be here? Oh — that ring of Moon fragments came in damn handy while we were vamoosing out of Earth orbit, as it turned out, since we needed a billion tons of matter. Thanks.

So here we are, nigh on two years later, still accelerating at a twentieth of a gee, nearly up to one-tenth c. Truth is, like I said, that's close to our top speed, and we'll shut down and be cruising on inertia soon, for various reasons. Right, because of the interstellar medium, partly that, and various other reasons.

A tenth of a light year from Earth out here, we're about a century from home. No, it's not a dirty planet, I told you, we live in space. Yes, in the region of Barnard's Star, Dr. Vasek, good job, you've managed to extrapolate out our nearly straight trajectory. I can see why your fellow primates gave you that shiny Nobel.

Here we are, and here you are, which was the biggest surprise I've had in ages. The thruster makes it impossible to look straight behind us while accelerating, so I assume that was your direction of approach. First thing we knew, you were right next to us, matching velocity, and I gotta say, kudos, that's an impressive feat.

I wouldn't have put money on your even being out of disaster mode in just two years, let alone making a faster version of our thruster and putting together that ugly thrown-together thing you arrived in. For a human structure it's impressively big, if nothing else.

Speaking of which — am I correct in thinking you've sort of engulfed my ship with your ship, so that the one is inside the other in like a big hangar? That would account for the notably poor view of the stars.

So you got our doors open, not sure how, but in you came, and there went poor Cool-Cool, and here we are. You can kill me, or you can haul me back to your planet, or you can hang around for a hundred years and meet my relatives. None of these options will gain you much.

Now, I'd rather light a candle than curse your darkness, my *H. Sapiens* friends. There is one card I've been holding onto, and I'm ready to lay it down and I think y'all will agree it makes up for that whole laundry list of grievances you keep yellin' about. You remember I said we don't get old, where I come from. How would y'all — see here, Madame Secretary General, I'm going to speak right to you, I always felt we had a connection. Madame Secretary — Jiao — I notice you're of a certain age, and your little human body is startin' to deteriorate and malfunction, so pretty soon it'll break down and you'll be 80 kilograms of rotting organic waste, *nicht wahr?*

Fine, however much it is, I'm no expert on human mass; don't know why you picked out such a trivial — anyhow, you're gonna die soon. All y'all, somehow you go about your lives and mostly waste time even though you're never more than just a few Earth decades from being stinky dead sacks of garbage.

Hey, hey, whoa now, don't shoot the messenger! Seriously, folks, please, I'm speaking literally, fingers off the triggers. Please! Surely is a lot of guns y'all brought with you.

I do have a point, yes, that being: how would all y'all — that's the whole human race, but especially you, Jiao — like to fix that stupid problem with your bodies where they fall apart so quick?

That's knowledge you can't steal from our computer 'cause it ain't there. But we've got biomanipulators aboard this ship that can fix you up in no time, and you can take 'em all back to Earth. Here, let me show you —

Ow! Ouch! Hurts! Stop stickin' me! I can't take pain, ow, sumbitch! We gave up the whole pain experience way back when, we don't even have — goddamn! — don't have any words to express pain, that's why I have to use your stupid dirtball savage words — ouch!

Fine, yes, I was lying about the biomanipulators, I just wanted at those controls. You give me ten seconds access and I'll flood this ship with enough ionizing radiation to kill the shit out of every one of you. Nothing but a pleasant tingle for me. Yeah, obviously you're not gonna let me, now, but it would've worked.

You want to know something? I'm glad you people are gonna destroy yourselves. That much is obvious just from your short history. You're like that cartoon coyote of yours, blowin' himself up and such. You're also the bird and the Acme company at the same time, but mostly the coyote, a filthy animal scavenger with an overheated brain and no long-term judgement. Just walkin' off the cliff, thinks he's fine 'til he looks down — Hey, you don't like that metaphor, pick another one, your whole body of artistic endeavor is puerile self-obsessed metaphors and whatnot. Buncha pants-wetting finger-painting halfwit children playing with matches.

One more thing you need to hear. The instant your stupid lumpy spaceship came into view, we — me and Cool-Cool — we sent a burst transmission to our people. They'll see everything that's happening here, in a few years when our message arrives.

That's right — even if you kill me and take my ship and your great-grand-children finally arrive at my home after you've shriveled up and died of old age, they'll be walking into a world of hurt. My folks is got thousands of habitats, and they'll have 90 years to prepare. Hell, they'll probably meet you on the way and reduce you to monatomic dust—

No, clean out your ears, Madame Secretary, I told you, it's a hundred-year trip. You're opening the hangar? Well, it's about time. Okay, now we can see something, let me point out—

That's — that ain't possible. That's Barnard's Star, that's what I'm looking at? What you call it Barnard's Star, yes? That's — home. We're right on top of — Creeping Christ, I can see our biggest habitat from here.

Ah. Yeah. Well now. So you did it, didn't you? You people. Well now, that takes the cake. Y'all babbling, short-lived, floundering, mindlessly violent bunch of primitive biologicals snuck past the physical limits of the universe and cracked the speed of light. Just FTL'd right on through. Katano was right.

Hey! Think a minute! You didn't lose your stupid Moon in vain then, see? We gave y'all a dream, and you made it happen, that's a win-win! From where I'm standin' you got no cause at all to be mad — Hell, friends, you oughta be thankin' me!

Ouch! Ouch! That's my vestigial generative organ!

You people, oh you ... I hate you people. I hate you.

Shit.

HUMAN ALTERED
Dara Brophy

Eells stumbled back to the ship, happily singing a half remembered song from Earth. "Something, something … and I knew it complete…" He reached the ship. Yeah. Another tour. Dragging through his pockets he found his plan B, a sober pill. He dry swallowed it and waited. The world came back into unwelcome focus. Another three months in the HMS Shitshow. He dragged his sorry ass back to his berth.

Captain Reid watched his human return. His engineer, for the love of all the gods, stumbling back to his ship. He watched as the yellow/red/blue balance that he had learned was human sleeping developed.

"We launch now. Before it wakes up." The mining vessel Shahetow left the dock.

Reid hated having a human. No one else was allowed to service the engines, so he was having to put up with it. The insanity of allowing one species to control most of the interstellar hardware sat badly with the captain. His people had owned the stars for generations before these blind savants had arrived. The humans had arrived into the galaxy with nothing but a bag of spanners and an open mind. Within a generation they had "fixed" everything so much that no one would touch a machine if they had gone near it. It was only a matter of time before "Human Altered" became a common sign, then a T-shirt and a religion.

Then a warning, and finally a law.

Insurance would disavow any injuries, loss or death from an accident unless you had a human engineer or could prove no human had "had a look" at your equipment.

Eells walked through the engine compartment. The refit was over; he could smell the new wiring drying out. The hum of the converters was steady. Still, it sounded off. It would take a month or so before it sang again. He lived to give these gentle giants a voice.

Time to report to Reid. The previous engineer had told him that the Captain could see well into the infra-red. Nocturnal hunters somewhere in the bloodline, he guessed. He debated mentioning human vampires. Probably not.

Captain Reid prepared himself for the human. Honestly, why couldn't they have a proper shell. Talking to a human was like watching a fireworks display. Except they were surly and argumentative. He raised the lights and equipped his sensor dampeners.

"Welcome back, Engineer," mimed the captain in his traditional dance. Eells just waited. He waited for the correct moment to sit down.

"Hello again, Captain. The refit seems fine. It will take me a month or so to get the system back to peak performance. I reckon we are running at eighty percent now."

This, this was why he didn't like humans. His engineer didn't dance, just sat there like a bored bonfire. He had paid for the best engineering. The finest upgrades. And this, this tree swinging biped said he could add twenty percent performance. And he would. No one other than another human would understand how, but it would happen.

"I am grateful for your efforts. Your bonus will, of course, reflect that. However, I have news. The weapons array has been declared off limits to humans. Apparently allowing humans access to ship weapons is now a war crime. Please leave them alone."

Eells shrugged. The weapons on this tin can were ones he could build as a child's science project. He wondered which one of his people had taken an interest and why. Generally they didn't like Xenos seeing them play with guns. They got nervous.

"Are we expecting hostiles? Did I miss a briefing?"

The captain had learned about human curiosity. Tell them before they find out. And they will find out. Long ago he had watched a human engineer corrupt a kitchen appliance to find "sports results." In the middle of a war. In a deadzone. And it worked. "One of the edge systems had declared all foreign traders to be spies. Don't worry; we are far from them. One of your colleagues was attacked and, well, the reports are classified, but she reacted badly. They are still recovering survivors. Of the system, not the ship."

Eells raised his eyebrows at that. His heat signature shifted. "Perhaps, Captain, I could have a look at the transporters? I feel they lack a little something?"

Reid relaxed, his tail unwinding from the chair. He had expected protests. Excellent. Finally a human that understood.

"Of course; all other systems are yours! Just not weapons."

"Fine by me."

Eells was deep in thought when he grabbed a coffee in the canteen. Why the transporters? Well, it was a delivery system. He reckoned he could play about with this one. Best not mention it to the captain.

The following day, Reid's second officer called his office.

"Captain, the human is making the warning noises. It's rebuilding the aft transporter. It just showed its teeth when I asked what it was doing. Apparently you authorized an upgrade."

"Stars protect us. Which noise? Is it the 'humming' or the 'whistling'?"

"Both, sir."

The Captain definitely wasn't running to find his engineer, but it was close.

Eells was deep in thought as he disassembled the transporter. That was the problem with Xeno tech. They had a good idea, then a generation later they had another great idea and slapped that on top. After a few generations, the thing was a mess. A lot of Mankind's reputation for genius was simply digging right back to the beginning and integrating things properly. The captain arrived to find Eells deep into his transporter, parts carefully piled around him. The human didn't even notice his arrival. It was making the "humming" sound.

No one was quite sure why they did it. Some xenobiologists maintained that it had evolved to warn people that something dangerous was underway and that you should stay back. Reid certainly felt like that. "Engineer Eells, may I ask what you are doing? We will need this transporter shortly. If you dismantle it, I cannot get the ore into the hold. We will lose days of work."

Eells poked his head out of the machine. "Hello Captain, didn't hear you come in. Don't worry, she'll be up and running before we hit the asteroid belt. I'm just boosting the range and capacity a little. When they designed these, they didn't have the power available that we have now. Should speed up collection by maybe forty percent."

Reid was torn. That was a massive bonus to the ship, but it meant yet another system that only a human would dare touch. "Isn't boosting it that much dangerous?"

Eells waved his face about in a way that Reid recognized as indication of a negative. "No, Captain. In fact it's safer now. I'm upgrading as I go along. All the fields will be harmonized for once. I can give you a much narrower focus; means we can grab a lot more of the small stuff. Should improve our take as well as our speed."

The Captain let out a long hiss. This was how the humans had taken over. One system at a time. With these improvements, his shareholders would be ecstatic. And everyone would try and match the improvements. So everyone would need a human, and it would cost him more to keep his one.

"Commendable, Engineer Eells. Can I expect the same from the forward teleporter before we begin?"

The human waved his face about again. This was the positive.

"Aye Captain, there or thereabouts."

Now resigned to it, the Captain simply said, "Carry on then. Let me know when you are finished."

Eells continued his work, reflecting that sometimes people, of all types, didn't see the obvious simply because they were used to normal. Not allowed on weapons? Here he was playing with field generators designed to rip entire asteroids apart. You could keep your antique plasma cannon. The captain now had something much better if they needed it. One day he might even tell him.

The Shahetow moved back to base two weeks early, with full holds and a happy crew. Eells had tuned the engines to his satisfaction and refined his work on the transporters.

The improvements gave Reid another advantage when it came to unloading the ship quickly. The crew picked up another major bonus as docking fees were cut. The other mining ships started asking about it. They were told to ask the human. Many drinks later, Eells was stumbling back to the ship again.

He had given his fellow humans a description of the upgrades, as well as a quiet word about its other uses, if they ever needed it. Normally the friendly competition between the engineers would have kept his mouth shut, or at least wearing a big shit-eating grin while they tried to figure out how he'd done it. But not this time; not when it might mean lives at risk. When it came to safety, all for one and one for all.

Meanwhile, out in the asteroid belt was a very disgruntled ship. The Retaz was unusual in that it didn't have a human on board. The engineers had blacklisted it years ago for smuggling and war profiteering. Hardscrabble mining was bad enough, but as the word filtered out of major improvements in the delivery of ore, the price began to fall.

The owner of the Retaz and its crew were an insectile race, who realized that this was going to cost them a lot of money. "It's the humans again," the crew complained. "Destroying our traditions! Our business is ruined. This ship is cursed!"

The captain knew his crew. He had scraped the barrel hiring them and they were an ugly bunch at the best of times. This was not the best of times. "Perhaps ... perhaps we should get a better ship," he told them. "One with these improvements. One with a human and a full hold." The crew went silent. It didn't take long to work out that the captain wasn't talking about buying a ship. This was piracy. One after another, they agreed.

"So be it. The next ship that comes out, we take. The Retaz might be a rubbish mining vessel but she still has the weapons from our smuggling days." You didn't need much stealth in the asteroid field. Just turn off the lights and stay off the comms. The Retaz waited.

Elsewhere, Eells had just finished putting the compulsory "Human Altered" signs on the transporters when the captain called. "Engineer Eells, your improvements have made a substantial contribution to our success. Thank you. I was wondering if you had any other ideas?"

Eells was surprised. The Captain had seemed reluctant to engage before. Perhaps his shareholders were pushing him. "Well, Captain, I'd like a really good look at the scanners. They look like they could do with some attention."

"Of course, whenever you wish. Your help is appreciated."

Reid ended the call. Since his last run, every other captain, his shareholders and customers had showered him with praise. And money. Apparently letting the human adjust the transporters had been an act of commercial genius. Now they wanted to see what else he would do. So be it. He was resigned to dying in whatever disaster resulted. At least the human couldn't blow the ship up using the scanners.

Eells happily pulled the array apart. His suspicions were right. Some of these sensors were older than him. He enjoyed the EVA; always nice to get out of the ship and see space properly. He knew some of the crew found it creepy and weird that humans would happily spend time on the outside of a moving ship, but he regarded it as a perk.

Over the weeks, he fabricated and installed something more suitable. Then he moved to the bridge and began rebuilding the scanner console. He added a few more "just in case" functions, buried in the diagnostic menus.

He was just calling the captain to tell him the job was finished when the weapons array exploded.

The captain called him first.

"What have you done! I told you to stay away from the weapons! What lunacy have you inflicted on us now?"

Eells tried to explain that he had not touched the weapons, but the captain wasn't listening, so he just turned the sensors back on. On the screen he could clearly see the ship that must have fired on them.

"Captain, we are under attack."

"What, who would attack us?"

Eells watched the unknown ship close the distance. Apparently it still believed that it remained hidden.

"I don't know Captain, but I'm watching them approach."

Reid ran to the bridge.

The crew watched as the ship came closer. Eells activated a couple of the new functions. The enemy ship was suddenly identified as he pinged their backup transponder. He guessed anyone with evil intentions would turn off the primary one. Half the ships didn't even know that a backup existed in all civilian craft. Idiots.

"It's the Retaz. Anyone know it?"

The Captain hissed. "Yes. Roughneck scum. That's a smuggling ship; we can't outrun it."

Eells wasn't sure about that, but he preferred to fight anyway. No one was going to shoot up his ship for free.

Captain Reid was seething. If he was forced to surrender his ship, that was it. He would never get a Command again. No weapons and not enough speed to escape. The policy was clear. Evacuate the ship and run, hoping that no one died. He turned to the crew. "Begin the evacuation. We must abandon ship before they arrive."

Eells was astonished. What did the captain think he was doing? He had no plans on spending weeks in an escape pod, hoping that these fuckers didn't shoot them out of space. "Captain, I need to do some urgent repairs to the transporters." Take a fucking hint, Captain.

Reid stared at the human. He must have lost his mind. "What are you talking about?"

"Captain, I need to recalibrate the transporters immediately. Then you might find evacuation unnecessary. Bearing in mind that humans aren't permitted to use weapons, remember."

Slowly Reid realized. The mad human had a plan. He must always have had a plan, ever since Reid had forbidden him access to the weapons array. He couldn't order a human to fight. But he could let him use everything else.

"Of course, Engineer Eells. Feel free to do as much … recalibration as you like."

"Thank you, sir."

On the screen, a red line appeared between the two ships. Eells took over the transporter control and began aligning the aft and forward fields. He gently fed power from the engines until the fields stood at over four hundred percent of normal output. Slowly they reached out to the red line.

Reid watched. The human practically glowed with concentration. No wonder the galaxy didn't want them on weapons. He began to wonder what had happened in the edge system that had attacked a human engineer and her ship. No wonder it was classified. He imagined that if this worked, it would be classified too.

The Retaz approached the red line.

"Attention Shahetow, surrender or perish! You have no weapons and we can outrun you. Flee, and we will allow your emergency pods to leave. Oppose us and you will all die. Leave your human on board."

Eells looked up from the controls.

"Well, now it's personal. Fuck you assholes."

He watched as the enemy crossed the line. He waited until he was sure they were in range. Then he attacked.

The transporter fields ripped through the ship, tearing the engine apart. The ship crumpled under the assault. Then Eells retracted the fields, grabbing tons of ore from the hold. Once again the fields reached out, slamming the ore through the Retaz. And again. And again.

He looked levelly at Captain Reid. "Captain, the teleporters are calibrated. Our scanners seem to be picking up some wreckage. It looks like someone collided with an asteroid." Reid had never seen such a cold-blooded execution. Eells seemed unmoved by the carnage. What were these Humans, on every ship, in every station? Fixing, improving. Perhaps guarding.

"Thank you Eells, we will investigate the … accident and report it. It is unlikely anyone survived the impact."

"I'm sure you're right, Captain. I'll just go over and check. Just in case."

"Carry on, Engineer Eells. Don't forget to mark the scanner as 'Human Altered.'"

MIMICRY FOR FUN AND PROFIT
Mara Lynn Johnstone

When I signed up to be the only human on a ship full of tentacle aliens, I expected three things. The air would be unpleasantly damp. My crewmates would occupy spaces that I wouldn't think of, so I'd need to make sure I didn't step on anyone. And I'd get a reputation as the tall one who could reach high shelves without climbing them. While these were all true, I was surprised to have my voice, of all things, treated as a Special Talent.

It came up right away, when I met the captain and greeted her with a phrase in her own language. It was all I knew, and I thought it would be passed off as a thoughtful gesture. I'd practiced the phrase on the ride through the spaceport; my pronunciation was surely terrible. But since the language honestly sounded to me like a mix of squeaks and flatulence, I considered it a success that I could say it at all without dissolving into unprofessional giggles.

My masterful effort at keeping a straight face was met with goggle-eyed surprise that looked downright comical on a rusty-orange octopuslike alien. But the captain kept her cool, introducing me to the handful of crew-mates I'd be making deliveries with. The rest of the conversation was thank-fully in Galactic Standard.

They were impressed again an hour later when I reported a mysterious sound from the hover engine by imitating it: "Kind of a faint *whirr*, then a *screech-chunk*." Apparently this was amazing where they came from; who knew? I would have loved to introduce them to a parrot, and really blow their minds.

As entertaining as it was, my talent was just a passing curiosity as we made our rounds between planets. Something to joke about, a cure for boredom, a source of harmless pranks. ("Something chirped; is there a pest onboard the ship? There it is again!") But when we made our final delivery run, my human vocal cords got to do something far more important.

We were bringing construction materials to a newly-terraformed moon, a place staffed with busy robots and a few stressed-out organic types there to oversee everything. They were on a schedule to get ready for the inhabitants to arrive. Due to an error somewhere, they'd run short on a specific type of welding rod. Thanks to us, they got them in time. But they also had another problem.

"We caught some saboteurs," said Tavi the construction head, her antennae twitching uneasily. Her species was new to me, with a strong resemblance to an Earth beetle, all iridescent green and faceted eyes. Oddly pretty as bugs go, and just this side of creepy. Not that I would ever say so out loud. Especially when she was telling the captain about people trying to wreck her operation.

"Did they already do damage?" asked Captain Rominom. She stilled her orange tentacles in respect, paying polite attention.

"We suspect so," said Tavi. "They haven't admitted to anything, but there are traces of a certain plant in their cargo hold, which is known for spreading quickly. We fear they have placed some nearby, but..." She fidgeted, rubbing forelegs together. "I just can't spare the workers to look for it. If we knew where exactly to *send* the workers, they could remove the problem without losing us too much time, but not if they have to explore the entire area. Could we call upon you to do another task for us?"

Captain Rominom spread her tentacles wide. "But of course! For a fee."

They haggled while the rest of us waited in respectful silence. I took care not to draw attention, since I was by far the tallest here, and it would look bad if I bent down to whisper to a crewmate during negotiations. I definitely wanted to, though. Of the other four tentacular spacefarers, three did excellent observational humor, and one was an unexpected pun master. Fweeht, Nifitini, and Po all came from the same world. Jeremy came from a multicultural hub that gave him both a nontraditional name and a delightful way with words.

He was muttering something to Nifitini now, palest blue beside dark gray. If not for me, he would be the light-colored one who stood out among the rest of the crew. As it was, he was just one bundle of tentacles among many.

The captain wrapped up the conversation and waved for the rest of us to follow Tavi. The construction head scuttled around the corner to a bright courtyard where a little two-seater spaceship waited with its hold open. Tavi reached inside to grab a yellow leaf off the floor. She made sure we all got a good look at our quarry.

I could smell it from arm's length. Minty and powerful, like weaponized toothpaste. I didn't say anything, but a glance at my crewmates' wrinkled faces told me their opinion. Not just me, then. Good.

Tavi gave us directions to where the ship had been captured, and waved us on our way. She was a very busy iridescent beetle alien, with much to do.

"Onward, crew!" the captain declared, twining two tentacles together much like a human would rub their hands greedily. "Let's find some invasive plants."

It was a quick flight on a spaceship such as ours. In no time at all, we were walking among purple-green plantlife, looking for anything yellow.

No luck so far. We found lots of springy moss and giant fern things, growing on all sides of a landscape studded with natural rock pillars. I assumed they were natural, anyway. Who knew what the terraforming of this place had included. All I could say for sure was that it was nearly up to the standards of the high-end insectlike clientele, and that those folks had a neighboring clan who were still bitter about not claiming the place first.

I was thinking about bug alien politics when a tentacle as rigid as a safety bar brought me up short. Captain Rominom whistled a sharp sound of alert. She held the position, blocking me on one side and Fweeht on the other, while staring forward.

Something tumbled onto the path a few lengths ahead of us. It didn't look dangerous. Spotted and brown, fluffy, equipped with half a dozen limbs and no coordination. Tavi had stressed the fact earlier that all of the animals here were both small and harmless, so I didn't see what the captain was worried about. When a second one trotted over to the first, I was still mystified. They were a little weird-looking, what with the face tentacles, but who were we to care about that?

Then the big one stepped out from behind a rock and roared at us.

Oh, I thought. *Oh no.*

The crew scrambled in panic while I froze. None of us carried weapons. Why would we, looking for plants in a place sworn to be safe? Even our delivery ship wasn't armed. We were no match for this kind of predator: the size of a hovercar, with toothy mandibles and tentacles that seemed designed to horrify my human hindbrain. And it was clearly protecting its babies, which played around its ankles, meeping happily.

The captain shoved me forward.

"What—"

"Make the noises the little ones are making!" she said. "This is your time to shine!"

Oh. I swallowed. *I guess it is. Here goes nothing.* With a deep breath and what I hoped were calming hand gestures, I faced off with the terrifying thing and did my absolute best.

"Meep. Mew. Meer?"

It had stopped growling, and was watching in what looked like confusion. A shuffling noise behind me said that the rest of my crew had lowered themselves to an unobtrusive height, and were wriggling backwards to safety. Great idea.

"Meep meeeek." I sank into a crouch, hoping that I looked nonthreatening, instead of like I was ready to spring. The creature didn't attack. The babies remained oblivious, tussling in the moss and rolling forward to bump against my arm. I didn't move. Changed my noises a little to match their play fight. They ignored me.

The parent didn't. I'd been glancing down at the babies when it moved, so I jumped in surprise when an enormous paw appeared in my field of vision to bat the little ones further along the trail. They went happily, with renewed meeping.

Then before I could react, the big one was behind me, fastening its mandibles around a mouthful of my shirt. Breath on my neck, squirming tentacles, bristly whiskers; it was a miracle I didn't pee my pants. I found myself hauled off my feet by the alien tiger-thing, and dragged down the path like a particularly long kitten. I had to grab the front of my shirt to keep it from choking me. Even my best efforts left me gasping for breath.

Then the creature leapt straight up, and my vision grayed around the edges.

My senses returned as I lay on moss, under a fern, at the top of one of those pillars. The tiger had disappeared.

Where'd it go? I wondered. *Am I out of the way here, or — Ahh!* My vision was full of fur and tentacles as it sprang up to the top again.

I scrambled back against the fern. The creature set one of the babies next to me, then jumped back down.

Oh. Oh dear.

I wasn't food, or I would have been mauled instead of carried gently. Nope. I was family.

The communicator at my hip chirped, and I scrambled for it before the tiger came back.

The captain's voice came through with no preamble. "You have over-performed. Tell it to let you go."

"I don't know what the sounds mean!" I exclaimed. "I'm just copying the babies! And it might eat me if it thinks I don't belong here."

"Understood. We'll figure something out."

The tiger sprang into view again with the other cub in its mouth. I shut off the communicator before it got suspicious. To say I was uneasy about this would be an understatement.

In something of an anticlimax, Mama Tiger lay down in the shade of the fern and pawed at her babies to cuddle close. Including me. I ended up on my side in the fetal position with my head against a cub and my back against the alien tiger's belly, and I tried my hardest not to be *incredibly concerned*.

I waited. It was a long wait. Plenty of time to wonder how the saboteurs had gotten creatures this size into the hold of their tiny ship, and to wonder whether those minty leaves worked like catnip. Releasing this kind of predator here would certainly wreak more havoc than any invasive plant would.

I tried to listen for signs of a plan from down below, but I couldn't hear anything over the growling purr that Mama Tiger was making. And the sound of her licking the other cub. Picturing those mandibles, I dearly hoped that my crewmates would think of something before it was my turn.

They did. Oh bless them, they did, and it was brilliant. Inspired by me.

A faint chattering sound from ground level caused all three of the beasties to lift their heads like dogs hearing the dinner bell. It sounded again, and Mama Tiger stood with a chirrup that I took to mean "Stay here." She flowed off the edge to land far below with more stealth than something so big should be allowed.

The chattering stopped, then started again from farther away. It sounded like there were a few of them, whatever they were.

Then there was Mama again, apparently having decided that this was the perfect time for a hunting lesson. She grabbed one baby, came back for the other, then for me. I took a deep breath and clutched my collar. She was gentle. It was still terrifying. She clung to the side of the pillar and slid down awkwardly instead of leaping headfirst, which I deeply appreciated. I would have broken approximately all of my bones otherwise.

As it was, I made it to the bottom with only a few bumps and a wild heart rate. The creature let me go with a pat urging me forward. She chirruped at the babies and trotted off, her movements transitioning into the silent stalking posture of catlike creatures everywhere.

The babies bounced after her. I kept close, bending over a little and feeling silly. Did I dare run? Was this the plan? She would hear if I tried to use the communicator.

Speaking of which, I thought in surprise as something caught my eye. A comm unit like mine lay at the side of the path, at roughly the spot where the chattering sound had come from. *Oh, I'm starting to get it. Clever crewmates.* I made a note of where it was and hurried along.

The ferns and pillars were close together here. Close enough to hide a family of tentacle tigers earlier, and some sort of trap now. I kept my eyes open as we approached a corner to the sound of a chorus of prey animals.

Mama Tiger crouched, listened, and peered around the edge. She twitched her tail (which was split in two; how did I not notice the tentacle tail before?) then crept forward in utter silence. It was frightening to watch. The cheerful clumsiness of the two cubs balanced it out, though. They crawled around the corner, and I brought up the rear.

I saw what was very clearly a tarp thrown over something large, about the size of the wire cage we'd been hauling bricks in. A slit was cut in the tarp, with the flap pinned back over the doorway. All I could see inside was darkness. I heard the chattering of prey, and I was pretty sure I smelled meat on the breeze.

Is that the chicken I was saving? Oh, fine. A good cause and all.

I couldn't see any tentacular crewmates, but I had no doubt they were hiding close by. Mama Tiger was easing her way up to the door. I walked as quietly as I could, grateful for the moss. She reached the entrance, sniffed thoroughly, then crawled inside.

I was starting to get alarmed at the lack of a visible plan, then a dark orange tentacle emerged from under the tarp to wave at me. The captain was waiting at the door.

Got it. I meeped softly and scooped up one of the babies, setting it inside after Mama. The other one went just as tamely. I heard chewing sounds from inside the cage.

Then I heard an almighty CLANG as the door shut in my face, followed by the captain jumping down to check the lock, and other tentacled crewmates appearing from all directions. Mama Tiger roared and pawed at the door, but it was solid. I stood well back anyway.

"Good job, team!" said Captain Rominom. "That couldn't have gone better."

I tried to laugh off my speeding heart. "It was a little dicey there at the beginning."

"You were amazing!" the captain told me, while the rest of the crew backed her up. "We would have been eaten without you, instead of alive and many credits richer. Do you know what the going rate is for a healthy family of SneakTeeth?"

"Is that what they're called?" I said, still taking deep breaths. "Can't say I disagree with the name."

Beside the captain, Jeremy did an intricate tentacle flail. "You've never heard of them? Did you imitate their calls on the *first try?*"

"Um, yes? It wasn't that hard," I said. "Kinda like a housecat."

Captain Rominom held up a tentacle in declaration. "Double shares of the bounty for our crewmate of the hour!" There was unanimous approval at that, along with the tentacle alien equivalent of applause.

Since tentacles don't make a proper clapping sound, this meant a rousing chorus of blowing raspberries. I grinned for two reasons. I pretended it was just for one, and thanked them humbly.

We kept the tarp in place while ferrying the cage back to the ship. That cage had been on the hoversled this whole time; more good thinking on the captain's part. Po ran to get her communicator and make sure we hadn't left anything else behind. Jeremy filled me in on the relevant details about this particular species, which was endangered and difficult to relocate.

"I don't think anyone's tried impersonating one of their young before!" he said. "This might be the start of a new trend."

I shuddered. "Just don't ask me to do that again. Noises yes, being dragged up a cliff, no."

"I thought your species liked climbing things," he said far too innocently.

"That was *not* climbing. Climbing involves getting there under my own power, with no teeth at my neck."

"Picky picky."

We made our triumphant return to the compound, and Tavi met us outside, having heard the news on our way over. She got a timid look at the creatures in the cage (standing back and flinching when Mama Tiger snarled). After taking pictures of them to show her bosses to account for the expense, she paid Captain Rominom an amount that left her *very* pleased. We said our goodbyes and headed for space.

When I first lifted the tarp to feed them, I was greeted with a chorus of growls. In response, I began setting chunks of synth-beef through the bars, and did my best imitation of the growling purr that Mama Tiger had made up in her makeshift nest.

A face full of mandibles and feline curiosity appeared at the bars. I waggled my fingers at her and held out more food.

The babies pounced on the first pieces, meeping happily. I purred louder.

Mama Tiger reached her face tentacles gently through the bars, and took a piece from my hand. I wanted to scritch her scary kitty head, but held out more food instead.

Maybe with the next meal, I thought. *Plenty of time to make friends.*

THE LANGUAGE OF EMOTION
Bill Rogers

The landing pod plunged into a downdraft. Whitemane squealed in terror. "Belt, may you break your legs in gopher holes!" he said, forming the words with the silent, tiny fingertip motions of his herd's secret language, Smallsign.

"There is no reason to curse us. How did we offend?"

The little ship shuddered and then rolled nearly inverted as the turbulence got even worse. Whitemane snorted and rolled his eyes. Their whites showed all the way around. His ears were folded back and his lips trembled. "How? *How* did you offend? You incompetent meat-eating idiotic machines! You're trying to kill us! Stop trying to crash this pod. *How did you offend us?* Gods, how could even computers be as stupid as you!?"

In the corner of his eye, Belt signed back. Belt used the full-size gestures of Language, of course. There was no reason for Belt to use Smallsign. Belt projected its persona to Whitemane's eye via a tiny mirror on the equitaur's bridle. Nobody but Whitemane could see it.

"It's no surprise that we-the-computer-Belt are stupid. After all, you-the-stallion-Whitemane programmed us. We might have been geniuses if others had done the job."

Whitemane stopped trembling and perked up his ears. "That's a joke. We-the-stallion-Whitemane never programmed you for humor. Are you sure you haven't developed intelligence?"

"How would we know? Could you prove that you yourselves are intelligent?"

"And now philosophy! You surprise us. Are things really going well? Will we live?"

"Calm your fears. You are not alone. Our trajectory is perfect. We have gone subsonic and are mere minutes from landing. Might we ask why, if you fear them so, you agreed to work for the Hukai? It seems illogical."

"They pay well, and quickly. They might enjoy killing us, but they'd much prefer to just stay away from us." He shuddered. "That's good. They are so ugly!"

"You risk your lives just for money?"

"Our herd needs it."

"We are only computers, but we think it is unfair that you must lead the wolves away when you yourselves get nothing for your courage. Tell them-the-mare-Herdleader to risk their own lives, and leave us to browse in peace."

"We will be granted our own lands, should we survive this."

"Ah! Congratulations! That explains much. Your mare-friends are worth the risk. We land in twenty heartbeats. There is a strong crosswind; this may be rough. Brace yourselves."

The buffeting let up a bit. Then everything went silent. Whitemane took a deep breath and started to relax. And the landing craft crashed into the ground, an impact nearly hard enough to break his ribs. He screamed, a horse's high squeal of terror.

"Calm yourselves! We're down and safe."

"Down!?" Whitemane gasped. "But we still accelerate ... No, that's right. Truly, fear is the killer of minds. It shames us that we-the-stallion-Whitemane forgot this world's excessive gravity. Won't our hosts compensate for it? Surely even the Hukai wouldn't expect us to work when we weigh so much we can't even stand?"

"Local gravity is about twice our standard," the machine said. "They are compensating. Calm yourselves, they come!"

The pod rocked a bit, and rocked again. The gravity faded to normal. A few moments later the little ship's cabin split in half and swung open.

Whitemane rose to his four hooves and blinked, astonished by the sheer normalcy of his surroundings.

He faced a brightly-lit, grass-carpeted habitat colored in soothing greens and blues. At first glance, it resembled the sort of cheap but acceptable quarters a traveler might rent for a night or two. But everything about it screamed that none of the Herd People had designed this place.

For one thing, there was the art collection. Even the most modest room needed a few choice artworks to calm the soul; these should be arranged in harmony with the lines of the architecture and the views of the gardens outside, with a care that made the arrangement as important as the art itself. But these rooms were cluttered with a haphazard assortment of inferior pieces that seemed to have been dumped at random.

Speaking of views of the gardens, there weren't any. Of course the Hukai would not have provided a habitat large enough for even a modest meditation garden, but Whitemane had expected some holographic fake windows at least. These rooms had only one small window. It looked out into darkness.

He stepped out of the landing pod and around an inferior sound-garden, typical of those found at bus stops. It sat incongruously in the middle of the floor. There was no breeze to turn its sails, no flowing water piped in to contribute sounds of nature and to operate the heavier chimes. That was a pity. He was very afraid; he could have used some soothing music just now, to help him meditate away his fears and to mask the roar of the methane wind blasting past outside.

Stepping over an abstract sculpture of cheaply-synthesized marble, the kind one might see in a boiler room, he approached the window. Below it was a video display screen, showing an image of a horse-headed centauroid like himself. Cartoon-like in its simplicity, it stood square on its four hooves with its arms hanging limp at its sides. It also faced Whitemane square-on.

Whitemane twitched his fingers. "They seem to have tried to provide decent living quarters. Yet their translator-picture faces us directly. Estimate please: Is this threat to attack us deliberate, or are the Hukai merely ignorant of our etiquette?"

"Insufficient data. We suggest you speak to them."

Whitemane snorted in amusement, even as his stomach clenched with fear. "That's useless advice! What else could we possibly do?" But since there were no other options, Belt was right. Shrugging his shoulders, standing facing somewhere off to the side of the window as was polite, Whitemane switched from Smallsign to Language.

"We have arrived as you requested. We are ready to work."

Lights flashed in the darkness outside, glowing from a Hukai's body itself. They illuminated it enough that Whitemane could see its ugliness. It had six eyes and as many legs. It was a huge vomit-colored monster of a bug. The sight of it almost made him jump out of his skin.

As its lights flashed, the cartoon image on the screen made the signs of speech. "You are being Whitemane, signal archaeologists wide known?"

He tapped a hoof on the floor and bobbed his head. "We are."

"Retainer twenty thousand standard moneys as agreed being in account you now. Habitat adequate for you surviving?"

"Living conditions are adequate for mere survival."

"Atmosphere storm strong, being danger. In distress press red button wall. Landing pod being safety capsule if breach. Second shelter capsule being in back sanitary room passage, brown doorway."

"Your concern for our safety touches our hearts. What do you want? What was so critical you couldn't contract us over hyperlink?"

"Alien transmission duration passage of time twelve hour six-tenths total, broken several pieces, plus repeatings. You translate."

"What sort of transmission?"

"Standard Class One radio, being highly in frequency. We fear because it being beamed to us, aliens know of our location. You will understand and tell if making-transmit creatures being threat, being not threat, to Hukai."

Whitemane snorted, trying to force down his growing terror of being trapped inside this tiny space, deep in this poisonous atmosphere, dealing with a species whose cruelty was legendary because they valued no life— not even *their own*. Dealing with creatures who had so little concept of beauty that they denied it even existed. He must remain calm, he must remain professional! He forced himself to understand what the bug had said, and to form a logical reply.

"Perhaps the aliens are a threat to all Treaty species. The aliens may have beamed their signal to us, not to you."

"If threatening you, you worry for yourselves. Hukai being worry for Hukai only. You will understand transmission?"

"We can't tell you whether the beings who sent the transmissions are a threat. We may be able to tell you the meaning of the transmission, but you have to decide for yourselves whether the senders threaten you."

Belt signed in the corner of his eye. "Your heart rate and blood chemistry indicate approaching panic attacks. You should breathe deeply and close your eyes for a moment. They-the-stallion-Lawgiver said: Emotion destroys our minds. Fear makes us all fools, anger makes us all killers. We will dream that we walk in green pastures. We will think on things of Mind and Beauty. The fear and the anger shall—"

Whitemane shook his head and Smallsigned back, desperately. "We need no sermons! Stop speaking! Put your hands at your sides and keep them there! Do not distract us!"

The bug hesitated for a few moments, flashing away. Other shapes stirred in the murk beyond the glass, lights flashing on them too; other bugs, a rolling swarm of things horrible beyond belief, surrounding him. Surrounding him everywhere. There was no escape at all. There was nowhere he could run. His heart raced. He couldn't see the rest of his surroundings, he saw only the roiling mass of insects. He fought to control his breathing.

The bug at the window seemed unaware of his growing terror, or perhaps it just didn't care. "Acceptable," the picture signed. "You will understand transmissions quick, before eight days, fee five million standards. Much quick! Your failure being unpleasant you."

Whitemane trembled. He felt his ears fold back against his skull, felt his lips tense to bare his teeth. He shifted his hooves until he faced the window directly. Belt's persona signed desperately in the corner of his eye, something about stress hormones, neural overloads, and not doing anything stupid, but he didn't feel like paying attention.

"We can do our best. We-the-stallion-Whitemane are the best signal-archaeologists in Treaty Space, in the entire Cluster. If we can't do the job for you, nobody can. If we fail, you need not pay us."

The bug flashed its lights. "No. You accepting contract, you being not fail. You will understand transmissions, yes yes! Before eight days for five million standards."

"We can't do that," Belt signed. "Not enough time!"

Whitemane felt his heart pound. He could barely hold his head up, he was so frightened. He saw his reflection in the window, jittering on its hooves, stepping forward in the most threatening posture possible, making signs, promising something insane as he, the real Whitemane, looked on in helpless horror.

"We will crack the signals in two days, for twenty million standard."

"Accepted. Being failure not!" The image on the video screen went motionless.

Whitemane fell to his knees. He shook. His surroundings seemed to darken as he nearly fainted.

"Well, now you have done it," Belt signed. "We tried to tell you to calm yourselves, but you would not listen. There is no way out except to solve their problem. We suggest you get to work."

He panted and raised his head again. "We have been cornered-mad!"

"Do you think we do not know? They should give us, your computers, drugs to knock you down when stress hormones approach the level of insanity. Your pulsebeat and blood chemistry were as if wolves were tearing out your throat. But stop trembling. Breathe deep, think on things of Beauty and of the Mind, and get to work. Did you have any ideas when you told the bugs we would have an answer in two days, or did you just rear up in panic?"

Whitemane took a deep breath and picked himself up off the floor. The carpeting had spared him from any injuries; good. "It was panic. But if we thought anything, it was that a signal from a species primitive enough to use radio should be simple. Any encryption they might have used will be as rudimentary as the senders' technology. If we can't understand them in two days, we probably can't understand them at all."

"True. We can hope that your stupidity was not quite as stupid as it seemed."

"Also, the Hukai said these signals were beamed toward our star cluster. That means the aliens sent them to us deliberately. There's no reason for them to do such a thing unless they want us to understand their message. Therefore, the signals should be their version of plaintext — no encryption at all. Let's find out. What is the form of the first message?"

"Binary data. 1,679 values, at a carrier wave frequency of 1.47 gigacycles per heartbeat."

"The Fountain Frequency. They send their signals to us at the frequency defined by water. That could be coincidence, but it likely means they're based on carbon, water, and free oxygen, as we are. What else? If they meant their signal to be understood, they would have used some obvious mathematical trick to make it easy for us to decode. What's the numeric significance of 1,679?"

"Analyzing. Results. 1,679 is the product of two prime numbers, 73 and 23."

"That old trick again! It's probably a rectangular matrix; either 73 units wide by 23 high, or vice-versa. Show it to us."

In the corner of his eye, Whitemane saw Belt's persona pull a scroll out of midair and unroll it for him. The patterns on it were interesting indeed. Nodding, he got to work. Anything was better than worrying about what the Hukai would do to him, when he failed to fulfill this impossible contract.

*   *   *   *   *

Out of all the clutter of artworks in these rooms, the little bronze statuette he'd found hidden behind a particularly hideous bit of artificial topiary was the only good thing. It was more than just "good"; it was a miracle.

It was a simple and elegant little figurine of a female race-dancer, on her belly on the ground, holding an injured foreleg. It had to be one of the sculptor Spindrift's race-dancer series, masterpieces of art that were all the more remarkable because they found beauty in the raucous, passions-infested world of a mere physical contest. He'd seen other figurines in the series on display in museums. Here he could not only see one, he could touch it.

It was a work he didn't recognize. It might be a lost work, unknown at home, unseen by any of the Herd People for hundreds of years. And the subject matter was unique.

Others in the series told stories of pride, action, and triumph. This race-dancer was different. He could feel her pain, her defeat, the tears in her eyes, and yet the sculptor had given her dignity and beauty. Perhaps more beauty than any of the others … She went straight to his heart in a way the Lawgiver wouldn't have approved.

What a wonder! And what stories this little statuette could have told. Surely, there was tragedy in it. How many good people must have died for this masterwork to have fallen into the hands of the Hukai, who were in all of Treaty Space the species least likely to understand it?

"Yet that is not the greatest wonder," Whitemane signed slowly.

"What are you trying to tell us?"

"We apologize." Whitemane shrugged and tried to bring himself back to the job at hand, even as his free hand still caressed the little statue. "Our calming exercises had us lost in contemplation. We found ourselves struck with astonishment, thinking about what endures and what does not.

"All these things we build, all the works of art like this masterpiece in my hands, all the great buildings, all the events of history; the lifespans of these are nothing compared to that of a simple radio beam. Did these strange creatures know, when they sent their transmission into space, that they might be creating their civilization's longest-lasting artifact? Think on it: If this signal truly was beamed from its most likely point of origin, the Neighbor Galaxy, it's been on its way to us for over ten thousand standard years. Perhaps as much as thirty or forty thousand."

"We are computers, and you did not program us for wonder. And yet even we can recognize that this information is exceptional."

"Have we decoded the message completely?"

"We cannot tell you. We still do not know whether the central image is a picture of the senders' body form, or another binary number. But probability is high that our interpretation is accurate enough to satisfy the Hukai."

"Now we know much of the aliens," Whitemane signed slowly, musing. "As we suspected, they're water and carbon-based oxygen breathers. They tell us they come from the third planet of their solar system. There are enormous numbers of them. They sent us this message using a radio dish; we'd have known that anyway, of course.

"We don't understand their biochemistry, but it appears the aliens might have a typical long-chain genetic molecule. As it seems to be a representation of a double helix, probabilities are high that it's one of the DNA or RNA variants. That should reassure the Hukai. These aliens aren't methane-breathers. They wouldn't want Hukai worlds." He shuddered as another blast of the eternal gale outside rocked the habitat, roaring. "Who would?"

"Perhaps the Hukai are eager for war. War against a species not advanced enough to resist them."

"We-the-stallion-Whitemane believe the Hukai only want survival. Knowledge, beauty, and wonder seem lost on them; fortunately, the so-called 'glory' of conquest seems to be lost on them also."

"Perhaps. Speaking of survival, your fatigue and stress chemicals are reaching dangerous levels. You should sleep."

"But we still have most of the messages to decipher!"

"We are your expert systems. We have already determined most of the remaining messages are two- and three-dimensional matrices, based on multiples of prime numbers, as the first message was. We can apply your methods to decode most of this material while you sleep. Only the last message seems to be beyond us; a continual sine wave with some tiny variations in frequency. That will require your full attention. You should be well-rested when you begin work on it."

"We should sleep, then. But we are afraid!"

"Courage! The herd goes with you. You are not alone."

That was a lie! But Belt was almost as good as a person, and Belt was right about Whitemane's fatigue. His legs were about to tremble right out from under him. Bobbing his head, Whitemane walked to his cushions and settled down to rest.

*   *   *   *   *

"Have you been analyzing the last message in background while we finished the others?"

"You ordered us to. Why then ask? Of course we did."

"Have you found any hints on how to crack it?"

"No."

"Try a Class 6 cipher. The aliens like prime numbers; start a substitutional key based on the lowest primes and work your way up."

"A cipher on what? How? We cannot even determine the digital encoding of this signal! There must be bits of data, but we cannot detect them. The signal is merely a constant carrier wave, centered around a single frequency."

"Then it has no meaning. Yet the Hukai thought it did. They included it with the other transmissions. They must have determined that it contains some data."

"We-the-computer-Belt cannot detect any."

"Analyze the signal in detail."

"We can detect no binary data. We repeat, the signal is just a carrier wave. Its only property of interest is that the frequency shifts by a tiny percentage. The frequency shift is not consistent with 'Doppler' shift or any other natural cause. The frequency shift appears to be random. However, the entire pattern of frequency shifts repeats itself exactly each ten minutes. The pattern of frequency shifts must therefore be the message. Yet we analyze the shifts, and find no digital pattern to correspond with them in any meaningful way."

Time was slipping away, and he had no ideas. It was too much for Whitemane. "We are going to die here. We will fail, and the Hukai will collapse this habitat on us. We'll be crushed like a mouthful of soft grain. Belt, record everything we have done here. Record to our mare-friends that we love them, and would have had them be our harem for life, had the gods allowed. Our regrets to the herd for failing in our duties to them. Put it in your permanent storage, multiple redundant copies. Use your disaster-hardened memory."

"We comply. But why?"

"If we are to die, we would like something of us to remain. Perhaps when we die your memory will survive. Perhaps the Hukai will send it home, or someone else will find it some day." He looked down at the bronze figure of the defeated race-dancer, still beautiful in her defeat. But a defeated race-dancer didn't face death at the hands of soulless methane-breathing bugs. His own destruction meant the statuette's too, most likely. That hurt; that brought the approaching doom to him with a clarity he had never felt before.

"You are cornered-mad again. What are the chances such a message could ever reach people who cared? But take courage! There are still six hours. We have only the last message to decode."

Whitemane dropped the statuette, sprung to his hooves, and spun in circles, but there was nowhere to run. "It doesn't contain data!" he signed, his arms flailing wildly in a shout. "We wouldn't think it is a message at all, except it repeats itself again and again! We will die here, we will die!"

He threw himself on the cushions and curled himself into a tight ball again, trembling all over. His foamy sweat broke out all over his body as he shivered.

Suddenly Belt's projected image became two, and then four, and then he seemed to be surrounded by a great herd. Whitemane felt something wet spray onto his nose, and he could smell them; dozens of people, crowded close around him. Slowly, his trembling eased. He took deep breaths, calming himself.

"Thank you. Thank you for bringing us back."

"That is our most important function," Belt signed. The phantom herd vanished from his eyes as quickly as it had formed, leaving only Belt's persona signing to him. "Now, calm yourselves and think. Leave the last signal alone and consider other questions for a moment. The Hukai will want to know why the aliens sent this message directly to Treaty Space. How could they know we were here?"

Whitemane snorted. "Why worry? No species primitive enough to use radio could threaten us, or the Hukai."

"But they must have known we were here. How?"

Whitemane stood and started to spin again. Then he stopped, stock still. His eyes went wide in wonder.

"We have it. We understand! They didn't know."

"But they must have known! They beamed the signal to us!"

"No. Employ basic thought-discipline. The aliens couldn't know we were here. Logic, therefore, tells us they didn't."

"You have fallen into a paradox. How could they know to send it here, and not know to send it here, at the same time?"

"They *didn't* know," Whitemane repeated. "They played the odds and got lucky. We know, mad as it seems, that they wanted to send a radio signal to announce themselves to aliens. With their crude technology, concentrating all power into a narrow beam was the only way they could project a powerful signal far enough out into the sea of stars for anybody to hear. Since they weren't starfarers, as far as they knew each star they saw had an equal probability of harboring civilization. Given that level of knowledge, where was their best probability of success?"

Belt pondered for a moment. Its clock speed was so fast that the hesitation was probably for effect more than anything else. "Given that the probability of success was equal for each star, logic suggests they would have sent their signal toward the highest concentration of stars they could see."

"Which, if they *are* in the Neighbor Galaxy, would have been here. This globular cluster. Treaty Space."

"Extraordinary! I estimate a high probability your analysis is correct. But why would they have announced themselves to a hostile universe?

Were they such warriors they were sure they could defeat any comers? If so, the Hukai are right to fear them."

"Perhaps they thought interstellar war was impossible. It would be impossible, or nearly so, if the speed of light were the unbreakable barrier that most primitive races believe it to be. Thinking nobody could attack them, they wouldn't see any danger in drawing attention to themselves."

"We think you are right. You surprise us with your insights."

"We thank you. But why the multiple messages later? Why the attempts to jam each others' signals? That's insane! Refusing to send messages to the stars is prudent, but jamming one signal with another, stronger signal, just makes the senders more obvious."

"It hints at herd-madness."

"Yes. The poor aliens must have had conflict on their world. Different herds, each with its own philosophy of rule, so cornered-mad with fear that each herd could see only evil in the others. Until they became so full of herd-hatred that they would oppose each other in all things, just for spite. Even to the stupidity of trying to jam an interstellar message."

"That is a high order of insanity, but historical files include 1,733 known examples of such behavior. In 95% of known cases such herd-madness led to war, as on our homeworld before they-the-stallion-Lawgiver created the Herd of Herds. In 62% of known cases, it led to extinction."

"War…" Whitemane shuddered. "We dreamed of war last night. We dreamed of the screams of the dying. We dreamed of monstrous armored vehicles rumbling across the pasturelands, smashing everything. We heard fires roar and buildings collapse. We heard the mares of our harem we have yet to form, we heard our foals yet unborn, screaming as they died. We couldn't see anything, or smell; we only heard. It was only sound, but our hearts nearly burst at the terror of it. We wouldn't have believed mere sound could frighten us so."

In the corner of his eye, Belt's projection shifted side to side on its hooves. Its body language showed approximately Level 3 uncertainty. "We would try to interpret your dreams, but they are too strange. Sounds. A dream of only sounds. We have never encountered that. Your mind's deeper levels, and perhaps even the Herd-Souls themselves, must be trying to tell you something. There is truth there. Reach for it!"

Whitemane froze in place, staring at nothing. "Sounds," he signed.

"Yes, you dreamed of sounds. What of it?"

"Sounds! In the last signal the aliens sent, what is the frequency of the variations in the carrier wave?"

"We do not understand your question."

"You know the center radio frequency of the signal. The radio frequency shifts around this center by some amount. But for now, ignore how much the frequency of the carrier wave varies. Instead, count the number of variations themselves. How many different variations in frequency pass by per heartbeat?"

"Give us one moment … Done. The changes in frequency occur at different rates, varying from 10 to approximately 22,000 per heartbeat."

"We think we sense light in the forest. What if the last message is more primitive than we could have imagined? What if it's analog?"

"Then there is no way we can decode it."

"If it *is* analog, there's nothing *to* decode! 10 cycles to 20 kilocycles per heartbeat covers much of our own range of hearing, which is not unusual for creatures our size. If the variations pass at an audio frequency, they may in fact represent an audio signal. Assume this is so. On the hypothesis that this signal represents a sound wave, do you have the means of demodulating it?"

"It should be possible."

"Do it."

"Referencing archaeological library: Obsolete communications, subcategory analog signals. Analyzing … Programming to digitally simulate a modulated-frequency signal detector circuit from the Sixth Dynasty.

Altering design to accommodate the observed carrier frequency and signal bandwidth. Calculating … Debugging … Ready."

"Execute."

Exotic sounds, alien and marvelous and musical, filled the habitat. Whitemane froze in place, his eyes wide with wonder, as he heard the gift the aliens had sent into the darkness of space.

"Play it again."

Belt did.

"Again."

"No. Your life-signs indicate that this signal is causing you to experience dangerously strong emotional responses, in previously unknown patterns. Does this signal disable you? Is it overwhelming you and making you cornered-mad? Is it a weapon?"

He shook himself. "No, not a weapon. We understand it. We understand!"

"Then we suggest you prepare your report for the Hukai. They come soon."

Whitemane took a deep breath. Reluctantly, he tapped the floor with his hoof and bobbed his head.

"Yes. They can never comprehend it. Yet we must try to explain it to them."

"We are ready to record your findings."

"No. We will give our findings to the bugs directly, by sign-of-hand."

"Is that wise?"

"Play the signal again … No, it's not wise, but we must do it."

Again the music played. The methane wind rocked the habitat, the darkness beyond the window held terror, but he was unaware of these things. He let the sounds carry his soul away from this place, as he decided what to have Belt check, what to analyze and have Belt analyze, and what to tell the bugs.

He stooped low to pick up the fallen statuette, the race-dancer who was beautiful in her defeat. He stroked her bronze nose. "It's all right," he whispered. "We understand it all."

* * * * *

Something moved in the murk. The cartoon of a person on video display came alive. "It being two days, and fulfillment of contract being due. Tell your understanding," it signed.

"Our computer is now transmitting our translation of every message but the last."

The bug paused half a minute. "Correct," the image signed. "Our understanding is it being same. Tell understanding last message."

Rage gripped him. He was at the glass, baring his teeth, rearing to strike it with his forehooves, before he knew how he'd gotten there. The bug outside flinched back, as if it were about to run away.

Whitemane screamed. He spun in a circle, three times around, grinding his teeth, spittle flying from his mouth. Somehow he forced himself to a stop, although every muscle in his body ached with rage, with the need to lash out.

"You pack of meat-eaters! You understood all but the last message, but you made us waste time translating them all? *In the name of the Herd-Souls and the nine hells, **why**!?*"

"Data redundancy check. Being need to know you understand. You understand goodly. Now tell understanding last message. Transmit."

Whitemane took a deep breath and turned to face not quite toward the glass. His rage faded away, replaced by a strange kind of pity. The poor, sad Hukai! They were as ugly inside as they were on the outside, and there was absolutely nothing they could do about it.

"We understand the signal," he signed, with gentleness in the motions of his hands and arms. "But we can't transmit it as digital data, because it isn't that at all. It's a language of a type previously unknown, something completely new to us."

The giant cockroach stood dark for quite a long while. Finally it flashed a message. "Explain."

Whitemane twitched his fingers and his computer played the sound again. "This message confused us because it is analog, representing sound. It was too simple for us to understand, at first. The gods laugh at us for that. It was a message in sound, but sonic communication must have seemed natural to these aliens. It appears their form of speech may have been vocal."

"Sense of atmospheric vibration speak using are inferior oxygen-breather lifeforms, yes, sometimes."

"You are our clients. It would be impolite to contradict you. You can't hear sound yourselves, can you? We know, we know, you won't tell us anything about yourselves, but basic logic says a sense of hearing would be little use to beings who live in a constant methane gale."

The bug stood motionless and dark. The sounds of the alien transmission ended, and then started again from the beginning. Whitemane lowered his head, as if exhausted.

"We have analyzed these sounds for you. As you say, some oxygen-breathers have languages based on sounds their bodies make; languages of the standard type, conveying words, concepts, requests, and thoughts. Perhaps these aliens did, too ... but if so, this isn't it. It's a different kind of language altogether.

"These sounds were generated by artificial devices, made of various materials including wood, brass, stretched strings and organic membranes. The frequency spectrum shows this clearly. These sounds aren't speech from the throats of living creatures."

The sorrow in the alien sounds built. It was the agony of loss, given a language of its own, and it was the most lovely thing Whitemane had ever heard. It made him want to curl up and mourn all who had ever died, but the strong emotions didn't drive him mad the way the Lawgiver said emotions always did. Instead, they filled him with a sense of beauty and perfection. They drove his emotions to the heights of insanity, yet calmed him and gave him strength at the same time. That was good, because he had to keep talking. His life depended on it.

"There were perhaps a hundred or more sound-making tools, and tiny variations in their output indicate each was operated by a living being, not a machine. These aliens must have valued this activity as much as anything in life, to put so much effort into it.

"We think these aliens achieved something unique. They had not one language, but *two*. What they sent us here, the very last of their works, their greatest achievement, was unique in the galaxy. It is a story written in their second language, their Language of Emotion.

"Their other messages tell us about them. How they grew in number and power. Then they sent competing messages, and jammed each others' signals. That speaks of herd-madness. They lost themselves in struggles for herd dominance. That can only end in war."

"War?" The bug shifted.

"Yes, war. But you don't have to worry. Listen to this: Sorrow. Then they climb out of sorrow, triumph, but sink back into the sorrow again. Everything is cut off by a sorrow so powerful we are surprised that even you soulless bugs can't feel it. Everything ends.

"The message couldn't be clearer. They destroyed themselves. Their message says 'We have vanished, and we have taken with us everything we dreamed, everything we created, everything we were, and everything we could have been. Mourn us.'"

The bug flashed. There were other flashes in the murk. They went on for a long time.

Finally the image signed "Agents instructed fund transfer. Leave now."

"They're gone, bug. And whatever they were, they took great beauty out of the universe when they died."

"Worthless. Failed Second Great Test; built technology, yes yes, but destroyed selves with." Then the video screen went blank, and the monster behind the glass went away.

Whitemane spun. He grabbed the precious race-dancer figurine. Hugging it like a lost love, he leaped into the landing pod. If he tarried, they'd probably collapse the habitat on him, even though he'd given them everything they wanted, and more.

"Is your data safe?" he signed to Belt as he shoved the figurine into a storage chamber and grabbed for his shock harness.

"Redundant copies made. Launch in thirty heartbeats. Soon we will be back with our herd."

"Yes. But our-the-stallion-Whitemane's world has changed forever. The Language of Emotion has changed us."

"We cannot see how an alien language could have any such effect on you."

"No? We believe otherwise. Time will tell."

*   *   *   *   *

Ruff tapped on his data pad, getting the story down for the folks back home. He kept the pad turned so it hid his claws from this leaf-eater. Whitemane was a nice enough fellow, but predators' claws did tend to make the Herd People nervous.

"But why? Why would they send this last message to us? How could it possibly have helped them, when they faced their own extinction?"

Whitemane answered in handsigns, but the computer he wore around his waist translated these into sounds Ruff could understand. Whitemane's belt said, "When we-the-stallion-Whitemane thought we would fail in our contract, when we thought the Hukai would kill us, we told our computers to record our story in their permanent memory. We wanted some tiny chance to be remembered. It must have been the same with these aliens.

They sent us this, in the forlorn hope that somewhere, someday, somebody would hear it and remember them."

"That is a tremendous story. I'm astonished to discover that you, the Founder and Director of the Institute, didn't invent High Music yourself!"

"No; it was the gift of an alien race who went extinct twenty thousand years ago. We-all-of-us owe them much for the joy it brings us. We-the-stallion-Whitemane owe them far more.

"We owe them our meaning in life, our purpose, our beloved harem, our foals. We owe them this land, these mountains and streams, lands where we-the-stallion-Whitemane can run for a day and a half in any direction and never see anything that isn't ours. It is much to owe a race dismissed by our philosophers as worthless."

"I take it you don't believe in the Three Great Tests, then?"

"Philosophy simplifies the world for us; that is its purpose. But it simplifies things too much. When are real-world questions ever so clear-cut as philosophical ideals?

"We do think the Three Great Tests have *some* truth. They warn us of the dangers we all face, even now. Can we develop technology? Can we avoid destroying ourselves with it? Can we live in peace, or at least mutual indifference, with other starfarers? There are few questions more important than these.

"Yet by the standards of the Three Great Tests, the Hukai are worthy, even though they have never created anything good or beautiful. Even though their lives are mere *existence*, with no purpose, without even pleasure. And by the standards of the Great Tests, these poor dead aliens, who gave us so much, were worthless.

"We-the-stallion-Whitemane cannot accept the judgment of the Great Tests. We say life should be more than just ... brute survival."

Ruff tapped on his computer pad. "I agree with you."

"We knew you would. We saw you when the students played their new major-work this morning. We saw the light in your eyes. We know how high your hearts can soar."

At those words, Ruff felt a warmth he never would have thought he could feel toward a leaf-eater. He smiled. "It was wonderful. The emotions it raised took me to another world. It is what I imagined the First High Music itself must be like."

Whitemane turned his head and tossed his mane. "Have you never heard the First High Music? It is time you did. If you wish to understand, you must."

He twisted his upper torso to reach back and pull something from his left saddlebag: It was a complex device of steel strings and polished wood, and Ruff knew it was called a keyharp.

Whitemane braced the instrument between the shoulder of his right foreleg and his chin. He fingered the chord keys with his right hand, took up the plectrum in his left, and began to play.

The theme was simplicity itself; at first, just one note repeated again and again, unchanging for several measures. But beneath that one note, the alien composer had woven a progression of chords of impossible depth, as if trying to show that hidden in a single note, even in just one of the dozens of possible notes, there is more beauty than anyone could possibly know.

And then the melody moved, and built. Whitemane's computer began to produce the sounds of accompaniment as the equitaur himself followed the melody where it led; sorrow, triumph, the crashing, heartrending minor chord that ended it all.

Ruff could hardly breathe. Shaking his head, he finally whispered "It is … beautiful. Beautiful beyond words."

Whitemane put his keyharp back in his saddlebag and looked off across his lands for a long moment. "Yes. As lovely as anything we can ever hope to create. Feel their sorrow and think on it. Marvel as we do at how these creators can still touch us, after so much time, across such great gulfs of emptiness.

"We-the-stallion-Whitemane love the sounds of their last message. It makes us think about fate and the stars, and fills our hearts with a great joy and a great sorrow. In that lies the other message hidden in the transmission, the one we never told the Hukai."

Ruff blinked. "What? How could you possibly bring yourself to conceal a truth from those, those, those creatures when your life depended on what you told them?"

Whitemane turned away again. He might be watching the sun set behind the mountains; it was hard to tell.

"We didn't tell them because they could never understand. They are true philosophers; they place no value on that-which-exists, and concern themselves only with abstractions, ideals. For the Hukai, an exchange can only be total win or total loss. Beings can only be worthy or worthless. Never both; never anything in between; never first one, then after a while the other.

"These lost aliens taught us a greater truth. A truth that fills our hearts with great sorrow, yet also with great joy and hope.

"For through their High Music, they tell us that space is great and eternity is long. They tell us that, as measured against the Universe, nothing lasts. All things rise to whatever glory they can reach. All things fade away again, and it is as if they had never existed.

"The lost aliens tell us that in the end we all win, we all lose, and none of us are worthless. And thinking upon this in these sunset hours, we remember the poor, foolish creatures who invented the Language of Emotion … and we mourn them."

Ludwig van Beethoven

Symphony No. 7 in A Minor, Op. 92

2nd movement *allegretto*

ABOUT THE AUTHORS

Jules Blymoor (they/them) is a writer, tailor, leftist agitator, and student of psychology at the University of British Columbia. They'd love to talk to you about D&D, vinegar, socialism, and storytelling as an expression of love! Jules can be found at @softlysuited on tumblr, for writing or questions.

Lauren Glover is an archaeologist who enjoys writing in her spare time. Having travelled around the world excavating and doing research, she has plenty of experience in investigating how weird humans are through what they leave behind.

Jennifer Lee Rossman is a queer and disabled nerd who has never been accused of having an overabundance of diplomacy. She is the author of over 40 short stories and two books. Some of them are even good. Read more of her work on her website http://jenniferleerossman.blogspot.com and follow her on Twitter @JenLRossman.

S.Park (yes, you can just pronounce that "spark") is a queer, genderqueer and transhumanist author who's been writing since the age of six. Said writing ranges across at least half a dozen genres and all over several different universes, covering everything from the silly to the erotic. Home life involves a toddler, two cats, and a very nice partner, so writing isn't a full time job, but it's still very rewarding, and S.Park won't stop until the ideas dry up, which probably means never.

Maree Brittenford is an Australian who now lives in the alien environment of California with two cats (who occasionally choose to associate with her), and also her husband and children. In addition to writing, she enjoys frequently rebuilding sections of her house.

Harrison Salzman aimed for a career in Vancian magic and landed in software analysis. They have started approximately ten thousand stories and finished nearly six of them. Currently, they live in New York with thirteen definitely imaginary cats and one probably real husband.

M. L. Winslett has been writing since they could write letters from the alphabet. Their writing aims to bring happiness and spark the imagination of the reader. This writer greatly enjoys food, tea, and the company of cats, until they act like cats. If you have cats, you understand.

Jay Mendell is (allegedly) human and definitely alive, largely because of a terrible curse that forces them to write constantly or their normal human body will fail them. You can find them in the catacombs with a new story that you just *have* to check out, or on Twitter (@ijaymendell).

Jane Colon-Bonet has always thought that there is little else more human than cooking. They are very fond of baking, and believe that writing stories is very much the same activity. Language cooked up in a variety of scrumptious ways to be shared with the people we love and strangers alike.

Thaís Polegato de Sousa is a writer, translator and pop culture aficionado. Yes, the last one goes with the professional occupations too, as she might as well be getting paid for it, with the level of energy poured there. Not that she is. But humans have done weirder things.

Liz A. Vogel is a writer of science fiction, fantasy, espionage, mystery, and anything else that'll hold still long enough. She's also chair and co-founder of Narrativity: A Convention for Story (www.narrativity.fun). She loves the idea of this anthology, because she's always thought humans were weird.

E. A. Greene is a writer and avid notebook collector living in North Carolina with her mother, her cat, and an excessive number of chimney swifts. She spends her free time rolling dice with her gaming group, weight-lifting, and finding new ways to entertain the cat.

K.B. Elijah writes for various international anthologies, and her work features in dozens of collections about the mysterious, the magical and the macabre. Her own books of short fantasy novellas with twists, The Empty Sky and Out of the Nowhere, are available on paperback and Kindle now. www.kbelijah.com

Janna Kaiser might not be able to escape the tiny blue dot she has inhabited all her life, at least not bodily. But in her mind she is free to explore what might be out there, hoping you enjoyed the brief journey she took you on. She's happy to be human – and to be able to wonder if we really are the weird ones.

Chris Bannor is a speculative fiction writer who lives in Southern California. Chris learned her love of genre stories from her mother at an early age and has never veered far from that path. You can follow Chris on Facebook @chrisbannorauthor.

K. Winter Walker-van Aalst: If not found in a library, check the mountains, their balcony garden, and wherever their kitten is playing. Winter's inventory includes glasses, dice, knitting needles, a pride flag, and probably a few bones or insects. They study biology at UC Berkeley, but their interests range from language to physics.

Garrett Gantt, as you might have guessed, is a writer and a poet, with a particular fondness for science fiction and fantasy stories. He's currently working on obtaining his Bachelor's in Nursing while pursuing his lifelong dream of becoming a novelist. He will continue on this path until July 14, 2071, when he will disappear under mysterious circumstances following a last reported sighting in Newport, Oregon. Until then, he can be found on social media on Twitter, Facebook, and Instagram.

annie nguyen is a traveling martial artist (and advanced roomba) who spends her time exploring the people and places of this world and those beyond imagination. From Texas to Australia to Japan to Pennsylvania, she continues to build her map of this life. After all, there is wonder in wandering.

Elizabeth A. Allen lives in Vermont. She has edited four local history books and published one, *Mary's Diary.* Her book reviews have appeared in *Out in the Mountains, Curve Magazine,* and *Tangent Online,* among others. Her fiction has been anthologized in *Unbound, Master Works, Painting It Black,* and *Gender Who?*

Olivia Gordon, Trekkie and knee sock enthusiast, has been a ghost for three years and a writer for much longer. Some of her favorite things include reading, music, and sloths. She plans to write stories for the rest of her life.

Diana van der Schouw, online known as TimeglitchD, is a Dutch artist and author currently studying IT in college. She likes to explore topics such as AI and extraterrestrial life, but also has a never-ending love for dogs which may or may not be obvious in most of her work.

Kit Harding is herself an alien (or perhaps an enchantress?), happy to be embarking on her writing career. You can find her discussing writing, gaming, and fandom culture at writerkit.dreamwidth.org.

Charles D. Perry lives in Texas as a part time page and part time game programmer. He is currently locked in a never-ending battle with his arch-nemesis Boredom.

Maggie Maxwell has been writing stories that make physicists roll in their graves since 1994. She currently lives in Durham, NC with her husband, the ghosts of all the plants she's killed, and a large number of overworked and underpaid bookshelves.

Manuel Royal, like Tristram Shandy, was born with a broken nose. He will die. In between, he lives and writes in Atlanta, Georgia.

Dara Brophy (aka yousureimnotarobot) trained as a sculptor, ended up as a teacher. He has a house full of teenagers under quarantine. His work is on Royal Road and HFY/Reddit, including the other forty-odd stories in the Human Altered universe. He gives thanks to all the engineers and military that have advised him, even if they advised him to stop.

Bill Rogers was born in Michigan shortly after the last ice age, and in all the years since hasn't quite managed to get out. He works in environmental protection. He writes for fun occasionally, mostly SF and fantasy; it saves on needing to remember the details of real history. Under no conditions let him read you his poetry.

ABOUT THE EDITOR

Mara Lynn Johnstone grew up in a house on a hill, of which the top floor was built first. She split her time between climbing trees, drawing fantastical things, reading books, and writing her own. There may have been an imaginary friend or ten. She went on to gain a Master's Degree in creative writing, a husband, a son, and three laptop-loving cats. She enjoys writing, drawing, and spending hours discussing made-up things. She can be found on social media and at MaraLynnJohnstone.com.